For Uri and Marlena —
With a friendly tip
of Schwartz's fedora.
Cheers,
Larry Karp

The Music Box Murders

A Mystery

by

Larry Karp

A Write Way Publishing Book

This is a work of fiction. Names, characters, locales and incidents are either the product of the author's imagination or are used fictitiously, and any resemblance to actual persons, living or dead, is entirely coincidental.

Write Way Publishing
10555 E. Dartmouth, Ste 210
Aurora, CO 80014

First Edition; 1999

Acknowledgement: "The Song Is You," written by Jerome Kern and Oscar Hammerstein II. Copyright©1932, PolyGram International Publishing, Inc. Copyright Renewed. Used by permission. All Rights reserved.

Acknowledgement: Cover photo courtesy of Olin & Brenda Tillotson

ISBN 1-885173-58-X

1 2 3 4 5 6 7 8 9

Dedication

For my friend, Jack Cady.
This one's for you, Jack.

ONE

People die. You're a doctor, you adjust–either that, or specialize in Dermatology. I'm a neurologist, a clinical professor at Manhattan Medical School down on First Avenue and 30th, and in my more than twenty years of practice I've done my share of death watches. But I still got knocked sideways one morning last December when my good friend Shackie woke me with the news that Harry Hardwick was dead.

"...seemed fine at the party last night," I mumbled into the phone.

"He was," said Shackie. "He was murdered *after* the party."

I came fully awake, all systems on ready alert. Another perk of twenty-odd years of medical practice. I rolled onto my side, folded the pillow in half with my free hand, and propped my head against it. "Harry murdered?" I said. The words sounded incongruous, grammatically incorrect.

"Shot." Shackie rushed on, a full question ahead of me. "Muriel came downstairs this morning, and found him lying on the floor in his cylinder music box room. I thought you'd want to know."

I looked at the alarm clock. Nine-thirty. Time for a quick music fix. Like Jimmy Durante's old tune: "Start Off Each Day with a Song." I reached over and pushed the start lever on the antique Swiss music box I keep on the night table, within easy reach from the bed.

Convenience, that's the thing. I live in the Gramercy North

Apartments, across First Avenue from Man Med hospital. How many New Yorkers own a thirty-second commute? When I get a hurry-up call in the middle of the night, I play a couple of tunes on that music box while stuffing myself into my clothes; then I ride the music across First Avenue and into the hospital.

"Verdi, right?" said Shackie. "*La Forza del Destino.*"

I'd been humming softly along with the music. "Yeah. My Nicole overture box, the one by my bed."

"Thomas, I'm sorry. You're upset, aren't you? But I did think you'd want to know."

"I do, Shackie," I said. "I'd have been upset if you hadn't called."

Did you hear what I said there? Can you believe for a minute I *wanted* to hear somebody blew a mortal airhole through Harry Hardwick? I know about John Keats, and how beauty is supposed to be truth and truth beauty, but that's a pile of sophomoric crap. Keats died at twenty-six, remember? Without a generous coat of varnish on our truth, I doubt many of us would make it past twenty-six, or would even want to. It's not truth but stories that get us through our long days and even longer nights. Stories are beautiful. Truth's ugly as sin.

I went to the kitchen and brewed a pot of coffee, then sat sipping and brooding. What a way to start a vacation. I'd penciled myself in for a year-end holiday, two weeks' worth. Starting that morning, my partners would cover my practice. But one of my patients had stroked out at nine o'clock the evening before, which meant I'd gone charging out of Harry Hardwick's annual Christmas Extravaganza, the event of the year for the New York Music Box Collectors' Association, practically before it began. Then, a few lousy hours of sleep later, here comes a wake-up call telling me someone shot Harry Hardwick.

Who murders a force of nature? It was impossible to picture Harry dead. He'd grown up poor on the West Side of

Manhattan, but he had brains and balls, and didn't stay poor for long. By chance or design, he trained in electronics in the Army. When he came back from the Second Big War he borrowed a little money on the GI Bill and opened Hardwick Electronix. From day one, Harry plugged into the post-war mood. He knew what people wanted better than they did, and sooner. Hardwick TVs were the top sellers in New York markets between 1948 and 1953.

By then Harry was well past his fifth million, living in an elegant old brownstone on East 62nd and planning his big push. In less than ten years the Hardwick chain stretched from sea to shining sea. If it was electronic, Hardwick made it, sold it, fixed it.

Then came computers. To most people at the time, Univac was either a joke, a mystery, or both. To Harry, it was an embryonic gold mine. Less than five years after he introduced the Hardwick PC, Harry's name made *Fortune*'s list of America's ten wealthiest men.

That's when he discovered music boxes. It happens to a lot of men in their mid-forties. Get a new hobby or a new wife, the joke goes, and Harry never did things by halves. He got both. Now he had a third B–bucks–to go with his brains and his balls. Within a surprisingly short time he filled his 62nd Street brownstone with the finest and rarest antique music machines. Say this for Harry: he was generous. He liked to play host. Three times president of the New York Music Box Collectors' Association, Harry's home served as hub of the organization. Real collectors were always welcome for a visit, and researchers were given carte blanche with cameras and note pads. Parties were frequent and well attended.

And invariably, the center of activity was the big man with the shining dome and beaming moon face. Harry was everywhere at once. Bantering, showing off new acquisitions, telling jokes and listening to them, talking up possible deals–

Harry never sat pat. The thought of him lying motionless on a marble slab in a morgue didn't work.

The phone rang me out of my funk. "Thomas Purdue," I snapped into the mouthpiece.

"Hey, Doc," sang the voice at the other end, "I got a hot one."

It was Broadway Schwartz. "You do, huh? Don't let it cool off. What's happening?"

"One of your favorite kind of music boxes–the little ones you wind up with a big clock key."

The bugle call to the chase. A sure cure–the only sure cure–for the depressed collector. I stood up, bare feet and all, because with this kind of excitement who can sit?

"Okay, Broadway. You want me to come by your place? I'm free all day."

"Not this time," Schwartz chirped. "Guy has it knows what he's got, and it's too rich for me to do spec. Go take a look, have a listen. If you like it, make your own deal, and figure ten percent for Broadway. Fair enough?"

"Fair enough. Shoot."

"It's up on the West Side. On Amsterdam, between Seventy-Fourth and Seventy-Fifth, east side of the street. The Gotham Antiques Mart. Owner's a guy called Marty Abramowitz. Big guy, fat. Kind of bald. More'n a little on the greasy side."

"You're not overly specific. But all right. Is he open yet?"

"Is he open? For Christ's sake, how do you figure *I* saw it? Hey, it's ten-thirty already. If you don't get your heinie in gear, somebody else is gonna pick this baby off. And oh yeah ... there's something different about it. Kind of unusual."

My stomach stirred, not from hunger. At least, not food-hunger.

"You know how Swiss music boxes've got lines cut round and round on the cylinder, right? Well, this one's got those ring-lines, but also it's got lines straight along the lengthwise of the cylinder. Makes the thing look like a checkerboard. You ever see one like that?"

Harry Hardwick, alive or dead, suddenly never existed. My stomach rolled into a tight knot beneath my ribs.

"You snooze, you lose, right? You know how it works."

"I'm on my way, Broadway. Talk to you later."

Broadway Schwartz is a picker, one of those characters who make the antiques trade run. Whether in an attic, a basement, a cheap auction house, or a junkyard, the picker is always on the prowl. A good picker is never put off by dirt, scuff marks, or rust. His nose can smell a good item a block and a half down the street from a flea market; his eye can distinguish the McCoy from a fake at twenty paces, and his memory instantly spits out the names and phone numbers of every client who collects or deals in a particular line. A picker might pay fifty bucks for an item, then pass it to his client for a hundred and a half. If the client happens to be a shopkeeper, *he'll* put a price sticker of three hundred or three-fifty on it. It's an impressive money chain. If Alan Greenspan ever asks me for advice, I'll tell him he's missing the boat by not paying more attention to the Broadway Schwartzes.

I first ran into Schwartz fifteen years ago in a downtown flea market. As I haggled with a dealer over a little German disc music box, I could feel two intense brown eyes taking in the exchange from under the wide brim of a well-worn black fedora. When I finally walked away with my prize, the little man followed. At a safe distance from the dealer, he congratulated me on my bargaining skills, and introduced himself. He told me if I'd invest a little of my time in his education, he would make me the biggest collector of antique music boxes in all five boroughs, plus New Jersey.

So, I gave him music box lessons–why not? For his part, Schwartz delivered. If I never did get to be Numero Uno among

New York's music box folk, that was a matter of my own limitations. No way could I compete with Harry Hardwick's bucks. And to face a fact–unpleasant as that always is–Harry probably had me beat on those other two B's as well.

Early on I learned that Schwartz's eye puts Kodak's best to shame. That checkerboard cylinder design my little picker had just described over the phone is the identifying characteristic of something sensational. It sounded as if Broadway Schwartz had found a rigid notation box.

What's a rigid notation box? It's the top of the line, the musical crown jewels, la crème de la crème de la crème. Its music is exquisitely beautiful, and it is exquisitely coveted by people like me. I've been collecting music boxes for nearly a quarter of a century, and I've seen and heard exactly eight rigid notation boxes–none of them for sale.

Maybe I'd snoozed, but I wasn't about to lose. Not a rigid notation box. Shaving and breakfast could wait. I was out the door before eleven. By a quarter after, I was off the subway and working my way uptown on Amsterdam Avenue, head down into the biting December wind.

As soon as I saw the green awning with the white letters, I recognized the Gotham Antiques Mart. Like most collectors, I cruise shops more or less regularly, covering one or two neighborhoods a day. Over the years I'd been in this place several times. I'd never found anything–but it's been a while since antique music boxes were so plentiful that a collector could find them with any degree of regularity.

The Gotham's warehouse-like room was divided into five aisles by back-to-back rows of glass-front display cases, all crammed with china, glass, and silver. In the rear of the shop was furniture.

For specifics, that's as far as I can go. Some collectors have encyclopedic ranges of interest and knowledge, but I'm narrow. Just the way my mind works, I guess. In medicine, I trained as a neurological specialist, and whatever reputation I may have came through my research on the effects of music on brain function. "That's Dr. Purdue, Soother of Savage Breasts," the second-year med students say when they point me out to freshmen. It's the same way with my collecting: antique music boxes are the beginning and the end. I can't tell a piece of Doulton porcelain from Wedgwood, or Tiffany glass from Lalique, nor could I care. They don't play music. Furniture to me is just sticks cut and arranged in vaguely different patterns to make tables on which to put music boxes. For all I know or care, Hepplewhite, Chippendale, and Sheraton could be a firm of lawyers.

So, once inside the Gotham, I wasn't about to spend time looking around the shop. I'd come for one item and prayed it was still there. I had no reason to play cute.

The dealer sat behind the counter. As I came in, all I could see was the shag-rimmed top of his head above a copy of *The Daily News*. When I closed the door he looked up. His face was fat and round; grease shone on his forehead. If Schwartz had described the music box as accurately as he had the dealer, we were all three golden: the dealer had a sale, Schwartz had a commission ... and I had a once-in-a-collector's-lifetime treasure.

The fat man nodded, the customary and noncommittal greeting to the antiques customer. It meant if I was only here to kick tires, he really couldn't stop me, so I should go right ahead. Just don't bother him. If I saw anything I was serious about he'd open the cabinet for me.

"You've got a music box," I said.

Down went the newspaper, all the way to the counter. Behind gold-rimmed glasses, the dealer's dark eyes glittered. He worked his tongue around the inside of his lips as he gave me the quick once-over. Then, he bit on his thick lower lip. But he didn't say a word.

That seemed like an odd reaction to a customer, but antiques dealers tend to be more than mildly odd. It's nothing like shopping at Macy's. "You have a music box," I repeated, deadpan. "A little one, you wind with a clock key."

He smiled. Then, he nodded twice, quickly. His wattles shook like jelly. "Okay, buddy," he said. "Hang on. I'll show it to you."

The man was a professional. Some antiques dealers see a prospective customer dressed in a gray work shirt and jeans, with stubble on his face and a nice red pair of sleep-deprived eyes, and they say, "Well, I *do* have one ... but I'm afraid it's quite expensive." In other words, don't waste my time. This guy knew better. He'd undoubtedly seen people who looked a lot grubbier than I did right then reach into their pockets and start peeling off hundred-dollar bills with as much concern as if they were buying ice-cream cones for their kids. It works the other way around, too. Some of the most notorious deadbeats and check bouncers in the antiques world dress as though they were on their way to the Mayor's Inauguration Ball.

The dealer slid off his stool with an "Ooph," and disappeared down low, under the counter. He resurfaced in a blink, holding a small, rectangular wooden box about eighteen inches long. Just a plain fruitwood case, well-worn, with little brass handles at each end, set within recesses. My poor heart went to pounding fast, with those little extra beats that make it hard to breathe and even more difficult to talk. With exaggerated care, the fat man set his prize between us on the wooden countertop. A little smile flickered around the corners of his mouth. Finally, he lifted the lid.

"Nice one," he said.

"Yeah." That's all that would come out. Just a little "Yeah."

Once again, Schwartz was right on target. The surface of the brass cylinder was deeply tarnished, but what the hell–this music box was some hundred and sixty years old. And tarnish or not, I had no difficulty making out the checkerboard pattern on the cylinder. The teeth on the comb were finely cut, thin as needles, more than two hundred of them in the twelve inches of the comb's length. "Francois Nicole" was impressed on the middle of the comb, behind the teeth–he being the master Swiss craftsman in music boxes during the early nineteenth century. No question about it. I was gawking into the heart and soul of one of the most magnificent musical creations of all time. I was eyeballing my ninth rigid notation box.

I could have sworn that the dealer actually picked up on the thumping in my chest. He chuckled, and reached over the top of the box to push the start lever. "Guess you wanna hear it, huh, buddy?"

The cylinder began to rotate, slowly, and with the first chord every hair on my body jumped straight to attention. There's a delicate precision to the music on rigid notation boxes that lends an other-worldly quality to the sound. Nothing here of the "tinkly music box"–that slanderous line from the idiotic mouth or pen of some lunkhead who either has never heard mechanical music at all, or can only remember his auntie's glitzy little jewelry case with its authentic eighteen-note, made-in-Japan modern musical movement and an ugly plastic blob of a ballerina on top, twirling to the tinkle.

Goddamn it to hell, *real* music boxes do not tinkle. Delicate though the sound of a fine music box may be, the tones are rich and full, and in the very best of the best, they fairly tremble in the air with the emotion of the man who first heard those notes in some special place inside his skull, and who then took pains to set them to the surface of the cylinder so that we, listening, might share his vision.

The first tune came from the overture to *The Magic Flute*, a rendition more light and gay and airy than any ever heard in any opera house. Next was a portion of the *Figaro* overture, and after that, a selection I did not at first recognize, but then it came to me: *Idomeneo*, also by Mozart. The fourth tune was a passage from the overture to *Don Giovanni*, the most haunting, heart-wrenching presentation of this piece I'd ever heard.

By the time the music stopped and the cylinder clicked to a halt, the music box was shimmering in my watery field of view. An all-Mozart rigid notation box. Whatever it cost, whatever it took, this treasure was going home with me, never to leave. It would go in my coffin with me. To hell with the harps of heaven.

The dealer brought me back with a phlegmy chuckle. "Does sound good, don't it?"

"Yes, it does." I looked up, right into his eyes. "Very nice. What do you need to get for it?"

He chuckled again, and his ocular glitter ratcheted a couple of notches higher. "It's one of the best I've ever had, buddy. Cost you six thousand. You knew that was the deal, right?"

I tried to remember what Schwartz had said. As best I could recall, he hadn't mentioned a specific price, just told me the box wouldn't come cheap because the dealer knew what he had. Well, Abramowitz *did* know he had a very nice music box–but just how nice, he didn't have a clue. Which was understandable. Most music box collectors prefer the disc-playing machines, the Reginas and the Polyphons and the Symphonions, with their bright, loud, "big" sound. Not many people care much about cylinder boxes. Consequently very few people would even notice a checkerboard pattern on a cylinder–let alone recognize its significance.

Most fine, early cylinder boxes sell in the two to three thousand dollar range, so Abramowitz had set an asking price double that. Pretty stiff, he must have thought, but it wasn't, not really. That checkerboard cylinder went right past him. He didn't know that on the extremely rare occasions when rigid notation boxes are sold, their price has been as high as $25,000.

So, there I was, being offered the music box of my life, and at roughly twenty-five cents on the dollar. You'd think I'd have plunked down the money, grabbed the music box, and run. But I didn't.

Collectors are funny people. Never mind that the dealer

had already shot off every one of his metatarsals. *He* didn't know that. If Abramowitz had made his pitch while the music was still playing, I'd have reached into my pocket like an automaton, forked over his asking price, and said thank you. But unfortunately for him, the effect of music is almost as evanescent as its physical presence.

I gave Abramowitz my best professionally puzzled look, and said, "Excuse me. I thought you said six thousand. What *is* the price here?"

The dealer's round face relaxed into a genial smile. "Your ears're fine, buddy. What's the matter–that doesn't sound reasonable to you?"

"Frankly, no," I said. "It's high. Very high."

He was a pro, no question. Without letting his smile flag in the slightest, he managed to get just the right amount of disdain and faint condescension into his expression. "High, huh? Well, what would you think if I told you that this here music box ..." He paused, just long enough to give the edge of the opened lid an avuncular pat, "came outta the O'Shacker collection. The Charles O'Shacker collection."

At that point, I didn't know what to think. Charles O'Shacker–or Shackie, as I called him–had been a very good friend for a very long time. Shackie earned his living restoring music boxes, and he owned a small, definitely first-rate collection. But he'd never had a rigid notation box. And, if he ever *did* have one, it would never have found its way into this place. Not under any circumstances.

My silence was making Abramowitz impatient. He picked roughly at some skin behind his left thumbnail, then looked up at me. "You *do* know who's Charles O'Shacker?" he finally said.

"Sure," I said. "Anybody who collects music boxes knows who's Charles O'Shacker."

"Well, then," Abramowitz moved smoothly into grand intonational mode. "It was him who sold me this box." He shrugged. "Needed money. Happens in the best of families." Another phlegm-soaked chuckle.

The odor of horseshit was overwhelming. Shackie lived alone, and very simply. If someone stiffed him on a repair job, he'd likely just shrug and go on with the next piece of work. Shackie was the last person I could think of who'd sell a music box–*any* music box–out of his collection for need of money. So, in our little game of Haggle, it was now advantage Purdue.

"Okay," I said quietly. "Maybe it *was* O'Shacker's music box, but we're not talking about Winston Churchill, or the Emperor-God of China. Charles O'Shacker's name isn't worth two bits on a music box price. And besides, no collector who needs money is going to sell his very top machine. You know that." I jerked a thumb at the rigid notation box. "Six thousand dollars' worth? Uh-uh."

Abramowitz's chummy smile did a slight fade as lines tightened around his mouth. He drummed his fingers on the countertop, a fast-running staccato. "Well, all right, buddy, okay. If *you're* some kind of a big-time collector, you tell me. What's this box worth, huh? You give *me* a price."

I took a deep breath. We were getting serious. "It's a nice cylinder box," I told him. "A very nice cylinder box. Cylinder boxes sell for two to three thousand, in good condition. Which this box is."

You'd have thought I'd spit straight into his merchandise. He clapped his fleshy hand to his forehead. "*Oy*, buddy! I'm used to *goniffs* in this place; three times now I've been held up. But all they do is stick a gun in my face and take the dough outta the register." He gave me a withering look. "I ain't never yet had a *goniff* try and rip me off by slinging bullshit in my face."

To close the discussion, he lowered the lid on the music box and moved his hands as if to lower it behind the counter.

I fought the impulse to pay his six thousand. *Play the game*, I told myself. *You're winning*. "As long as we're talking bullshit," I said, keeping my voice level, "why don't *you* tell *me*. What's the most you've ever sold a cylinder music box for? A small one. Like this." I rested my hand on the lid.

Dark light glittered in Abramowitz's piggy eyes. The left corner of his mouth twisted upward in subtle acknowledgment. The game was still on. He shrugged again, his round head telescoping between his round shoulders. "...you think I am, anyway? Some kinda freakin' encyclopedia? Jeez, buddy, I been selling antiques for thirty years now. I've sold hundreds of thousands of pieces, and you want me to remember what's the most I ever got for a music box? Tell you what. I give ten percent to dealers, so I'll make you the same price. That's six hundred off; fifty-four hundred bucks, okay? What could be fairer'n that?"

"Turn the numbers around," I said. "Forty-five."

"Forty-freakin'-*five*?" Abramowitz glared at me as though I'd spit a second time. "Hey, in case you ain't noticed, it's still a week and a half 'til Christmas. And just for the record, I ain't jolly old St. Nick. Now, let's quit screwin' around. Money talks. Bullshit walks. Gimme five; that's it."

"Forty-five," I said, very evenly, being careful to keep every trace of frustration or annoyance out of my voice. "That's more than I've ever paid for a small cylinder box, and I'll bet it's more than you've ever sold one for. It's also halfway between three thousand, which would've been my price, and your six. What could be fairer than *that*?"

Abramowitz cupped his chin in the palm of his hand, and proceeded to radiate weary righteousness at me. "Are we talkin' cash?"

"Sure, cash."

"Cash *money*?" This Abramowitz was one persistent fat son of a bitch.

"Green cash money," I said, and started to reach into my pocket.

"'Cause at that price I don't take no check. And for sure, no Visa or MasterCard."

He didn't want to take a bad check or risk a stolen credit card. There's also the point that checks and credit cards represent traceable income. I always have a good handful of money with me when I think I might be buying a music box.

I pulled my wallet out of my pocket and started to count out pictures of Franklin onto the wooden surface next to my music box.

All of a sudden, Abramowitz looked as though one of his hemorrhoids had infarcted. "Hey, buddy." He actually whimpered. "You got forty-five hundred bucks in bills ... in your *pocket*?"

I stopped, and eyed him. He was actually pale. "Sure," I said. "That much in change gets kind of heavy. And I just had my hernia repaired."

"You're some kind of wisenheimer," he said. "Just hold on for a minute, huh?" He trotted around the edge of the counter and chugged to the door where he threw the deadbolt. He gave his sign a quick flip so that the CLOSED side faced toward the sidewalk. "Christ Almighty," he wheezed, as he did his quickstep waddle back to the counter. "You're a frickin' mugger's dream come true. Walkin' the streets with forty-five hundred bucks in your pocket? The *goniffs* say a prayer for guys like you before they get in bed at night."

Takes one to know one, I thought, but didn't say. I just smiled, counted out the bills, and laid them on the counter.

As Abramowitz's sausage fingers closed around the pile he actually licked his lips. I thought he might slobber on his take. He counted the money, then slid it off the counter with all the slick insouciance of a Vegas croupier. Probably stuck it into a box hidden down below.

"Congratulations," he said. "You just got yourself one hell of a deal on a fantastic music box."

I smiled again and closed the lid.

His grin turned crooked. "You don't exactly give nothing away, do you?"

I shook my head. "I'm like you, a low-overhead operation. No freebies. No loss leaders."

He chuckled, bent over with a "whoof," then bobbed back

into view, waving a brown paper bag. "From Gristede's," he said, pointing at the red logo. "We'll put your music box in here. The *goniffs*'ll just think you been to the supermarket for a coupla melons."

I slipped the bag over the music box. Meanwhile, Abramowitz picked up a pen and bent his head over a receipt book. "What's your name? For the record, that's all."

"Purdue. Thomas Purdue."

He nodded, filled out the page and tore it off the pad. "Here you go," he said, with a grand flourish. "Enjoy."

I put the bag with the music box under my left arm, and slid the receipt, that little slip of paper saying *Antique Music Box - $4500*, inside.

Abramowitz came from behind the counter and led me to the door. "Come back again, Tom. You never know when I might have another one of these little beauties for you."

"Fine, but that's Thomas. Not Tom."

He gave a broad shrug. "Tom, Thomas, whatever. It's your name, buddy. Far as I'm concerned, customer's always right." He waved and closed the door behind me.

Turning from the doorway onto the sidewalk, I bumped squarely into a tall young woman in a gray Persian lamb coat, nearly sending her flying through the plate-glass storefront. I grabbed at her arm to steady her, then mumbled a quick apology. She pulled roughly away and hurried past me into the shop. So much for good will toward men.

I started down Amsterdam, moving as rapidly as possible through the mass of holiday shoppers. I clutched my package tightly under my arm, so no *goniff* could push it out from behind and take off down the sidewalk. I didn't feel the concrete beneath my feet. I barely noticed the savage December wind whipping around corners of buildings, blasting into my face. I had my love to keep me warm. I couldn't wait to show her off to Shackie.

But unfortunately, I couldn't show her to Harry Hardwick. You can't brag to a corpse.

Two

Where Broadway crosses Amsterdam at 72nd Street, I zipped to the middle phone on a Ma Bell Triple-Header. Balancing my music box carefully on the little ledge beneath the phone, I punched in Shackie's number.

The damn phone rang and rang and rang. I hopped up and down, first on one foot, then the other. I was shivering, only partly from the cold.

Finally, Shackie said hello, a question. His voice sounded distant.

"In the middle of a box?" I asked.

While Shackie was doing a restoration job, he was in another world. I was lucky he'd heard the phone at all.

"Thomas?" he finally said.

"Yes, good old Thomas. Who were you expecting, Francois Lecoultre? F. W. Ducommun?"

Lecoultre and Ducommun were two of the first-generation Swiss music box manufacturers, contemporaries of Francois Nicole. Shackie insisted that while he was working on a music box, he always communicated with its maker. He said this kept him faithful to the original musical vision. He also claimed the makers guided him through those sticky wickets that inevitably pop up in the course of a complex restoration. People tended to laugh at Shackie, or at least roll their eyes–but then these same skeptics would go on to tell me about the uncanny insights of their astrologers, or the incontrovertible evidence to prove space aliens abducted Judge Crater, or how Jesus had reached out personally to them and changed their lives. I listened to them almost as politely as I listened to Shackie.

Shackie clucked into the phone. "You're making fun of me."

"No, I wouldn't do that," I said. "Just kidding around. But, listen—I've got something to show you."

"O-o-oh. Something like what?"

"Something like with wood on the outside and metal inside, and you wind it with a key."

"You got a goodie!" Shackie's voice went up a full octave.

"A very goodie. I'll be right over with it."

"But what—" Shackie was practically screeching.

"You'll have to wait and see," I said, and hung up the phone.

Shackie's place was on 16th, between Seventh and Eighth Avenues, 2,000-odd square feet of undivided loft on the top floor of a building formerly commercial. Not a tony neighborhood—but the tax returns of music box restorers don't exactly set IRS auditors to drooling.

From the hallway, you walked directly into Shackie's workshop. Walls lined with storage space for supplies, tools, and sick music boxes. Desktop workstations stood here and there, each set up for one particular type of repair work, and arranged to coordinate efficiently with Shackie's wood and metal power tools. There were lathes and drill presses, saws and grinders. A large, gas-fired kiln rested on a sturdy stand against the south wall, under an amazing assortment of gluing clamps hanging from a square brown pegboard. Floor-to-ceiling was easily twenty feet, which allowed Shackie to construct a platform for his living area, accessible from the workshop by a flight of ladder-stairs along the north wall. Nothing fancy: a combination bedroom-sitting room and a walled-off bathroom. A simple wooden railing around the platform prevented Shackie from pitching down into the shop during a somnambulistic episode.

I knew the place well. Unless I was out of town, I spent at least a part of every weekend and a couple of evenings a week in the shop with Shackie. Consider it therapy, cheaper and more effective than any shrink. All my life my head has been full of gorgeous music, both new arrangements of old tunes and altogether new tunes that no one but me has ever heard. No one ever will, either, because I don't know how to let them out. Dinking around over a piano keyboard was useless, studying music theory even worse. That music is locked inside my head, and knowing it's going to die with me could drive me crazy. Talent without ambition is sad, ambition without talent even worse.

Fortunately, there's an anodyne. The sound of a music box in restoration is a soothing unguent on my incurable wound, the only palliation I've ever found. I apply it as frequently as I can.

Shackie must have heard me coming up the stairs. As I swept through the open door past him, he eyeballed the grocery bag under my arm. "Is that it?"

"Nice. No 'Hello, how are you?' Just 'Is that it?'"

He didn't hear me, just shoved a partial music box carcass to make table-top space. "Put it down here. Let's have a look."

Passion will always win over reason or courtesy. I smiled as I slipped my treasure out of its mundane camouflage and laid it on the table before my bug-eyed friend. He touched the right-sided brass handle lightly. Slowly, ever so gently, he lifted the lid.

What happened then was a shocker. Shackie plainly did a double-take. He gave his long ponytail an automatic flip back over his shoulder, bent from the waist to peer inside the case, then quickly straightened and turned around. "Thomas ..." he said, eyes clouded with concern, "where did you get this box?"

This was not what I'd expected. "I stole it," I snapped. "What kind of a dumb-ass question is that?"

"This is Harry Hardwick's rigid notation box," Shackie said, calmly. "Where did you get it?"

"Excuse me, but it's *my* rigid notation box. I bought it at a shop up on the West Side. Less than an hour ago, in fact. What the hell are you talking about?"

"You were at Harry's party last night. Remember the big demonstration? When Harry got everyone into the cylinder box room to show off his new rigid notation box–the one he'd picked up only a few days before?"

"What time was this big demonstration?"

Shackie checked his watch. It must have told him the answer, because he looked back to me and said, "Ten o'clock. Right at ten, in fact."

"Which could explain a lot. If you'll remember, my beeper went off a little after nine. By ten o'clock I was in the Man Med emergency room, ordering tests on one of my patients who'd had a cerebral hemorrhage. He hung on 'til four-thirty in the morning. I thought that might be a little late to go back to Harry's, so I went home instead, ate a pint of Ben and Jerry's mint chocolate chip, and went to bed. Which is where I still was this morning, Mary Sunshine, when you called to brighten my corner. So: if Harry Hardwick put on a demonstration of a rigid notation box, I missed it."

"Hmmm." Shackie nodded mechanically. "That's a shame. You'd have enjoyed it."

"I'm sure I would have, but think for a minute: How could this box have been at Harry Hardwick's at ten o'clock last night, when first thing this morning it was sitting in a shop on Amsterdam Avenue, waiting for me to buy it?"

Light shrug. "That's what we have to find out. But we won't get anywhere until you open your mind. Stop swimming against the current."

"Shackie, sometimes you *have* to swim against the current. Otherwise, you'll go over the falls."

"Only if you're certain that going over the falls is necessarily a bad thing."

"Only if you're certain that a fractured neck and quadriplegia are a good thing."

"But you might *not* fracture your neck. You might only be shaken up a little. You might be taken to a hospital for observation, and the nurse who checks you out might be the soulmate you've been searching after for years. And if you hadn't gone over the falls, you'd never have met her."

Shackie was a New-Age guy, crystals and color healing, even that Farina-with-no-salt music. Nothing in Shackie's world ever went wrong. Occurrences occurred, happenings happened, Shackie adjusted. Why waste time and energy fighting the forces of the universe? Makes sense to some people, I suppose. But marches are so much more stirring than madrigals that I can't help smiling and wishing the torpedo-damner good fortune as he barrels along, bathed in glory, on his way to victory or death. John Brown's body lies a-moldering in the grave, but his soul keeps marching on.

"Shackie, goddamn it, stop. Swimming and currents are neither here nor there. It's all very straightforward. I bought this music box in an antiques shop this morning, and it's mine."

"I'll prove to you it's not," Shackie said.

"Oh?" The word sounded mild enough to my own ears, but I noticed I'd placed my hand on the rigid notation box.

Shackie pointed at the three little numbers stamped into the brass at the upper left of the music-box bedplate. "Serial number four-three-two. Same as Harry's. And the program is all Mozart. *Magic Flute. Figaro. Idomeneo. Don Giovanni*. Am I right?"

I didn't say anything.

"And something else. The music doesn't sound quite the way it should."

"Aha!" The drowning man clutched frantically at the straw. "The music on this box sounds more than all right. It's lovely, in fact. Beautiful."

"Basically, yes." Shackie kept coming at me. "It's a wonderful program; what would you expect from a box like this? But it isn't exactly right. The music's ... well, here, let me show you."

He turned the box on; *The Magic Flute* began to play. We listened in silence through the entire tune. As the music stopped, he looked at me and said, "See what I mean?"

"Frankly, no, I don't. It sounded just fine to me."

"It's unbalanced. Uneven ... in a funny kind of way. The notes from the lower, oh, quarter of the comb don't have the body they should. And the treble notes are very thin. But the mid-range ... *those* notes are too strong. They overpower bass *and* treble. Strange ... I've never run up against that situation. I told Harry I'd like to work on the box, get it to sound right. Here–listen one more time."

He turned on the music.

Again, we listened. I remembered the time in med school when one of my pediatrics professors handed me a stethoscope and pointed at a sad-looking little boy staring at us from behind the bars of a crib. "Classic mitral stenosis," the professor said, and described the characteristic loud, harsh, diastolic murmur. But when I put the stethoscope to the kid's chest I didn't hear any murmur at all. Just a normal lub-dup, lub-dup. Sweat popped out on my forehead; I listened so hard I thought I might shit in my pants. Finally the professor asked what I thought of the murmur. "I'm sorry," I said, ready to trot over to the Dean's office and hand in my resignation, "I don't hear a murmur." At which point the professor smiled and said, "Right! There *is* none. You've just learned the first lesson of medical practice: Don't trust anyone."

So, I listened to *The Magic Flute* with Shackie. Was he correct? *Was* the sound unbalanced, with loudness shifted away from the bass and treble in favor of the mid-range notes? Shackie's ear was phenomenal: Many times I'd watched him fuss for hours, trying to get rid of some little damper or pin noise that to me was barely noticeable–assuming I could hear it at all. I tried to focus my attention in turns on the volume of sound coming from each third of the comb, then tried to play off the regions against each other. Like listening with three ears. *Was* there any imbalance there? Maybe ... maybe so. Just the tiniest bit. "But these early cylinder boxes are all one-of's," I said. "Could be this one left Nicole's workshop sounding this way."

The look on Shackie's face suggested I'd just called his mother a name that wouldn't be listed even in *Krafft-Ebing*. "Francois Nicole wouldn't have sold a box that didn't sound exactly right," he said.

If I'd laughed at the height of dudgeon in Shackie's voice, I wouldn't have been a music box collector. Put it this way: If there'd been K-Marts in Geneva in 1840, they would not have carried Francois Nicole music boxes. So, once I agreed with Shackie that the tonal qualities of this particular music box were not all they should have been, I also had to agree that the problem was one of deterioration. And the chance that two such fine and rare boxes had gone down the same peculiar chute would have had to be about the same as finding teeth in hens or snow in hell.

Which Shackie knew. He pointed at the phone. "I'm going to call Muriel. Maybe someone walked off last night with Harry's rigid notation box."

This was getting worse by the minute. If Shackie called Muriel Hardwick and shot off his innocent little yap, my rigid notation box could end up in police custody. For that matter, so could he. Remember who supposedly sold the box to Abramowitz? I reached for Shackie's hand. "I wouldn't do that."

He looked up at me, silently asking why not.

"You *can't* call Muriel now," I said. "For God's sake, her husband's been shot, she must be beside herself, and you want to go asking questions about a missing music box?"

Shackie bit his lower lip. "Then we've got to call the police."

"No. I don't think we should call the police, either. Listen, here's an idea."

Shackie looked doubtful. "You're trying to pull something, aren't you?"

"Me? Pull something? Shackie, come on. For one thing, we don't know for sure yet whether this actually is Harry's music box; for another, we don't even know whether Harry's box was stolen. And there's something else–something I haven't told you."

"Oh, God. There's more?"

"Yes. The dealer who sold me this box told me *you* sold it to *him*. He said this music box came from the collection of Charles O'Shacker."

Shackie never raises his voice, which at times can be exasperating. Like this time. "But that's ridiculous. I've never had a rigid notation box. It came from Harry's collection, not mine."

I wanted to shake him. "Jesus, Shackie," I moaned. "Don't you see? The last thing to do right now is go running to the police. If Harry's been murdered–"

"He *has* been murdered. Muriel said."

"Fine. Harry *has* been murdered, excuse me. And if his rigid notation box really was stolen, then whoever did it–and presumably killed Harry in the process, right?–sold it to this dealer and told the dealer he was you. *You*–Charles O'Shacker. Who murdered Harry and stole his music box."

Shackie suddenly went pale. "But I didn't. I wouldn't ever do a thing like that."

"I know that, but the New York City Homicide detectives have no idea what a fine fellow you are. They'll hear that story, toss you in the dungeon, and charge you with grand larceny and first-degree murder."

Shackie lowered himself into one of his swivel work chairs and looked up at me, all of a sudden ten years older. "Well ... what are we going to ... *do*?"

"We're going to have a talk with the dealer who sold me this music box. We'll go up there, you and I, and see whether he recognizes Charles O'Shacker."

Light flooded back into Shackie's eyes. He jumped out of his chair. "That's great. And when he doesn't recognize me, we can go to the police. Wait, I'll get my coat."

He was halfway across the room toward the ladder.

"Not so fast," I called after him.

He froze. "What do you mean, not so fast?"

"I mean a couple of things. Before we tackle this character, let's put a little ammunition in the gun ... so to speak. First, we'll see what Frank the Crank might be able to tell us about our dealer friend. Then I'll send Broadway Schwartz up to the shop to do a little pumping."

Shackie stood there, finger to lip, nodding gravely. "Yeah ... okay, sounds reasonable," he finally said. "As long as it won't take too long."

"It won't. And one more thing. I'm going to line up a witness–somebody to walk into that shop with us, and then be willing to testify that this slob of a dealer didn't know the real Charles O'Shacker from Godzilla."

Shackie's face brightened again. "Oh, that's a *won*derful idea. I don't know how you always manage to think of all these things. Do you have anyone particular in mind?"

"I thought Sarah might be good."

He smiled, slowly at first, then with all his face. My wife's parents missed the boat by not naming their little girl Earnest. No one has ever accused Sarah of telling a lie, probably because she never has. Which is why we've lived in separate apartments for the past six years. Cohabitation with someone who barrages you night and day with missiles, mortars, and bullets of truth is no picnic.

"I'll take her to supper tonight," I said. "She'll do it." I reached for the rigid notation box.

Shackie laid a hand on my arm.

I gave him the fisheye. "Yes?"

"Leave it here," he begged.

"What, are you crazy? My new rigid notation box?"

"I want to check it over. See if I can't find out why it doesn't sound right."

"Forget it." I slid the box into the Gristede's bag.

"But, Thomas–"

"Don't even think about it." As I put my topcoat back on and tucked the bag under my arm, I checked my watch. High noon. "Come on," I said, in a tone of voice a little softer than my usual. "Let's go see what Frank the Crank has to say. Then–after we've got everything sorted out–*then* maybe we'll check the box over. We. Together. Kapeesh?"

"All right." Shy smile. We were still friends.

THREE

Frank the Crank's real name is Frank Maar. No man was ever better nicknamed–not Mack the Knife, nor Leo the Lip, nor Attila the Hun. For one thing, Frank runs a shop named Wind-Me-Up which specializes in antique clocks, phonographs, and music machines.

For another, there's his personality.

I've never seen a person with more impressive mood swings than Frank's, and keep in mind what I do for a living. I've tried for years to get him on some effective medication, but Frank is convinced that drugs are chemicals and chemicals are poisons and why would any reasonable person willfully swig down a glass of Drano? So on Frank goes year after year with his own natural body chemicals wildly out of control, careening madly from extreme geniality to incredible hostility, then back again. One day he'll sell you anything in the shop at less than wholesale and even throw in some literature or a couple of phonograph records. But on other days you'll walk in, say "Hiya, Frank," and he'll yell at you to shut the hell up and get the hell out. Which you would be wise to do, and quickly.

From Shackie's, Wind-Me-Up was a short block cross-town to Seventh, then downtown to 12th Street and down a short flight of concrete steps to the basement of an old apartment building. Frank's hole-in-the-ground is a collector's paradise, 500 square feet invariably packed with super items. Edison Opera and Maroon Gem phonographs. Gold-plated Victor-Six gramophones. Rare music box/phonograph combinations. There might be musical automata, French-made, more than a hundred years old, with a lovely lady-doll playing the harpsichord, or a furry cat turning the crank of a little street organ. How Frank manages to keep turning these things up, year after year after year, I can't begin to say. He tells me he ought to go into politics because he always has his ways and means. Not that I think he'd take in anything hot—Frank's crazy, but he's also honest. On the other hand, he knows who isn't. In New York's antiques world no one knows more about what's going on than Frank the Crank. Which was why I wanted to talk to him.

As we came through the door, Frank looked up from behind the counter in the rear of the shop. He grinned and waved. "Hiya, Doc. And the good *Señor* O'Shacker. What can I sell you boys today?"

"Great," I whispered to Shackie. "It's an up day."

The unshaded light above Frank's head reflected off his shiny dome. With his probing blue eyes, hollow cheeks, and short salt-and-pepper beard, Frank in his up mode puts me in mind of a mildly amused fox. "I got a nice little Edison Fireside, and you know how often you get a chance at one of those," he said. He pointed at a small phonograph with a graceful swan's-neck horn, on a shelf to his left. "All original and absolutely mint, not a scratch on it. Perfect decals. For you, special, a quick sale. Five-fifty. And I'll throw in twenty good cylinders, half two-minute, half fours. No dreck. How can you say no?"

"Only because I don't collect phonographs," I said. "Otherwise I'd be at your mercy. What I'm after today, Frank, is information."

"Oh?" The foxy look intensified. "Doing a little research, are you?"

He took a bite out of a half-eaten donut on his desk. Frank eats constantly and he's still a leather-cased skeleton. I'd love to put his thyroid gland to the test, but he won't hear of it. The bastard's serum cholesterol is probably below 100; he's a human detoxification machine. When I'm lying in my pissed-up bed, paralyzed and speechless after my third stroke, Frank the Crank will still be sitting in his little shop, selling Edison phonographs and scarfing greasy donuts.

"You might say that, Frank," I told him. "Research on a person, actually. But it does involve a music box."

"Like what person?" Frank's ears seemed to wiggle themselves into better hearing position.

"Marty Abramowitz. Owns the Gotham Antiques Mart, on Amsterdam between Seventy-Fourth and Seventy-Fifth. You know him?"

"Fat Marty?" Frank the Crank grinned. "'Course I know him."

"Well enough to tell me how honest he is?"

Frank arched one eyebrow. "Honesty's relative, Doc. Compared to what? Or to who?"

"How about compared to you, Frank?"

"Oh, *well.* Doc, what can I say?" Frank was going to have his fun; I needed to be patient. "Compare a guy to the soul of honesty–that's a tough thing. Let's just say they come worse than Marty Abramowitz. Of course, they also come better. Not a lot of dealers have ever cobbled a Reginaphony."

Nearly a hundred years ago the Regina Music Box Company tried to head off Edison's new invention by building a combined music box and phonograph. These hybrid Reginaphones were expensive even then and not many were sold. Today they're highly sought after by collectors. Highly enough that occasionally an unscrupulous dealer or collector will take an ordinary Regina music box, add more or less proper phonograph parts in more or less proper places, and voila! The Reginaphony.

"Abramowitz did that?" I said. "I'm amazed."

Frank chuckled. "Not by himself, don't worry. Marty ain't got the smarts for a solo job. He did it with Nussbaum."

"Randy Nussbaum? The gambling-machine collector?"

"That's the guy. You know what *he's* like, Doc. Far as Marty was concerned the Reginaphony was strictly business. But for Nussbaum it was fun and games. The schmuck went bragging all over town about how he got the phonograph parts off Walter Remler, stuck 'em on the Regina, set the thing up in Abramowitz's window, and gave some new young collector a hot tip to Marty's shop. Marty got twelve thousand out of the kid, which the two of them split. That the kind of thing you want to know?"

"It's fine for starters, Frank," I said. "Now let's get to basics. This Abramowitz has been talking to me about a music box, but I'm suspicious. Is he someone who'd handle hot merchandise?"

Frank the Crank scratched at his chin, and let his eyes wander upward. "W-e-l-l-l, let's see," he said. "Put it this way, Doc. Marty's not what you'd call a professional fence. If a sixteen-year-old kid came on to him with a bag of costume jewelry, Marty'd toss him out in the street. But you *could* say Marty's ethics go by a sliding scale. The more money he could make and the less risk to his own heinie, the more he might take a flyer. So if you feel any heat when you put your hand on a music box in Marty's shop, you wouldn't be crazy to pay attention." Frank jerked his head in the direction of the brown bag on the counter. "And if you're sayin' you're afraid that paper bag's about to go up in flames, maybe you'd better get it out of my shop. Like now. And fast."

"No sweat, Frank," I said quickly. "That's just some melons from Gristede's."

I had to laugh as Frank twisted up his face and pinched his nose between thumb and forefinger. "P-U—musta been a mounted cop just went by. What the hell they feeding those poor animals? You ever smell such terrible horseshit?"

Shackie giggled. I reached into the bag. "Between us, Frank. Kapeesh?"

"Sure, Doc, you bet." A good game is wine and caviar to

Frank the Crank. "Mum's the word. Absolute soul of discretion. Let's see what you got there."

As I slid the rigid notation box out of the bag and put it on the counter, Frank whistled. He opened the lid carefully and peered inside. "Not very big," he muttered, "and no bells or any other fancy shit." He straightened and studied my face. "But quality, right? Good stuff, and early, yes?"

"Very early and very good, Frank."

"And very expensive?" Light danced in Frank's eyes.

"Not as expensive as it should have been. I paid Abramowitz twenty cents on the dollar, but I don't think because he was trying to dump a hot machine. I figure he just didn't know what he had."

Frank nodded thoughtfully. "Probably right. To listen to Marty he's an expert in everything, a regular Renaissance man of antiques. Maybe he knows his glass pretty good, and his chinaware, I'll give him that. And furniture a little. But music machines?" Frank made a spitting noise of disparagement. "Frankly, he don't know the Nicole Freres from the Andrews Sisters."

Shackie laughed. Frank grinned. "Thanks, *Señor* O'Shacker," he said. "Good audience always appreciated."

I pointed to the checkerboard pattern on the cylinder and quickly explained its meaning to Frank. His eyes widened. "So you made yourself a nice little killing, huh?"

Frank's expression told me he had not missed the look that came over Shackie's face. He chewed on his upper lip for a moment. Then he began to speak, very slowly. "Okay, Doc—time to drop the other shoe. Hit me with the punch line. You got a valuable music box off Marty Abramowitz for peanuts, good for you. But I'm a dumb kid from Hoboken and I fail to see why it is you're so interested in Marty's morals. And also why *Señor* O'Shacker gets that very funny look on his face when I say you made a killing. Fair's fair, Doc. Your turn to talk."

I wanted to brain Shackie. Frank the Crank is as curious as any cat but he never acts as if he'd heard what curiosity can do to cats. The last thing I wanted was for him to go snooping on his own, trying to get answers from other sources. Better to enlist him on my side, right from the start. I gave him the hardest look I could manage. "Mum's the word, Frank? Scout's honor?"

He put his hand over his heart, looked at the heavens, and said, "Cross my heart and hope to die."

I didn't dare look at Shackie. "Okay, Frank. Here's the story. You know a collector named Harry Hardwick?"

"Long Green Harry?" Frank grinned. "Very wealthy man. Sure, I know him."

"Correction: Sure, you *knew* him."

Frank cocked his head and studied me like a curious sparrow considering the world from a telephone wire.

"Harry is now a very *dead* man. Somebody shot him last night. Furthermore, Shackie says that Harry owned a music box that answered to the general description of this one. What we don't know is whether whoever blew Harry away also pulled a quick double-play with his rigid notation box: Hardwick to Abramowitz to Purdue." I didn't bother to tell Frank who Abramowitz had said that somebody was.

"Hoo, boy." Frank pulled a grimy handkerchief out of his pocket and wiped it across his face. He flashed the foxy grin. "The light's startin' to shine, Doc." He leered into my face. "Am I right to say it ain't, well, *convenient* for you to ask the widow if that music box is still in the house?"

"One hundred percent right."

"And also you're not in any kind of a hurry to hand it over to the cops. Not with possession being nine-tenths of the law."

"It's nine *points*, not nine-tenths. But yes."

Frank looked annoyed. "Don't get technical with me. Points, tenths, same thing. If there's ten points of the law, and possession of a thing is nine of them, then it's also nine tenths. It comes down to the fact you got yourself a nice little treasure, and you don't want it to get away from you. Way I see it, you got two choices: You could lay low and hope nobody ever gets past Abramowitz to you. Or you could try and find out just how the box *did* get to Fat Marty in the first place. Me, I recommend the second route. You sit tight, you give the other side a chance to screw around with you. Better *you* should screw with *them*. Find out who sold the box to Abramowitz, maybe we could figure a nice quiet way to get the guy over to the cops."

I heard that "we." Frank the Crank with his spring wound to the snapping point.

"Let's see what I can find out, Doc," he said, holding out his hand like a traffic cop at a conversational intersection. "On the QT. Mum's the word. Soul of discretion. You ain't got a thing to worry about. Go home and listen to your music box. I'll be in touch."

We were about to open the door to the street when Shackie said, "Thomas ..." in that tone that means real trouble when it comes from your wife or your boss. Shackie was neither of the above, but I still went on full alert.

"What?"

"Let me take that box home with me. It's driving me crazy."

"Shackie–"

"Just 'til tomorrow. I'll give it back first thing, I promise. I bet I can have it fixed by then. Think how good it'll sound."

I sighed. I wish I'd done more than that, something like saying no and sticking to it. But I didn't. Shackie had me literally at a weak moment. Not enough sleep, no food since supper the night before. I needed to find Schwartz and get him cracking. Also, I thought I should pay a condolence call on Muriel Hardwick. Seemed like the decent thing to do, and besides–if I happened to find out whether Harry's rigid notation box was stolen, what would be wrong with that?

So I was going to be busy until evening. Which meant I'd have to carry the rigid notation box all over town—including right into Chez Hardwick—unless I wanted to take time to go home first and leave it. I didn't like either idea. Besides, I was not about to admit it out loud, but if Shackie said there was something wrong with the sound of a music box, then there was.

I glared at my friend, trying to look menacing. "You'll give it back first thing in the morning? Promise."

"You bet." He made a grab for the bag.

"Not so fast." I pulled it away. He stumbled, nearly falling on his face. "Shackie. You also promise you will not—repeat, *you will not*—try to return it to anyone whom you may at any time decide might be its rightful owner?"

"Oh, Thomas, come on."

"Promise, Shackie. Also promise you won't say *any*thing about it to *any*one."

"All right, for heaven's sake. I promise."

"All of it?"

"All of it."

My stomach took a flip as I slowly handed him the bag. It would be safe, I told myself—safer than my shlepping it all over New York. Who in the world would take better care than Shackie of a rigid notation music box? Besides, it would never occur to my New-Agey pal that a promise made under duress isn't worth the paper it's not written on.

"Keep it under wraps," I said, as I opened the door.

Shackie, clutching the bag with both hands under his left arm, went out ahead of me. "Don't worry." He smiled over his shoulder. "It'd take Francois Nicole himself to find it while I'm not working on it."

"Good." I shut the door behind us. "Give Francois my best and say thanks for me."

He didn't bat an eye. "Sure will," he said and waved back at me.

I'm not a sentimental guy but my eyes still go watery when I remember Shackie, his muffler sailing in the wind behind him and the Gristede's bag tucked under his arm, dodging through the crowds on the sidewalk like a scatback. But all I did then was check my watch. A quarter after one. By now, Schwartz would be close to finishing for the day at the Chelsea Flea Market.

I ducked into a 14th Street deli, grabbed a cheese Danish which I gobbled and a Styrofoam cup of coffee which I gulped as I humped it uptown on Sixth Avenue to 25th. Half a block away from the flea market, I saw Schwartz jawing with one of the dealers. He was an easy pickup, a little man in a black snap-brim fedora, arms and hands flying in every which direction. Tie Schwartz's hands to his sides, and he'd be incapable of speaking a complete sentence.

I paid my two bucks at the gate, glided over to my loyal picker, took him by the arm, and shepherded him toward the chain-link fence. "You can have him back in five minutes," I said to the dealer he'd been talking to, a chunk of a man with a cold-blotchy face. The dealer snickered and rubbed the sleeve of his coat across the underside of his nose.

Schwartz gave me the up-and-down. "Whoa," he said, all grins. "You don't mind me sayin', you're lookin' pretty scruffy."

"Thanks. Credit's yours. I didn't think I needed a soup and fish to buy a music box from Marty Abramowitz."

"Hey, right." Schwartz, ever on the uptake. "You get it?"

"I did. Thanks; I owe you. But no ten percent deal. That's a box I've been looking for since day one and it's worth a hell of a lot more than the forty-five hundred bucks I paid. Figure *twenty* percent for you–"

"Jeez, Doc–"

"Plus another hundred for appreciation."

"Doc! A *thousand bucks*?"

You don't often see Broadway Schwartz at a loss. His mouth

opened, closed, then opened again. "For that tip you're givin' me a K?"

"For that tip and a little work."

"Work? What do you mean, work?" Schwartz eyed me with caution.

"Don't worry. Nothing that'll give you a hernia. Here's the story: There's a chance—just a chance, mind you—that my music box is hot. If it is, I need to know. That Abramowitz slob fed me a prize cock-and-bull story. According to him, he got the box from Shackie."

"Shackie?" Schwartz guffawed. The dealer nearest to us, a little gray-haired woman in a maroon knitted hat, turned to look. I glared at her; she suddenly decided to rearrange her table full of plastic holiday ornaments. I nudged Schwartz and mouthed, "Keep it down."

Schwartz looked appropriately chastened. "Oh ... sure, Doc."

"Don't let him feed *you* that line. See what you can find out. Whatever, even if it's nothing, you get your thousand. Fair enough?"

Schwartz set his hat lower against the wind. "I'm on my way. That's better money than I'm gonna get here." He moved toward the gate. "Call you late this afternoon; you be home?"

"I'll make a point of it," I said and followed Schwartz out the gate. But then I remembered what he'd said about my personal appearance. I rubbed my fingers against my chin. Maybe I wasn't exactly in shape to make a condolence call. Better stop home after all, I thought. Shave and a shower, chop-chop.

FOUR

In the hot shower, I thought about Shackie, alone in his loft with my rigid notation box, and felt the way I did back in med school when one of my classmates beat me out of a Saturday night date with Sarah. She was a young staff nurse on Labor and Delivery, and I was crazy about her. Just a glimpse of Sarah down a hospital corridor and my head was filled to bursting with gorgeous melody. *I hear music when I look at you. A beautiful theme of every dream I ever knew.* Locking her up in marriage seemed like a great idea at the time–better than to burn and all that.

More great advice from those good folks who bring us the conventional wisdom. Within a couple of years Sarah's silky voice went lead-heavy, and that irresistible soft questioning in her eyes became a stony, intractable demand. What she wanted from me I didn't have to give. She said I was selfish and egocentric and my priorities were thoroughly screwed up. For fourteen years we stuck it out; talk about repenting at leisure. Finally, Sarah pronounced me hopeless and moved into an apartment in a small walkup building on Second Avenue between 24th and 25th. She never filed for divorce, though, not even for a legal separation. Go figure.

Whatever, that's been the Purdue *modus vivendi* for the past six years. More married than not, but definitely with separate bedrooms. Sarah went to work at Planned Parenthood's Teen Pregnancy Prevention Program. My mind's eye can't help seeing her as a raging white-caped crusader, ferociously pressing condoms, pills, and assorted sociological flapdoodle onto snickering teenaged girls.

But it makes sense to her and I've tried to give what I could. Planned Parenthood salaries are not munificent, so I pay Sarah's rent bill as well as my own, plus her basic living expenses. Plus a little more here and there whenever it's needed. Why not? We couldn't make it as husband and wife, but somehow and despite all our best efforts we accomplished something more impressive. We developed into friends.

As soon as I got out of the shower, I flopped across the bed and dialed my friend's number—and got her machine. In a way, that made things easier. "Hi, Babe," I chirped into the phone. "Listen: I'll pick you up at six-thirty; we'll go to the Brasserie." Then I added, quickly, "It's important ... *very* important. See you."

Now, if she had other plans, she'd cancel them.

I reached over to drop the receiver back into its cradle. Then I stretched long and hard. I closed my eyes, just for a minute.

Next thing I knew I had the phone off the hook and was saying, "Thomas Purdue" into the mouthpiece.

"Hey, Doc. It's Broadway."

The room was dark. I craned my neck to check the time on the alarm clock above me on the headboard. 5:17. Goddamn it! No condolence call this afternoon.

"What'd you find out?" I said.

"I ain't sure: maybe something, maybe not. I went up to Abramowitz's and said to him did my client buy the music box, and he said yeah. I asked him for how much and he said don't I trust my clients, so I told him sure, up to a point. He got himself a laugh outta that. Okay, he said, it was forty-five hundred, and my client was lucky to get it because right after he left, somebody came in and asked about music boxes and she was real disappointed when he said he had one but he just sold it. I asked him was there any chance he'd be gettin' more, and he said he guessed that depended on whether the guy who sold it to him needed more dough. But when I tried to find out anything about the guy, Abramowitz made like a Cherrystone. Sorry, Doc."

"It's okay. You're still in for the thou. Catch up with you tomorrow."

The Brasserie is east of Park Avenue on 53rd. It's been there forever, serving the best onion soup in the city, twenty-four hours a day, seven days a week. First time I went there was with my dad and mother one Saturday after a matinee performance of *My Fair Lady*. Some one-two punch for a ten-year-old: Julie Andrews and The Brasserie's onion soup. I still take either every chance I get.

When Sarah and I walked in, it was still early, not yet busy. The maitre d' led us past the small flocked tree with its blinking lights to a quiet table in a back corner. The waiter brought us menus, then glasses of wine.

Sarah raised hers in my direction. She could still make my heart pound. Her hair was shorter now and more gray than brown, and she was a pound or two overweight, which she thought was unattractive. I didn't, though, not at all. If only she'd remember where she lost that tender gaze that used to melt my heart.

"You've got a funny smile on your face," she said. "What are you thinking about?"

"Just trying to figure how I can get you to go to bed with me."

"For heaven's sake. You're worse than when you were a horny medical student."

"Thank you. What do you say? Is tonight the night?"

"No, it's not. And if that's why you've invited me here, you're wasting both your time and your money."

"*Why* not? *Why* won't you go to bed with me?"

"Because I don't go to bed with married men."

"But it's you I'm married to."

"We're separated, remember?" She couldn't stop the smile.

I sighed, a big phony one. "Oh well. Just thought it might be fun to beat Harold's time with my wife."

We clinked glasses. Sarah looked at me the way my mother used to and shook her head. We sipped our wine.

This was one of our games. After Sarah moved out she took up with a guy named Harold Bresler. She wasn't about to get married again, she insisted, but people, well ... they have their *needs*. So Harold was need-satisfier, I was friend, and never the twain would meet. Higamus, hogamus, woman's monogamous, and Sarah did *not* want scenes. I had the key to her apartment and was not to worry about using it; when it was need-satisfying time she went to Harold's place. My wife's always been an SOP person. Establish rules, know them, play by them. Play fair and play square.

Sarah put down her glass and studied me. She always complains I make her nervous because she never knows what might be coming next. "All right," she breathed. "What is it that's so very important?"

"Before we order?"

"Yes, before we order. I want to be able to enjoy my dinner."

This from the woman who would never go with me to an Alfred Hitchcock movie. Sarah labors heroically under the delusion that if one exerts proper effort and sticks firmly to her guns, she *can*, by George, impose order upon her world. Eliminate uncertainty, make it safe.

I was tempted to tweak her a bit, but since the favor I was after was hers to give or withhold, I restrained myself. "It's about Shackie. He needs some help."

Sarah took a long swig from her wine glass, then lowered it slowly. "Shackie needs help," she repeated.

"Shackie needs help," I echoed.

"Then why isn't *he* here? To speak for himself?"

"I'm the man in the middle," I said. "He's my friend; you're my wife. He asked me for help. I'm asking you."

"What's the problem?"

Enter the middle-aged lady bureaucrat. Eyes slitty, lips tight. Fingers drummed on the table.

"A nasty bit of mis-identity," I said. "An antiques dealer on the West Side sold a music box which may have been stolen from a certain collector. The dealer says Shackie sold *him* the music box; Shackie says not only no, but hell no. So here's the story: Tomorrow morning the three of us–you, Shackie, and I–will go over to the shop and talk to the dealer. Shackie'll pretend he's been there recently, but the dealer won't know him from Adam. Then if it's ever necessary, you'll be able to testify to that. See?"

Sarah looked doubtful. "I don't see what you need me for. You'll be there; you can testify."

The waiter approached, holding his order book at the ready. I waved him off, mouthing, "Few minutes."

"That wouldn't work," I said to Sarah. "Shackie and I are good friends, so your word would be more convincing." Before she could object, I leaned forward across the table and continued. "Besides, you know how Shackie is, poor guy. He's all in a stew about this, worried sick. Why, as soon as I mentioned that you might be willing to help, his whole attitude–"

"You told him I'd do it? How could you have the nerve?"

"I didn't tell him you would. I told him I'd ask you. There's a difference."

"Some difference!" She grabbed her glass, took an angry sip at the wine. "All right." The words, angry and grudging, forced their way past her lips. "You've got me. I'll do it. But really, you do have a nerve."

"Wonderful." I patted her hand. "That'll mean a lot to Shackie. It could be very important to him–say, if this thing ever does come down to a matter of who's telling the truth."

I saw steel in her eyes. Now, *I* got uneasy.

"Let me ask you something: What if that dealer takes one look at Shackie and says, 'Hello, Mr. O'Shacker. Do you have any more music boxes to sell?' Then what?"

"I wouldn't ask you to tell a lie. If that's what happens and then shit hits a fan, you just tell whatever you heard."

"Really? You're not telling me one of your stories, are you?"

"Absolutely not. Straight truth."

Well, it was ... at least as far as it went. Of course I wouldn't ask her to tell a lie. No point. Easier to persuade Sarah Purdue to parade naked down Fifth Avenue on the Fourth of July than to get her to tell a lie. But if Abramowitz did recognize Shackie, Sarah's testimony would be the least of my friend's troubles.

What I did not tell Sarah, though, was the identity of the buyer of that possibly-stolen music box. Or that her testimony might be of help to him in establishing legal ownership of the box. I also didn't bother to say anything about Harry Hardwick. Why confuse an issue with unnecessary detail?

Sarah humphed quietly and picked up her menu. I looked over mine. Rack of lamb sounded wonderful, a rare rack of lamb. The waiter came over and asked if we were now ready.

"I'll have the vegetarian angel-hair pasta," Sarah said. She delivered a sharp glance, right to the hearts of my eyeballs. "And another glass of the same wine, please."

I licked my lips slowly. "Make that two pastas," I said, returning the glance. "And two glasses of wine. And, oh yeah, a bowl of onion soup for me."

When I ordered the pasta, the expression in Sarah's eyes made my stomach lurch. It was almost gentle. As the waiter walked away, she whispered, "Thank you," across the table at me. Then she added in a louder voice, "You know, you really can be sweet when you want to be."

She meant thank you for not ordering blood-rare rack of lamb and ruining her entire evening. Sarah believes all animals should be treated with kindness and respect, which makes for a broad definition of cannibalism. Which was why I ordered the pasta. When someone else's view of the world seems a little goofy to you, try redirecting your own spyglass. Move over a couple of yards and peep through a different knothole. See if that makes a difference. The only thing more contemptible than proselytizing is making fun of the evangelist.

So I'd go veggie for the night. Nothing wrong with angel-hair pasta. I had no trouble imagining my revolted wife's face as I savored each forkful of lamb, and like standing on the corner watching all the girls going by, you can't go to jail—or hell, for that matter—for what you're thinking.

"If you won't go to bed with me, will you at least hold my hand?"

"Yes." Sarah smiled. "That would be all right." She extended her palm across the table top, and nestled it comfortably into mine.

I hear music when you touch my hand. A beautiful rhapsody from some enchanted land.

Some things don't change.

Sarah crooked her neck to look at her watch.

"Not to worry," I said. "You don't have to meet Mr. Harold 'til when? You said you've got an eight-thirty curtain."

"But I don't want to run in at the last minute. Tripping over people's feet as the house lights go down."

"Relax. It's only seven. We'll be done in plenty of time. Trust me."

That got me a world-class fisheye, but I didn't mind. No bad feelings. Just part of the game.

FIVE

A couple of minutes before eleven the next morning our little intelligence team got off the Uptown Local at 72nd Street. As we stepped out of the kiosk onto Broadway, the wind hit us like a club of ice. Shackie drew a sharp breath. I pulled my muffler tight around my throat, took Sarah by the elbow, and leaned into the blast.

While we waited to cross to Amsterdam, I felt a tug at my sleeve. A man in a ragged black overcoat had his hand out. I pulled a fistful of change out of my pocket, pressed the money into his shaking palm, and curled his fingers around it. "Thanks, mister," he mumbled, then turned and shuffled off into the crowd.

Sarah humphed. "You didn't do him any favor. He'll only go buy more liquor."

Alcoholic delirium tremens is nobody's idea of a romp in the park. I've treated my share of DT'ers and if it's not a kindness to drive the snakes and green Martians back into the jug, at least for a while, I don't know what is. "He needed money, I gave him money," I bellowed into the wind. "What he does with it is up to him."

I didn't convince her. I didn't expect to. It's a free country; believe what you want.

Just below 73rd on Amsterdam, we passed a clothing store, windows all red and green crêpe paper bunting and spray-on snow banks. A loudspeaker broadcasted Sinatra's earnest assurance that he'd be home for Christmas.

Sarah turned to look at me, eyes shimmering. "Did you say something?" she shouted through a whistling wind blast.

I shook my head. "Just humming along with the music."

She pulled her arm away and started walking faster. When I hum or sing along with music it's as if I'm having a pleasant conversation with the singer. I do it automatically, and Sarah hates it. She says it makes her feel as if I think she's not there. I used to tell her she could sing, too, but she always said no, that would spoil the music.

Approaching the Gotham Antiques Mart, I saw we had a problem. No way were we about to have a nice little chat with our friendly neighborhood antiques merchant. A small crowd on the sidewalk in front of the shop jostled and rubbernecked behind a length of thick yellow tape. A sweaty, beet-faced policeman breathed smoke out of both nostrils into the cold air on the other side of the tape barrier, inside the open doorway. His face said No Passing Me and No Kidding. I looked past him, into the store. The place was literally crawling with cops, some down on the floor behind the counter, others writing in little notebooks. A couple paced up and down the aisles exactly like antique collectors, but paying scant attention to the contents of the display cases. Rather, they seemed to entertain hopes of snatching a treasure from beneath or between those cases.

Shackie poked an elbow into my rib cage and whispered, "I think we ought to get out of here." Sarah just stared.

I held up my index finger to Shackie, and looked at a young woman standing to my left. Whether with excitement of the moment or from chronic bad nutrition, the clarity of her blackheads and reddened pustules against her chalky skin made her a walking ad for Clearasil. Under a green, knitted cap, her dark hair hung lank and lifeless. I touched her arm gently and out of the corner of my mouth said, "Hey, what's happening?"

The woman gave me a quick once-over, the New Yorker's ritual reflex assessment of a stranger. "They killed the guy owns the antique store," said the woman. "Probably serves him right, too, you ask me. I oncet tried to sell him some champagne glasses, they belonged to my Grammer, they were over a hunderd years old, easy. And you know what he wanted to give for them? Ten bucks! Ten ... lousy ... bucks! Said they were just cheap glass. I been tellin' my Mommer like forever now, the guy sells hot stuff. You oughta see some of the people go in there with things under their arms. Druggies and pimps and teenage nigger boys who you know couldn't have nothin' good to sell 'less they stole it. I bet it was one of *them* did it. Got pissed at the cheap Jew bastard and blew him away."

I nodded, very gravely. Then I slipped her a private smile, a little conversational grease. "How do you know so much about him?" I said. "You live around here?"

"*Around* here?" The young woman snorted like a mare in heat. "Hey, Mister, I live right up*stairs*." She wrenched her arm free to point toward a window two stories above the shop entrance, where an older woman–probably Mommer, I figured, or maybe Grammer–was peering out with anxiety smeared across her face, thick as movie makeup. "They live–the Abramowitzes, I mean, Mr. and Mrs.–they live on the second floor and we live right over them. And I been watchin' the characters comin' and goin' in and outta that shop for better'n five years now."

Her voice was as mean as her appearance. Even outside, in the cold winter air, she stank of stale cigarettes.

"I was sleepin' last night," she went on. "About one-thirty in the morning I hear this bang-bang, just like that. Didn't think anything about it: I figured it was just a bus backfirin' or somethin'. But when I got up this morning there were the cops, all over the place. So I went down to see Mrs. A, see if she knew what happened. And guess what? Her husband got shot last night, in the shop. She found him when she went down about seven o'clock 'cause he hadn't never come back to bed. I bet you anything what I heard wasn't no bus backfire. Bet I heard them shootin' him."

Basking in the reflected glory of having been somewhere important at an historical moment, she turned a coy smile on me. She did not want her story to end.

I returned the smile with interest. The best I-care-you-share look I could manage. "But that's peculiar, isn't it?" I said. "That Mr. A was in the shop at one-thirty in the morning? Not many antique shops stay open that late."

She gave me a look of pity. "I already tol' you," she whined. "He was buyin' hot stuff."

"But you don't know that for sure."

Her hands assaulted her hips. "Well, hey, mister. It don't take too much brains to figure it out. Mrs. A, she told the cops some guy called her husband up just a little after midnight, said he had to see him right away and no, it couldn't wait 'til the next morning. She even knows the guy's name, at least sort of, 'cause her husband told her after he hung up the phone."

It seemed as if the whole world had stopped breathing. I wanted to put my hand over the woman's mouth to stop the words I knew were on the way. But the irresistible force rattled on. "It was Olshansky, something like that. Mrs. A didn't get it clear. But the cops, they said they thought it would help a lot."

There's irony for you. Shackie's great-grandfather was named Moishe Olshansky. He was Jewish, as orthodox as they come. But between his middle-European pronunciation and the impatience of the Irish recording officer on Ellis Island, Olshansky became O'Shacker when he entered the United States. Things often are not as they seem.

I led my thwarted crew across 75th Street, then half a block uptown to Piu Bello Gelato. Sarah looked doubtful. "Ice cream? In this weather?"

I opened the door and moved her along, inside. Shackie followed us. "Best gelato in the city. Maybe in the world. You can have a pastry, though, if you'd rather. And a cup of coffee or espresso. We need to talk a little."

We took a table all the way in the rear, draped our coats over the vacant chair, and sat down. The cold had brought out high color in Sarah's cheeks; she looked delicious. She glanced my way, made a little clucking noise with her tongue, and shook her head sadly. "That poor girl," she said.

That's my wife. "That poor girl." Two people dead, Shackie in big-league trouble, the ownership of my rigid notation box in question ... all right, she didn't know that, of course, but still. Item Number One had to be That Poor Girl.

The waitress trotted up, order book open. Shackie and Sarah ordered coffee; I asked for a mocha and a small dish of vanilla gelato.

"Right away." The waitress smiled extravagantly, executed a little pirouette, and flounced off.

"She's a slob," I said.

Shackie narrowed his eyes in thought. "She looks nice enough to me," he said, gesturing with his eyes at the departing waitress.

"Not *her*, dummy," I said. "I'm talking about that poor girl outside the antiques shop, Little Miss Diarrhea-Mouth. 'The cops said that Mrs. A said that she sorta kinda heard her husband say–'"

"Relax, Thomas." There was an unusually soft edge to Sarah's voice. "You don't have to work so hard." She patted Shackie's arm. "Whatever that poor girl said, I'm not about to believe Shackie killed anyone. Shackie's not a killer, for heaven's sake. If that name really was O'Shacker, then *I* say it was someone pretending to *be* Shackie. Using his name."

People are always surprising you. As the waitress set down the cups in front of us, Sarah flashed me her I-win, you-lose smile. Marriage as a competitive sport. I was not about to complain, though. Actually, I wanted to kiss her.

"Guess there's nothing else to do here," I said. "Not any more. I'm going to go pay Muriel Hardwick a condolence call. Shackie–want to come?"

Before Shackie could answer, Sarah said, "Why? Who died?"

"Uh ... well, Harry died," I said. "Harry Hardwick."

"I didn't know he was sick," said my wife. Slowly but very clearly, she was moving into polygraph mode.

"He wasn't," I said. "It was actually ... quite sudden."

"Heart attack? Stroke?"

"Well ... kind of a stroke," I said. "With a bullet. Out of a gun. It happened after the party the other night."

Shackie filled the silence with a soft cough.

"After the party," Sarah finally echoed. "Who did it?"

I shrugged. "Don't have a clue."

Shackie waved his hand like a little boy asking permission to go to the bathroom. "I think I'll pass on the visit, okay? I've been working on a ... a very nice music box, one that hasn't been playing the way it should. But I think I've got the problem solved."

"Oh yes?" I said. I was careful to not look at Sarah.

"Uh-huh. I worked on it 'til four in the morning. Then, I got to talking with Pierre Legrande."

"Pierre Legrande?" This was a name I'd never heard.

"Yes." Shackie was suddenly all brightness. "Pierre started off as Francois Nicole's apprentice–then later, he had his own watch- and clock-making shop. He solved the problem for me. Tell you what, Thomas. You go see Muriel and then come on by, and I'll show you the box. I think you'd really be interested."

I glanced at Sarah. Best I could tell, she hadn't caught on. "Sure," I said. "I can do that."

"I'll go to Muriel's with you," Sarah said.

"Oh, that's not necessary," I said, much too quickly. "I don't want to waste your time."

"It's no problem," said Sarah, much too firmly. "I'm free 'til two; then I'm going to the Philharmonic. Muriel lives on what, Sixty-Second?"

"Yes," I said. "Between Park and Madison."

"Fine," Sarah said. "We'll cab over there. Then afterward, you can go to Shackie's and I'll come back here to Lincoln Center. I haven't seen Muriel in quite some time. Besides–a wife ought to go with her husband to offer condolences."

If it hadn't been Sarah, I'd have been highly suspicious of her motives. But Sarah operates by the book: Emily Post's book, Miss Manners' book. For her to come along with me was the proper thing to do. Worse, it was convenient.

So I said fine, come along. I'd only have made the situation more difficult by trying to dissuade her. *Nolo contendere.* Don't swim against the raging torrent.

SIX

Muriel Hardwick looked like no recently-widowed woman I'd ever seen. Makeup impeccable, eyes clear and bright. No throat-catch as she told Sarah and me the story. But her careful paint job couldn't quite gloss over a tightness around her eyes or parentheses left and right of her perky mouth which seemed to suggest that whatever she might say should be regarded as qualifying information.

Muriel had been Harry's third wife and considerably younger than her husband. Word was that this particular May-October affiliation would not last beyond the coming January. Which might have helped explain Muriel's matter-of-factness as she told us how she'd gone downstairs the morning after the party and found her spouse on the floor of his cylinder music box room, clotted splatters all over the shelves and music machines behind where he'd been standing when someone fired a bullet straight through his heart.

"Died instanter, of course," Muriel said in a voice full of smoky London fog.

Sarah, of course, was all sympathy. "Oh, I just can't imagine anything more awful."

"It *was* ugly, quite." Muriel lit a cigarette, inhaled deeply, then blew the poisons out of the right side of her mouth so as not to directly contaminate her guests. Her smile was cynical and also very attractive. Lovely white, even teeth.

We were sitting in the drawing room. Harry had done a

first-rate job of redecorating his home to showcase his treasures. Since the house was now officially in mourning, the heavy maroon drapes should have been drawn to create proper Victorian mid-day darkness. The giant gilt-framed mirror on the far wall should have been covered. But the drapes were wide open, permitting the weak December sun direct access, and my view of the three of us in the mirror was unencumbered. Which wasn't surprising. Muriel never pretended that antique music boxes and Victorian furnishings did anything for her. As far as Harry's obsession went, she was just along for the ride. There being no other transportation in town, she had no choice.

At that moment I would have agreed there was something to be said for Muriel's attitude. Barely ten minutes in a wingchair with its overly straight back and rounded, raised woven seat and I was ready to audition to play Quasimodo. Sarah, sitting in my chair's mate, looked comfortable enough, but Sarah would never let it be assumed or even implied that she was not satisfied with every aspect of her hostess' hospitality. Muriel sat on a small sofa facing us, shifting every couple of minutes from one buttock to the other.

"I guess there're going to be some changes here," I said as I watched her squirming nether parts.

Sarah let me know without a word that that kind of talk was not acceptable.

Muriel chuckled. "Perhaps. But I'm not sure just what sort of changes. To be frank, I'm not certain I shall stay here altogether."

"Oh, really?"

She took a long drag on her cigarette, then blew smoke. "Yes, I'm afraid so. I simply don't care for old things–and this is an old, dark building. I might prefer a nice condo, don't you know. Over on the East Side and up high, where the sun has no trouble coming through."

"Well, you don't want to make any major decisions," Sarah said firmly. "Not for six months, anyway."

Muriel laughed again. I thought I knew what she was thinking. The conventional wisdom holds that money can't buy intangibles, but that's wrong. Of course money can buy intangibles, and chief among those is immunity from the conventional wisdom. With what she stood to inherit from Harry, Muriel could buy a condo tomorrow, have it furnished to her specifications, move in, and leave the brownstone unoccupied but looked after. In six months or six years if she decided the move had been a mistake, she could make a phone call and have all her things brought back. Just like that.

"I'd sure hate to be your mover," I said.

Muriel expelled another mouthful of smoke and shook her head. "No problem there. If I do move house I'll be traveling light. And if I stay, well ... there's going to be a lot of empty space. At least for a while."

"You're going to sell the collection?" My own words left me light-headed. All these marvelous music machines hitting the market at once–literally tons of superb items, many of them one-of's. What an auction that would be.

"Yes, just as soon as possible," said Muriel. "The minute the lawyer tells me I may. I'll no more than have to pick up the phone and Lucas Sterne will have the lot out of here."

From the heights to the depths in one quick tumble. "You're going to have Lucas Sterne dispose of ... all this?"

"Why, yes." She was suddenly on full alert, studying me intensely. "Do you think he's not the right man?"

That was not a question I could answer properly with a simple yes or no. Lucas Sterne, Prop., owns and operates the Lucas Sterne Music Box Emporium, located at 42 East 56th Street, precisely at the center (as defined by Lucas, naturally) of the antique music box world. He's a slim young man in his mid-thirties who affects black pullovers and slacks to match, and arranges his thicket of dark curls so it cascades down his forehead to flirt with a pair of wide, dark eyes which I suspect he would describe, if pushed ever so slightly, as soulful.

Lucas is a curious living mixture of the highly admirable and the intensely abominable. His interest in and enthusiasm for music boxes is genuine; I once saw him reduced to tears by the music from a particularly lovely clock base music-works by Henri Lecoultre. This at a moment when he had nothing to gain from such an emotional display.

On the other hand there's no one like Mr. Sterne for pursuit of the main chance; he's Lucas-at-the-Rathole for all NYMBCA's elderly, frail, or faltering. Lucas sends cards on every birthday, pays afternoon visits religiously on Sundays, calls to inquire after the well-being of any member over sixty who happens to miss a meeting. When one of our geezers falls ill, Lucas is at the bedside, the quintessence of helpful sympathy. *Such* a nice young man! Before the undertaker gets a collector's body out of his late house, our boy has the widow's signature on a contract. Since many of our older folks set up their collections back in those glory days when people were giving antique music boxes away, sometimes even paying collectors a small fee to haul the damn things out of their attics, Lucas can offer wholesale prices that make him appear the soul of generosity but which in fact represent nothing short of grand larceny. Small wonder Lucas Sterne is the only full-time music box dealer in the city who can swing the rent on a fancy showroom in midtown Manhattan.

So, what to say to Muriel? "Lucas does sell a lot of collections. But I can't see how he could possibly give you anything like fair value for what you've got here. Not for a collection like Harry's."

Muriel corrugated her forehead and stubbed her cigarette in a small amber glass dish in the outstretched hands of a bronze, winged nymph. "Harry and his little art nouveau gewgaws," she muttered absent-mindedly, then blinked as if to clear her mental vision of distractions. "Lucas tells me he can sell the entire collection as such," she said and clapped her hands. "Bang, just like that."

So Lucas was going to broker the Hardwick collection. Smart move. No capital outlay, very little work, a quick return, and you can figure for yourself what ten percent of a ten-million-dollar collection comes to. Or more accurately, twenty percent. In this situation Lucas Sterne would hardly overlook the enchanting possibility of the double commission. *Caveat emptor et vendor.* Especially since a buyer at that level would likely be Japanese, German, Dutch, or Swiss–someone not at all likely to sit down and compare notes with Muriel.

"Well ..." I said, then paused to smile at Muriel. "As long as you know the value of Harry's machines, I guess you'll be okay."

Muriel returned the smile with interest, her response to my bit of *lèse majesté.* "Not to worry–Harry kept an inventory, a very careful one. He kept track of when he bought each piece *and* what he paid for it."

"I guess that shouldn't surprise me," I said. "Had it on computer, did he?"

Muriel laughed fully and openly. "The President and CEO of Hardwick Electronix? Surely you don't imagine he had boxes of file cards. No, Harry designed his own program. I've always wondered why he didn't make it available to other collectors–at least the ones in your association."

Bingo!

I scratched at my chin and tried to look thoughtful. "I wish he had," I said. "None of the commercial programs are any good for mechanical music. I've tried them; they're all more trouble than they're worth. I certainly would like to take a look at Harry's program sometime ... when it would be convenient."

"Well, there's no time like the present, is there?" Muriel stood up quickly, and smoothed her skirt. "It's no trouble. Come on, then."

Sarah and I rode Muriel's wake out of the drawing room, across the entry hall, and into a medium-sized room directly opposite. This was Harry's study. A big walnut desk and a high-backed red-leather swivel chair showed where the once-Prez and CEO used to sit with his back to the window. On the opposite wall were built-in shelves, filled with books. *Crime and Punishment* stood next to *Madame Bovary*, then Adam Smith, then of all things, a copy of *Gray's Anatomy*. Absolutely no order, no sense. Only Harry's extensive collection of mechanical-music literature was grouped, stacked top to bottom in the shelves at the far left.

Sarah was launching eyeball-daggers in my direction. This was inappropriate behavior, highly so, on the part of both bereaved and consoler. Where was the mandatory weeping and rending of garments? Where the patting on arms and saying of "There, there now"? Instead, here we were, poking casually among the dead man's effects. We were snooping, for God's sake, the two of us guilty of nothing less than criminal spiritual trespass.

But inactivity is the greatest ally of sadness. People *feel* better when they're doing things. So if showing her late husband's computerized inventory system was helpful to Muriel, I wasn't about to argue. Especially if I might thereby just happen to pick up the information I'd come for.

Muriel bent fetchingly over the computer on its stand next to Harry's desk. Out on the sidewalk, the line of little staked trees at the curb whipped sharply eastward in the wind, then returned slowly to neutral position. A man and woman walked past, light-stepped in spite of the wind. One of them must have said something funny because they both laughed. Hand in hand, they swung their arms between them as they went along, not seeming to mind that they were both wearing gloves. Love in the Day of the Ubiquitous Condom. I felt something sharp and sad deep inside my chest.

Muriel turned on the CPU. The machine booted; she typed in MUSEUM. An entry menu appeared and she selected VIEW CONTENTS. From a list including CYLINDER MUSIC BOXES, DISC MUSIC BOXES, AUTOMATA, ORGANS, and ORCHESTRIONS, she highlighted ORCHESTRIONS. Rows and columns filled the screen.

"They come up in alphabetical order," Muriel said. "But you can regroup them according to any parameter or combination of parameters you wish."

Sarah wandered over to the bookshelves. She picked one book, then another, riffling pages as she browsed. She was not going to participate in this travesty of condolence.

"It's incredible," I said.

What I meant was the scope of Harry's collection. Orchestrions are giant mechanical one-man bands, usually comprised of a piano or an organ with accompaniment instruments like drums, bells, or cymbals. Some orchestrions play their music from pinned barrels but most use coded perforated cardboard or paper. These things are huge, sometimes more than ten feet across and eight feet high, and they do not come cheap. For a collector to pay forty- or sixty-thousand dollars for one is not unusual, and the rarer ones bring six figures. Most collectors find that even if money is not a limiting factor space is, so it's uncommon to find more than one or two orchestrions in even a big mechanical music collection. But here was the first page of Harry Hardwick's orchestrion list, with twelve entries arranged in neat columns showing the name of each machine, its estimated age, condition, date of purchase, source, purchase price, and restoration cost. A quick add indicated Harry had something in excess of $600,000 worth of orchestrions on the first page alone.

I gave Muriel a golly-gee-whiz smile, the look new collectors get on seeing their first extensive collection of music boxes. Then I slid down into the seat, mumbling a non-interrogatory "Do you mind," and pushed SCROLL DOWN. Eleven more orchestrions came into sight. I kept pushing the SCROLL DOWN key. By END OF LIST I'd scanned the descriptions of sixty-two orchestrions with a total worth of between three and a half and four million dollars. True, some were duplicates, but the word for owning two very rare Encore Automatic Banjos is opulent, not jejune.

"Muriel, this is marvelous!" I said.

Have you ever noticed how families develop their own private languages, both verbal and body? From the bookshelves, Sarah paused long enough to flash me a look I had no trouble deciphering as a Cease and Desist Order. For answer I gave her a wink. To Muriel, who smiled, that wink meant, Hiya Babe, isn't this just amazing? To Sarah, it meant, Go ahead and take the goddamn high road if you want, but my errands happen to be along the low road and you'd better not do anything to stop me from getting to Loch Lomond. Amazing how much intelligence you can get into a wink.

Sarah got it all right, every unspoken word. She tossed off a military turn and went back to shuffling through books.

"Let me look through this a little," I said. "I might be able to adapt it to my own collection–on a much smaller scale, of course."

"Yes, certainly, go ahead," said Muriel. "Harry never did show it to you, did he?"

"No, he never even mentioned it. And I've never been in this room."

Muriel smiled wryly. "Few people were. This was his *sanctum sanctorum*. When he wasn't inside he kept it locked."

While she was talking I exited ORCHESTRIONS and went into VIEW-AUTOMATA. I scrolled through some 350 entries, nearly twenty-one pages, net worth roughly three million. I repeated the procedure with the 485 disc music boxes, thirty-two pages, a little more than two million. Then, I looked at the cylinder boxes: 427, twenty-nine pages, one and a half million.

I took a hard look at one entry in that cylinder-box list. It identified a rigid notation box by Francois Nicole, serial number 432, twelve-inch cylinder, 211-tooth comb, four Mozart overtures (*The Magic Flute, Figaro, Idomeneo*, and *Don Giovanni)*, in full operating condition. Most important, it had been bought on December tenth for $22,500, from Sophie Soleski.

That done, I scrolled through the miniatures. I'm sure

they were impressive, but I wasn't taking in the information on the screen. I was wondering about Sophie Soleski. Soph is one of the founding members of NYMBCA, a delightful octogenarian who's been selling music boxes from her place in Greenwich Village for more than fifty years. I'd have to talk to Soph–because now I had to accept that Harry's rigid notation box and mine were one and the same. I didn't like it, but since it was so I needed to know it. Ignorance is never bliss. At best it's a handicap, at worst highly dangerous.

I stood up. "I'd love to have a copy of this program, Muriel," I said. "If you wouldn't mind, I'll come back another time and talk to you about it."

She shrugged. "Why should I mind? I was always telling Harry he should be more generous."

We went back down the entry hallway into the kitchen. Muriel put on a pot of coffee. "Do the police have any leads?" I asked. "Do they know ... well, why?"

Muriel rolled her eyes. "Not really. They think it was probably someone who was at the party."

"One of the NYMBCA members? No."

"Well, actually, yes. There was no sign of breaking and entering, nothing destroyed, and they estimate Harry died at about two or three in the morning. I went to sleep about one-thirty, but you know how Harry was. A real night owl and then up in the morning with the robins. He only needed three or four hours of sleep, and one-thirty a.m. was the middle of the day for him. I went off to bed and as far as I know he went off to play with his toys. But when I got up in the morning it was obvious he hadn't been upstairs at all. *That* seemed a bit unusual. So I went looking."

The coffee was ready. Muriel poured three cups and handed them around. She leaned against the counter and sipped at hers, then looked at me over the edge of her cup. "And there he was ... in the cylinder room."

This was too much for Sarah. "You don't have to tell us all

over again, dear," she said. "I'm sure it must be terribly painful for you."

"Oh, I'm all right, never mind. It *was* unpleasant, of course—but now they've come and taken him away, and ... it's all been cleaned up ... well, I'm pretty much over the shock. No bother talking about it."

Muriel sounded almost chipper, as if the subject under discussion might have been a half-eaten mouse in the vestibule, left by the cat and quickly disposed of by the butler. I looked at Sarah and without a word told her, you lose again. She replied, just as silently, that if she were ever inclined to use such language she'd tell me to go screw myself.

"But why do they think it was one of the party guests?" I said, as off-hand as I could manage.

"Because a music box was stolen," said Muriel. "The police are assuming one of the guests hid somewhere, maybe in a closet, and then after he thought we were all asleep he tried to nip off with the music box. Harry must have surprised him in the act—so he killed Harry."

I shook my head sadly, but said nothing. I didn't want to appear particularly curious about which music box had been stolen.

After coffee we left. Sarah said all the Right Words on the doorstep. You have our deepest sympathy. We're available if you need help. You have only to call. Muriel also played the scene according to Hoyle. It's so nice to have *real* friends. I'm sure I shall be just fine, thank you. But should the need arise, I'll not hesitate to call. The two women hugged and kissed cheeks; I shook hands with Muriel.

At the sidewalk Sarah glanced back over her shoulder, making sure the door was closed. "Pretty cold fish," my wife sniffed. "How long were they married?"

"Not quite five years. It was a few months after the big Sotheby's auction in London—the one with the fantastic automata, early cylinder boxes, and miniatures."

"I should have known you'd time something by its relationship to an auction. Or a sale or a music machine get-together." Her voice was like the icy wind, whipping out from between buildings, stinging my face. The sun was behind the clouds now. Snow coming.

"You asked. I'm pretty sure Harry met Muriel in London when he went over for that auction. They were married only a month or two later."

"Humph." Sarah clearly did not approve. "Older men can be foolish, especially wealthy ones. They're easy bait for some ambitious young gold-digger. I don't understand why they don't just go to a brothel. It'd be so much cheaper in a lot of respects."

We were approaching Fifth Avenue. Sarah took my arm as the holiday crowd pushed and shoved us every which way. At the corner as we waited for the light to change, a scroungy Santa waved his bell over a red kettle, looking like one of Harry's automata. "Come on now," I said to Sarah. "You're being pissy. Maybe it was different between Harry and Muriel."

"She didn't seem exactly heartbroken."

"She's British, for Christ's sake," I said. "Stiff upper lip, you know. Those Brits have the decency to not go bawling and sniveling in public every time something goes wrong in their lives. Damn it, Sarah, you're being unfair to her."

The light changed. I took a step into the street, but Sarah stayed behind on the curb. The right corner of her mouth twitched and her hand seemed to be trying to move toward her purse. She looked like someone about to throw a full-fledged grand-mal seizure.

"Are you all right?" I called, then rushed back and grabbed at her hand.

I instantly saw she was both all right and furious. She jammed her hand into her purse and came out with a photograph, which she thrust without a word into my hand. The crowd swirled past us, hurrying to get across the street during the green.

I clutched the picture tightly. It was an ordinary 4x6 glossy color print, but there was nothing routine about the subject matter. Two people, a man and a woman, were lying jay-naked on a bed. Neither seemed aware they were being photographed. They were too busy concentrating on the business of the moment, which appeared to be wholehearted fellatio. The man's eyes were closed and he had a silly little smile on his face. I looked more closely, blinking my eyes for clarity. No question. The man was Harry Hardwick; the woman was Muriel.

"Jesus," was all I could say.

"Try this one," Sarah said, passing me another picture.

I pulled her back from the street corner, toward the Chemical Bank Building behind us. Once inside the glass-enclosed cash machine area I marched her to the counter, as far as possible from the machines and the waiting line. Not complete privacy, but good enough. And the wind wouldn't blow the pictures out of our hands and away forever down Park Avenue. I looked at the second picture.

This one was a posed shot. A naked man and a bikini-clad woman were grinning at the camera. The man had a big-time hard-on which the woman was holding in a hot dog roll. Her mouth was open, ready for the first bite. This woman was definitely not Muriel, though, and the man wasn't Harry. So far as I knew, I'd never seen either of them before.

"Well?" said Sarah.

"Well, what?"

"Well, what do you think of ... *that*?"

"Hard to say. I wonder if they've got mustard and sauerkraut on that roll? Ketchup'd be perverted."

I don't know why I did that. I had nothing to gain by provoking Sarah, but her tone was so prissy and irritating that the words just came out. She glared at me and made a move to stamp her right foot. Next thing she'd be out of there, across the street, and I wouldn't hear a word from her for at least another week.

Which would not do. "Look, I'm sorry," I said quietly, and grabbed her arm. "It was just a manner of speaking, a little verbal shorthand. These pictures are shocking, they really are. All right? Do you recognize the guy in the hot dog roll? Or the woman?"

Sarah made a face of utter disgust and shook her head.

"Where did you get these, for Christ's sake?"

"In a book." She almost smiled.

I stared at her.

"Harry's bookshelves," she said. "Where I was browsing, remember? One of those books wasn't a book. It was supposed to be a summary of nineteenth-century economics but it was actually a box. And it was full of these."

"Full?"

Sarah nodded. "Some of Harry, some of other men. The ones with the other men looked like this one, posed. The ones with Harry didn't."

"Hidden camera," I said.

"I didn't think one or two would be missed. So I took them to show you."

"Why?"

She flared up, then remembered where she was and that we were not alone. "I thought you'd be interested," she said, quietly enough, but not so quietly that I could miss the sharp edge on the words. "I mean, really! The way you were pumping Muriel."

As she heard her own words, she reddened; as she saw I had caught on, she went scarlet. I thought she looked delectable. She saw that, too. "Well, I don't know what you're up to," she said. "Two murders, a stolen music box, Shackie in trouble. I just thought they might ... *help* you and Shackie. So I took them."

I bent forward to kiss her forehead. "Thank you. You're absolutely wonderful and I appreciate it." I slipped the pictures into my shirt pocket. "I'll tell you more later. You're going to the Philharmonic now, right?"

She checked her watch. "If I don't hurry I'll be late."

I took her by the elbow, shoved us both through the door and to the curb, where I flagged a cab. Payment for services rendered. She shouldn't keep Harold waiting, the son of a bitch, or miss any of her concert, not on my account. I dropped her at Lincoln Center, told her I'd see her later, and told the driver to take me to Seventh Avenue and 16th Street.

SEVEN

As the cab barreled down Broadway *allegro con brio*, I slipped the two photographs out of my pocket and copped another peek. Muriel and Harry, my God! Who in hell had taken this picture and why? For that matter, how? A camera behind a hole in a nearby wall? Privacy's getting dicier every day. We're rapidly approaching a time when it may be crazy to *not* be paranoid.

The lady in the other picture, the posed shot, was a slim brunette with a mischievous smile. She was wearing a yellow bikini and was down on her knees, holding the hot dog roll in both hands, all set to take the first bite. The guy was big, with lots of teeth and slicked hair. I'd never seen him before, but he definitely was not Harry Hardwick. He stood proudly, chest-out and hands on hips, grinning for the camera. The woman was looking up at him out of the corners of her eyes. Definitely a pose, but whether for porn sales or just the work of dedicated amateurs, I had no idea.

I stared out the window. According to Sarah the box was full of pictures like these. Who'd shot them and how did they get to Harry? Did Muriel know of their existence? Did she know Harry had them?

And how could I get my hands on the rest of them?

We were coming up on 16th Street. I slipped the pictures back into my shirt pocket, then had a second thought. People do occasionally get mugged and robbed on the sidewalks of

New York. I took the pictures back out and worked them down inside my jockey shorts. Like I said. Paranoia is getting to be less crazy every day.

Shackie's place was four flights up. I took the stairs two at a time. My heart was pounding, not from the exercise. I was an ardent swain dashing forth to meet his *inamorata* now restored to health by Merlin of the Music Boxes. I gave the door a vigorous knock. Someone said come in.

Someone. To this day I can't tell you whether the voice was Shackie's, but at that moment who was thinking? Not me, that's for sure. I threw open the door and rushed in.

I had a momentary impression of chaos; then I heard a loud, cracking thud and saw a display of white fireworks on a red background. Then my head exploded.

I woke to a fierce pounding behind my eyeballs. By reflex I ran my hand over the top of my head, which turned out to be a bad move. The lump above my left ear confirmed my diagnosis that I'd been cold-cocked from behind, but the light pressure of my hand set off the fireworks again, along with a major wave of nausea. I had to lie still for another few minutes. Then I got slowly to my feet, sliding my way up the door, holding the knob for balance.

I blinked. Shackie's loft was a war zone, the floor covered with tools, clothing, kitchen pots and dishes. The place looked as if it had been done over by a colossal MixMaster. "Shackie?" I called out. My voice sounded strange to my own ears, weak and wavery.

There was no answer.

I started to make my way through the mess. It wasn't easy. Workbenches were overturned, all their drawers emptied and tossed aside. Music boxes that should have been neatly stacked on the shelves at the far end of the room were scattered on the floor. Parts under restoration were tossed every which way. In the back of the room and to the left, where Shackie cooked and ate, not a drawer was in place, not a pot or a plate or a fork where it should have been. Everything in heaps on the floor. But no sign of my rigid notation box or any of its parts. I wasn't sure whether that entitled me to feel better or worse.

Looking up into Shackie's sleeping area, I could see only the front foot and a half. Still, it was clear that the same whirlwind had run rampant up there. The floor was covered with shirts and pants; pajama bottoms were draped over the railing. In my odd-sounding voice, I called Shackie's name again and again.

Very slowly, clutching the side rail, I started to climb the stairs. I was pretty sure I wasn't going to like what I'd find up there and I couldn't have been more right. Drawers had been pulled out of the bureau, emptied upside down, and slung off to one side or the other. The door to the little closet was open. Against the light from the bulb inside, a shadow spilled out of the closet onto the floor of the room. Three steps closer and I could see Shackie, hanging by his neck from the clothes hook on the back closet wall. His feet were only about four inches off the ground and a step-stool was on its side in front of him, as if it had been kicked free.

What I did I can't explain. I walked calmly over and shook my friend by the shoulder. "Shackie, wake up. Come on, now. Wake up."

It was like shaking a hanging bag of putty. Shackie swung ever so slightly, first to the right, then to the left. His eyes were open, his pupils wide, and his mouth was twisted into a grotesque shape somewhere between the classical masks of comedy and tragedy. His congested tongue lolled from the left corner of his mouth. I put my ear to his chest, heard nothing, and then grabbed for his left wrist. No pulse. I let the arm fall and grabbed the right. With no better result there, I tried to feel a transmitted heartbeat in his neck, below the rope or above. I looked into his eyes; they stared right through me. Whatever they were seeing they didn't like.

That was as far as I could deny the obvious. People die. You're a doctor, you adjust–either that or go insane. But a cerebral hemorrhage in a long-term hypertensive patient is one thing, a rope around your pal's neck something terribly different. No adjustment here, folks.

But no insanity, either.

And suddenly, even, no headache.

Propelled by a cold fury, I ran downstairs to the kitchen area, found a bread knife on the floor, and took it back upstairs. With my left arm around Shackie's chest, I sawed through the rope in three quick strokes. Shackie's head rolled forward and plopped onto my shoulder. I'd set myself, thinking he'd be heavier–I'm no iron-pumper–but I had no trouble carrying him to his bed. The mattress had been slashed, then pulled off the box springs, which had also been cut from top to bottom and side to side. With my right hand I wrestled the mattress back onto the springs; then, carefully, I laid Shackie down. He was still looking in horror at whatever he'd seen ... or was seeing. With my thumb, I closed first one lid, then the other. Goodnight, sweet prince. I worked the noose off his neck and threw it to the floor as though it were contaminated by plague bacilli.

I patted Shackie's limp hand. It felt like a mackerel on ice. I started to walk away, back down the ladder steps.

But as I turned to leave, I noticed a sheet of paper on the table next to Shackie's bed. I'M SO ASHAMED was printed in big block letters.

"Ashamed?" I asked the air. "Ashamed of what?" I glanced back at Shackie. Ashamed was the last thing he looked.

At least he looked comfortable now, lying on his bed, the rope off from around his neck and his eyes closed against all horrors past and future. What else could I do for my friend?

Find the son of a bitch who killed him.

Taking at least minimal precautions to not go ass-over-teakettle down the ladder, I went back to the shop and walked over to the farthest back corner. Then, systematically, I started to search.

Back and forth I prowled, covering the floor line-by-line across the room. My desperation grew with every fruitless pass. When I got to the front of the shop without seeing either my rigid notation box or any of its parts, I started again. I checked every item I passed on the floor, pawed through every pile. New messes from old. My rigid notation box just wasn't there.

I don't know how long I searched. I might be there yet, moving robot-like through the detritus of my friend's life, but for a heavy pounding at the door. I jumped a foot. The knock came a second time, even louder. "Police," I heard someone yell. "Open up."

I staggered to the door, pulled it ajar, and found myself staring stupidly into two grim faces beneath blue policemen's hats. Behind them, a little to the right, a third cop aimed a pistol directly at my chest. His twin was off to the left. It occurred to me I might have heard sirens a few minutes before, but in the middle of New York City who's going to think anything about a siren scream here and there?

I didn't stop to consider what the situation must have looked like to the cops. "He's dead," I said dully and pointed to the loft. "Up there."

The two cops in front looked at each other, then back at me. Behind them, the pistol twins batted neither eye nor gun. Slowly, I raised my hands over my head. "I don't know who did it," I said. "I came in and got hit. I found him when I came to."

The two front cops pulled *their* guns and cautiously moved inside. One aimed his pistol at the lower shop area; the other crouched and pointed his weapon upward, toward the sleeping area. Despite being still under cover by the Hallway Sharp Shooting Boys, I was beginning to feel less confused and terrified. On the other hand, I was getting angrier by the second—though exactly at whom I wasn't sure.

"He's dead, I told you," I snapped. "Put those stupid fucking guns away."

One of the cops turned to face me. I don't think I've ever seen such an unpleasant expression on a face, anywhere, any time. "Lie down," he snarled and motioned to the floor in front of me. "On your face, hands behind your head. Move it."

I got only one word into my objection. "But—" The cop took me by the collar, pressed a foot behind my knee, and gave me a hard shove downward. I went to the floor like a sack of Idaho russets.

"On your face," the cop snarled. "And keep your goddamn face *shut*."

He started frisking me. I remembered the two pictures inside my underwear, between my body and the floor. Always better lucky than good. I didn't think the cop would search me there.

He had my wallet; I heard him riffling through the cards. "You Thomas Purdue?" he said. "You a doctor?"

"Yes," I muttered into the floorboards.

"Okay. Sit up."

I turned over and worked myself into a sort of Buddha position. I glared at him; he glared back harder. He held my wallet out to me; I took it and put it back into my pocket. I heard the other cops moving around in the loft.

"You this guy's doctor?" the cop asked me.

"No," I said.

"So what're you doin' here?"

"He's ... he *was* my friend," I said. "We were going to do some repair work on an antique music box. I knocked on the door, heard somebody say come in; I came in and got hit over the head." I pointed to the top of my head, being careful not to touch it. "When I woke up I found him, up there."

"Was it you called nine-one-one?"

"No," I said.

One of the other cops stepped forward. "Okay. So, you walked in, got hit, woke up, found your friend dead. Then what?"

I paused. It was going to sound very funny if I said I'd spent however long it had been searching the room for a music box whose description I was not eager to enlarge upon right then–particularly to the police.

It was story time.

"Then nothing," I said. "I woke up, found my friend hanging in the closet, cut him down, put him on the bed, came back downstairs ... and then, you guys were at the door."

The cops looked around. Someone else had come into the room–or better, two someones. They wore white suits, and one carried a black leather bag. Paramedics, an ambulance team.

The cop who'd been questioning me nodded a hello and jerked his head at me. "Says he got hit," the cop said. "Knocked out. He's supposed to be a doctor."

I didn't recognize either of the paramedics. They wouldn't have been from Manhattan Medical; this was St. Vincent's territory. The one holding the bag was a friendly-looking kid, not much over twenty, with a blond brush cut and a face full of freckles. His partner was darker, Italian or Greek I thought, and maybe ten years older.

Freckleface asked, "How do you feel?"

"Just peachy," I told him. "I've been knocked cold, my best friend's been killed, I've been thrown on the floor and frisked ... I feel just great, thanks. How about a little racquetball?"

The kid's face beamed friendly sympathy. "You're a doctor?" he said. "What kind?"

I had to hand it to him. Young guy, but lots of poise and savvy. He was being tactful about telling me I was behaving like a schmuck, making his life harder for no good reason.

"I'm a professor of neurology over at Man Med," I said. "Thomas Purdue." I held out my hand.

The kid gave it a fraternal shake, one medical professional to another. "Having any symptoms, Doc? You know. Nausea? Dizziness? Can you walk?"

"Nothing specific. I just feel like I've been hit. Hard."

I pointed to the left crown of my head. He peered at it, then ran a finger gingerly over the area. It hurt like hell and I told him so.

He looked properly pained. "Sorry. That's quite a mouse you got there. Any idea what he hit you with?"

"I didn't see a thing," I said. "Not the person, not the weapon."

The kid ran me through a quick neuro exam, testing my reflexes, looking into my eyes and ears, checking my neck for stiffness. He glanced up at his partner. "Wanna get the stretcher, Johnny?" he said.

Johnny nodded and walked out the door.

"Hey, wait," I shouted. "I don't need a stretcher. And I don't need to go to the hospital." I started to my feet.

The cop put a heavy hand against my chest.

"Dr. Purdue, come on." Freckleface talking. "You know better. You've been knocked unconcious. We'll take you over to St. Vinnie's, have them check you out. You know–make sure there's no subdural or subarachnoid hemorrhage."

I did know better. He was right–an injury of the kind I'd had can cause dangerous bleeding inside the head. But all I wanted to do right then was get the hell out of Shackie's place and away from the cops. I'd get an examination at Manhattan Medical, and if it was okay I'd go back to my own place and lie down. If I started feeling drowsy I'd head right back across the street. And when Sarah came back from her concert she'd keep an eye on me through the night.

"Not necessary," I said to the paramedic. "I'm okay; I just want to go home. I'll sign an AMA for you." It's always tickled me that the initials of the American Medical Association are the same as the acronym for "against medical advice," the statement a patient signs when he wants to withdraw from treatment.

The cop loomed up big in my face again. "Sorry, but you ain't signing nothing, Doctor," he said. "And you ain't going home, not now, anyway. You're going to St. Vinnie's with the team here and I'm going right along with you. If it wasn't for the fact you got hit over the head, you'd be on your way to the station by now. So do what the team says and figure you're getting a good deal."

Freckleface looked embarrassed. A nice kid. Johnny walked back in, a rolled-up stretcher under his arm. He and Freckleface opened it onto the floor. I made a face; the cop made a worse one. I shrugged and moved onto the canvas. Johnny took an IV pack out of the bag and moved toward me.

"Come any closer to my vein and I'll break your fingers." I smiled at the young men.

Before the cop could object Freckleface said, "I don't think we need an IV, Johnny. Let's get him in." They moved to each end of the stretcher, lifted me up, and with the cop marching at the head of the parade, took me down the stairs and outside. I waved to the little crowd on the sidewalk as they loaded me into the City of New York meat wagon.

EIGHT

They gave me the million-dollar workup. X-ray series, CAT scan, ultrasound, MRI–God forbid a professor of neurology should die of an undiagnosed intracranial bleed. Fortunately, none of the procedures required me to take off my shorts.

Also fortunately, all tests were negative. "No fracture, no subdural, no subarachnoid hemorrhage," said Dr. Carl Ransom, the young staff neurologist who'd been lucky enough to be on call when I rolled in. "But you know how it is, Dr. Purdue. Delayed bleeds aren't at all uncommon up to twenty-four hours; I'd feel much better if you stayed here that long. You'll have a private room on the Neuro Ward, of course."

Of course. I looked at my shadow-cop. No point arguing. Even if I won I'd lose. Better to lie in a comfortable bed at St. Vinnie's than be hauled away downtown to sit in a hard-back chair in a crummy station house. I checked my watch. "Four o'clock tomorrow, then, right?"

Dr. Ransom laughed. "Fair enough. Four o'clock tomorrow, I'll sign you out."

While I waited for them to wheel me off to my room, I asked the cop to let me call my wife. "I don't want her to come home and find me missing," I said. "She'd be worried." He nodded grudgingly and listened while I told Sarah's machine I was all right but that I'd been hit over the head, was at St. Vinnie's for tests and observation, and she should get a cab and come down when she could.

Then I lay back and went along for the ride. Before I hit the bed in my nice private room I was asleep.

I woke to a dispute in the hallway outside. A moment later Sarah burst in, frantic. "Thomas, what *happened*? Why did that policeman have to search my purse before I could come in?"

I saw the cop peering around the corner. "He wanted to be sure you weren't bringing me a hacksaw. Or a semi-automatic assault pistol." I held my arms out, husband-like, and she rushed up and hugged me. "I'm okay," I whispered into her ear. "I really am. Just don't say *anything*. About Muriel or those pictures or Harry Hardwick or that dead antiques dealer." Then I let go of her and sat up.

"Thomas, *what* is going on?"

Why is it that a woman who's never been a mother still knows how to sound exactly like one? "Be quiet," I said, very softly, and indicated with my head and eyes the cop outside. The motion set off a minor display of intracranial fireworks.

Sarah slapped her palms against her legs and blew out two lungs full of exasperation. "I came home from the concert, found your message, didn't even take my coat off, just rushed right down here. And what do I find? You're in a hospital bed, in police custody no less. I think I'm entitled to *some* explanation."

Well, all right. Easy enough. I patted the bed sheet next to me. "Sit down and I'll tell you."

She made it obvious she didn't trust me, but she did sit down. I put my arm around her waist and told her the same story I'd given the police a little earlier. That I'd gone to see a music box Shackie thought would interest me, I'd been hit over the head, and just a few minutes after I woke up, the police were pounding on the door.

"But how did the police happen to come by?" Sarah asked.

"Good question. I'd like to know that myself. Maybe a neighbor heard the commotion; the place looked like a tornado had gone through it. Or maybe the killer called the police. After he'd left."

I could see gears grinding behind her eyes. "Thomas ..." She rubbed my hand gently, a bad sign. "You don't suppose, do you ... I mean ... Well, is it at all possible that Shackie really *did* kill himself–"

"No, that's ridiculous. He–"

"Let me finish. Maybe ... maybe Shackie needed money, let's say. For *some* reason, whatever, maybe Shackie stole Harry's music box, Harry caught him, and Shackie panicked and killed Harry. Then Shackie sold the music box to that dealer. Maybe the dealer tried to blackmail Shackie. So Shackie killed him, realized he was in over his head, couldn't see any way out, and killed himself. It's possible."

"No," I said.

"It *is* possible."

"Goddamn it to hell, the frigging sun just might rise in the west tomorrow. Now, listen, would you? For one thing, even Shackie would've had more sense than to give that dealer his real name. For another, why would he have gone to all the trouble of tossing his own place before he hung himself in the closet? And for Number Three: Shackie just plain would not have killed two men and stolen a music box. Never, ever, not for any reason. I know that and so do you. Enough! Now, I need you to do something for me."

Sarah got the same look on her face that I imagine I got when she started rubbing my hand. "I'm listening. But I haven't promised."

"Go get some dinner. And while you're there, get me a sandwich and something decent for my breakfast tomorrow, I don't want to eat hospital food. Then stop back at my apartment. Get me my pajamas and razor, and pick up the couple of books on my night table. Okay? Is that too much to ask?"

She smiled. Sadly, but still a smile. "Thomas, you are *so* self-indulgent. Don't you ever think of anyone else?"

I wanted to get Sarah into my apartment ASAP, but I didn't want to tell her why. So if it helped her to slip my feet into a well-fitting pair of shoes, I wasn't about to resist.

"I don't have to. You do it for me."

She gave me the mandatory fisheye. "Why I keep doing these things I simply don't know." She bent over and dropped a quick kiss on my forehead. "I'll be back in a couple of hours."

Sarah walked out; a man walked in. He didn't look like a doctor. Even dangerous physicians generally don't *look* threatening. This guy was big but not in the least fat, and he had angry, spiky, sand-colored hair. His eyes were twin lakes of blue ice. A scar curved its way down his cheek from the corner of his left eye. He nodded at me; I nodded back.

He flipped open a leather billfold to flash a badge in my face. "Donald Robinson. Homicide."

"Detective," I said.

He grunted a sort of agreement and settled down in the chair next to the bed. Then he thrust his legs out in front of him and set his eyes on me, hard. He probably figured that was intimidating. He was right.

"Doctor," he rumbled, "can you tell me what you were doing at Mr. O'Shacker's this afternoon?"

I hate it when people address me by that patronizing word, "Doctor." "Well ... Most of the time I was lying on the floor, being unconscious."

Robinson smiled, but very clearly not because he thought I was amusing. "O-kay. Let's start again. Why did you go to Mr. O'Shacker's place today? And what time did you get there?" Then, before I could say a word in answer, he added, "And one more wisecrack out of you, you're going to the prison ward. For a hell of a lot longer than you'd like."

Point made. I've been on the prison ward down at Bellevue, but only on the treating end. No way did I want to spend even a minute there as an inmate.

"I went for the same reason I usually go there. Shackie was a music box restorer; I'm a collector. We were good friends. He said he had an interesting music box he was working on, he thought I'd like to see it. When I knocked on the door, right about two o'clock, someone–I don't know who–said to come in and I did. I had just long enough to see that the place was a shambles; next thing I knew, I was on the floor with a major headache. I got up, looked around, went upstairs, and found Shackie hanging in the closet. I cut him down, put him on his bed, and then went back downstairs. That's when your troops arrived. That's it."

"Mm." He nodded again. "You didn't stop to think that you were tampering with evidence? Cutting the body down, moving it to a different place. Not as though you really could have done anything to help your friend."

I decided this was not a guy to play poker with. Or buy antiques from, for that matter. I gave myself a stern warning: Don't mess around.

"I guess I didn't think at all," I said. "But I'd been hit over the head and then I woke up to find my best friend hanging in a closet. I'll admit, it sounds stupid now. I'm sorry."

Robinson grunted and scratched at his left ear. "What kind of a music box was it he wanted to show you?"

Well, so much for not messing around. Story time again. "I don't know," I said. "Both of us were interested in the older machines, ones from the early part of the nineteenth century. It'd probably have been one of those, one with some unusual feature."

"Did you see any music box like that while you were there?"

"I'm sure there were–or are–some of those boxes there. That's the kind Shackie really liked to restore. But I'd never be able to tell which one he meant. He didn't give me any clue."

"Mm-hm. Had you and Mr. O'Shacker had any arguments recently?"

I laughed. "I don't think Shackie and I had an argument

in the twenty years I've known him. We had nothing to fight about. Why do you ask?"

Ice eyes glaring. "I'll ask, you answer. Do you know a man named Abramowitz? Marty Abramowitz?"

"No-o-o," I said, dragging the short word out to three syllables. "I don't think so."

"He owned the Gotham Antiques Mart, a store up on Amsterdam near Seventy-Third. You ever been up there?"

"I'm sure I have," I said. "I go to every antique store in the city from time to time."

"Been there recently?"

It occurred to me that the cops might have found Abramowitz's receipt book with my name in it. But given what Frank the Crank told me about Abramowitz, that particular receipt probably found its way into the trash the minute I walked out of the store. No receipt, no sale; no sale, no tax for Fatso to pay. But even if the cops did have the receipt, I'd have an out. Head trauma can do funny things to recent memory. Let Robinson thrust an embarrassing slip of paper under my snout, now or later, and I'd plead amnesia–must have been that crack on the head; sorry. If I had to, I'd show him an ordinary cylinder box in my collection and swear it was the one I'd bought. The receipt, remember, just said "music box."

"I ... don't think so, no."

I held my breath. Robinson nodded without registering any reaction. "The other night, you were at Mr. Hardwick's party?"

"Yes, of course. Everybody in music boxes in New York goes to Harry Hardwick's parties."

"What time did you leave?"

"A little after nine."

"Kind of early, wasn't it? The party didn't break up 'til after midnight."

"Yes, it was early. My beeper went off; one of my patients had a stroke. I ran into the Manhattan Medical ER and stayed there 'til about four-thirty in the morning, when my patient died. You can check it out."

"I *have* checked it out. Did Mr. O'Shacker seem in his usual frame of mind at the party?"

I shrugged. "Best I could tell, he was just Shackie."

"Mm." Noncommittal nod. "I don't suppose you got a look at the guy who hit you."

I shook my head. "I wish, the son of a bitch."

Robinson made a face that could have been distaste but turned out to be simply a silent announcement that he was finished. He started to get up. "All right, Doctor; that's all I have to ask you. When they discharge you from the hospital you're free to go."

"I'm not a suspect then?"

When most people smile it makes you feel good. But there are exceptions. Like Detective Robinson. "No. The case looks pretty clear to us. Your friend stole a music box from Mr. Hardwick. He sold it to an antiques dealer; we have evidence of that. Then he got worried and killed the dealer to make sure *he'd* stay quiet. After that, either his conscience started up on him or he knew we were closing in, so he decided to go the easy way. You interrupted him while he was getting ready to hang himself so he knocked you unconscious. Then he wrote that note and killed himself."

"That's ridiculous."

"Oh?" For the first time, Robinson looked faintly amused. "You think so?"

"Yes, Goddamn it, I do. Shackie wouldn't even kill the roaches in his apartment. He was no murderer, not even a thief. And besides, there're all kinds of inconsistencies. Like why would Shackie mess up his own place?"

Robinson shrugged. "People who commit violent crimes tend to be unstable. They can have temper tantrums–throw things around, like little kids. Your friend knew he was at the end of the road. Maybe it wasn't enough to just kick a wastebasket."

"But–"

Robinson held up his hand. "Doctor, I appreciate your feelings about your friend. But that's still the way the evidence adds up to me."

"*What* evidence? What are you talking about?"

Robinson stared at me.

"I know you don't have to tell me," I said, speaking much more softly now. "But listen for a minute, would you? Shackie was the best friend I had in this world. He's dead, not from natural causes, and I don't know why. It'd help–a lot–if you could tell me *something*. It's going to be all over the papers and the TV, anyway, isn't it?"

Dragging information out of people is no less important to a doctor than a detective, and if I have to say so myself, I'm pretty good at it. Robinson studied me for a moment, thinking God knows what. Then he said, "Two things. One, the antique dealer's records listed him as the seller of the music box. Two, the dealer's wife told us that O'Shacker called her husband about one in the morning today. Said he had to see him right away; it was urgent. The husband never came back from that meeting down in the shop."

"Wait a minute. Did anyone actually see–"

Up went the hand again. "You asked, I told you. If that helps you, fine. But that's it."

Worser and worser. I said thank you as humbly as I could. Then I leaned back on the pillow and closed my eyes. All right, I told myself. At least I won't have the cops getting in my way.

Sarah kissed me awake.

"Hi, Babe," I said. "Got my stuff?"

She laid a plastic bag on my roller-table. "Pajamas, razor, toothbrush, toothpaste, books," she said. "As ordered." Then she produced a big brown paper bag. "Dinner and breakfast." She opened the bag; the smell of corned beef filled the room. I was suddenly starving.

"Sandwich, potato salad, cole slaw," announced my wife. "And a prune Danish and cinnamon coffeecake for breakfast. Will that do?"

"For an army," I said. "A small one, anyway."

"Well, you can eat what you want and leave the rest. Would you like me to get the sandwich out of the bag for you?"

"Thanks. I'm not helpless, just confined." I pulled the sandwich out of its wrappings and wolfed a big bite.

"The policeman's not out there anymore," Sarah said.

I swallowed, then mumbled, "I know. Guard's off. Case closed."

"Did they catch who did it?"

I told her what Robinson had said to me, then added, "He and you are on the same track."

Sarah didn't answer. I thought she was being tactful but I should have known better. "I have to tell you something."

I stopped eating. I knew what she had to tell me.

"Your apartment. It's a mess. Someone got in and threw your things all over the place."

"The music boxes, too? Are any of them damaged?"

She smiled and shook her head. "I knew you'd ask so I checked them–at least as well as I could. They seemed fine. I'm not sure if any are missing, of course–"

That I wasn't worried about. The only missing music box hadn't been in my apartment–which was why the killer had gone on to Shackie's place. He knew I'd bought that rigid notation box from Abramowitz; he also knew if he didn't find it in my apartment, there was only one other place it would be. So he was somebody I knew. It was a start.

"Tell you what," I said. "Maybe before Shackie messed his own place up, he came over to mine–while we were at Muriel's–and messed up my things."

"It doesn't sound likely," she said.

"But possible."

"Don't be sarcastic."

"I feel sarcastic. Two of my friends have been killed, one of them is being framed for murder, I've been hit over the head and knocked unconscious, and my apartment's been ransacked. I'm not having a nice day."

"I'm only trying to help."

"Yes, I know. All right. I'm sorry."

She lowered her eyes and started to rummage in her purse. "There's one other thing. Here." She handed me a tape and my little portable cassette player from the den. I just stared at her.

"It's the tape from your answering machine. I thought you'd want to hear it."

I put the sandwich down, slipped the tape into the machine, and pushed the play button. A man's voice began to speak, very odd-sounding. Almost like the voice that drones those endless lists of choices on voice mail menus. "Dr. Purdue," it said. "I would be very interested in purchasing your rigid notation music box. I can offer you a price I think you won't be able to refuse. I will call again." End of message. The recording timed the call at 10:32 AM.

That was while we'd been outside the Gotham Antiques Mart. "Hmm," I said, sounding like Robinson.

"What's a rigid notation box?" Sarah on the uptake.

"A kind of cylinder box." I waved my hand. "Has very nice music."

"And you have one?"

I nodded. "I have a lot of music boxes." I picked up the sandwich again.

"Thomas, there's something very funny going on."

"If there is," I mumbled through the corned beef, "I'm not entertained."

"You know what I mean. Look, I'm not stupid. Someone—whether Shackie or someone else—killed Harry Hardwick and stole his music box. The music box turned up somehow in that Mr. Abramowitz's shop. Then *he* was killed, too. Then both your apartment and Shackie's were ransacked, Shackie was killed, and you were hit over the head. And now here's someone calling you, wanting to pay a price you can't resist for a certain music box you have. Am I supposed to believe that's a coincidence?"

I pretended that my mouth was too full of sandwich to permit me to talk. If I owned up to what apparently I alone knew about the travels of that rigid notation box, it might force Robinson to reopen the investigation. And if he did, to whom might his suspicions turn, pray tell? Also, if that rigid notation box was somehow still in existence, the fewer people who knew about it, the better were my chances of getting it back. So I swallowed my food and said, "It's possible."

"Thomas, damn you!"

"No, seriously. Sarah, the world's full of coincidences. I know who that guy is; he's a pain in the ass from Chicago who's been trying for six months to buy my rigid notation box. He's a broker, working for some big Japanese collector. The collector wants a rigid notation box, but there aren't many rigid notation boxes around. *And* most people who own them don't want to sell them. That's it. It has nothing to do with what's going on."

"Are you telling me the truth? Or is this another one of your stories?"

If I was telling her a story to start with, she was silly, wasn't she, to think I'd admit it was a story? "Sure, it's the truth. Scout's honor."

"You're no Boy Scout," she said sternly. "But all right. When are you getting out of here?"

"Tomorrow," I said.

"Fine. I'll come by and take you home. I'll help you clean up. And I'll stay over for a couple of nights–I'll sleep on the living room sofa–and keep an eye on you. And while we're there you can show me your rigid notation box."

Life isn't easy. There's always some well-meaning person threatening you with help.

"But you're not interested in music boxes," I said.

"If those rigid notation boxes are so nice I'd like to at least hear one. What time should I come by?"

Dr. Ransom had said he'd sign me out at four. What the hell: in for a penny, in for a pound. "Evening," I said. "The neurologist told me he'd sign me out about six o'clock."

"Good. I'll come right from work. See you then. But if you don't mind I'm going to go home now. I'm exhausted." She bent over and kissed me lightly on the forehead. "Do take care of yourself, please, would you?" she said. "I'd miss you. I really would."

"I'll be good. See you tomorrow night."

It's terrible, that short-term memory loss after acute head trauma.

Nine

At four-twenty the next afternoon I walked out the front door of St. Vincent's Hospital, a free man. The back of my head was still sore but other than that I felt all right. No need for Sarah to load me into a cab, help me up to my apartment and into bed, cook my dinner, bring me a tray, and clean up afterward. She'd even feed me if I'd let her. Goddamn it to hell, it's not my fault she never had a little boy to worry over. No reason I should be punished.

Besides, I didn't have a rigid notation box to show her. I needed to do something about that.

I walked up to the corner of Sixth Avenue, buttoning my coat as I went. A sad-faced little Sal Army waif, red-nosed and watery-eyed, was swinging a bell over a scabby red kettle; even in her woolly maroon coat and pants she was shivering. Frostbite in the service of the poor: the gangrenous badge of honor. I pulled a bill out of my wallet and dropped it in the kettle as I went past. "God bless you," the girl quavered after me.

I felt like anything but a merry gentleman. All day the sun had been behind clouds and now, not yet four-thirty, evening was clearly coming on. The weak light filtering into the stone canyon around me took on a purple cast. New York winter twilight, darkness deepening by the moment, sun extinguished before five o'clock in the afternoon. It seemed as if the whole world were dying an unreasonable and premature death.

I had to get out of there.

At the corner of Seventh Avenue I turned uptown and shifted into overdrive. I hustled past scuzzy flophouses and dark office buildings where guys were already huddled up in doorways, staking their claims to sheltered spots for the night. Sarah would have been glad to tell me their problems were worse than mine.

I headed east on 14th, then back uptown on Fifth Avenue. At 34th I made a brief run toward a cross-town bus, but the thought of my recently-ransacked apartment pulled me up short. I wasn't ready for that, not yet. I crossed the street and pushed on along Fifth into the East 40s, into the crush of the shopping crowd.

It was five o'clock and pitch black, but lights in shop windows were bright. All around me people laughed and chattered. Their talk became white noise, fragments of speech in a weird foreign language. Talk about being a stranger in a strange land. When someone looked my way, his smile faded in a hurry and he walked quickly past me. Thomas Purdue, M.D., Dark Presence at New York's Christmas Party.

Off to my left I heard music. I wasn't so far gone that I could walk past music–not even a canned version of "Hark the Herald Angels Sing." I followed the sound with my eyes. There was Rockefeller Center, down at the far end of that Art Deco channel of shops. In front of the building, the gigantic decorated Christmas tree swayed in the wind. I shoved my hands into my coat pockets, crossed the street, and made my way down the corridor, shops to my right, row of white-wire herald angels with golden trumpets directed skyward on my left. Directly past a little espresso stand I came to the observation platform above the ice-skating rink.

From behind the railing I looked down to the ice. Skaters glided past, oblivious, every one of them, to Prometheus stretched out on his rock high above them. Every now and again one of the skaters, usually a little kid, took a tumble and then quickly got up laughing, ski pants covered with white shavings. When I was that age, my father sometimes closed his office an hour early to bring me here. While I skated, Pop would stand pretty much where I was now. I'd see him as I zipped past, a tall man in a gray coat and gray hat, watching his son intently as though in doing that he was somehow skating too, gliding along at my side, telling me how I *should* be skating. And at that point, I invariably stumbled and went down hard on the ice.

My father had his way of doing things, but his way was never mine. When I was six or seven I wanted to play the piano. Pop insisted that before I could touch a keyboard I needed to learn musical theory and how to read music. He locked the piano fallboard over the keys, then brought home books and tormented me with them for weeks until I took to hiding them under my bed. The upshot was I never learned to read music, never learned musical theory, and never discovered how to coax music out of a piano.

This little tale became one of the recurring stories of my life. Our med-school professors made sure we understood that only if we did research might they possibly grant us a bit of space to squat beside them at the top of our profession. Practicing doctors? They were grunts, a sorry lot of medical Neanderthals. I told my faculty advisor I'd like to investigate the influence of music on human emotions.

He took a long look down his nose in my direction. "Then you're interested in the hypothalamus," he informed me. "You need to start by posing answerable questions–questions that will get you funding so you can carry out your work. What you want to do is design and perform carefully structured investigations of the physiology and biochemistry of the hypothalamus."

That wasn't at all what I wanted to do. I told my advisor that I was sorry, it was *not* the hypothalamus I was interested in, and I certainly did not want to design *or* perform carefully-structured investigations of its physiology or biochemistry. Nothing, I told him, could possibly withstand that sort of dissection and still be alive. So ended the interview. At graduation, he sought me out to shake my hand and say with heavy sarcasm, "Good luck in your studies of the soul, Purdue."

I thanked him and walked away. Arguing with any true believer is a waste of your time and his. The assertion that only in musty laboratories can you find answers to your questions about the nature of man is as limiting as the notion that God is to be encountered only in churches.

I waved at a small boy in a blue ski jacket who'd just gotten back up on his skates and was looking in my direction. Either he didn't see me or his mother had told him never to wave at strange men.

The swaying tree lights above the skaters were hypnotic. Music blared from the loudspeaker: *O come all ye faithful ...*

Some joy, I thought. Some triumph.

A young couple skated past hand-in-hand, the girl wearing a red knitted cap with a pom-pom flying behind it. My heart leaped. Winters ago, before we were married, Sarah wore a hat like that. With wind stinging my eyes and making me blink back tears, that girl in the hat could have *been* Sarah. Round red cheeks, laughing, she looked around for her boyfriend. She held out a hand, he grabbed it, and they skated off together, arms swinging between them.

I'd forgotten how Sarah used to laugh. Once she could light up any room she was in; now all she did was spread wet blankets over any joyful flame that threatened to get the least bit out of control. Where was that laughing Sarah now? Dead? Gone forever?

Or was she still here but somehow invisible to me? Maybe I just wasn't looking in the right way. Or in the right place.

O little town of Bethlehem, how still we see thee lie.
Above thy deep and dreamless sleep the silent stars roll by.

My shoulders started to shake. I couldn't stop them. I

rested my hands on the brass railing in front of me and snorted back a sob. Somebody to my right turned to look. I was mortified. I wanted to run off, but couldn't seem to move my feet.

Yet in thy dark streets shining, the everlasting light.

I was crying now, no holding it back. The tears ran down my cheeks, went splat on the rail.

The hopes and fears of all the years are met in thee tonight.

I tightened my grip on the rail. Out there below the Christmas tree I saw a semi-circle of half-erect, hairy men and women wearing rough-cut animal skins, gathered around a massive bonfire. The people raised their arms, following the sweep of the flames up toward Prometheus. They shouted, they screamed. They implored the sun not to go away forever and leave them in eternal icy darkness.

My tears were stinging my freezing cheeks. I don't know how much longer I'd have stood there and what else I might have seen, but at that point someone pulled at my sleeve. I looked down and blinked into a woman's face.

You couldn't have called her pretty. What showed of her face where it wasn't hidden by her green muffler and the hood of her down coat was pocked and rough; little red and violet lines ran outward from the corners of her nose. Wisps of hair more salt than pepper hung down over her forehead. But once I looked into her soft gray eyes I no longer noticed any of her other features. I thought in fact she was beautiful.

"Here, Mister," she said. "Have a nice hot espresso."

She pushed a red-and-green paper cup at me. I took it between both hands and drank. As I swallowed, the warmth spread through my entire chest. I smiled at her and said thank you.

"Think nothing of it," she said. "You got a nice smile, Mister, you know that? Keep it up there, and you'll be feeling better in no time at all."

If I believed in angels I'd have to admit they sometimes appear in strange disguises. The woman's name was Mildred–

she never did tell me a last name–and she was waiting for her husband, who duly arrived some ten minutes later and took her away. In our few minutes together I thanked her for her kindness and explained I'd just lost a dear friend. She said she understood: when people get to our age–*our* age, for God's sake, I'm forty-five–we've all managed to lose a good friend or two and she was sure I'd get over it. I just had to get into a support group. And get involved.

Well, one out of two isn't bad. I couldn't quite bring myself to tell her if I needed support I'd go out and buy myself a truss. But getting involved was another story. There, she was right on the button.

I'd get involved, all right. I patted my chest, where the tape recording of my phone solicitation was resting quietly against those two nasty pictures. Maybe they'd work together and generate some ideas. Revenge may not be much, but it beats hell out of moping around Manhattan, breaking into tears in public places.

There was something else. Whoever knocked Shackie off and me out had probably also kidnapped my wonderful rigid notation box. Very likely it was now sitting in some collection, if not in New York, then somewhere. Moreover, the fact that the killer had called me the morning of the day before probably meant he'd gotten to Abramowitz's sales book before Abramowitz pitched the receipt with my name on it. That would explain how the killer knew I had the machine but Robinson literally didn't have a clue.

As I moved away from the ice rink my step was brisk and firm. I looked back at the base of the Christmas tree. The gang of hairy pagans had taken their bonfire and gone back to wherever they'd come from. Very soon now for both them and me, the days would start to get longer. But not for somebody. For some son of a bitch the sun was going to go out.

I felt my spirit lighten as if a palpable load had suddenly

been lifted from my shoulders. One kind act, ten minutes of simple human generosity, and I was cured. Don't talk to me about answerable questions, Professor. A quick nod to Prometheus and I set off toward 49th Street, head up, singing along with the canned Christmas carols. People looked at me and smiled.

TEN

I got back to my apartment a little before seven. Someone had cleaned the place up. Guess who. After six years of not living there, my wife still knew which drawer to put my shirts and underwear in, and where to stash my socks. Books were neatly lined up on their shelves. If Sarah hadn't told me someone had torn the place up, I'd never have known ... but no, I'll take that back. I'd been writing an article on Jean Billon-Haller, one of the second-generation Swiss music box manufacturers, but now my desktop was bare. No books, no magazines, no papers, no dust. As usual, Sarah had been more than perfect.

From the middle of the living room I scanned the east and west walls, twin honeycombs of vertically-divided shelves. Each nook held a small to medium-sized wooden box. Some were plain; others were beautifully inlaid with exotic woods, brass, pewter, and enamels. Together, the 128 of them made up the greater part of my collection of antique music boxes, each with something special to say, each in its own voice. For over an hour I stood before them, listening to them in turn.

Everyone was present, accounted for, and in good health. One hundred twenty-eight lovely music boxes.

But there should have been 129.

My musical cuckoo clock on the mantel chimed eight. Time to go talk to Sophie Soleski. As the clock's music-works swung into a lively rendition of Eduard Strauss' "*Bahn Frei* Polka," I danced into the bedroom to get a clean shirt.

When the phone rang, I reached to answer it, then froze. My would-be rigid notation box buyer–or maybe Sarah trying to check up on me? I pushed the volume button on the answering machine to HIGH and waited, one cuff buttoned, the other open. During the outgoing message, the phone clicked off.

I buttoned my shirt, threw on my heavy down jacket, and trotted out the door.

Sophie lived in the Village, on the first floor of a small apartment building on Bleecker, close to Sixth Avenue. There were two apartments on each level, and when Sophie's husband Peter was still alive the Soleskis occupied the entire ground floor. This was no extravagance–not when you remember they'd lived there since right after the war, rent-controlled from day one. The second apartment had been Peter's workshop. Both Soleskis were old-time cultured Europeans, able to talk rings around me in art, literature, music, world politics, or Freudian psychology. In those palmy post-war years in Greenwich Village, antique music boxes fit right in. Peter fixed them, Sophie sold them. They were quite a team. Peter used to take walks, drink beer, and argue into the night with e.e. cummings. Marianne Moore once brought William Carlos Williams to meet the Soleskis, and the old doctor-poet insisted on watching Peter restoring a comb at the workbench. "Peter Soleski at *his* clavier!" Williams said, chuckling, playing off on Wallace Stevens' title. Peter and Sophie were equally amused and honored.

Unfortunately for my plans Soph wasn't alone when I rang her bell. "Thomas, how nice to see you," she said and kissed me on the cheek. "Come in; Barton Moss is here, too. I haven't had so many attractive young men in my parlor at one time since I was eighteen."

Sophie turned eighty-two last year but looks easily fifteen or twenty years younger. Her face is virtually unlined and she stands very straight, just an inch or two shorter than I. She wears her neatly-combed gray hair like a cap of steel. NYMBCA members argue whether Sophie's debt is to genetics or estrogen preparations. My opinion is that it's determination.

I glanced past Sophie and nodded at Barton Moss. "Forget him," I said grandly and kneeled at Sophie's feet. "Come away with me. We'll spend our winters in Monaco and our summers at Baden-Baden-Baden. We'll have twenty-six children and never a moment of unhappiness."

"Thomas, you're impossible. Do you know that?"

"Only highly improbable, Soph. But you love it."

"Yes, of course." She extended a hand down to me. "But get up before you throw out your back. Come on, now. Behave yourself."

I got to my feet. Barton Moss was still standing in the middle of the parlor, shuffling his feet and looking generally uncomfortable. Picture Ichabod Crane with mild chorea. "Hiya, Barton," I called, and went in to shake hands. "What brings you into the city on a freezing December night?"

Apparently that was a wrong question. Barton pulled back his hand and shot me a dirty look. "Came in to see Sophie," he muttered at the rug.

"Thomas," Sophie said quickly. "What would you say to a big piece of my strudel?"

I remembered I hadn't eaten since lunch. "I'd say, 'Hello and goodbye, big piece of strudel.' Especially if it had a cup of coffee with it for company."

Sophie laughed and marched off toward the little kitchen. "With some ice cream? Vanilla fudge? Ben and Jerry's?"

"All three," I shouted back.

Now that Sophie was out of the room, Barton Moss seemed even more on edge. He picked at a fingernail. I looked around. Sophie's collection was not large, but the machines she and Peter had kept over the years were real prizes. On a stand at the middle of the wall to my right was a plerodienique, a big music box with interchangeable cylinders set up to telescope as they rotate, thereby producing long-playing musical selections. There were four or five superb early cylinders by top makers: Francois Nicole, of course, and Francois Lecoultre. Reymond-Nicole. Ducommun-Girod. Opposite the plerodienique was a Symphonion Eroica, a magnificent upright machine that played three discs simultaneously, a proto-stereophonic system. Next to this was a large automaton, a life-sized acrobat in colorful circus silks who inverted himself to balance by one finger atop a ball. I walked past the acrobat to the dining room table, looked at what was on it, and turned to Moss. "I didn't know Sophie had a Regina with bells. Nice—but it needs some help, doesn't it?"

"Mmm. Guess so." Moss kept his eyes on the carpet. He looked up as Sophie came back into the room, carrying a mountain of strudel and ice cream on a plate in one hand and a steaming cup of coffee in the other. I took them from her and sat down at the table, next to the bell box. "Wonderful," I said, and took a big bite. "Marvelous dinner, my dear." I pointed my fork at the Regina. "Is this dessert?"

Sophie chuckled and glanced at Barton.

I slouched down in the chair, clearly settling in. "Oh, I won't be home until morning," I sang, and eyed Barton. Then I took another big bite of strudel.

Barton Moss gave me a look of unalloyed hatred. He shuffled toward our hostess. "Guess I'll get going, Sophie. You can call me, okay?"

"Oh, don't leave on my account, Barton," I sang out.

When Sophie turned to see his reaction, I screwed up the corner of my mouth and jerked my head in the direction of the door. I was lying, my look said privately to Barton. Beat it. Piss off.

He turned without another word, grabbed his coat off the rack by the door, and stamped out. The door slammed behind him. I noticed he grabbed both coat and doorknob with his right hand.

"Not especially strong on the social graces, is he?"

"Thomas, you were not nice to him."

"No problem. It was easy." I filled my mouth again.

"Ach!" Sophie shook her head sadly and sat down next to me. "He's such a *naar*."

"What was he doing here, for heaven's sake?"

"Well, what are you doing here, for heaven's sake?"

"I was hungry. Lonesome for good company. Happened to be in the neighborhood. All of the above. But it's a short run from First Avenue and Thirty-Second Street. *I* don't live in New Rochelle, like Barton does."

"All right, Mr. Buttinski. You want to know why he was here? It's no big secret. He was trying to persuade me to give him some of my repair work."

I nearly blew my mouthful of strudel into her face. "Barton Moss? Wants to do *your* repair work?"

Moss is a music box restorer–or so he represents himself. Sophie calls him a garage mechanic, which is her way of saying he hasn't got proper respect for either his own work or that of the Swiss clock and watchmakers who manufactured the machines. Antique cylinder music box components were cut to incredibly close tolerances: a thousandth of an inch here and there is often critical. When a mechanism refuses to go back together or run properly after re-assembly, an experienced restorer asks himself where he might have missed a trick, or even got a bit careless. Barton's approach is to give the balky music-works a stiff knock with a mallet. Which by itself is bad enough. But Barton also drinks more than is good for him, and gossip was that while soused a couple of years ago he managed to destroy a nice music box Harry Hardwick had entrusted to his care. Words, at the very least, were exchanged; some versions of the story had Harry and Barton rolling around on Barton's greasy concrete workshop floor, exchanging pokes and punches.

"He wants to do anyone's repair work, not just mine. Since Harry Hardwick took away all his business, Barton's been pretty badly strapped. You have to feel sorry for him. Even if he is a garage mechanic."

I didn't have to do anything of the sort, I thought, but I wondered why she apparently did. "Soph, tell me ... just what was it that happened between Harry and Barton? I know they had a scene, but I don't know the details."

She sighed. "Peter did all Harry's cylinder box restorations, and when Peter died Barton gave Harry quite a little rush. Finally, Harry gave him a couple of jobs. Barton had the sense to ship out the tough parts–cylinder repins, fine comb work–to Arthur Williamson in England. Harry didn't know that, of course. He was pleased with the work, so he gave Barton some more valuable boxes. Unfortunately, Barton went off on one of his binges at just the time Harry decided to put the heat on him for keeping a very fine Falconnet cylinder box for too long. So Barton started to take the box apart before he was dried out. The upshot was, he dropped the comb on the concrete floor. Shattered it to bits."

I stopped eating. Falconnet music boxes are exquisite and there aren't many around. The thought of Barton Moss trying to work on one while he had DTs made me red hot. "Better Barton should have gone head down on the concrete. The world would be better off with the Falconnet still here instead of him."

"Shush. That's no way to talk."

I just stared at her. Didn't even smile.

She sighed. "Ach, you collectors. You live in a different world. Actually, Barton almost *did* go head down on the concrete when Harry saw that comb. Harry told Barton he'd do all he could to see that Barton never got another music box to fix, not from anyone."

"And Barton's been in the hole ever since?"

"Deeper and deeper. If only he'd stay off the sauce–but that would require some character. Which is not what Barton Moss has to spare, I'm sorry to say. Anyway, he came to see me when he heard about Shackie. Shackie's been doing my repairs since Peter died. Barton says he needs work desperately: the bank is about to take his house. We were looking at this Regina when you came."

Interesting. Barton Moss had been nursing a grudge against Harry Hardwick a hell of a lot longer than he could ever nurse a bottle of cheap booze. And with Shackie out of the way, Barton could make a pitch for Sophie Soleski's repair work. I didn't think the voice on that message tape was Barton's. But who could be sure?

Then I remembered something else: "Didn't I see Barton at Harry's party the other night? After the big fight, what was he doing there?"

Sophie shrugged, then smiled sadly. "That was Harry for you–such a fair man. He never did give Barton any more work and I'm sure he never invited him to the house for dinner. But Barton's name is on the NYMBCA roster, and Harry's parties were NYMBCA functions ... so there Barton was. Walter Remler was there, too, for that matter."

Remler collects erotica, musical and otherwise. Most of his musical items are spectacular, but a lot of the nonmusical pieces turn me the wrong way. Still, there's no finer line than the one between titillation and nausea, and if I can't help wiping my hand on my pants leg after a shake with Walter Remler, that's as likely to be my problem as his.

"Harry and Walter had a terrible argument a couple of years ago," Sophie went on. "Something to do with a machine Harry was after and Walter bought. Harry thought Walter had been underhanded; he called him every bad name I've ever heard. And of course Walter's story was that Harry was a sore loser. But Walter's in NYMBCA so Walter got invited to Harry's parties. I say good for Harry. He was a fair and decent man."

I nodded. "Well, I hope you didn't tell Barton yes–about your repair work, I mean."

"We never got that far. But I wouldn't have, you know. I couldn't. I'd be better off with a ticket on the Titanic."

I swallowed the last bite of strudel. Sophie offered me seconds. I shook my head and patted my belly. "You're right; it couldn't work. Not after fifty years of having your machines restored by Peter and Shackie. I mean, imagine ... oh, say you had something really fantastic–maybe a piece you wanted to sell to Harry Hardwick. Something like ... I don't know. A rigid notation box? But it didn't play exactly right. Shackie would have set that straight for you, no trouble. But can you imagine yourself giving a box like *that* to Barton Moss?"

All of a sudden Sophie was watching me very closely.

"If it were yours to sell."

She still said nothing.

"If it were worth, oh, say, twenty-two thousand, five hundred dollars. And had a marvelous program, all Mozart overtures. Would *you* give a music box like that to Barton Moss to work on? If it were yours ... to sell?"

Sophie swallowed hard. "Thomas, we've been good friends for more than twenty years, now, haven't we? So please just tell me in plain words. What are you trying to get at?"

"I'm trying to get at where that rigid notation box came from. The one you sold to Harry Hardwick on December tenth. Who sold it to *you*?"

She was trying very hard not to show me how upset she was. Light approach for starters. "Oh, come on. Are you unhappy I didn't offer it to you? Well, I couldn't. *Harry* called *me*. He knew I had it and he wanted it."

"How did he know you had it?"

Enter the Woman of Steel. Sophie rose from her chair and stood over me. "Thomas, really! I don't think this is any of your business. In fact, I think you're starting to be unpleasant."

I pushed my chair away from the table and looked up at her. This was no way to behave toward an eighty-two-year-old lady, let alone one who'd been your friend for a bucketful of years. But when a really wonderful music box–like a rigid notation box–suddenly becomes available you can bet a bundle there's an ugly reason. Its owner died or is dying. Or is being divorced. Or has suffered a major financial reverse. Overly-sensitive collectors don't usually have first-rate collections. Also, overly-sensitive investigators don't usually solve their cases.

"You're right," I said to Sophie. "I *am* being unpleasant because I'm *feeling* unpleasant. Furthermore, you're wrong about whose business it is. I've lost two friends, somehow because of that particular music box. Rigid notation boxes don't grow on trees, Sophie. Where did you get it? And how did Harry Hardwick know you had it for sale?"

She lowered herself into the chair like one of her clockwork automata. I reached across and took her hand in mine. "Soph, I'm sorry," I said. "I really am. But as far as the police are concerned, Shackie killed Harry and stole his music box, fenced it through a dealer, killed the dealer, and then felt so ashamed he killed himself. Now, if you really think Shackie could have done that, fine; don't tell me anything. But if you think it's as crazy as I do, help me. I won't get you involved, I promise."

She raised her head; it seemed to take a tremendous effort. All of a sudden, she looked eighty-two years old. "Shackie was like a son to Peter. The only son he had."

I nodded. "I know."

She chewed her lip. "I wish I could help you, but I'm not sure I can. The very day that music box came in Harry called me. Not two hours after I'd opened the crate. He said he knew I had a rigid notation box and he wanted it. Well, you knew Harry. Inside of half an hour, here he was. He looked, he listened, he wrote a check. I asked him who told him I had it, but he'd only say he had his sources."

I laughed. No point arguing that. Harry Hardwick maintained an army of pickers, battalions of Broadway Schwartzes deployed world-wide to search out, seize, and ship to New York the rarest and choicest of antique music machines. One of them must have tipped Harry that a rigid notation box was being shipped to Sophie Soleski. "But where did the box come from? Who sold it to *you*?"

No collector likes to divulge a source. Dealers are even more reluctant. Other good stuff might be in the wings; no point giving a freebie to your competition. Sophie's lips moved but nothing came out.

"I won't cut you, Sophie. Tell me."

"Gordon and Maida Westfall," she whispered.

"In London?"

She nodded. "They've been very good to me. For more than thirty years Gordon and Maida have sent me wonderful music boxes. Early ones–the kind you can't get over here. They've sent them in as-found condition so Peter or Shackie could restore them and I could sell them and feel proud."

I gave her hand a ceremonial kiss. "Our secret," I said. But then a thought occurred to me. "Who *is* going to restore for you now? Now that Shackie ..."

That was as far as I could go. My voice stopped talking. Sophie patted *my* hand. "I don't know. I just don't know. Not Lucas Sterne. He wouldn't dream of helping his competition. And even if he did I wouldn't trust that sniveling little weasel. If you want to know the truth, I'm scared. Do *you* know anyone better than Barton Moss?"

"I have to know someone better than Barton Moss. Give me a little time."

Her laugh was hollow. "I'm eighty-two years old. A little time is what I've got."

ELEVEN

The walk back to my place from Sophie's felt like a hike along a treadmill. Nothing was falling into place. Sophie bought the rigid notation box from the Westfalls; one of Harry's scouts found out and tipped his boss. But what about Barton Moss? Easy enough to picture sloshy old Barton air-conditioning Harry's chest, but setting up and carrying out a complicated frame-and-kill routine on Shackie? I didn't think so.

I knew Gordon and Maida Westfall, but not well enough to call them out of the blue and start asking questions. Not a good idea to risk a short conversation at the end of which I'd be holding a phone in one hand and an empty bag in the other, the cat now five blocks down the street and running fast. Better to go by the Creed of Willie Sutton. Willie robbed banks, he said, because that's where the money was. But Willie didn't just pick a bank to rob and run right in, gun at the ready. Had that been his approach he'd have died long before he ever became a legend. Willie thought a job over, doped the situation from A to Z before he ever made a move. We can all learn from the masters.

The message light on my phone was blinking when I came in. It was Sarah, a breath of fresh air straight from the North Pole. "Please call me whenever you get back," she said. "If you can spare a moment."

I erased her voice and dialed her number. "Hi, Babe," I chirped when she answered. "What's up?"

"Well, what's up was obviously you. Two hours sooner than supposedly scheduled."

"I beg your pardon?"

"Don't be cute. I was at St. Vincent's to pick you up at six o'clock, only to find you'd been discharged at four. Would you like to explain yourself?"

"What's to explain? The doctor came by at four, said I was fine and I could leave. So I left. What were you doing there at six?"

It helped me to picture the confused look on her face. "What was I *doing* there? I was there because you asked me to be there. You said you'd be getting out at six o'clock, and I should meet you then and come home with you. Or don't you remember that?"

"No. I'm sorry, but actually, I *don't* remember that. I hope I didn't inconvenience–"

"Oh damn you! Don't talk to me like that, 'I hope I didn't inconvenience you.' I'm not a clerk in a department store."

"All right, I'm sorry. But they were keeping me under observation for a reason. Head trauma does have an effect on a person's memory. I suppose–"

"Stop it. I know you. You don't need a hit on the head to forget something you don't want to remember."

Time to cut this short. "Sarah, look: I said I'm sorry and I am. But the fact is–"

"I said stop it. You don't know a fact from your Aunt Yetta's alligator purse. I hate it when you lie to me. Can you at least manage to tell me where you were until now? It's nine o'clock; that's five hours since you were discharged. I've been calling and calling. I've been frantic."

"I'm sorry. Okay, here's what happened: When they let me out I started to come home, but I just didn't feel like sitting around here by myself; I was feeling low. So I walked up to Rockefeller Center and watched the skaters for a while. Then I walked back down to the Village and had a little supper. After that I came back here and found your message. That's the truth. Every word."

So I left a few words out. Sue me.

She blew a sigh into the receiver. "All right. I don't know why I ... forget it. Are you feeling all right?"

"Much better, yes. Thanks."

"Do you want me to come over?"

"Sure. We can go to bed–"

"I should have known. Goodbye." Her phone crashed down in my ear.

Shame she's got such a temper. I was going to tell her if she didn't want to get into bed with me she could still come over, tuck me in, sit by my side through the night, check my reflexes every hour, and make sure I didn't stop breathing. And I'd play my rigid notation box for her. That's exactly what I was going to say, but she never gave me the chance. Now she was so mad she'd probably stay miles out of my way for the next few days and not distract me while I was trying to figure out who had killed my friends and stolen my rigid notation box.

I was up early the next morning so I could catch Broadway Schwartz before he left on his morning rounds. Broadway lives in Yorkville, in a third-floor railroad walkup on East 84th between Second Avenue and Third. The vestibule and hallways in the building are dingy and badly lighted, and after continuous occupancy by five or more generations of German families the smell of sauerkraut is permanently embedded into the plaster of the walls. But inside, Schwartz's apartment is immaculate, thanks to Trudy, his live-in companion. Trudy's a sweet little dumpling with round, red cheeks–Betty Boop gone middle-aged and just a bit to the dowdy. She cooks, cleans, and says very little, which I suspect is a prerequisite for living in close quarters with Broadway Schwartz. Whether Trudy is Broadway's wife, girlfriend, cousin, sister, or any combination thereof I have no idea. I don't even know whether her last name is Schwartz–nor do I care. Not my business.

I knocked on the door a little before seven. Schwartz, hat on head, let me in and led me into the kitchen. Trudy, at the oven, gave me a smile and a nod, then put a cup of coffee and a plate with a fresh cinnamon roll on the little square kitchen table. She motioned me to take a seat.

Schwartz looked me up and down. One eye narrowed. "Something must be up. I mean, to get you coming here so early."

"Something *is* up." As quickly as I could, I told him what had happened over the past eighteen hours.

He whistled and leaned forward. "Oh, jeez, that's awful—poor Shackie. It's a joke except it ain't funny. Shackie wouldn't have known which end of the pistol to point. And if he did, Harry Hardwick would've grabbed it right outta his hand, and shoved it ..." He paused just long enough to regard Trudy. "Well, anyway. It's crazy, the whole thing."

"Too bad you're not a cop, Broadway. They've got it down as a package deal. Quick and dirty."

"It's both of those things all right. But it's also bull. Somebody's walking around who killed three people."

I nodded. "And I want to find him before the number goes to four." I pulled the cassette tape out of my pocket. "Got a player?"

Schwartz pushed back from the table and disappeared into the bedroom. Almost instantly he was back with a little battery-powered cassette player. I dropped in the tape, he pushed the START button, and we listened.

The puzzled expression on Schwartz's face lasted only until my odd-voiced caller mentioned a rigid notation box. Then his eyes bulged. "Hey, you hear that? Rigid notation box."

I shushed him quiet. "Listen," I whispered.

At the end of the tape, Schwartz scratched at his forehead under the brim of his fedora. "A deal you can't refuse, huh? There're two ways you could take that."

"Three. One way, the other way, or both. But that isn't a voice you recognize, is it?"

"Lemme hear it again."

I rewound the tape. Schwartz listened carefully, concentrating hard. At the end of the short message, he shook his head and said, "Sounds like a robot, you ask me."

"Someone trying to hide his real voice?"

"Sure. That'd make sense."

"If so, it's probably someone I know. Or *we* know."

"Yeah ..." Schwartz drew the word out to three syllables. "That makes sense, too. But I don't recognize his voice at all."

"Well, try this." I slapped my two pictures down in front of him. "Recognize any of these people?"

If the mention of a rigid notation box a moment before had made Schwartz's eyes bulge, now they threatened to pop out of his head. "Jeez, *Doc*!" He whistled, then quickly covered the pictures with his hand while he glanced over his shoulder. Trudy seemed to be giving all her attention to a pot on the stove. Slowly, Schwartz lifted his fingers and peered through them as if he were looking through a keyhole. "That's Harry Hardwick and his wife," he said. "But the floozie in the other picture ... and the guy with the hot dog ... them, I don't know. Never saw either one in my life."

I was disappointed. If anyone knew the Hot Dog Man, I figured Broadway Schwartz would.

"This's dynamite, Doc. Where the hell'd you get these?"

I gave him a mild fisheye.

"Don't mean to intrude. Just asking."

I told him about Sarah's find among Harry Hardwick's library books.

"Your wife found these?" Schwartz laughed, a nervous chuckle. "And she *gave* 'em to you?"

Leave it to Sarah. I don't think I ever saw Broadway Schwartz embarrassed before. "Yes. I'll admit, I was surprised, too."

"You never can tell about people."

"Maybe so. But we can tell a little about the person who made that phone call. For one thing, he wants a certain music box very badly. For a second thing he's already killed three people to get it."

Schwartz gestured with his head toward the cassette player. "You could take that tape to the cops. Then they'd have to look somewhere else than Shackie."

I shook my head. "I don't think the police would be impressed by a man saying he wants to buy one of my music boxes. I'd have to do some explaining about which music box he's after and how I happened to get *my* hands on it. *And* why I didn't tell good old Detective Robinson the straight truth in the hospital. What do you think would happen then?"

Schwartz waved off any further explanation. "Yeah, sorry. Dumb idea. So where do we go from here?"

I caught the "we." I smiled.

Schwartz caught the smile. "You're in, I'm in. You said it yourself: Whoever this guy is, he's killed three people already. My job's to make sure *you* don't get to be Number Four. Some day my Trudy might get sick again."

Six or seven years before, Trudy–who never complained of anything–got up in the morning with a severe headache. Her doctor talked to her by phone, called in a prescription for Fiorinal, and told her to get some rest. Several hours later Schwartz called me, frantic. Trudy's speech was slurred, she was becoming increasingly somnolent, and the doctor had said it was just the effect of the Fiorinal. I got her right over to Man Med Hospital, diagnosed a leaking aneurysm in a small artery on the surface of her brain, and lined up a good neurosurgeon to clip it before it blew out altogether. When Schwartz took Trudy home, he made sure I knew he was forever in my debt. Now in his own way he was reminding me.

I didn't argue. Nobody can live for you anymore than they can die for you, but I had the feeling I was going to be doing a bit of traveling through rough *terra incognita*. It might be nice to have a native guide.

I took the tape out of the player, and put it and the two

pictures back into my pocket. "What say we start with a little antique-ing? Could you bear company?"

"Sure, why not?" The little man stood up and grinned. "Better have your running shoes on, though, Doc. You've got to move fast, you want to keep up with Broadway Schwartz."

He wasn't kidding. If Napoleon had had Broadway Schwartz on his payroll he'd have ended up Emperor of Russia. Schwartz knew which dealers sat quietly in their back rooms at eight o'clock, a courtesy to their loyal picker trade, and which ones wouldn't open their doors to Jesus Christ before ten. In between shops, he worked in four appointments to look over the contents of apartments, two with dealers doing estate sales, the other two with the owners themselves. Without retracing a step we covered the entire territory from the Battery to 14th Street, River to River, and when we were finished Schwartz had close to $1200 in his pocket that hadn't been there before. He also had goodies stashed away with some twenty dealers. After lunch, he would go back, pick up the stuff–from memory; he kept no notes–and distribute it to the proper new owners. Very little, if anything, would go back to Yorktown.

Just before noon, I steered Schwartz into a deli on 14th Street and sprang for sandwiches and coffee. He asked me whether I'd gotten any ideas.

"I might've," I said. "From watching you deal, seeing stuff move so fast. Maybe we ought to track the travel of the one solid lead we've got–the rigid notation box. The Westfalls sold it to Sophie Soleski and somehow Harry Hardwick knew she had it. But Harry had people everywhere; our chance of grabbing the one guy in London on the other end of that particular pipeline is zero. But if we check out where the Westfalls got the box we might find something interesting. Any way you cut it, rigid notation boxes almost never come up for sale."

"Sounds good to me," Schwartz mumbled through a mouthful of corned beef.

"Problem is, I've only met the Westfalls a couple of times," I said. "I don't know how far I'd get with them. They might not talk to me at all–or they might not give me the right answers."

Schwartz's face brightened. "I know a guy in London. Al Resford."

"Thanks. I know some guys in London, too."

"No, no, Doc. This Resford, I call him The Gardener. Know why?"

Mr. Gallagher and Mr. Shean: Who says Vaudeville is dead? On charged Schwartz, straight to the punchline. "'Cause he's good at digging up dirt. Him and me, we've done business since forever. You want me to call him? See what he can find out?"

"Why not? What can we lose?"

That's never a question you should ask the wrong person. But Schwartz grinned, wiped his mouth, and looked up at the ceiling. "Gordon and Maida Westfall, right? Antique music box dealers, Gray's-in-the-Mews, London."

"I'm impressed, but don't you want to write it down?" I reached into my pocket for a pen.

"Nah." Schwartz waved his hand, then pointed to his head. "I got it right here, alongside of all the deals from this morning. I write it down, I'll only lose the paper. You ain't got no worry–soon's I get back this afternoon, I'll call Big Al."

Schwartz reached for the check; I beat him to it. I looked at his hand lying over mine. With my free hand I rubbed behind my left ear; it was still swollen and sore. "I didn't know you were a southpaw."

"Oh, yeah. Lefty Schwartz, they used to call me when I was a kid. Heck, they called me Lefty 'til I started in as a bookie, back in 'fifty-three. Then, I got to be Broadway 'cause of the hours I used to keep. Long as the lights on Broadway were on, I was on."

"You know, I never have heard your real first name."

Schwartz was on his feet, ready to go. "You never will. Talk to you later." He was out the door before I'd paid the check.

TWELVE

As I left the deli it occurred to me that Frank the Crank might have picked up some information about Abramowitz, so I detoured down to 12th Street. I might as well have saved the time. Frank was head-down on the desktop at the back of the shop, and if he hadn't looked up as I came in I'd have left without a word. When Frank is hosting his Black Angel–that's what he calls his depressions–he's worse than hopeless. But he saw me. "Whaddaya want?" he growled.

"Hi, Frank," I called out. "Just came by to say hello."

"Go screw yourself. Get out of here."

Frank's head plopped back onto the desk and I went out the door. If he'd found anything about Abramowitz it would have to wait another day.

There were two messages on my answering machine when I got back to my apartment. The first was a terse demand from Barton Moss to call him as soon as possible. The second was from a Melvin Madrid, who identified himself as an attorney and said he had an important matter to discuss with me. A couple of teasers. I took them in chronological order.

Moss answered on the third ring. He sounded as if he'd been drinking–no surprise there–and he wasted no time in getting to the point. "How'd you like to get sued for libel?" he snarled.

I thought about the next message, the one from Melvin Madrid, Attorney With Important Matter To Discuss. "I'm sorry, Barton," I said. "I don't think I know what you're talking about."

"Oh, I think you do." The coy lush at his irritating best. "But in case you forgot or something, I'll remind you. I was trying to get some repair business from Sophie Soleski last night, remember? Since your little faggot buddy O'Shacker got nailed, she needs a repairman. And I need work."

"What you need is a punch in your ugly mouth, you drunken slob."

"Oh, and I suppose you're gonna give it to me, huh? Big-shot doctor. You try, and I'll knock every friggin' tooth out of your head. You got some goddamn nerve–telling Sophie Soleski I'm not good enough to do her repairs."

So that was the basis for the proposed lawsuit. He meant slander, but what the hell. Libel, slander, as long as you're healthy.

"Don't try and deny you said it," Moss yelled. "She told me. When I called her this morning she said you 'recommended against it.'"

"I did more than recommend against it; I told her that as a repairman you're a clown, except what you do to music boxes isn't funny. Like Falconnet music boxes. To be specific, like Harry Hardwick's Falconnet music box. Which reminds me, by the way. Did you go back to New Rochelle after Harry's party the other night?"

"What, at that hour of the night? You crazy? Naw, I stayed over at Nussbaum's; that's what I always do when I come in the city and stay late."

Wasn't that interesting. Business and strange bedfellows and all that. The Nussbaum-Moss Reginaphony Factory?

Moss paused for a moment, then said, "What the hell business is it of yours, anyway? Where I went after Hardwick's party."

"Nothing important. I just thought maybe it was you who shot Harry. You'd have enjoyed that, wouldn't you?"

"Harry Hardwick!" The words came through the wire as pure venom. "That miserable prick. One lousy little accident, could have happened to anybody. Yeah, sure, I'd have enjoyed offin' Harry. But I didn't. You ask me, though, Harry got what he damn well deserved. That phony asskisser Lucas Sterne, sneaking into his bed and sticking it to his wife all the time. And then gettin' blown away. He had it coming and you want to know the truth, I was glad to see it."

Not being Broadway Schwartz, I was busy scribbling on the phoneside notepad, "Check Sterne–thick with Muriel?" while Moss was finishing his tirade.

"Sounds like you've got the good word for everyone today, Barton," I said. "Let me tell you something. Yes, I told Sophie she'd be better off with no repairman at all than with you. And as for your libel–or slander–suit, what I'm going to do right now is call your idiot shyster back and tell him that putting repair tools in your hands would be an act of criminal irresponsibility, and furthermore I'd be glad to say it in court and prove it. Now bug off. And don't try to hassle Sophie, either. You bother her anymore and we'll see whose teeth end up where."

I should have been ashamed of myself but I wasn't. It actually felt good. What's more, it worked. As Sophie had said, strength of character is not one of Barton Moss' strong suits. When he spoke again, he was actually whining. "Hey, take it easy, huh? I didn't call any lawyer. Just don't be a bad guy and tell Lucas Sterne what I said about him, okay? I was thinking maybe I could get some work from him."

"I won't say a word to Lucas," I said. "In fact, good luck. You guys deserve each other."

"Oh, great, thanks," Barton gushed. "I really, like, appreciate that."

I almost told him to remember me in his will, but I caught myself. I wasn't going to say that to anyone right then, not even Barton Moss. I just slammed down the phone.

Barton said he hadn't called a lawyer, but Barton was the

last person I'd take at his word. While I dialed Melvin Madrid's number I went over what I'd say to make it abundantly clear to this attorney what a lying sack of shit he had for a client.

But Melvin Madrid's opening remarks blew my embryonic speech clear out of my head. "Oh, Dr. Purdue," he boomed. "I'm glad to hear from you. We need to talk. You've come into a little inheritance."

His tone brought forth images of Wurlitzer theater organs. Up went my guard. "I didn't know I had any rich uncles, sick or otherwise."

"Well, I don't know about that," said Mr. Madrid. "But you did have a very good friend. Mr. Charles O'Shacker. He's left you his entire estate." There was a moment's pause, then I heard Madrid say, "Dr. Purdue? Are you still there?"

"Yeah. Sorry. What's one more little shock among friends?"

"Pardon me?"

"Nothing. Okay, Mr. Madrid; I'm with you. Where do we go from here?"

"Can you come down to my office so we can sort things out? The estate's not a big one, as I suppose you may know. But problems can arise even with smaller inheritances."

"Especially where Thomas Purdue *et ux* are involved," I said, and then added quickly, "When would you like me to come?"

"I'm free this afternoon between two and three-thirty."

My watch said one-twenty. "I'll see you at two."

Melvin Madrid was a big man, just about my own age, heavy, but not fat, with sand-colored hair carefully combed and a face full of freckles. His suit was an expensive one, the Brooks Boys' finest dark-blue striped worsted, and he wore it with the carelessness that only wealthy men can afford. An unwary opponent might take him for a clumsy bear, but the shrewdness in his gray eyes as he shook my hand said they'd be foolish to do so. This was a bear who'd deliver a clout when you least expected it and knock you into the next county.

Madrid motioned me to sit in a tan leather chair across

from his desk. "You've got a sense of humor," he said, "judging by our phone conversation."

"It helps me to go on living. At least it has so far."

He nodded, watching me very closely. Then he smiled. "We all need all the help we can get." He stirred in his chair and reached out to pick through some papers on his desk. "My dad and Charlie's father were friends. Sam O'Shacker did Dad's accounting; Dad was Sam's lawyer. Dad died first, so I took over what he was doing for Sam. Part of my job was to look after Charlie. I've done the best I could."

"I'm sure you did," I said. "Not always an easy assignment, was it?"

He let out a little chuckle that meant I'd said a mouthful. "Sam never understood Charlie–but for that matter neither did I. Spending his life fixing old music boxes." Madrid's eyes narrowed. "And all that business about talking to dead clockmakers."

"Well, it's about as far as you can get from balancing ledger books," I said. "Shackie never understood how his father could get off on making sure Column A and Column B added up to the same number."

I stopped short of saying it didn't sound very interesting or exciting to me, either. Tactful Thomas Purdue.

"I'm sure." Madrid swiveled his chair and sat up straight to face me directly. "Well, it takes all kinds. Charlie was a good kid, even if he was a bit flaky, and Sam loved him. Sam's big fear was his son might end up broke on the street, so he willed a trust fund for Charlie. He wanted to be sure Charlie'd never have to worry about money, or piss away a straight inheritance. But now Charlie's dead."

Madrid shook his head as if that could deny the truth. "I just can't believe Charlie killed two men and then himself," the lawyer droned. Again, the head shake, more vigorous this time, but no more effective.

"He didn't," I snapped.

"Oh?" Madrid was suddenly wide awake, eyes boring into mine. "How do you know?"

Schmuck! Even when I tell myself to be careful, off goes my tongue. Too late now to simply back off my pedestal of indignation; Madrid was too sharp a cookie to let me get away with that. Charlie O'Shacker's friend would have to borrow a leaf from the late master's story book.

"I just know," I said, as hotly as I could manage. "I knew Shackie for twenty years. Back when I was new in the practice he and I used to fool around with psychological and personality tests. And I've never, before or since, had anyone score lower in hostility, aggression, *or* greed." I banged my fist on the desk: neurologist as loyal friend and borderline wacko. "No, it's impossible. He could *not* have done it!"

Madrid relaxed a bit in his chair. He coughed. Witness dismissed.

I relaxed a bit in *my* chair.

"Well, anyway, Dr. Purdue. As you may or may not know, Charlie was an only child."

I nodded. I knew.

"Both his parents are gone, and his closest relatives are an aunt and uncle in L.A., and their two kids. Charlie hadn't seen or spoken with them in at least ten years. Four years ago, I finally managed to sit Charlie down here long enough to make up a will. He told me you were his best friend and he wanted to leave you his entire estate. We talked about it for a long while–not that I had any objections. I just needed to be sure that's what he really wanted."

My tongue wanted to say that when people say what they really want, that usually *is* what they really want. I bit it.

"He told me he was sure," Madrid continued. "So that's the way he wrote it up. He dies, the whole works goes to you. Trust fund, condo, tools ... everything. Not a whole lot of money, really, but a decent income from the trust. About sixty thousand a year."

Sixty thousand dollars a year! The way he'd chosen to live,

no wonder Shackie never seemed to have any money worries. But 'condo'?

"Excuse me," I said to Madrid. "Did you say condo?"

Madrid eyed me curiously. "Yes. Why?"

"Condo where?" I said.

"Where he lived, of course. And worked. That's a condo; didn't you know that?"

I shook my head. "We never talked about it."

"He had a life insurance policy on it," said Madrid. "So it's yours now, free and clear. What do you think of that?"

I couldn't say anything. I blinked hard. Melvin Madrid shimmered in his chair on the opposite side of the desk. "There is one complication, though." he said. "Nothing serious ... but I hope you can help. It has to do with Charlie's customers."

"Oh, God." I'd never thought of that. All those music boxes, in parts, all over the floor of that huge workshop.

"I see you understand."

"Yes, of course. Well, I'll certainly do what I can. Where do you want me to start?"

"Here." Madrid picked up a phone message slip from his desk and passed it across to me. "This lady's the only one to call me ... so far. She heard about Charlie on the TV news, started making inquiries, and found her way to my office. She said she left a music box for repair earlier this month. If you wouldn't mind calling her–"

"No problem. But how do I–"

"I was going to say." He handed me a small manila envelope. "Here's the key to Charlie's condo; it's a duplicate I kept in his file. Even though the police have finished their inquiry, we generally wait 'til the probate process is completed before we give property over to the heirs. But let's say I'm giving you access now so you can be of assistance to counsel. Just don't do anything definitive. No capital improvements, anything like that."

"Fine." I put the keys into my pocket, then read the phone message: Ms. Marisa Morgan. 762-0437.

"That's it," said Madrid. "If you'd give her a call and follow up, I'd appreciate it. And if any other customers get in touch with me I'll refer them directly to you."

"Fair enough. That's it for now?"

Madrid nodded. "I'll be calling you in a couple or three weeks to wrap up the probate. Sign papers."

I thanked him and got up. We shook hands. I was on my way to the door when Madrid said, "Oh, Dr. Purdue. By the way ..."

I turned around.

"While you're at Charlie's, maybe you could look around a bit. If you turn up his accounts book, that'd make it a lot easier to locate his customers."

I laughed. "Fat chance. The father was the accountant, remember?"

Madrid gave me a weak salute as I left.

Once I passed the secretary and got out into the hallway, I relaxed enough to smile to myself. A person doesn't shake free of his genetic inheritance. Whatever had led the father into accounting had guided the son into the precise work of music box restoration. Shackie wouldn't in a million years have kept a balance ledger, but a log book of his jobs was a different matter. He wrote a fresh page for each machine, begun on acceptance of the job. Name of client, date, type of machine, manufacturer (if known), lengths of both comb and cylinder, number of tunes, musical program (if known), any unusual features. Then, during the restoration process Shackie recorded the number of teeth in the comb and the tuning scale, along with any defects or unusual features. Finally, he catalogued every detail of restoration. Shackie wrote his autobiography in those five-and-dime-store notebooks, the account of a twenty-year love affair with antique music boxes. He kept the notebooks in the bottom right drawer of his central workdesk in the shop. With luck they'd still be there or scattered about on the floor.

Either way, I thought I'd be able to find them. But I wasn't going to tell Melvin Madrid. Or anyone else.

THIRTEEN

It was nearly three o'clock when I left Madrid's office. Another dark day threatening another premature night. I started downtown on Central Park West. At Columbus Circle I ducked into a coffee shop, had a quick cup, then slipped into the phone booth.

Marisa Morgan wasn't home. Her cheapie answering machine treated me to a few pathetic electronic bars of *"Fur Elise"* and asked me to please leave a message at the beep. I introduced myself, said I'd be at Shackie's between six and eight, and if she'd meet me there I'd do my best to help her find her music box. Then I went back outside, leaned into the icy gusts, and headed crosstown on 56th Street toward the Lucas Sterne Music Box Emporium.

There were three customers in the shop when I walked in. Lucas in his customary crow suit–black turtleneck shirt and black trousers–was playing a 15½" Regina in a magnificent hand-painted case for a youngish woman made up and dressed to the nines. An older woman and a young man browsed quietly among the other machines. No one I knew. These were noncollectors, wealthy citizens wondering if it might be fun to give something different this year, and say! Why not an antique music box? Why not, indeed? Lucas would be the last to argue. That handpainted Regina was a honey; any knowledgeable collector would have been happy to cart it home for eight or nine thousand dollars. I figured double that for the well-heeled but unsophisticated Lucas Sterne shopper. Peering over the woman's shoulders I saw I was right on. Sticker price, seventeen-five.

"That's just fine, my dear," I heard Lucas say as the music ended. "You *should* look around. And when you do, and you've discovered Lucas Sterne has the best selection *at* the best prices, I'll be here waiting for you."

I've never been able to figure how he gets away with that treacle-and-oleo delivery but he always does. The woman smiled. Lucas took her hand, bussed it lightly, and bowed ever so slightly from the waist. No doubt about it. She'd be back before Christmas, checkbook in hand.

Lucas watched her out the door, his face a massive simper. "Well, the good Dr. Purdue," he said from the corner of his mouth. "To what do I owe the honor of this visitation from the elite?"

"Just wanted to talk to you, but I can wait." I indicated the other two customers with a nod of my head.

"Tire-kickers," Lucas whispered. He turned the simper back on and called over his shoulder, "If you'd like to hear any of these wonderful music boxes just let me know." Then to me: "You can't waste any more of my time than they would. What did you want to talk about?"

"Music boxes."

He laughed. "Somehow we are not surprised. But I don't imagine I have anything sufficiently fine and early to even remotely tempt your exquisitely cultivated musical palate."

"Probably not. But there's a box in Harry Hardwick's collection I'd like to get."

"Oh, really." You could almost see Lucas's ears prick up, like a fox terrier's. "And which one might that be?"

"The rigid notation box. The one he had at the party."

Eyes and mouth flew open in mock surprise. "Oh, my. We're aiming at the top, aren't we? But don't you think you might be rushing ahead at a bit unseemly pace? And for heaven's sake–why should you be asking *moi* about it? Of all people."

When Lucas slips into snide overdrive I want to grab him by both ears and shake hard. Lucas can be an insufferable snot when he wants–which is a great deal of the time.

"I'm asking *vous*, because word has it Little *Vous* are in line to sell Harry's things."

He smirked. "One should not believe all the nasty rumors one hears."

"When they come from the horse's mouth I believe them."

The smirk grew wider. "Oh, do tell. And just what horsey is it who's been whispering sweet nothings into your pink little ear?"

I'd do better if I could control my stupid tongue. I should have played along in Lucas' silly verbal ping-pong game, given him a clever sliced shot that might have thrown him enough off balance that he'd swing, miss, and fall on his face. But instead I slammed the ball as hard as I could, hoping it would fly straight down his throat, whether or not it hit the table first.

"You know very well which horsey's been whispering, Lucas. That swishy little filly you've been buggering in your spare moments. Equus Murielus. When hubby's away, horsey will play, hmm?"

I was a success. I wiped the smirk right off his face. "You filthy pig," he hissed. "Get out of here."

"Lucas–"

He did a military about-face and strode over to his male tirekicker. The man had the lid of a cylinder box open and was peering inside. "Oh, you've made a marvelous selection," Lucas purred. "One of the finest cylinder music boxes. A Nicole Freres, circa eighteen fifty."

I shot a quick glance inside. "Sorry. You must be a little tired today. Nicoles were marked on the bedplate or the comb or both. This one has no mark. And that tune card is not one Nicole ever used; it looks like Bremond's to me. And it's a lever-wound box, no earlier than eighteen seventy. An eighteen fifty Nicole would have been wound with a key."

The man looked at me, questions all over his face. Lucas decided to pretend I didn't exist. "Let me play the music for you, sir," he said, and pushed the start lever–with his right index finger and thumb, I noticed. "Now listen. Isn't that gorgeous music? An utterly outstanding machine in all-original condition. Just cleaned up a bit."

"Not so gorgeous," I said. "Or original. The cylinder's been repinned, and poorly. That's why the music is so harsh and plucky. Look at the comb: three of the teeth have been replaced, see? Over toward the bass end. The box must have had a bad run. There's probably been severe damage to the governor ... yup, just look at the second wheel there, how it's wobbling. The bearings must be shot."

Lucas wheeled around, face white, lips purse-strung. "Thomas, if you're not out of here by the time I count to three, I'm going to call the police."

"Go ahead, call. I'll insist the box be shown to an independent expert–I'll bet Sophie Soleski'd be glad to give an opinion. I'll also bet the judge will direct you to thank me for saving you from grossly misrepresenting your merchandise." I pulled out my pocket notepad. "Would you give me your name, sir? Address? Phone number?"

The man backed away from the music box as if he was afraid it might blow up in his face. He edged away from us, then turned suddenly and shot through the doorway. I started to move toward the woman, notebook out and ready. "Excuse me, ma'am," I said. "I'm sure you couldn't help overhearing–"

She was already moving crab-like toward the door. "Oh no, no. I'm sorry. I didn't hear a thing," she twittered. "I'm not going to get involved ..." Then she was also out through the door and gone.

I put the notebook back into my pocket, then turned around and shook my head sadly. "*O tempora*," I moaned at Lucas. "*O mores*. Terrible, isn't it? Nobody wants to get involved."

Lucas was studying me, curiosity rapidly overtaking his anger. "I don't have any idea what's happened to you, but I really would be grateful if you'd get out of my store, at least until you're back to behaving in a civilized fashion. Now–"

"Can it, Lucas. I'm not feeling civilized, and I don't intend to apologize for it. Three people have been murdered over a music box–"

"Two," Lucas interrupted. "Shackie was a suicide."

"That's just my point: Shackie didn't kill himself and he didn't kill Harry or that Abramowitz character, either. Now listen: I don't care who you spend your nights with, but I suspect it might be embarrassing for you if it gets into wrong ears that you and Muriel are more than business acquaintances. Like for instance, Harry's lawyers' ears."

"You bastard! Harry and I made this agreement more than five years ago–before he even married Muriel. I found him some very nice things over the years and he was grateful. So he specified that in the case of his death–"

"That might be even more embarrassing. You arrange with the husband to sell his music boxes if he ends up dead, then you start sleeping with his wife. And then, guess what? He ends up dead. Which is going to make both you *and* his wife very rich."

"I'm going to call my lawyer."

"Blow it out your ass, Lucas. You're not going to call anyone. What you're going to do is answer a few questions for me and hope I'm so pleased with your honest answers I'll continue to keep our little secret. Kapeesh?"

The doorbell sounded and a woman started to walk in with a small child. Lucas jumped to his feet as if I'd goosed him. "I'm sorry, madam," he said. "But we're closed."

She looked at her watch. "But it's only a little past four," she said. "Your sign says you're open 'til five."

"I'm very sorry; we have an emergency." Old Honey-Lips, smooth as silk. "Please accept my apology. I'll be open again at ten tomorrow. I do hope you'll come back then."

The woman looked doubtful as Lucas ushered her out the

door; then he threw the lock and turned the sign–with his right hand–so the CLOSED side faced outward. "Come over by the desk in back," he said. "Where no one can see us."

I moved slowly, not taking my eyes off him. He sat down behind his little desk. If he moved a hand toward the drawer I'd jump him. But he just looked at me and said, "All right. What do you want to know?"

I lowered myself tentatively onto the edge of the desk and said, "Whatever you can tell me about that rigid notation box. Somebody wants it badly enough he's killed three people."

Lucas shook his head. "I can't tell you much. Harry had just gotten it, from Sophie Soleski, he told me. He was very pleased–as well he might have been. It was lovely."

"It sounded all right to you?"

A faint smile creased Lucas's face. He leaned back in his chair. "Yes. You must be talking about the scene Shackie made at the party. He insisted the music wasn't balanced and wanted to work on the box. Harry asked me what I thought."

"And?"

"I told him it sounded fine; I wouldn't do a thing to it. He laughed and said it sounded fine to him, too, and that Shackie was pestering ... he said Shackie was pestering the life out of him. I told him *my* advice would be to not let Shackie or anyone else near it."

"Except maybe you, of course? Lucas Sterne, Master Restorer?"

Lucas simpered, then shrugged. "I told you: I didn't think that box needed any work–by anyone, myself included. That's what I told Harry. And that's all I know about it. The next morning I heard about Harry–"

"How did you hear?"

He paused a moment. "Muriel called me. She told me Harry had been shot and the rigid notation box was missing." He took a breath, then decided to go on. "I know Shackie was your friend, but facts are facts and they all make sense." He started ticking the facts off on his fingers. "One, Shackie tried to get Harry to let him take the rigid notation box home from the party. Two, Harry said no. Three, Shackie got upset, killed Harry, and grabbed the box. Four, Shackie panicked, tried to get rid of the box. Five, the dealer heard about Harry on the news, caught on, and tried to blackmail Shackie. Six, Shackie killed him, got terminally scared, and bailed out. If you ask me, you're wasting your time at best. At worst, you're going to make yourself a great deal of trouble."

"I didn't ask you," I said, and got up.

Lucas shrugged again, stretched, and rose. "Suit yourself."

I started toward the door; he came after me. "That's all right, I'll let myself out."

I buttoned my coat quickly and pushed my way into the rush-hour swirl on the sidewalk. Make a new friend every day, that's my motto. I had to admit if only privately that Lucas' theory about Shackie, Harry, and the rigid notation box did make some sense. Harry Hardwick and Lucas Sterne insisting the rigid notation box sounded fine just could have thrown Shackie into a major snit. I could picture Shackie going far enough to grab the rigid notation box, perhaps giving Harry a shove in the process. But having a pistol in his pocket in the first place, then pulling it out and shooting Harry dead? Sorry. Not Shackie.

And besides. If Shackie was the killer, who was my voicemail caller?

No way, my friend, I said in my head to Lucas. *That's where your brilliant idea leaks like a sieve. That's where you're wrong. You, Robinson, and everyone else.*

I squeezed my way onto the packed subway train and was down at Shackie's a few minutes past five. It didn't look any better than the last time I'd been there. I needed full concentration to step through the mess of power and hand tools, supplies, music boxes and parts of music boxes that lay scattered between door and desk. I was sure the police hadn't been nearly so careful. Shackie would have been beside himself.

Shackie kept his workbooks in the lower right desk drawer, so I started burrowing through a disorderly mound of music boxes to the right of the desk. Just a couple of minutes and there they were, four black-and-white, covered notebooks. They must have been flung mindlessly out of the drawer, nothing about them to interest the killer. I sat down in the little swivel chair and started reading.

There in neatly-inked lines was every detail of construction, reconstruction, repair, and restoration of every music box Shackie had ever worked on. As I leafed through the pages I noticed something I'd never taken account of in all the years I'd known Shackie. You've seen 18th- and early 19th-century handwriting—that exuberantly flowing script with S's that look like F's, and graceful arching sevens with horizontal crossbars neatly placed through their midriffs. Well, Shackie's notebooks could have been written in Switzerland in 1830. If anything, the antique mannerisms became even more pronounced when he was describing the help various makers had given him during difficult restorations. Gooseflesh popped up on the back of my neck. I looked up and scanned the room, then laughed at my own foolishness. But the sound of my laughter in that empty room only made my neck hairs stand up straighter.

Part of Shackie's ongoing testament was to record the name of the owner for each music box he worked on. Most, I recognized. Some were collectors long dead, members of the Lucas Sterne Hall of Shame. A few, all single entries, were people I didn't know. These were probably non-collectors, people with one or two music boxes as heirlooms or decorator items, who'd somehow found their way to Shackie for repair work. The names that came up often were all familiar. Harry Hardwick was there, of course, and so was Sophie Soleski. It tickled me to find Lucas Sterne's name on several pages, he who advertised and boasted that all his restoration work was done on the premises. Well, fair enough. He didn't say which premises, did he?

Two names seemed incongruous: Jackson George and Sammy Shapiro. George collected miniatures and animated pieces, early stuff and very expensive. I thought he'd have patronized the one or two experts who specialize in restoration of miniatures, but over the past couple of years George had sent Shackie five pieces. One, a musical pocket watch, was supposedly still in the shop. As for Sammy Shapiro, I'd never in a million years have guessed Shackie did work for him. Sammy is a wheeler-dealer, a non-collector who belongs to NYMBCA purely for buy/sell opportunities. His favorite dish is pigeon, and a new NYMBCA member sets him drooling. To Sammy, a repair job means quick and cheap, just-make-it-run–the kind of work Shackie would never do.

It was getting close to six. I put the notebooks into the drawer, closed it, and then set to searching the room much as I had the day Shackie was killed. But I found no box or component bearing even a fair resemblance to Francois Nicole Serial Number 432. I covered the entire floor of the workshop, looked into every drawer and under every toppled machine tool. I even forced myself to go up the ladder to Shackie's living space. While I was there, I felt distracted, not able to take my eyes off the still-open closet. Finally I shut the door.

Then back downstairs. When I can't see something I'm looking for, I try a different point of view. I began to work my way east-west across the workshop floor, rather than north-south as before.

I'd only gotten a short distance when I heard footsteps outside, coming down the hallway. A woman, high heels. The footsteps stopped. There was a knock.

"Yes?" I called out.

"Mr. Purdue? I'm here to keep an appointment with Mr. Thomas Purdue."

I hopscotched to the door and opened it.

The lady smiled. "How do you do?" she said, and extended her hand. "Mr. Purdue? I'm Marisa Morgan."

I shook her hand and motioned her inside. "Pleased to meet you," I said.

"Thank you for being so kind."

She unwrapped a long red scarf from around her head and neck, and shook free a cascade of shiny black curls. Everything about her was highly colored: bright red cheeks, brilliant blue eyes, flaming lipstick. She unbuttoned her coat. Her dress was fire-engine red. A small gold leaf-shaped pin below her left collar drew attention just by being so uncharacteristically understated.

"No trouble," I said. "Shackie was a good friend. It's the least I can do."

Her smile brought more light to the room than any of the fluorescent fixtures above us. "Yes, Mr. Madrid said he thought you might be able to help." She looked around the room; the smile faded. She clucked her tongue against the roof of her mouth. "How very awful. It looks like a cyclone's been through."

There was something odd about her speech. I couldn't place it. Definitely not New York.

"It's bad, all right. We may have to do some hunting for your music box. Can you describe it for me?"

While I spoke she was sizing me up. "Are you in music boxes, too, Mr. Purdue? Do you repair them?"

"Yes and yes, but I'm a collector, not a professional restorer like Shackie was. I work on my own music boxes, just part of the hobby. Why?"

"Well, you see: I brought Mr. O'Shacker my music box only last week. An antiques dealer said he was the one to repair it. And I *was* very impressed when I met him. He seemed so knowledgeable."

"He *was* knowledgeable. *And* the right person to repair your music box. Especially if it was a good one."

"I'm not an expert at these things. It's the only music box I own. I've always loved them but I've never had money to spend on them."

Now, *I* studied *her*. Considering coat, dress, scarf, and jewelry I guessed she was wearing a couple of thousand dollars. To look at her, money ought not to be a problem. But that can be deceiving. A lot of well-dressed people have listened to my music boxes and said, "Oh, they're so beautiful! But so expensive! Some day I'll get one." They won't. They'll die with packed dresser drawers, bulging closets, loaded shoeracks, empty bank accounts, and unoccupied collection shelves. A matter of priorities. But apparently Marisa had taken the plunge.

"What was the matter with your music box?"

She shrugged delicately. "Well ... I don't know, not exactly. He said something about dampers and cylinder pins and ... oh, some sort of French word–"

"Terminage?"

Her face brightened. "Yes. That was it. He said it meant something like making sure all the pins on the cylinder were bent just so, so when they plucked the comb teeth the sound would be proper."

"Yes, that's exactly what it means." I thought for a moment. "Your music box must have been a good one if it was worth having that sort of work done on it. It's time-consuming and frankly, not cheap. In an ordinary music box you wouldn't hear enough of a difference to make it worth doing."

"Isn't that interesting? That's just what Mr. O'Shacker said. Do you think ... that *you* might be able to do the work for me, Mr. Purdue?"

I shook my head. "I've got neither the time nor the expertise. But no one can do anything 'til we find your music box. What does it look like?"

"It's not big." She held her hands apart as if showing the size of a trout she'd caught the day before. "Very pretty, though. The case is plain wood, not inlaid the way some music boxes are, and you wind it with a big key. It plays four songs, all of them from Mozart operas. And the cylinder looks funny–funny-different, I mean. Rather like a checkerboard."

Was there no end to this? Half the population of New York might've had their hands on my music box during the past couple of weeks. I flashed an expression of professional perplexity, as if Marisa had described an incongruous set of disease symptoms. "It *does* sound like a nice one. Any other identification you can think of? Something we can use to look for it?"

She thought for a moment, then raised a finger. "Oh, yes ..."

I waited.

"On the comb–behind the teeth. The name of the manufacturer was there; Mr. O'Shacker showed me."

"Ah. From the way you describe the box I'll bet it was Francois Lecoultre."

She started to say yes, then shook her head. Her brow creased. "That sounds familiar, she said. "But not precisely right."

Neither does your way of speaking. "Hmm. How about Raymond-Nicole?"

"That's so close. Both are. But neither's the one."

"Oh, well." I sighed. "Let's see what we can find, why don't we?"

We spent the better part of the next hour going through the littered minefield that was once Shackie's workshop, looking for a music box I knew we weren't going to find. After about twenty minutes Marisa touched my arm. "*I* remember now–it's been driving me mad ever since you asked me–the name of the maker, I mean. It *was* Nicole–*Francois* Nicole. *That* was the name on the comb."

"Francois?" I was all innocence. "F-r-a-n-c-o-i-s?"

"Well, no. Not exactly. It was abbreviated: F-r-a-n-c. And then a little 's,' a half-space elevated. Mr. O'Shacker said that was the way Francois Nicole signed his combs."

"Well, that *is* something," said Dr. Enthusiasm. "Very unusual, very rare. Very, very nice. Tell me if you don't mind: where on earth did you find such a music box?"

"Oh, just beginner's luck, I'm sure. I was browsing one day in a shop up on the West Side, a great big place called the Gotham Antiques Mart. I saw it there. And it was so pretty I couldn't leave it."

"This was just about a week ago?" I tried to keep the quaver out of my voice.

"Why, yes. I wonder were I to go back if he might have another?"

"I doubt that. You were lucky to find one. Why don't we look some more?"

In the middle of the third go-round Marisa gave a short cry and grabbed at my arm. She'd caught her heel on the edge of a toppled lathe. I caught her and pulled her back; she came up with both my arms around her. She felt nice and smelled even nicer. I got that funny feeling in the pit of my stomach.

"Oh, dear," she said, pulling away just enough to look up at me. "How clumsy. I'm terribly sorry."

I released my hold on her. "My pleasure."

She laughed politely, then her face turned serious. "I don't think we're going to find my music box. Whoever was here must have taken it away."

"I suppose that's possible. I'm sorry."

"Never mind," she said, and looked at her watch. "Oh my. How late it's gotten. Have you had your dinner?"

"No, not yet." I could still smell her face powder; some of it must have rubbed off on my cheek. "Would you like to go have a bite? I'd be happy to–"

"Oh, no thank you. I couldn't possibly take more of your time."

That was not a refusal; it was a story. It meant I just needed to work a little harder. I didn't mind. So far she'd only muddied my already-murky waters, but some further conversation might be enlightening.

"Don't even think about it. I'd enjoy talking to you. Maybe I could help you find some sort of replacement. That is, if your original music box never turns up."

"You're very kind," she said, then seemed to recollect herself. "*I* know—why don't we go to my apartment. I'll make a quick dinner."

"Oh, well, uh ..." I scratched my head. She had been telling me a story, all right, but maybe a different one than what I'd thought. "*Come into my lair," said the spider to the fly.*

"It'll be no trouble at all. I insist!" A teasing smile spread out from the left corner of her mouth. "You're not ... afraid, are you?"

"'Course not. Your name's not Virginia Woolf, is it?"

"I beg your pardon?"

"Just a joke. It means how silly of you to think so. Sure, if you really don't mind—"

"If I minded I wouldn't have asked. It's settled then." She walked over toward the door, picked up her scarf and coat. "I make a lovely cheese and mushroom omelet. Come along."

Marisa lived on Second Avenue between 52nd and 53rd. Not as plush a neighborhood as I'd have thought, but fashionable enough. The apartment itself was small: direct-entry living room, bedroom in the back, and a small kitchen off to the right. There was a peculiar starkness about the place, lots of white paint, walls decorated by only a few garden-variety travel posters. A sofa-bed, a few chairs, and a coffee table were Danish Modern recycled through Salvation Army. Odd. Marisa's apartment said nothing about her. Maybe it was like her jewelry, I thought. *She* was supposed to be the centerpiece, the focus of all attention.

While she was making her lovely omelet I took the opportunity to copy down the number on her telephone. By the time she set the sizzling pan down between us at her little white-topped table, I was starving—but not so much that I failed to notice the way she handled her utensils as she ate. Suddenly some things fell into place.

"Wonderful," I said.

Her eyelashes fluttered becomingly. "I'm glad you like it."

"You're not from New York, are you?"

If I'd hoped to take her aback by the sudden talk-twist, I failed. She laughed lightly and said, "No, I grew up in Milwaukee, then Dad moved his business to St. Paul. I only came to New York earlier this year. Are you going to ask me why?"

"Sure. Why?"

"I worked with Dad from the time I got out of college 'til last year. We ran a travel agency. It was fine ... but in a way that was the problem. Last year I turned thirty. I had a good job; I was making enough money; Dad and I got on well enough. I'd been married; I'd been divorced. And I felt, oh ... I suppose you could say, in a rut. I wanted to try something different, somewhere more exciting."

"Before life passed you by," I said.

"You're making fun of me." She was a pretty pouter.

"No, not at all. I meant it. I was thirty once. Also forty."

Her smile was a heart-melter, but she was still telling me stories. The question was why. She was no more from Milwaukee or St. Paul than I was. People from Milwaukee and St. Paul—just like people from New York—cut their food with the fork in the left hand, knife in the right. Then to eat what they've cut, they put down the knife, shift the fork into the right hand, pick up a piece of food, and transfer it to the mouth with the concave side of the fork uppermost. But Marisa cut her omelet with single firm slashes; then with the fork still in her left hand, convex side still up, she fed the pieces directly into her mouth. Which is the way kids learn to eat if they have English mums rather than American mothers.

And her speech—that was also British. She had the accent under control, but not so her cadence, phrasing, and word choice. She and her Dad got *on* well, not *along*, which is what she'd have said if she really were from Milwaukee via St. Paul. And terminage was supposed to make the pins "just so." Jolson used to sing a funny song about a Latin from Manhattan. It wouldn't be nearly so humorous if this classy chiquita turned out to be a psychopahth from Bahth.

When we put down our forks, each in our own way, Marisa pushed back her chair, leaned across the table and kissed me. "Leave the cleaning-up; just be comfortable. I'll only be a moment." She vanished into the bedroom.

She didn't close the door behind her, and through the open doorway I had no trouble following her progress by shadows on walls. She stepped out of her dress, then peeled off her underwear, piece by piece. Thus reduced to native condition, she bent over. I heard a drawer open. Getting something comfortable to slip into?

Or maybe getting something a bit more lethal? Like a knife or a gun?

I looked across the austere living room at the door to the hallway. What could this luscious thirty-one-year-old crypto-Brit with a morbid fascination for rigid notation boxes possibly want from me? Not my body, certainly, or my money.

How about my music box or my life?

I edged out of the chair, grabbed my coat off the sofa, and moved quickly and quietly to the door. A few seconds later I was doing a nice broken-field move down Second Avenue, running like hell.

FOURTEEN

I got out of bed the next morning with a nasty post-noncoital depression. My old psychiatry professor, Dr. Morris Bloom, used to tell his medical students that all they ever needed to know about sex could be summed in one Yiddish sentence: *Ven der putz shtet, licht der sechel in drerd*. "When the penis stands up, common sense is dead and buried." True enough, but a person would have to be awfully low in the *sechel* department to risk losing his literal head over even a very attractive piece of tail.

Besides, after fifteen years of intimate association with Sarah, all other tails looked second-rate, no matter how I regarded them.

I sighed, picked up the phone and dialed Schwartz's number. Trudy answered. She laughed when I asked if Broadway was around. At nine-thirty in the morning? I had to be kidding. I asked her to have him call me as soon as he could. "Tell him to go through my beeper; Manhattan Medical Hospital, have them ring Dr. Purdue."

Soggy corn flakes and marginal milk are lousy morale boosters. I tossed half the bowlful into the sink and dropped a couple of pieces of wheat bread into the toaster. Then I couldn't seem to sit still and wait for them to pop. I'd been making an outright pest of myself, asking questions of Sophie Soleski, Lucas, Muriel, even Barton Moss. Any of them could have been in some way involved in the murders. And even if they weren't, NYMBCA is a tight group. So by now most of the membership probably knew Thomas Purdue was being determinedly snoopy. Sooner or later I was going to start making the killer nervous.

The toast popped up. I popped up. I'm sure we looked funny but we were not amused.

Down at the Wind-Me-Up, Frank the Crank was bubbly. "Hey, the good doctor," he greeted me. "I been wondering when you were coming by. I got some good stuff for you."

I didn't say a word about having been there the day before. I can never tell whether Frank remembers what goes on when he's in the throes of one of his funks or whether he's a true Jekyll-Hyde, one personality unaware of the existence of the other. There are times I'd love to get him into my office for a few hours, but right then was not one of those times. "Do tell," I said from across the counter. "And tell all."

He pointed at his pile of donuts. "Have one. Fresh from Nedicks."

I waved my hand no. "Thanks, I just had a big breakfast. I'll settle for your good stuff. What is it—machines or gossip?"

Frank's eyes sparkled. "You wanted dirt; dirt's what I got you."

"Good. Start shoveling." I walked around the counter and sat down next to Frank at the side of his desk.

He grinned and tapped twice on the desktop. "Okay. Abramowitz, to tell you the truth, I didn't do so well on. No record, just like I thought. He did do a few deals with Nussbaum besides that Reginaphony, but nothing you'd write home about. On the other hand, what I picked up about your pal Hardwick and his wife ... *that* you're gonna be interested in."

All I could think about was Mr. Wiener-Dick. I wondered whether I'd ever eat another hot dog.

"They were not exactly your Hallmark lovey-birds," Frank

said. "Word has it the young lady had more of an eye for the boys than a person might think was smart when she was on a big-time gravy train. Soon as Harry was on a plane the back doorbell started ringing."

"Anyone in particular?"

"Ho, ho, ho." Frank, enjoying himself to the limit. "Hey, it ain't exactly a secret–"

"I'm hopeless with that stuff. Eternal last link in the gossip chain. Come on. Give."

"Well ..." Frank's face broadcasted joy. He was in his glory, the standup comedian working his way to his big punchline. "I got it on the customary good authority that for the last couple of months or so, Mrs. H's little boy *du jour*'s been Lucas Sterne."

Confirming evidence. I decided to play dumb. "Lucas Sterne? Jesus, Frank."

"You surprised?"

"I sure think she could do better."

"Maybe that depends on what she's after. All men got the same equipment. But no two of them use it exactly the same way."

"I get the picture–and speaking of pictures, how about those photographs I showed you?"

"No luck there. I still don't have a clue who's the guy wearing the hot dog roll. Or the lady who's going to circumcise him with her teeth. But there *is* more about Hardwick and his wife. Word is, the big heave-ho was on the way. And on top of that Hardwick was doing a plan with his lawyer. Like before he pitches out the missus, he sets up a foundation and transfers ownership of all his machines. *And* the house. He'd keep livin' there, of course. But when he croaked, all his assets would go to the foundation to set up the house and machines as a museum and maintain it. Like an endowment."

I whistled. "That would've left Muriel *and* Lucas out in the cold, wouldn't it?"

"Thought you'd be impressed." Frank the Crank leaned back in his chair and smirked.

"I am. Be sure to let me know if anything else turns up, okay?"

"You know me. Ear to the ground. Nose to the grindstone. Soul of discretion."

I strolled uptown through the peak of New York's Christmas frenzy. Frank the Crank's information made for a good little story. Either Lucas or Muriel got wind of Harry's plan and called the other. They arranged to kill Harry after the party; then Lucas took the rigid notation box to Abramowitz's, told Abramowitz his name was Charles O'Shacker, and sold him the box. Then he killed Abramowitz so he wouldn't be able to testify as to what Charles O'Shacker looked like. It made sense.

Except for one thing. At that point Lucas and Muriel both would have had what they wanted. The cops were convinced Shackie had killed Harry, Abramowitz, and himself; Muriel stood to inherit all of Harry's estate; and Lucas was waiting for the official go-ahead to make *his* bundle on ten percent of Harry's brokered sales. They had it made. For them to jeopardize their freedom and fortunes to try to recover a $22,000 rigid notation music box made less than no sense. Good story, but the end was pure shaggy-dog.

Jackson George lived on the twenty-first floor—the entire twenty-first floor—of The Blenheim, a luxury apartment hotel on Central Park West. His monthly rent would've kept me in food, shelter, movies, and ice-cream cones for a year. He was nearly as wealthy as Harry Hardwick had been, but where Harry wore his fortune like a rumpled old gabardine suit, Jackson George wore his like a neon sign.

In their approach to collecting, Jackson and Harry were also very different. When Harry was offered a machine he wanted, he dug deep and paid the asking price. Jackson, however, pulled a lemon-sucker face. So much money! You're trying to take advantage of me. Which was very likely true—but that's why Harry Hardwick's collection was the finest in the world, while Jackson George's was merely first-class. It's also why Jackson George hated Harry Hardwick.

Jackson's apartment must have been assembled by a designer who painted by the numbers. The carpet was white. The furniture was that sinuous walnut-and-glass stuff, not a straight line to be seen anywhere. The upholstery was a spoiled-peach color. On the walls hung picture frames painted to match the upholstery, while the subjects behind the glass—mostly generic country scenes—accentuated the white and walnut. All style, no substance. Just like Jackson George.

Even with Harry dead, Jackson couldn't find charity in his heart. "It goes to show you," he said as we sat in his living room, looking out at the white expanse of Central Park below. "He was an imbecile to strut his stuff. Inviting all those people to his place—you just can't do that these days. It only takes one bad egg."

Jackson was a tall, angular man in his forties with the sourest soul this side of Arthur Schopenhauer. Goggling from behind his huge horn-rimmed glasses, he looked for all the world like a dyspeptic stork. But the stork had recently seen a bigger bird in his pond choke on a fishbone. Jackson was smug; Jackson was pleased. Jackson was smart; Harry was dumb. Jackson was alive; Harry was dead. Praised be the Lord.

"But 'All those people' are the New York Music Box Collectors' Association," I said. "If we didn't open up our collections we wouldn't have an organization."

"Nah-nah-nah." He shook his head and waved his hand rapidly back and forth. "There are plenty of members who have collections that aren't so ... well, so *tempting. They* should have the meetings. Consider the times we live in. It's all too easy to face temptation with a lethal weapon in your hand. If that rigid notation box had been mine I wouldn't have felt at all comfortable–not the way that low life Sammy Shapiro was behaving around it."

This was interesting. Shapiro always has a deal for you, but it's always cash-on-the-barrelhead. No business license, no inventory, no income tax. His is a highly mobile collection: in the front door, out the back. I asked Jackson what bothered him about Sammy's behavior.

"After Harry's demonstration, when Walter Remler was trying to listen to the rigid notation box–"

"Remler?" I said. "I didn't think Remler would be interested in a rigid notation box."

Jackson raised his head ever so slightly, the better to look down his nose at me. "Perhaps not for acquisition," he said. "But Walter has proper appreciation for artistry–even if the items he collects *are* a bit ... unconventional. He was trying to listen to the rigid notation box but Shapiro kept chattering away, poking him in the ribs, pointing at the music box. He wouldn't let Walter alone. Finally, Walter said some sharp words to him. Shapiro just laughed, but he did go away so Walter could listen to the music box in peace."

This didn't add up. Why should Walter Remler, erotica collector, be so interested in music on a rigid notation box? And why should Slimy Sammy Shapiro be so interested in Walter Remler?

Meanwhile, Jackson droned on. "Harry simply should not have hosted those meetings. I'm sorry to say it, but pride goeth before a fall."

He was sorry to say it. I imagined Harry's response.

Jackson looked at me curiously. "I didn't know I'd said something funny."

"All depends how you look at it. One of the reasons I came here was on behalf of the Association. Harry put a great deal of life into the group. This is an opportunity now for you to step forward. I hope you can see that."

From the expression on Jackson's face you'd have thought I had pulled a gun out of my pocket and was sitting there pointing it at him. "*That's* why you came here? You think *I* should host meetings? With what *I* collect? You must be out of your mind."

Jackson George collected very small, very early, and very valuable mechanical musical machines. Very early means between 1790 and 1820. He owned watches, rings, fobs, snuff boxes, scent bottles, jewelry cases, all featuring magnificent workmanship in gold, silver, precious stones, ivory, tortoise shell, and mother-of-pearl. With as few as seven or eight teeth, the tiny and elegant music-works hidden inside these trinkets play arrangements of old French or English tunes that leave listeners in stunned and respectful silence. Price tags begin in the lower five-figure range and go up rapidly from there.

"I can just see it," Jackson whined. "I'll take my things out of ... safe-keeping, and set them on the dining room table there. Then after the meeting I'll consider myself grateful if I still have half of them. *And* if I'm still alive. I'm afraid you're wasting your time, and mine as well."

Of course Jackson George had never hosted an NYMBCA meeting. He never would. But that wasn't really why I'd gone there. "All right. I've got something else to talk to you about. I'm functioning as executor of Shackie's estate–"

He went off like a cherry bomb in the hands of an eight year old. "Oh that no-good ... so and so," he spluttered. On his feet, arms gyrating, head bobbing and weaving, he looked like Jake LaMotta trying to box his way through an epileptic attack. "After all I did for him. To–"

My turn to interrupt. "Wait a minute, after all *what* you did for him?"

He bent over me, pushing his face close to mine. "I gave him my things to work on," he shouted. "I don't give my things to just *anyone*, you know."

I made a point of slowly taking my handkerchief out of

my pocket and wiping my face while I glared at him. He backed off, but only a little. "Yes, it *was* irresponsible of him, wasn't it? Getting killed simply to inconvenience you. If I were you I'd never give him anything else to work on."

"He killed him*self*, Thomas–in case you haven't been told. After he killed two other people. And stole a valuable music box."

I told myself there was nothing to be gained by trying to convince Jackson George that Shackie didn't kill anyone, himself included. Nothing to gain, maybe even something to lose. "No one will ever call you a prince, Jackson, unless it's a mispronunciation. But never mind; I'm an equal-opportunity executor. Tell me what Shackie had of yours and I'll do my best to find it and get it back to you."

"Humph. Fortunately there was only one item: a very rare and expensive twenty-four-carat gold watch by Henry Capt, *pere*, a quarter-repeater with a *sur plateau* musical movement. I'd hate to tell you what I paid for it."

"Don't then." I took out my pocket notebook and scribbled in it. "The place is a mess, but I don't know that anything was stolen. I'll try to locate the cause of your poverty."

Either my sarcasm went past him or he decided to ignore it. "I hope you'll do it soon."

"I'm sure. But can I ask you one question?"

"You just did." He smiled smugly.

"I'll be damned. I'd never have accused you of owning a sense of humor. Why on earth were you even sending things like that watch to Shackie? I thought you'd have Bruce Carlson do it. Or Clive Williamson in London. Someone who specializes in miniatures."

"Oh, well." He scratched at the top of his head; I thought he looked embarrassed. "Those people ... they take absolutely forever; after all, they're *artistes*." He struck a limp-wristed pose. "And then they charge you an arm and a leg."

I laughed. I should have known. "And Shackie got the work done in three months for half the price."

Jackson didn't say anything.

"*And* the work he did was every bit as good as anyone's. Wasn't it?"

"Well, yes. Of course. Otherwise, I wouldn't have patronized him."

"You patronize everyone, Jackson." I got to my feet, picked up my topcoat, and slid into it. "I'll be calling you. Don't call me."

I got only a couple of steps toward the door when my beeper went off. Jackson pointed toward a phone on the end table.

"Thanks, but it's one of my patients. Private matter, privileged information. I'll go downstairs and use a booth."

He gave me a disgusted look and pointed past the dining room. "There's a phone in my study. You can talk privately there." He paused, then added, "I won't listen in."

I nodded thanks and went into the study. Green leather-topped partners' desk, leather chair, custom bookshelves. Nice to have money.

I dialed the hospital operator.

It was Schwartz. I told him to meet me at the Second Avenue Deli at 12:30.

As I was getting up from the chair I noticed a bit of bright red on the floor on the far side of the desk. I picked it up; it was a matchbook. On the cover was a cartoonish drawing of a short-haired woman wearing pants, a shirt and a tie. The George Sand Club, it said, at an address somewhere in London. I almost set it back down on Jackson's desk, but changed my mind and dropped it into my shirt pocket instead. Let Jackson George accuse me of stealing his matchbooks. Wasn't he convinced that given half a chance any NYMBCA member would walk out of his apartment with a pocketful of his tiny treasures? Oh, dem self-fulfilling prophecies.

I thanked Jackson as I came back into the living room. Then, as if a new thought had hit me I said, "Capt watch, huh?

Those don't grow on trees—certainly not on American trees. What do you do, Jackson? Go to England to find your things?"

His nasty smile said that was a pretty clumsy attempt and no, he wasn't about to give away his sources. But he'd throw me a bone. "*I* don't go after my things; my things come to me. I haven't been to England in ten years or more. Terrible climate, worse food, utterly impossible people. But I do have ... representatives there. The watch came out of Sotheby's auction this past September. It was the biggest auction of miniatures in years, more than a hundred and twenty lots. Mostly the Theodore Badger collection, but some other items were mixed in as well. Gold, jewels, tortoise, ivory; *sur plateau* movements, *barillets*. You can imagine what sort of crowd it drew. My representative was fortunate to come away with six premier items."

Especially considering the tight budget he'd undoubtedly been working with, I thought. His representative! Jackson George was not about to roll in the gutters with the *hoi polloi*. Me, I take every possible chance to go to England. I've never been treated badly there; in fact I've always found their hospitality delightful. But theirs is an old society and they are both sensitive to *parvenus* and not terribly tolerant of them. Somebody once must have really socked it to Jackson George. Which meant he was likely telling the truth when he told me he hadn't been to England in years.

So who dropped the matchbook in Jackson George's study? Someone from London who represented Jackson at auctions?

Back at my apartment the answering machine was going ballistic. As I came in it was taking message number 14. I let it finish, then picked up the lot. Six messages were from Shackie's customers: three NYMBCA members, three non-collectors. They'd been referred by Melvin Madrid. The fourteenth was Sophie Soleski. I dialed her number as soon as I had my coat off.

"Oh, I'm so glad to hear from you. Listen, dear, can I ask you for a favor?"

"Anything, Sophie."

"Maybe you shouldn't say that until you hear what it is."

I laughed. "I didn't say I'd do anything; I said you can ask anything. Fire away."

"Well, I know it's an imposition. But I sold a box to a very good customer with the sale contingent on his being satisfied with Shackie's restoration. It's a mandoline-basse box, a real beauty, and I'll admit I got a good price. But it's full of damper noises. Now my customer has heard about Shackie and I think he's one step away from asking for his money back–which frankly would be a real problem for me. Do you know how I might be able to get that box back from Shackie's? And then ... is there any chance you could do the damper job for me? I hate to ask, but there's no one else around right now I can trust."

People die. Life goes on. I told Sophie I was executor of Shackie's estate and I would look for her customer's box. And if I could, I'd do the repairs. "But dampers on mandoline boxes are the hardest to adjust," I said.

"Please. I know that. I've been in music boxes for longer than you've been on earth. And for more than forty years I was married to Peter Soleski."

"No insult intended, Sophie. It's just that I'm not a professional restorer. I don't know whether I can do a good enough job."

"I've heard your music boxes, the ones you've restored. *I* know you can do it, if you've got time."

Sure I had time. I was on vacation these two weeks, wasn't I? Somewhere between settling Shackie's estate and finding out who was killing New York's music box elite I'd work in a bitchy damper job for Sophie. "Don't worry about a thing, Soph. Tell your customer when he hears his box he'll think he's died and gone to heaven."

"I don't know how to thank you. We do learn who our real friends are, don't we?"

"You bet," I said, and thought, *also our real enemies*. But sometimes not soon enough.

***

Schwartz was even more animated than usual. He moved aside the pickle barrel on the table to show me a sleeper he'd picked up that morning, a little green agateware pot whose underside bore a Wedgwood and Bentley impression. "Guy had it thought it wasn't real Wedgwood because of that mark," Schwartz cackled. "I told him I could give him thirty bucks for it anyway." Then Schwartz explained that for a few years in the 1770s, Josiah Wedgwood had been in partnership with Thomas Bentley, and the fine pottery they produced was now the most valuable ever to have come out of the prestigious old factory. "If I get less'n a thousand for it I'll eat it," crowed my triumphant picker.

He'd also heard from his English friend. "Big Al says those Westfalls are five hundred percent honest. They been in business since the early nineteen sixties, got contacts all over England and then some, and nobody to say a bad word against them. He couldn't find out anything about where that rigid notation box came from, though. No scuttlebutt about a stolen music box. Al found out that much. He figures if the Westfalls did send over a rigid notation box they came by it fair and square. Best he could do."

"Then the monkey business must have happened over here. The Westfalls shipped a rigid notation box to Sophie, Harry's scouts got wind of it, told him, and he called her and bought it. But obviously someone else wanted it, and very badly. Of course, that someone might be English."

"Well, for that matter, Doc, he *could* be French. Or an Eyetalian or a Turk or an A-rab. So what?"

I told Schwartz about Marisa and how she'd said Shackie was going to work on her rigid notation box, which was identical to Harry's and mine, and which she'd bought a week before at the Gotham Antiques Mart.

Schwartz didn't look the least fazed. He nodded knowingly. "What do you think? That Abramowitz guy had a little thing going there? Turning out repos?"

For some reason the second R in repro is usually dropped

among the antiques crowd, so that a recently-manufactured copy of a valuable old piece becomes linguistically indistinguishable from a reclaimed automobile.

"No chance. Nobody's going to reproduce that kind of music box, not today. No one's got the skill or the time."

"But Shackie said the box sounded funny."

"Not funny enough to be a fake. Get off that track; there's only one box involved, but somehow it's done a lot of traveling."

Schwartz paused a moment, then said, "Here's something else: If your lady-friend from last night bought that music box a week ago, it don't jibe with Mrs. Soleski getting it from England two weeks ago and selling it straight off to Hardwick."

"Right on. Tell you what"–I grabbed a napkin out of the holder and wrote down Marisa's name and address–"do you think you can find out anything about her?"

A sly grin spread over Schwartz's face.

"Okay," I said. "What do you know that I don't?"

"Nothing, Doc–at least not yet. But you said go find out so I'll go find out. Just thinking about how, that's all."

Whatever was Schwartz's how, I knew it wouldn't be mine. But that's why *he* was going to check out Marisa. We live in an age of specialization. When surgery is indicated a neurologist calls in a neurosurgeon. For this particular procedure I figured there could be no better operator than Dr. Broadway Schwartz.

I pushed back from the table. "Find out what you can. I'm going over to Shackie's; I think I'd better get the place put back together. Meet me over there when you're done."

He saluted and was out the door.

I was not looking forward to my afternoon: housecleaning's not my thing. I thought of calling Sarah and apologizing, but finally decided against it. I needed to keep my eyes open while I was straightening and if I found anything, I probably would not want to explain. Better to let Sarah stay sore a while longer.

FIFTEEN

By four o'clock when Schwartz banged on the door, I had Shackie's place nearly squared away—tools back where they belonged, music boxes identified as to owners and labeled with yellow Post-it notes. There was surprisingly little damage; the killer had been considerate.

I groaned when I saw Sophie's mandoline-basse box. Its comb was fifteen inches long and had 182 teeth. Probably 130 would need dampers. Against my better judgment I played one of the six tunes. It sounded like a nest of crickets—probably not a working damper on the whole damn comb. I sighed and hefted the box onto a shelf.

No rigid notation box, though, nor any part of one. Since Shackie was waiting to show it to me, it seemed likely he'd had it on his workbench; the killer must have taken it. But if so, why did he tear the place apart? I shook my head. Every story, no matter how well it began, eventually crashed and burned in incongruities.

Schwartz stood in the middle of the room and looked around. "Wow, neat place, Doc. Shackie had it made. What a shame."

"In every respect. What'd you learn about my new lady friend?"

"Maybe something." Schwartz sat on a chair in front of a worktable holding a jeweler's lathe. "I talked to the super. If your chickie came from St. Paul it wasn't all that long ago. Like last week, to be specific. She gave 'Out of town' for her previous address and paid her rent in cash. No employer. No bank."

"When'd she get the furniture in?"

Schwartz gave me a pitying look. "Furnished."

"Oh. Sure, of course. Did he tell you anything else?"

"Sounds like he didn't have anything else to tell. She comes, she goes. Only one time with a guy." Schwartz smirked. "Last night."

"Great." I rolled my eyes and wondered what went through the head of this hawk-eyed super as he watched me fly down the stairs, slam through the door, and go barreling south on Second Avenue. "What was the price tag on this little conversation?"

"Three bills."

"That's what you paid the super?"

"I didn't say that."

"Well?"

Sly smile. "I didn't pay the super nothing. He talked for free."

"Chatty guy." I pulled out my wallet and counted three hundred-dollar bills into Schwartz's hand. If that was his rate for undercover work, so be it.

"People don't usually get paid for talking to cops."

"Excuse me, I think you've lost me."

"The three bills." Schwartz waved the hundreds in my face, then slipped them into his pocket and reached inside his vest. His hand came out holding a worn black leather case, which he flipped open in front of my face. Something lay shiny inside.

I grabbed it from him. "What the hell's this?"

"Police badge, NYPD. Detective Paul Bornstein at your service. Special Investigations, Plainclothes Department."

He pushed a billfold at me, opened to show an ID which said the bearer was Paul Bornstein, Detective, Special Investigations, New York City Police Department.

I raised an eyebrow.

"I got a friend, he makes real good IDs. Business I'm in, it comes in handy more than you might think."

"What did you do? Impersonate a cop?"

"You said find out; I found out."

His how wasn't mine. My how wouldn't have worked. His did.

"So the three hundred was for the ID. What about your time?"

"Hey, Doc? What about *your* time when you spent practically a whole entire day and night in the hospital with Trudy, making sure she got better?"

"That was my job."

"Yeah, sure. And it was *my* job to tip you to that music box and get you in all this mess in the first place. For which I got my commish and then some, remember? You're in, I'm in, like I told you before. What do you want I should do now?"

I looked at the police badge and ID. What the hell. Hang for a sheep or a lamb.

"Abramowitz's wife."

"Hmm." Schwartz chewed his lip.

"Maybe Officer Bornstein could find out something useful about who really sold her husband that music box. And then killed him."

Return of the cagey grin. "Know something? You ain't got much in the way of street smarts. But you do learn fast."

Back at my apartment I got two immediate phone calls, both from Shackie's customers. One was Harley Bostick, an NYMBCA member, the other a woman named Wilma Ryan. Both had left music boxes with Shackie; both had been referred to me by Melvin Madrid. I told them they could pick up their property at Shackie's between 7:30 and eleven that evening.

Then I returned the earlier calls, giving those people the same message. Five of the six thanked me politely, but one guy wanted me to bring his box over to his place: he said he thought that was the least I could do. I told him there were two things *I* thought *he* could do. The second was complain to Mr. O'Shacker about the poor service.

I fried a couple of eggs, poured a glass of white wine, sat down at the kitchen table, and picked up my fork.

The phone rang.

That's a doctor's magic trick. Touch an eating utensil and the telephone rings. Contact of a doctor's buttocks with a toilet seat closes the same circuit.

I grabbed the receiver. "Thomas Purdue," I snapped.

Click.

The killer? But if he'd taken my rigid notation box, why would he be calling me now? More likely just a wrong number. How often does a person realize his mistake and just hang up without a word? Medical students learn that the sound of hoofbeats is more likely to mean horses than zebras, and unicorns are even less likely.

I sighed, then reached across the table to my Italian aria box and pushed the start lever. *And there* La Traviata *sighed, another, sadder song. And there* Il Trovatore *cried, a tale of deeper wrong.* I ate my eggs, drank my wine, and pitched the dirty dishes into the washer.

Eleven music box owners came by Shackie's that evening. A few seemed embarrassed. They took their property, scrawled a quick signature onto the receipts I put in front of them, muttered thankewvermuch, and were out the door.

One older man balanced the scale. He went on and on about how he'd have never guessed Shackie was that type, and boy wasn't he lucky to be getting his music box back, it was a very rare and valuable one (it was neither but I didn't argue), and he was going to be a heck of a lot more careful in the future, I could count on that. Long before he finally left I was praying for the miraculous appearance of a bottle of chloroform.

The man who wanted personal home delivery service marched in glaring. He reached for his music box when I brought it down from the shelf but he wasn't about to sign the receipt, not without the advice of his lawyer. "Fine," I said, and pulled the box away. "Go call your lawyer. You want to be reasonable, you can take advantage of my good nature and go home with your box. But if signing a receipt makes you nervous, beat it. Have your lawyer call my lawyer." In the end he finally scribbled his name and went away muttering, music box under his arm.

Four owners were NYMBCA members. They talked about how sad it was that Shackie had stolen a music box, killed two people, and then committed suicide. I didn't try to convince them of Shackie's innocence, though. The fewer people who knew how deep in the situation I really was, the better.

The last customer came in around ten. She was a slim woman, mid-thirties, I thought, wearing a ton of makeup. Her sandy hair was done up neatly in a bun. A pair of nervous blue eyes took me in behind the safety of a pair of rimless glasses.

She introduced herself as Wilma Ryan, then worked off her gray gloves, finger by finger. "Thank you for being so helpful. I was sorry to hear about Mr. O'Shacker. He seemed like such a nice man."

"He was. A nice man *and* a good man."

Interestingly, she didn't argue that nice and good men don't ordinarily steal music boxes and gun people down. She nodded her head and said, "He was so *interested* in my music box. He said it was the kind he likes to work on."

Her box, on the table, was a medium-sized keywind by the Lecoultre Freres, circa 1840s, with a thirteen-inch cylinder. Its tune card listed selections from four Italian operatic overtures: *La Sonnambula, Rigoletto, I Puritani*, and *La Cenerentola*.

"It's a very good one," I told her, "the kind I like to listen to, myself. What's the matter with it?"

"It won't run." She pointed at the governor. "I bought it a

few years ago at the Winter Antique Show at the Park Avenue Armory. It was fine then. But it's been running slower and slower, and finally it wouldn't run at all. Mr. O'Shacker said the governor here was clogged with grease, and maybe the spring was, too. He was going to clean it for me." She wrung her hands. "Oh, I'm so disap*point*ed. I don't imagine you'd know where I could take it now, do you?"

The recurring-nightmare question. Sending Barton Moss a box like this would have been an act of moral depravity. Lucas Sterne certainly could have done the work–but I hated to send Lucas any business, just on general principles. I scratched my head. "If it just needs the governor cleaned I could do that myself. It might take only a few minutes. You in a hurry?"

She clapped her hands like a little kid promised a trip to the zoo. "Oh, right here? Now?"

"Sure. Let's give it a try."

I unscrewed the works from the case and set them down on the bench. Then I checked to be sure the spring was fully unwound. An inexperienced tinkerer can destroy a music box by disconnecting the governor with power remaining on the spring: without the restraining influence of the governor, the spring unwinds all at once, sending the cylinder flying around at tremendous speed. In an instant, teeth are knocked out of the comb, pins fly from the cylinder, and if the hack tries to stop the disaster by grabbing the whirling cylinder he receives a punishment to fit his crime as steel pins rip away flesh from his palm and fingers. This disaster is called a run. It's the most expensive tune a music box can play.

This spring *was* down; it would've surprised me had Shackie not let down the power as soon as he'd taken in the box. I unscrewed the governor from the bedplate, then disassembled it. Everything was covered with hardened black grease.

Wilma Ryan stared at my handful of small gears, brass plates, and screws. She looked vaguely worried. "You *will* be able to get it back together, won't you?"

I laughed. "Trust me. I'm a doctor."

Her laugh in reply was a bit tentative. "Really? *Are* you a doctor?"

"Sure. MBD. Music box doctor. You have nothing to worry about, my dear. Your child is safe in my hands."

She giggled.

I put the governor parts into a basket of fine netting material and lowered them into Shackie's ultrasonic cleaning machine. "Ten minutes. Want a Coke?"

She asked to use the phone to call her husband. "I'd better let him know I'll be later than I'd thought. Otherwise he'll worry."

When the ultrasonic cleaner shut off I pulled out the governor parts, dipped them into a rinsing solution, and spread them on the worktable in front of me. Wilma bent forward and gawked. "My goodness, they're so clean."

"That's the idea." I put on a magnifying visor and checked each of the three gears. "No damage; it was just dirt." Quickly, I reassembled the governor, dropped a bit of clock oil into each bearing, and applied light grease to the worm. I held it up and tested it with my finger. "See? Runs nice and free now."

I screwed the reassembled governor back onto the bedplate, then picked up the key. "Keep your fingers crossed." I wound the spring and pushed the start lever.

Music began to play, but far too slowly. Also I had no trouble hearing a distressing number of groans and chirps, calling cards of crooked cylinder pins and misaligned or missing dampers. I muttered a soft, "Damn!"

Wilma Ryan, on the other hand, seemed delighted. Her hands clasped her chest and there was a beatific smile all over her face. "Oh, my!" she said. "Isn't it beautiful! You're wonderful, Mr. Purdue."

When the music stopped I asked whether she really did think the box sounded beautiful. She looked puzzled. "Why, yes. Of course. Don't you?"

I shook my head. "Which isn't to say this is not a wonderful music box—it is. Just needs more work. Clean and grease the spring so it'll play fast enough. Then there're those squeaks and groans. Didn't you hear them?"

She looked frankly disturbed. "Well, yes, of course. Aren't they supposed to be there? The man who sold it to me said this was a rare music box with bird-song accompaniment. He said they didn't make many of them."

I felt my patience slipping. Some music boxes *were* made with a tiny feathered bird sitting either behind the cylinder or in a recess in the front panel of the case. As the music plays, the bird moves and appears to be singing, thanks to small wooden organ pipes hidden beneath the bedplate. But this early Lecoultre was no *piece a oiseau*—or better, it shouldn't have been. I explained the problem to Wilma Ryan, then showed her the crooked pins and the missing damper wires beneath the teeth.

The sight set her back, but only briefly. "Can you fix those, too?"

"Well ..."

I was going to tell her what was needed would require a good deal more than a few minutes' tinkering. But she grabbed my arm and said, "Oh, please say you can. I want it to sound beautiful. Whatever your fee is, I'll be glad to pay."

Whether it was her eyes or her voice I knew I was stuck. How could I send her out into the street with her sick Lecoultre in her arms? I said yes. "But it'll take some time. I won't be able to get to it right away."

"I don't mind." Wilma beamed at me. "How long do you figure?"

"Three months at least. I've got your phone number in Shackie's log book. I'll call you."

"Oh, thank you. I just can't tell you how much I appreciate it." She gave me a quick hug and cheek-peck. "I'll wait to hear from you." She snatched up her coat and was out the door before I could offer to take her downstairs and wait with her for a cab.

I picked up the Lecoultre and set it on the shelf next to Sophie's mandoline-basse box, then stared at them and shook my head. Two repair jobs—just what I needed. When the hell was I going to get them done?

Maybe I should move in here, I thought. Work on them at odd hours. I *could* do that: I owned the place now, didn't I? Music box repairs in my spare time? Not an unpleasant idea, not at all.

While that notion was drifting through my head I heard footsteps outside in the hall. Soft, but definitely a person coming closer.

I waited for the knock. None came. It occurred to me that all the people I'd called had already come and gone. Whoever was out there was a party-crasher.

I heard little scratching noises. Someone was picking at the lock. I grabbed the closest reasonable weapon off the workbench, a little ballpeen hammer, and tiptoed toward the door, thanking God for how well these old buildings were put together. No squeaks in the floor. I flipped the light switch off, then moved to the opposite side of the doorway. If the door opened, I'd be hidden behind it.

Whoever was going at that lock was not a pro. He scratched and scratched. I stood behind the door, barely breathing. My heart was pounding insanely and my head began to throb again, behind my left ear. I gripped the handle of the hammer as firmly as I could and held it ready. Somebody besides me was going to enjoy a big-time headache.

The lock clicked; the door sprung open just a crack. A triangle of light from the hallway flooded across the floor. A human shadow began to glide across the light.

I raised the hammer.

What do you imagine might be on your mind as you waited behind a door for someone to come into proper head-bashing range? I was afraid I might swing my hammer and crack the intruder's skull like a coconut, split it right in half. The cops would come, take the messy corpse away to the morgue, and take *me* away for assault with a deadly weapon, first degree murder, premeditated. Maybe it'd be smarter to grab a screwdriver, poke its handle into the intruder's back, and shout, "Stick 'em up."

Stick 'em up? What, am I crazy? Say something as idiotic as "stick 'em up" and this killer will turn around and blow me–unarmed me–into the next world alongside Harry, Abramowitz, and Shackie. What's one more murder among old pals? No, it was him or me and that ballpeen hammer wasn't so very heavy. I'd have to be careful not to pull my punch and just pong a little shot off his head that wouldn't even slow him down, let alone split his coconut.

Now the door was halfway open. The shadow moved forward, oozing across the floor to the right. No question, he was going straight for the light switch at the other side of the doorway. Once he turned it on, my advantage would be gone. He'd see me and shoot me dead.

I took a slow step forward, then a couple of quick ones. I raised the hammer high and swung it down with all the force I could get into it. There was quite a nice little thud as I solidly connected with the intruder's head. It helped that he was short. He let out a groan, kind of an "Uhhhhh ..." and went down in a heap.

"Gotcha, you son of a bitch!" I shouted. I ran over and turned on the light.

And saw I'd just cold-cocked Marisa Morgan.

She looked sweet. Fetching was the word that came to my mind. She could have been dreaming of sugarplums, lying on her side, head cradled on her left arm. Her peaceful face was lusciously framed by black curls.

I had a momentary panic: what if she were dead? I kneeled down and leaned over her. To my relief, she was breathing easily; I had no trouble telling she'd fortified her nerves with a smoke before coming up. Her pulse was strong and regular.

I'm such a quick thinker. Here I was, checking vital signs on someone who given half a chance might do *me* in—and there was her little blue leather purse, lying just beyond her outstretched hand. I scrabbled across the floor on my hands and knees, picked it up, undid the catch, and emptied the contents onto the floor.

What caught my immediate attention was a pistol, a dainty little thing with a pearl handle. Every bit as pretty and probably just as lethal as its owner, I thought. Not much else: wallet, a few keys on a chain, a half full container of Tic-Tacs, pocket-sized package of Kleenex. I picked up the wallet. Underneath it on the floor was a small blue booklet. PASSPORT, it said in gold script across the cover.

I flipped it open. There was a picture of Marisa, a good one, and underneath, her name and an address in London. Interesting, I thought—but on the other hand, didn't a mere $300 transform Broadway Schwartz, presto-chango, into Detective Paul Bornstein? Still, I copied the address into my pocket notebook.

I cruised through her wallet. A few credit cards, all in the same name, a driver's license with the same London address, and in the billfold section along with some tens and twenties, four fifty-pound notes.

I scooped up her belongings and put them back into the purse, gun and all. No need for her to know I'd snooped. She'd suspect, but that I couldn't help.

She was moving her hands a bit now, and her head; she moaned softly. At that point, it occurred to Dr. Quickthink that there might also be a gun on her person. I scrambled back to her, pausing just long enough to tell myself this definitely was not the time for delicacy. Moving as quickly as I could, I satisfied myself that there was no gun hidden in her clothing. Then I walked to the kitchen, drew a glass of water, and went back to wait.

About five minutes later her eyes blinked open. She raised her hand to her forehead, trying to shake away cobwebs.

"You all right?" I asked, and handed her the water.

She took it, I noticed, with her right hand, sipped once, and gave me a long look. Her expression was that of a cat whose tail had been stepped on, quite likely with malicious intent. "Thomas ... Did *you* hit me?"

The words were thick, and–I noticed–considerably heavier with British accent than they'd been the evening before. I nodded. "You're all right now?"

"I believe so." She sat up halfway, balancing her head on her palm. "What did you hit me with?"

I waved the ballpeen hammer at her. "I grabbed it when I heard you fiddling the lock. Would you like to tell me why you were breaking in?"

Picture kitty, caught red-pawed on the table where the meat for tonight's dinner was thawing. Who, me? Well, I swear I saw a mouse up here.

"Oh, I ... I don't know. Stupid of me, I guess. I got to thinking of my lovely music box, and I thought maybe if I just could look around here myself ... I see you've done a good bit of straightening. I don't suppose you ..."

She saw me shaking my head. Her voice trailed off. "Oh, well. I suppose it's gone, that's all."

"I'm afraid so." I reached out a hand and helped her to her feet. "Come on. I'll get you a cab to take you home."

"You're not going to call ... the police, then?"

"Heavens no," I assured her. "I've had enough trouble tonight already."

SIXTEEN

First thing next morning I called Schwartz to find out what Detective Bornstein had learned from Mrs. Abramowitz. "Mousey little thing, drinks more than is good for her," Schwartz said. "Also, she don't know diddly about her husband's business. All she could tell me was somebody called up Fat Marty about one in the morning the day he was killed and Marty said to him, 'Hey, O'Shacker, it really takes balls to wake a guy up at this hour.' Then he said okay, he'd meet him in the shop in half an hour. Mrs. A said she asked her husband what was so important it couldn't wait until morning and he just told her to mind *her* business, he'd take care of the antiques business."

"Nice guy, Abramowitz. A real charmer."

"You said a mouthful. Anyway, she went off to sleep and next thing she knew it was seven-thirty, alarm's ringing, and no Abramowitz in bed with her. So she went down to the shop and found him on the floor behind the counter. She called the cops. That's it."

"Hmm." I drummed out a little rhythm to think by on the tabletop. "Not much. But how about that question of hers–what the hell *was* so important to make Abramowitz go down and open the shop at one-thirty a.m?"

"Bet it had something to do with money," Schwartz chirped.

"Safe guess. What doesn't?"

Schwartz laughed. "So, what now?"

"I'm going back down to Shackie's for a while," I told him. "Couple of sick music boxes waiting for me."

"Sick music boxes? Hey, what about dead people?"

"I'm admitting them for observation," I said.

Admit for observation. That's where good doctors separate out from hacks. Doctors see a lot of patients who are clearly sick, but with no obvious diagnosis. So we admit them for observation. To the hack doctor that means put the patient in a hospital bed, order a few tests, and wait. If the patient's better in the morning, send him home. If he's dead, get the family to okay an autopsy. And if he's neither, call a consultant.

The good doctor, on the other hand, takes the term literally: he observes. He opens a file in his head with all current information about his patient. As time passes he adds in new developments: symptoms, physical findings, test results. And whenever the doctor's away from the bedside he keeps the file open—but he's careful not to look at it. He knows a diagnostic dilemma is like a teasing little kid running in circles around his grandpa. If Grandpa yells at the kid, waves his fist, threatens him, the kid moves farther away and teases even louder. Cagey Grandpa on the other hand pays the kid absolutely no attention—or so he makes it seem. To all intents and purposes he's wrapped up in his crossword puzzle. But he's watching out of the corner of his eye. Let that snotty kid dart up close, and zap! Out goes Grandpa's hand, gotcha! The kid's squirming like a fish and squawking like a parrot.

So a doctor learns. When there's a problem you can't figure out, open a mental file, put in whatever information you have—and then go concentrate on something else. Like fixing a music box.

Sophie's need was more pressing than Wilma's, so I took

down the mandoline-basse box from the shelf and set it on the work table. Mandoline-basses are lovely instruments, not easy to come by and not cheap. You know the way mandolin players embellish their music by rapid up-and-down strokes of the pick–well, a mandoline music box has lots and lots of teeth, with groups of eight or more tuned to the same note. Cylinder pins plucking teeth in rapid succession within one of these groups gives a mandolin effect to the music. Nice enough, but if the mandolin effect is carried into the low bass notes, the sound becomes organ-like–thus, the alternate name for this type of music box: organocleide.

That's the good news, all for the owner of such a box. The bad news is for the restorer. With that rapid plucking of comb teeth, cylinder pins need to be set spot-on, and damper wires beneath tooth tips have to be perfectly aligned. Otherwise notes will play out of sequence and there will be squeaks, groans, and whispers spoiling the music. When setting up the comb and cylinder for a mandoline-basse box, the restorer has to concentrate fully. No peeking into any open files in his head.

I lifted the comb, set the rest of the mechanism aside, and studied the dampers. Most were missing altogether and would have to be replaced. A few might only need adjustment. That's where I'd start. Cylinder pins, I'd look at later.

With a small pair of pliers I pulled the tiny brass set peg for the first damper. I reamed the hole beneath the tooth tip and slipped in a new wire, then pushed in the peg to hold the wire in place. Then with a small tweezer I shaped the wire to proper form. I started to hum William Tell, "The Prayer," Tune Number One on the box, so listed on the little card inside the lid.

I'm not sure how long I'd been at it when the telephone rang. I was working smoothly so I considered ignoring the phone. Then I remembered my open mental file. Before I left my apartment I'd call-forwarded my own phone to Shackie's. I sighed and set down the comb, then walked over to get the phone. "Thomas Purdue."

"Thomas, baby. How you doing?"

He didn't have to identify himself by name. The only person in the world to whom I've ever been Thomas, baby, is Sammy Shapiro, Wheeler-Dealer Extraordinaire of the New York Music Box Collectors' Association.

"I'm fine, Sammy. What's upmost in your feverish little mind today?"

Sammy laughed easily. No offense, all jolly good fellowship. Sociopaths are like that. They can be quite pleasant company while screwing you firmly to the nearest wall. "You are, 'cause you, my man, are the one who can help me. Melvin Madrid gave me your number. Said you can get me my things back from Shackie's."

"Oh, yes." I sounded as absent as possible. "What did you have?"

"Oh, couple, few boxes. Nothing super-spectacular. You know."

I did know, of course. Shackie's log book had told me three of Sammy's boxes were awaiting repair: a Regina disc machine needing tooth replacement, a medium-sized Paillard cylinder box, and a small Polyphon disc box with frozen star wheels. As Sammy said: nothing spectacular. "You'll have to be more specific," I said. "Tell me what you left with Shackie. If it's there, I'll give it to you."

"Thomas, baby. I'm hurt. What do you think, I'd rip you off? Take someone else's music box?"

"Perish forbid. Standard red tape. Customary bureaucratic nuisance. Lost and found in the 'nineties, baby."

He laughed again and then named his three machines. I told him fine, he should meet me at Shackie's in about an hour.

I guess you could call Sammy Shapiro a good-looking guy if you like them greasy. Slicked-back hair, shiny forehead, wide-set brown eyes darting in every direction at once. Dark blue suit with white stripes, patent leather shoesies. Definitely 'twenties-Chicago, but Sammy's gat is his mouth. He's gotten more mileage out of an ass' jaw than anyone since Samson.

His music boxes were waiting for him when he came in. He whistled. "You're impressive, Thomas, baby, know that? Got the place all fixed up, everybody's music boxes ready. You do good work, my man."

"Right and wrong," I said. "I do very good work, but I'm not your man."

Sammy ignored that. He stood in the middle of the workshop and looked around. "I don't know ..." he said. "I just don't know ..."

I ignored *that*. I wasn't going to play straight man to Sammy. With me he'd have to work for his con.

"I don't know who I'm going to take these boxes to," he finally said.

"Give me a break. You're with repairmen like a sailor with girls. I'm just surprised Shackie did any of your work."

I didn't have to say it straight out. I knew and he knew I knew that Sammy Shapiro's interest in restoration was purely mercenary. It had nothing to do with love of music or respect for the genius of the craftsmen who'd brought the machines into being. Perfection to Sammy meant "just make it play so I can sell it." But Shackie never did that kind of repair job.

"Come on, Thomas, money talks with girls, money talks with repairmen. Hey, what do you think, Shackie was some kind of vestal virgin? Give him enough bucks, he had his pants off and was bending over."

I must have gotten quite a look on my face. Sammy threw his hands up in mock surrender and said, "Hey, okay. Hey, my man, I'm sorry, all right? I shouldn't be talking like that about the dead. Shackie *was* a good guy ... even if he was a pain in the ass sometimes. Once, I wanted him to do a little put-together for me, you know, fake a Nicole. He damn near threw me down those stairs out there. I lost a bundle but hey,

I'll be honest with you. I always say you got to respect a guy's morals. That's the way Shackie was going to be, that's the way I'd have to deal with him. If bringing back a box all the way meant I could get more for selling it, then that made sense, right? These three boxes, that's the way it was. I gave them to Shackie, I said fix 'em up. *Carte blanche.*"

"I understand. Shackie did a complete restoration for what Lucas Sterne or Barton Moss would charge you for a patch-up job."

"Moss!" I thought Sammy was going to spit on the floor. "That bum. Drunk bastard. I wouldn't let him work on my grandmother's titties."

Sammy paused and licked his lips. Baseball pitchers sometimes develop mannerisms that tell opposing batters a curve ball is coming. Sammy Shapiro licking his lips meant here comes the jughandle. I faced him squarely but was ready to bail out of the batter's box if I had to.

"Say, Thomas ..?"

I didn't say a word.

"How about you? You want to make a few bucks here and there, little pocket change? Just for fun and games?"

I shook my head. "No time, Sammy. But thanks, anyway."

He jerked his head toward the workbench where Sophie's mandoline-basse box sat behind my mess of dampering tools and wire. Bright light from the gooseneck lamp reflected off the partly-dampered comb. "Looks to me like you've got time to do a job for Sophie Soleski. She may be a broad, but Christ, she's eighty if she's a day. What's she got to offer you I don't?"

There were any number of answers I could have given him, starting with nearly thirty years of genuine friendship and ending with the fact she'd never called me either Thomas-baby or my man. But all of a sudden it seemed a good idea to extend my talk with Sammy. I shrugged and shifted into Amiable Mode. "It's a one-shot deal, Sammy. She's in a spot, she asked me, and I said I'd try. Hell, I'm not even sure I can pull off a dampering job on a mandoline-basse."

"Hey, Thomas, baby, chill. I've known you for a few years, and modesty does not happen to be your thing. I can just about see you telling Sophie you can't hack it. The old Bellevue bulldog, that's what they called you when you were an intern, right? You'll sink your teeth into that comb and you won't let go 'til it says uncle. However long it takes."

Social laugh. "Believe what you want, but it's either going to go quickly or it's not going to go. I don't have time to repair other people's music boxes."

He didn't believe me, but he couldn't push any further, so he shifted his direction of attack. "Must be nice," he said through a crafty smile. "Having all the dough you need."

"I wouldn't know, but if you think I do, well, no one stopped you from going to med school. How the hell did you know this box was Sophie's?"

The only hope of getting an honest answer out of Sammy is to catch him off guard. He blinked at my nonsequitur, then grinned. "I like to know what's going on. That box was Arvid Ellingson's, up in Vermont. Sophie sold it to him back when you and I were still going around in shitty diapers. I told Arvid any time he wanted to sell it ... but he said he liked dealing with Soph." Sammy shrugged. "Free country, right? Anyway, last month Tim Rutledge told me Sophie'd found him this great organocleide, he'd have it as soon as Shackie got it in top shape. So there's your two and two, my man. That Soph's one cool old bird. The connections she's got—whew!" He shook his hand as if he'd touched a hot stove. "When the good stuff's there, she gets it. Like for instance ... that rigid notation box the late H.H. was showing off at his party last week."

Sammy's smile was teasing and sly. I opened my eyes as wide as possible and said, "Is *that* where Harry got the rigid notation? From Sophie?"

"Bet the farm." Sammy was very pleased with himself.

"You'll excuse me, but are you just guessing that? Or do you know it?"

"I have it on ... what do they say?" Sammy stroked his chin and looked at the ceiling. "Good authority."

"The famous source that shall be nameless?" I tried to get just the right amount of disbelief into my voice.

"Nope. It's the source called the horse's mouth."

I gave myself a stern warning. No horsey jokes this time. "Sophie?" blurted Mr. Naively-Incredulous. "*Sophie* told you that?"

"No, no. Harry did. Harry the Horse. I asked him, he told me. Hey, I know how everybody always walked on eggs around him. But I always figured his pants went on the same as yours and mine. I just asked him straight out. 'Hey, Harry, where'd you get a box like this from?' And he gives me a big smile, and says, 'From Sophie.' Come on, Thomas. You know as well as I do she's got every inside track in the game locked up."

"Hmm."

"What do you mean, 'hmm'?"

"Oh, I guess I'm just a little sore. I've been looking for a rigid notation box for more than twenty years, which Sophie knew. Why the hell didn't she call *me* when she got one?"

Sammy snickered. "Thomas, baby! *That*, I've got to tell you? You're not exactly starving, but you can't expect to get on the same playing field with Harry Hardwick."

"Maybe. But I can still be annoyed."

"So?" Sammy spread his arms grandly. "Maybe you ought to deal with some different people."

"Like you, I suppose."

"Why not? I'll find you a rigid notation box. You think I can't?"

"I wouldn't bet against you, Sammy."

"Okay, then. It'll cost you, though."

Always the catch. "I'll pay a reasonable price, but don't go making anybody an offer he can't refuse. Keep in mind what you just said about which stadiums I can play in and which I can't."

"Hey! Tell you what, my man."

Sometimes Sammy actually caricatures himself. Right then, he looked like Professor Harold Hill, clapping his hands and doing a little dance, ready to launch into his routine about why there was real trouble right here in River City.

"*You* tell *me*," Sammy said. "What's a rigid notation box worth? What should a guy expect to pay?"

"Oh ... eighteen to twenty," I said, and quickly raised a warning finger. "In top condition. No work needed."

"Okay then, there's your number. You'll pay that much for one?"

"*If* it's in top shape, Sammy. *Really* top shape."

He saluted me. With his right hand, I noticed. "You'll be hearing from me, my man."

After Sammy left, I went back to the workbench, but after a few more dampers I put down the comb. I couldn't get back into it. Sammy has that effect on me. Why all this interest in rigid notation boxes? You'd expect only dedicated collectors of early cylinder machines to even know what a rigid notation box is, and that definitely should have excluded Sammy–and probably Harry as well. But Harry only had to know he was pursuing something rare and wonderful, and he was off like a water buffalo in heat. Whoever whispered into his ear would have had to make sure he *did* know that.

That meant a highly knowledgeable tipster. Where?

Apparently in England.

I picked up the phone, switched the call-forwarding back to my place, and locked up.

Yesterday's brief sunshine hadn't lasted. We were back to dark, swirly gray clouds, twilight at noon. This murderer had chipped off two good-sized chunks of my life; he and the December darkness were working together, one at each of my elbows, hustling me along toward obscurity. That wouldn't do. I decided to pay an unannounced shop-call on Frank the Crank.

Walking into Wind-Me-Up, I inhaled the congenial aroma of old graphite-grease. "Hey, hey, the good doctor," Frank called out from the rear. "Just in time for lunch. Come on back."

I tried to work my way past two old men who were looking over an Edison Home Phonograph, but one of them collared me. "I can still remember the day my old man brought one of these home. It was for Christmas, nineteen and eight. Looked just like this one." He pointed at the price. "Can you believe that? Six hundred dollars. Know what he paid?"

"Twelve bucks, which included five or ten cylinders."

The coot looked me over and chuckled, an old man's phlegmy attempt at good humor. "Just about. Sure wish I'd have kept it. But who'd ever have thought they'd be worth this kind of dough?"

"Anything good gets more valuable as it gets older. Like you. I wouldn't have given a plugged nickel for you when you were a baby, just puking and screaming all day and night. But now? You're ninety if you're a year—"

"Ninety-one. I turned ninety-one the third of last August."

"Ninety-one. Gloriosky! Why, man, you're a treasure house of stories. You heard Sophie Tucker sing; you saw the Babe hit some big ones. Are you telling your grandchildren all about it?"

"Sheesh!" He waved his hand in disgust; his friend cleared his throat. "My grandkids, some joke. They don't give a hoot in hell. *Or* my great-grandkids. 'That's all dead and gone, Grandpa,' that's what they say."

"One day they'll want to hear. But then it'll be too late. Write it down for them. Take my word. They'll be grateful."

The old guy was staring at the Edison again. Or better, into it. "I'll never forget that Christmas," he murmured. "We listened to those records over and over and over. Nobody could believe it—a person's voice, and music, coming out through that horn. It was the closest thing to a miracle ..."

Frank leaned over the counter to poke my arm. "Back in 'seventy-seven when I first opened up, this store was full of old guys like that," he said *sotto voce*. "Never bought a thing, just looked. I played the machines for them, what the hell. It was worth the looks on their faces. But there aren't many of 'em left."

A stray notion popped into my head. "Put a cylinder on for them, Frank. Go ahead. I want to watch."

He gave me a funny look. But he wiped his hands on his jeans, walked around the counter, and picked up a Blue Amberol cylinder. He slipped it over the mandrel of the phonograph. "Here you go, Old Timer. A trip down Memory Lane, courtesy of Frank Maar's Wind-Me-Up."

It was Ada Jones, that comely songbird of eighty years ago, with a voice like thick cream and honey. She was singing "Don't Get Married Any More, Ma," one of her big comic hits. The old man who'd been talking to me was no longer with us in the shop. From his expression I suspected he might have been on the green of some upstate village, Fourth of July, 1921. There was a picnic lunch spread out on a blanket where he was sitting with his pretty sweet-sixteen sweetheart. Up on a white octagonal bandstand, a bunch of country musicians were backing a local chanteuse as she charmed the people with Ada's crowdpleaser. It was warm, the sun was shining, and life's possibilities seemed endless.

The second old man, however, did not look the least charmed by the phonograph music. He just stood with a hand on his hip and a jagged little smile at the corners of his mouth, watching his friend with far more derision than sympathy. No question, he voted with the grandchildren and great-grandkids. This was all dead and gone. Forget about it.

Frank the Crank pushed a donut at me and poured coffee out of a thermos into a Styrofoam cup. "Here you go, Doc," he said. "What can your humble shopkeeper do for you today? You didn't come in here to watch geezers listen to Edison cylinders."

The music stopped. The talkative old man pushed the OFF lever on the phonograph, then he waved his thanks as he and his friend headed for the door.

"Not really. I was wondering: You remember the music box I showed you the other day? The one with checkerboard squares on the cylinder?"

"Sure I remember it. My Alzheimer's hasn't gotten that bad yet. What about it?"

I bit off a piece of donut. "Frank, tell me something. Have you heard anything about people looking for that kind of music box lately? Or wanting to sell one?"

He thought for a moment, then shook his head. "Why're you asking?"

"Because it's a funny thing. These are rare music boxes, and valuable, but most people–including most collectors–don't even know they exist. When one is sold, it's usually on the QT, one hardcore collector to another. But all of a sudden, everyone in New York is desperately looking for one. I think I've heard 'rigid notation box' more times in the past week than I have altogether in the past twenty-five years."

"Hmm. Maybe so, maybe so." Frank took a huge mouthful of donut and chewed ferociously. It was his way of thinking. "But no, I ain't heard a thing about any run on those rigid boxes of yours. What I think is maybe you ought to try chewin' your cud over those pictures you showed me."

"What do you mean? I showed them to you; I showed them to Schwartz. We agree that's Harry and Muriel, and we don't know who the other woman and the guy are. What am I supposed to do? Have the picture published on milk cartons? 'If you've seen me anywhere, please call Thomas Purdue'?"

"Funny. No. What I'm saying is, you told me there was a whole load of those pictures but your wife only took two. How about getting the others?"

"I thought of that. But if Muriel Hardwick knows those pictures are there and then the whole load of them turns up missing—right after I've been in the room—she's going to make some connections, isn't she?"

Frank stuffed the rest of his donut into his mouth as if he had a grudge against the poor thing. "Doc. You're a smart guy, else you wouldn't have got through med school. Use your head. If she knew those pictures were there they wouldn't have still been there the first time you went. They'd have gone in a fire the minute Harry was laid out on the carpet. I'd say it might be a good idea if you found the rest before she does."

"I hadn't thought of it that way."

"You're welcome," said Frank. "I play records for geezers, I give answers to doctors. Now, I'll ask you. If I'm so nice *and* so smart—why the hell ain't I rich?"

All the way back to Gramercy North, Frank's phonograph geezers knocked around in my head. It was the way they looked, listening to that phonograph record. Something very familiar but I couldn't put a finger on it. I was a walking storehouse of disconnected information.

My telephone had one message, from 11:46 AM. I pushed the button, listened to the beeps, and finally heard Jackson George say, "I need to speak to you right away."

SEVENTEEN

Jackson George customarily spoke as if he were delivering silken words into sows' ears. But on my message tape he sounded very different: his voice actually shook. "I need to speak to you right away."

I dialed Jackson's number. His machine told me curtly that I'd reached 555-6842, and to leave a short message. I dialed again with the same result. It was a quarter past one, only an hour and a half since Jackson had left his urgent-sounding request.

I drummed my fingers a couple of times, then called Schwartz. Here I got lucky; he was home for lunch. He said he'd meet me in half an hour, in front of the Plaza on the south side of Central Park.

Next I called Muriel. She said she was doing well, thank you, and was sorry to hear I was having trouble setting up my inventory according to Harry's program. Yes, she said, she'd be glad to have me come by later, say about four, and take another look at the original.

Finally I took a deep breath and called Sarah at work.

I'd barely got out my request when she exploded. "I can't be*lieve* this. You have no shame whatsoever. *Or* pride."

"This has nothing to do with shame or pride. I need your help. It's important. You know where those pictures are and you can help me get the rest of them."

"Bad enough I took two."

"But you did. So it shouldn't make any difference to get the rest. It's for a good cause."

"Don't *you* talk to *me* about good causes," she snapped. "You are the most selfish person I've ever met. Whatever *you're* interested in and can benefit from is a good cause."

"Sarah, listen: Somebody killed two of my friends and he's not going to get away with it–whether you're willing to help me or not."

"Stop trying to manipulate me, or I'll hang up."

"Manipulate? Wait a minute. *I* didn't give *you* ultimatums. *I* didn't throw either-ors into *your* face. Sarah–"

"You're not fooling me. Even if the police *are* wrong and Shackie *was* murdered, you're not just trying to bring a killer to justice. There's something in this for you. I have no idea what it is but I'll bet a month's wage it's got to do with music boxes."

A broken clock's right twice a day. "Now listen to me–"

"I'll tell you what–"

My head began to pound. It's one thing when Sammy Shapiro telegraphs a curve ball. But Sarah Purdue is a fast-ball pitcher, every offering right down the heart of the plate. Her occasional off-speed delivery is unhittable.

"What, Sarah? *What* will you tell me?"

"I'll make you a deal. You want help from me–all right, you can have it. I'll go back to Muriel's and get you your ... your pictures. But then *you* have to help *me*."

"I always help you–at least when I can. Which is usually. You've got to admit that."

"This is a little different. Yes, I always *can* count on you in a pinch and I do appreciate that. But this time the deal is for you to help me help others, just for once. On Christmas Day. I want you to come down to the Union Mission on Third and Twelfth. We're going to cook dinner there and serve it to the homeless."

"Oh, for Christ's sake–"

"It won't do you any harm. For once in your life do something completely unselfish."

"That's ridiculous. Also, it's unfair. You do things your way, I do them mine."

"Fine. Go get your smutty pictures your way, without me. And I'll go feed the homeless my way, without you. That's the deal; take it or leave it."

I paused a moment and then said, very quietly, "Okay."

"You mean that? You won't renege?"

"Scout's honor."

"You're not a Boy Scout. You were never a Boy Scout. Say, 'I promise.'"

She drives me crazy. "I promise."

"'I promise I will help you feed the homeless at the Union Mission on Christmas Day.'"

"Sarah, this is childish–"

"Say it, Thomas."

"I promise I will help you feed the homeless at the Union Mission on Christmas Day."

I heard her sigh. "All right. It's a deal. I don't think you'll find it so terrible. Who knows–you might even decide you like it."

I gave silent thanks she couldn't see my face. The homeless didn't need Sarah to fill their plates and wish them Merry Christmas. They could fill their own plates and wish each other Merry Christmas, and they'd be every bit as well off. Better, maybe, because then they wouldn't have to avert their eyes downward and mumble an endless, humiliating litany of embarrassed thank-yous. But it made Sarah feel virtuous, so she did it. Talk about profiting from your own acts of charity.

"Stranger things have happened," I said.

"Mark my words, though: If you welsh on this deal I will never–*ever*–talk to you again."

As if exacting a promise under duress was a morally-commendable act. But that would have to be sorted out later.

"Where shall I meet you? And when?"

"Can you get off a little early and meet me at Park and

Sixty-Second, right up from Muriel's, a few minutes before four?"

"I can do that, yes. I'll need to be finished by six, though; I'm meeting Harold for dinner. But ..."

"What?"

"It's cold out. Please don't be late."

"Wait in the cash machine enclosure," I said. "We'll look for you there."

"Wait a minute. 'We'?"

"Schwartz and I. I'm bringing Schwartz along, too."

"Why don't you stop at the Armory and enlist the whole Seventh Regiment while you're at it?"

"You're funny. That's why I love you. See you at four."

It was only a few minutes' walk from the Plaza to Jackson George's digs at the Blenheim. Schwartz and I nodded to the doorman and went straight through the lobby, past the eight-foot Christmas tree full of ornaments, into the elevator. We got off at the 21st floor.

I knocked. No answer. I wasn't surprised and I certainly wasn't pleased. I knocked again, then rang the bell. Still nothing.

Schwartz was exercising his fingers, rubbing his thumbs briskly against the tips of the other four fingers on each hand. Placekicker warming up as the drive downfield begins to stall within field goal range.

"Okay, Broadway," I said. "Let's get inside."

I took two pairs of rubber surgical gloves from my pocket, gave one to Schwartz, and slipped the other pair on. Schwartz began to poke around inside the lock with some sort of pin. Beetle-browed in concentration, he alternately jiggled the pin with his right hand and worked the doorknob with his left. I passed the time by shifting slowly from one foot to the other, counting as I swayed back and forth. I'd reached sixteen when I heard Schwartz let out a little, "Ah!" As he spoke, he twisted the knob sharply. The door opened inward.

We slipped inside and closed the door quietly. The living room was empty, not a spot or stain on the white carpeting. Every book on the shelves was in place, the curvy walnut furniture unblemished. "I thought this guy collected antiques," Schwartz said. "But I don't see nothing here older'n five minutes. Place looks right out of *House Beautiful.*"

"He collects prestige. What he thinks will make people sit up and notice him. Never mind what he likes."

"What does he like?"

"Having people sit up and notice him," I said. "Come on."

The dining room, with its long, oval glass-top table was also unoccupied and undisturbed; so was the kitchen. In the bathroom Schwartz paused long enough to look closely at the gold-colored faucet knobs. "Hey, Doc." He pointed for me to look. Below the H and the C atop each knob was an inscribed *18K.*

"Just so no one should miss it," I said.

Schwartz whistled. "Some people know how to live."

The phone rang.

I took off at a gallop toward the living room and began to fumble with the voice-monitoring button on the left side of the answering machine. At the third ring the machine kicked in. "You have reached five-five-five, six-eight-four-two. Please leave a brief message at the tone."

"Mr. Congeniality himself," said Schwartz.

I shushed him. The ICM was clicking on. "Hello, Mr. George," said a woman's voice. "This is Marisa Morgan. We need to have another talk; it's really quite important. Would you please give me a call at your earliest convenience, seven-four-six, twenty-four-ten."

"Marisa Morgan?" Schwartz grinned. "Your little chickie from the last two nights."

I nodded. "She does seem to get around, doesn't she?" I pushed Schwartz toward the den and bedrooms. "Come on," I said. "Who knows how much time we've got? I'm starting to get antsy."

Our search ended in the den. Jackson George was slumped in his chair at the desk. His head was twisted sideways, resting on his left shoulder. At heart-level on his white shirt was a maroon stain surrounding a small burn-hole. His back was against the chair, which was nice since the exit wound probably bore a general resemblance to a small pizza.

Schwartz wrinkled his nose. "Jeez, it smells like a butcher shop in here."

There's an object lesson. What more than a century of Charles Darwin's polite and erudite words haven't managed to do for half the population of the United States is readily accomplished by ten seconds of sniffing around a heart-shot cadaver.

Schwartz made a move toward George. I grabbed his arm. "Better not touch him. Just look around. Check for papers, pictures–anything interesting."

Nothing we found was. Whoever made Jackson George Number Four on the Music Box Collectors' Hit Parade had wiped the slate clean. The desk top was clear; we found only bills in the vertical file cabinet and desk drawers. No list of pickers. No auction catalogs. Nothing whatsoever to suggest that a collector of antique mechanical musical items had lived here. I nudged Schwartz. "Let's check out the bedrooms."

We came to the spare bedroom first, spare in more ways than one. It held a neatly-made bed and a chest, all the drawers of which were empty. So was the closet. In the next room, George's own sleeping quarters, the bed was unmade–probably, I said to Schwartz, so anyone who came in wouldn't miss his silk sheets. I was about to go through the bureau opposite the foot of the bed when the doorbell rang.

The harsh insistent buzz sounded loud enough to wake the dead. Schwartz and I stared at each other. He raised his finger to his lips.

The bell rang again, then a third time. We stayed glued to our spots on the floor.

Then we heard the sound of a key in the lock.

Schwartz motioned toward the closet. We tiptoed over and quickly opened the door just wide enough to slip inside. I started to pull the door shut behind us, but Schwartz whispered hoarsely, "Leave it open just a crack, so we can hear."

We heard, all right. "Mistuh George," a voice said. "Mistuh George, you in?" It was a man's voice, the rough but deferential voice of a servant.

"Shit, what now?" I whispered to Schwartz. "Chauffeur? Cleaning man?"

In the narrow beam of light I saw Schwartz rummaging in his pocket. He pulled out a handkerchief and plastered it over his ample nose. "Mothballs," he wheezed. "Allergic."

"Mistuh George," the voice said again. "It's Robert. I got a package for you."

The voice wasn't moving any closer but Schwartz's agony was increasing apace. Snuffling, choking, he sounded like a small animal flushed from its burrow, not knowing which way to run. If he let loose a whopper sneeze we were goners.

"I'll just leave it on the dining room table," Robert said, as though he thought his words might somehow linger in the air to enter the august ears of the Lord of the Manor whenever he might make his return. A few seconds later, the door to the outside hall closed with a slam.

The closet door flew open as if by reflex. Schwartz shot past me, handkerchief to nose. He flopped on the floor, snorting and wheezing. It sounded like bathtime at the elephant cage. He blew a noseful into his handkerchief, then looked up at me.

He was a mess. Red eyes, red nose, water leaking out of every facial orifice. I went into the master bathroom, picked up a towel, and soaked it under the tap. Then I went back, took off Schwartz's fedora, and washed his face clean.

"Sorry," he croaked, breathing more easily now. "Mothballs and me, we just don't get along. Been that way ever since I was a kid. One time my bronchial tubes got so clogged up they had to put me on a machine; for a while they were thinking they'd have to cut into my throat. Whew!" He shook his head.

"We can stop at a drug store," I said. "Get some Benedryl."

"Uh-uh. Bad idea. That stuff puts me right to sleep." He reached for his hat, slapped it back onto his head, and got to his feet. "I'll be okay soon's I get some fresh air. Let's get out of here, huh?"

"In just a minute."

I went into the dining room. On the table was a long rectangular cardboard box with a Brooks Brothers label on the front. I was disappointed. I'd hoped the package was going to be small and square, from London or Paris, say, with something elegant, valuable, and musical inside. I hefted the box. "Just about the right size and weight for a jacket or a couple of pairs of pants."

Schwartz nodded. "Better not open it, 'cause when they find him, it's better if they don't start thinking about who opened it–especially when you figure we still got to get past that doorman."

"Good point. Okay, come on. Before somebody else starts knocking at the door."

With the paranoia of the unpracticed cat burglar, I opened the door to the hall and peered right and left. No one there, at least not that I could see. We slithered into the hallway, closing the door quietly behind us. Then we stripped off our surgical gloves, stuffed them into our pockets, and started toward the elevator. Halfway there, I nudged Schwartz toward the stairway. We ran down the stairs to Eighteen, where we rang for elevator service. When the car came, an elderly couple moved aside to make room for us.

As we walked through the lobby, Schwartz beamed. "Good thinking. You're gettin' the hang of it."

I hoped he'd be more circumspect in front of Sarah.

Schwartz's proper color was returning; already he was his usual jaunty self. We strolled out the doorway and started down the sidewalk while the doorman was helping an elderly woman into a cab. As we approached the corner Schwartz said, "Well, Doc, one thing at least you know: who *didn't* do it. Your pal Marisa."

"You're sure about that?"

"Yeah. It figures, don't it? If she called up to talk to him after he was already dead for a while, she couldn't have been the one who stiffed him."

"Or that's what she wants people to think. Suppose she comes in, shoots George, maybe grabs whatever it is he has that she wants. Then she takes off. She waits a couple of hours and calls to say she's got to talk to him. The machine records the time of the message, which is after George is dead. Kind of an alibi after the fact. Think about it."

"Hmm." Schwartz looked disgusted with himself. "So we're still on square one."

"'Fraid so," I said.

I herded Schwartz into a deli on Madison. "We're early. Coffee and a Danish before we meet Sarah."

I was not good company. I just sat there, sipping absently at my coffee and occasionally gnawing at a prune Danish. Something was bothering me, a connection that wouldn't quite come together. Static noises blurring the music; a camera just that much out of focus. Turn the tuning knob, adjust the lens ...

I put down the coffee cup.

"Aha!" Schwartz, perennially on the uptake. "I hear bells going off."

"I pounded my fist lightly on the table. "Yes!" I crowed at him. "That's it."

"That's what?"

I leaned across the table to talk quietly. "At Frank the Crank's this morning two old men were listening to a phonograph. The looks on their faces reminded me of something, but I didn't know what. One of them was totally wrapped up in the music, but his friend looked like he thought the first guy was a prize schmuck. And I kept thinking I'd seen them before. *Now* I've got the connection: Jackson George told me yesterday *he'd* seen Walter Remler and Sammy Shapiro listening to Harry Hardwick's rigid notation box. Remler supposedly looked like he wanted to eat the thing up; meanwhile, Sammy was giving him a hard time, cracking wise. No wonder I couldn't make the connection. I'd never actually *seen* it—except in my imagination."

"Walter Remler?" Schwartz asked. "The erotica collector?"

"Yes, and that's just the point. Remler collects erotica. Some of it's musical, but still. Why should he be drooling over a rigid notation box? And why was Sammy Shapiro calling him a schmuck?"

Schwartz looked doubtful. "Shapiro's always calling everybody in the world a schmuck."

I couldn't argue that. But there was still the matter of Walter Remler, New York's Number One man in the field of high-class porn. Show Remler a twenty-four-carat watch with a button that starts music playing and sets a tiny couple on the watchface to moving slowly back and forth against each other and it's a sure sale. But a rigid notation box? That shouldn't have brought forth anything beyond a yawn from Remler. It didn't make sense.

Maybe I needed to talk to Remler.

I checked my watch; it was a quarter to four. Couldn't keep Sarah waiting. Remler would have to wait a bit for the pleasure of my company.

EIGHTEEN

Sarah's face said Muriel Hardwick was bearing up just a little too well. "You're looking much better," Sarah said, as Muriel led us through the entry hall.

I thought the greeting came across more as accusation than an expression of sympathy, but if Muriel noticed she didn't let on. "Thank you, dear," she said, and pecked Sarah lightly on the cheek.

Muriel actually did look much better. Her light blue knit dress set off her eyes admirably, and those eyes were bright and clear. I sniffed as she leaned forward to buss me. Professional hair spray. She'd been to the hairdresser today.

She took out a package of cigarettes, tipped one into her mouth, and lit up. "Life goes on." She removed the cigarette from her lips–with her right hand–and blew out a mouthful of smoke. "Come in, do."

We followed her into the living room, where my strategy ran smack up against a complication. Lucas Sterne was sitting on the edge of the fainting couch. He gave us a phony smile. "Well, Thomas Purdue, what a pleasure. And Sarah." He looked at Schwartz. "I do believe I've seen you, but I can't quite make the connection."

"My friend, Mr. J. P. Schwartz," I said. "J. P., Lucas Sterne."

Schwartz stuck out his hand, which Lucas accepted in the manner of a delicate and refined lady whose darling cat has just brought her a mouse. "I been in your shop," said Schwartz. "Wonderful place. Nicest collection of music boxes in the city."

I swore I actually saw Lucas's ears prick up.

"Oh? Are you a collector?"

"More like an appreciator, maybe you could say," said Schwartz. "I'm into general antiques."

Muriel blew out a cloud of smoke and leaned over from the waist to stub her cigarette in the ash tray. Sarah saw me appreciating our hostess' hindquarters and disapproved, silently but very effectively.

"As I was saying," Muriel said. "Life goes on. The barrister–attorney–thinks we're quite close, really, to settling Harry's affairs. That's why Lucas is here. He's spent so much time, very kind of him."

"Lucas' kindness is legendary," I said. "I don't want to interrupt you or be a nuisance."

"Thomas' capacity for being a nuisance is legendary," Lucas twitted.

I smiled blandly. Mr. Grace Under Pressure. "Why don't you and Lucas just go on about your business, Muriel," I said. "Sarah and J. P. and I can take a quick peek at the computer by ourselves and then we'll be on our way."

"Oh, no. No trouble at all. We'd be interested to see what the problem is. Wouldn't we, Lucas?"

"Oh. Certainly." Lucas got up with dutiful weariness.

We walked single-file into the library.

"Yes, there certainly will be a great deal of change here," Muriel said. "Lucas is ready to sell the music machines. I've found a dealer in Victorian furniture who'll come in and remove all this bloody damned dark, heavy stuff. And there's a bookseller who'll empty out the entire library for me. He was in yesterday, looking through the books. No first editions, apparently; nothing really valuable. Harry wasn't as good with books as he was with his other investments."

I prayed the bookman wasn't particularly interested in nineteenth century British economics.

Muriel led me to the computer. I turned it on. Schwartz

watched over my shoulder. Sarah–I had to hand it to her. She flashed the computer a look of classic boredom, then wandered over to the bookshelves.

"Oh, yes." Muriel laughed. "I'd forgotten. Sarah's quite the little book-person, isn't she?"

"Always was," I said. "She's never had any interest in computers."

Unfortunately, Lucas Sterne didn't seem to have any interest in computers, either. He followed Sarah over to the books. "Well, Sarah, let's see where your tastes run," he said. "Are you a fiction or a nonfiction reader?"

"I'm afraid I don't classify quite that easily," she said, with the perfect touch of coldness.

The computer screen filled with an action menu. I chose to view CYLINDER MUSIC BOXES. The machine beeped, chugged, and grunted. Up came CYLINDER BOXES. I pretended to study the list.

"Oh, now, I'll bet that's not terribly interesting reading," I heard Lucas croon. "*The Economics of Britain in the Nineteenth Century*. Dry, dry, dry. But there–why don't you read *that* one. *Portnoy's Complaint*." He almost giggled. "You certainly won't fall asleep over *that*. Of course, you also may never eat another piece of liver."

"I'm sorry, Lucas," Sarah said. "I don't read smut."

I imagined myself jumping up, running across the room, and slugging the son of a bitch. It'd be bad enough to leave without the rest of the stash of pictures–assuming that yesterday's bookman had left them in the first place–but even worse to have them come out into the open right in front of both Lucas and Muriel.

Then Schwartz said, "Excuse me, please, Mrs. H. Could you tell me where's the bathroom?"

Goddamn it, I thought. Right *now* he has to go?

"Out the door, turn left into the vestibule," said Muriel. "Then the first right, into the alcove. It's at the end of that hallway."

"Thanks." Schwartz tipped the fedora and went out.

My eyes went back to the computer screen.

"Don't like the spicy stuff, eh?" Sarah hadn't put Lucas off in the least. "Well, let's see. What can we find that might be perhaps a bit less offensive to your sensibilities?"

I was just about to ask him to come over and look at the listing of a rare Malignon box with a forté-piano comb setup and hidden bells when Schwartz reappeared in the doorway. "Excuse me again," he said. "I'm sorry, but I can't find it."

Jesus, Dummy, I almost shouted. You haven't been gone long enough to look.

Then it hit me. Of course he hadn't been gone long enough to look.

Schwartz locked eyes with Lucas. "Would you mind showin' me?" he said. "Sorry to be a bother and all that, but ..."

Lucas rolled his eyes. Apparently it was not in his job description to suffer fools gladly, if at all. "I'll show you," Muriel said, and led Schwartz out the door. Lucas, that impossible bastard, turned back to the bookshelves.

I didn't have long; Muriel would be back in a minute. "Hey, Lucas," I chirped as I pecked randomly away at the keys on the computer keyboard. "Where do they keep paper here? I want to take a few notes."

Now he was thoroughly put out, hands on hips. "How would I know where they keep paper?"

"Okay, thanks. I'll go find some for myself." I walked over to the desk and pulled open a drawer.

"Thomas!" Lucas, now in highest dudgeon. "Don't go poking like that in those drawers."

"Why not? You never do know what you might find, poking around in other people's drawers."

I saw only pens and pencils, but I made a brief show of rummaging. "Oh, ho!" I said. "Ha ha *ha*."

"What, Thomas?"

Time was passing too damn fast. Bite, twerp, I thought,

and said, "Oh, nothing. None of *your* business, anyway. *You* don't poke around in other people's drawers."

That got him on the run. I moved my body to block him away, and at the same time pushed the drawer shut. He shoved me; I caught him sharply with a knee behind his upper calves. He let out a grunt and went down on the carpet.

"What *are* you two up to?"

Muriel, back from showing Schwartz to the *pissoir.*

"Lucas was helping me find some note paper," I said. "Very helpful guy, Lucas. He'll fall all over himself to give you a hand."

Across the room Sarah actually snickered. I looked over. Almost imperceptibly, her head went back and forth: no. Goddamn it to hell! She hadn't had time to get the pictures out of *The Economics of Britain* and into her pocketbook.

Her little laugh faded quickly. Lucas was already on his feet and halfway back to the bookshelves, glaring at me the whole way.

How long could this Three Stooges routine go on?

Muriel opened another drawer in the desk, took out a pad, and handed it to me. Strain lines had begun to appear around her eyes. I thanked her and went back to the computer.

I looked at the screen, clapped a hand to my head, and said, "Oh, crap."

Everyone turned to look at me.

"The computer," I said, all pain and misery. "It's crashed."

Muriel corrugated her brow. "What on earth is wrong?"

I pointed at the blank screen. "I don't know; it seems to have just died."

Right then, Schwartz strolled briskly back into the room. "The computer's crashed, J. P.," I said. "Can you make any sense out of it?"

Schwartz may be a world-class picker, but what he knows about computers could be put into a wrist-watch case and rattled. He grinned and said, "Shove over. Let me take a look."

He sat down in my place, pushed the fedora back on his

head, and muttered something unintelligible. Sarah, bless her heart, wandered over to peek. Lucas rode her wake. They stood behind Schwartz, craning their necks to see the screen. "Must be the hard drive," Schwartz said. "Yep, I think it's got to be. The hard drive must have crashed."

Sarah gave my hand a surreptitious squeeze. Hope rose in my chest.

"Ridiculous," Lucas sneered. "Lord knows, I'm no computer expert, but the screen's a total blank and if the hard drive crashed you ought to be seeing *something. I* think you've got a monitor problem. Are the cables connected?"

I shrugged.

"You people can figure this out," Sarah said, and walked away toward the shelves of books.

Schwartz was on his feet. "Okay, Mr. Sterne. Have a seat here and check out the monitor."

I pushed Lucas toward the chair. "Stop that," he groused. "I need to get behind the computer to check the cables."

He leaned over the back of the table, then let out a little cry of triumph. "Hah, yes! See here?" He held up a black wire. "It was hanging loose; must have not been pushed all the way in." With great ceremony he reached back and plugged the cable into the rear of the computer.

Out of the corner of my eye I saw Sarah at the bookshelf, her back to us. Her pocketbook was resting up on the ledge in front of her. To all intents and purposes, she was scanning a book.

"Screen's still dark, Lucas," I said.

"Eh?" His face was as black as the monitor screen. "Oh, all right. Here." He turned off both monitor and CPU. After several seconds, he turned them back on. The computer went through its booting routine, beeping, chugging, grunting, and flashing red, orange, and green lights. But the screen stayed dark.

Lucas blew out a long breath. "Well, I guess there's been

some damage to the monitor," he said. "Maybe there was intermittent power and it ... oh, I don't know. Blew something. I guess you need a repairman, Muriel."

Sarah now stood one section past *Economics*. Either she had the pictures or she was never going to get them.

Muriel rested a hand on my shoulder. "I'm terribly sorry. What a nuisance."

"Never mind." I smiled. "Really, there's no hurry. Whenever you've got the thing back working, why don't you give me a call?"

As she walked slowly over from the bookshelves Sarah's face was a mask, but she clutched her pocketbook firmly in front of her. "Ready to go, Babe?" I asked.

"If you're finished for now, sure." She smiled at Muriel, then shook hands cordially. "Please," she said. "You will call if there is any way I can help, won't you?"

I felt annoyed. Sarah was cool as penguin fur. She had talent to burn—but why did *I* have to find proper applications for it and practically force her to use it? Sad, what a waste. What a marvelous team we could be.

"You really are quite the reader, aren't you?" Muriel said. "Your place must be just wall to wall books."

"Oh, no." Sarah shook her head. "I don't like clutter. I borrow what I want to read from the library and then return it. That way I can keep my apartment orderly."

Muriel shot me a sly look and smiled. "Oh—you're not a collector, then?"

"Most emphatically not," said Sarah.

As we hurried down the sidewalk I asked Sarah, "You got them?"

"All the ones in that book," she called through the wind. "I couldn't check every book in the room, but as far as I could go I didn't find any more pictures. You'll just have to be satisfied with these."

"How many? About?"

"Ten or fifteen. Let's go back to the cash machines and I'll give them to you."

"No. I've got an idea. Let's walk over to The Regency and have a drink. It's only a few blocks–Park and Sixty-First. We can look the pictures over there."

She looked doubtful. "I really ought to go back to the office and finish up for the day. And then I've got to meet–"

I took her by the arm. "Finish up for today tomorrow. And as for Mr. Harold ... well, never mind. You've got time. Have something warm, a toddy, or something ridiculous, all full of chocolate and crème de menthe. Cocktails for three. We've earned a little refreshment, haven't we? A little celebration?" I steered her toward Park Avenue.

"You're impossible." She was smiling, though. "All right. You've convinced me. I guess I could really use a drink."

"That's the spirit," said Schwartz.

People laugh with relief. Coming in out of the savage cold to the warmth of the lobby in the beautiful old Regency Hotel, we were a high-spirited trio. I slipped the headwaiter at the cocktail lounge a twenty to get us a corner table all the way to the back. We threw our coats over the backs of our chairs and sat down.

In the front near the entrance a piano tinkled, overembellished Cole Porter. Sarah didn't seem to notice the music. "Oh, my." She giggled. "I didn't think I was going to be able to do it this time. That Lucas person just wouldn't move an inch away from me."

"I can't say I blame him," I said.

"For heavens' sake. He's ten–maybe fifteen–years younger than I am."

"So what? That's an in-thing: young men, older women. In ancient Greece there was only one Oedipus, but this is America. Every man a king."

Schwartz chortled. Sarah's color went up another notch and she said, "I swear! The stuff that goes on in your head–I'll never understand it." But she was still smiling.

"I thought maybe I could get him to show me the toilet," said Schwartz. "But I couldn't pull him offa you."

"No way." I shook my head. "Lucas likes the ladies. You didn't have a chance."

"Guess not." Schwartz looked thoughtful. "Lucky we got lucky, know what I mean? Like if the computer monitor hadn't gone blooey I don't know how we'd have gotten away with it."

"A person makes his own luck, Broadway," I said.

Both he and Sarah looked at me. "You mean you pulled out that cable?" Schwartz asked.

I nodded. "When I was on my way over to the desk."

"So why didn't the picture come back on when he plugged it in again?"

"Because I also turned the brightness and contrast knobs all the way down."

Schwartz chuckled, but Sarah seemed to find that hilarious. She laughed and laughed. She was still laughing when the waitress, an anorexic blond in a short black dress, set a bowl of peanuts and pretzel sticks on the table. Sarah blotted her eyes with a tissue, and asked for a glass of Chardonnay. I said that'd do for me, too. Schwartz ordered a pint of Schaefer.

"*Beer*, Broadway?" I said, and pretended to shiver all over. "What're you going to do for a chaser–jump in a snowbank?"

The waitress snickered. Schwartz shrugged. "We didn't have much money when I was a little kid," he said. "And beer was half the price of milk. Ma weaned me on Schaefer; what can I say? I guess I never got past it."

The waitress went away laughing. "Oh, the two of you," Sarah said. "You embarrass the life out of me."

Her eyes were shining, and the lines between her nose and mouth were barely visible. Recognition stirred; my heart leaped. "Hey, guess what," I said. "You're having a good time."

Her smile faded. She studied me.

"You *are*," I said. "You look marvelous. You got yourself into that picture heist and you're enjoying yourself now, too."

I leaned over to kiss her, but she moved back in her chair. "I did a job and I did it right," she said. "And now it's done." She lifted her pocketbook; I ducked. But she just upended it over the table, shaking out a shower of photographs and small strips of film negative, along with her wallet and keys. She snatched up the keys and wallet, shoved them roughly back inside. Then she jumped up, grabbed her coat off the back of her chair, and threw it on.

"Hey." I started to get up too, but she motioned me back. "If you'll please excuse me, I need to get back to the office," said the middle-aged, clipped-voice lady-bureaucrat. "I have responsibilities; people count on me. And I have to meet Harold at six; I don't want to be late." She lowered her gaze. "I'll see you Christmas Day."

Every line had miraculously etched itself back onto her face.

Schwartz looked after her as she disappeared past the piano into the lobby. "Jeez, Doc," he said, very softly. "That wasn't exactly the brightest thing in the world for you to say. If you don't mind me telling you."

I waved my hand lightly. "Paradise found, paradise lost."

Schwartz looked puzzled. "Excuse me?"

"Nothing," I said. "It wasn't the brightest thing to say, even if I *do* mind your telling me. Which I don't." I scooped the messy array of pictures into neatness, as if I were rearranging a deck of cards. "Wait'll the drinks come," I said. "Then we'll take a peek."

I told the waitress to leave the lady's wine, that she'd had to leave but I hoped she might come back. Which was as straight a story as you'll ever hear.

The first swallow of Chardonnay burned its way down to my gizzard. I threw down a handful of peanuts as oil for my troubled gastric waters. "Okay," I said to Schwartz. "Let's peep through the keyhole."

The pictures were impressive. Could Muriel possibly have known she'd been on camera? She appeared in every pose you could imagine, doing the most amazing things to and with Harry. Nothing was left to imagination. It was a silent still theater of the absurd, more humorous by far than erotic, a collaboration of the Marx Brothers and Eugene Ionesco, directed by the Marquis de Sade.

About halfway through the pile, a different picture caught my attention. There were two people in it, the same woman and man who'd done the hot dog pose. This time the guy with the toothy smile was wearing only a white sailor's cap, set at a jaunty angle. Hanging from his erect penis was a little British flag. The woman, in the same yellow bikini, also sported a sailor's cap. She was on her knees, mouth open and saluting smartly up at the man. Under the picture was printed "Brittania Rules the Waves."

The shot after that, a whimsical little piece, featured the same woman standing up, swathed chest to mid-thigh in a full-sized British flag. She stood, smiling coyly, an index finger against her lower lip, flanked by two men who were obviously masturbating. One was Wiener-Dick, the other someone I hadn't seen before. This touching scene was entitled "Getting the Union Jack Off."

I'd seen that woman before, and not so long before. It was the second picture, a face-on shot, that established the connection. Pull her long unrestrained hair up into a bun, give her a pair of rimless glasses, and there was Wilma Ryan.

I held the picture up for Schwartz.

He made a face. "So? Another dame, not Muriel. I don't know her; I don't know the guys, either one of them. What's the big deal?"

"The big deal is this woman left a music box with Shackie, for him to repair. And she came by last night to pick it up.

But she *didn't* pick it up. She called her husband and then persuaded me to hold onto the box and do the work."

Schwartz picked up the second picture. "She does stuff like this and she's got to call her husband to ask if it's okay to fix up a music box?"

"There's something else." I started dropping the pictures one by one onto either of two piles, as if I were dealing cards to Schwartz and myself for a little poker game. "Strange. Two constants here. Either Muriel and Harry are in a picture, or else this Wilma Ryan is. And how about these negatives?" As quickly as I could, I held them up to the light from the holly-wreathed candle in the middle of the table. "Twelve Harry-Muriel pictures, twelve negatives. But two pictures of Wilma and no negatives."

"Hmm." Schwartz pushed his fedora back and scratched at his forehead. "I don't get it."

"Neither do I. A statistician would probably tell us twelve out of twelve against zero for two isn't significant. But I'll bet it is. Wilma's phone number is on her page in Shackie's log book. Come on." I got up, stuffed the pictures into my pocket, and grabbed my coat.

The waitress rushed over. "More hurry-up calls?" she asked. "No time for another drink?"

I pushed a twenty into her hand. "Not tonight. Change's yours. Buy yourself a pair of nice warm leggings."

NINETEEN

"Broadway! Look at this."

Schwartz studied the page in Shackie's notebook. "Wilma Ryan," he muttered. "Fourteen twenty-one West End Avenue, five-five-five, two-seven-one-seven. Fancy territory."

"Look at the date she left the box," I said. "December fifteenth."

Schwartz squinted. "Not all that long ago—only four days."

"The day Shackie was killed. Last entry in his book. She left Shackie his last music box to fix, and then there she is in those porn shots hidden in Harry's den. More than a small coincidence?" I banged a fist on the work table. "This whole damn case is full of coincidences but none of them seem to lead anywhere."

I snatched up the phone and dialed Wilma Ryan's number.

"Van Ostrand Residence."

The answering voice was gracious, elderly, and female. It was status, class, money. Wilma, it was not. Maybe her mother? Wilma Van Ostrand Ryan? "Hello," I said. "This is Arthur Wagner. May I speak to Wilma, please?"

"Wilma?" The elegant voice was puzzled. "I'm sorry, Mr. Wagner. There is no Wilma here."

"Wilma Ryan? Is this five-five-five, two-five-one-seven?"

"Yes it is," said the voice. "But there are no Wilmas here, nor any sort of Ryans." She chuckled. "Young man, I'm afraid your lady friend may have given you a wrong telephone number."

"Oh, well," I said. "Sorry to bother you."

Schwartz could barely contain himself. "Somebody covering?" he whispered as I lowered the receiver into the cradle.

"Doubt it. She sounded for real."

Then I remembered the music box owners I'd called back the day before. That list was still on my telephone table. But my enthusiasm was brief. Wilma Ryan had reached me directly, hadn't she? Wilma and Harley Bostick. I hadn't called her. I didn't have her number.

I picked up the phone book and flipped to R. Nearly two full pages of Ryans. No Wilmas, but several W's. No Ryan of any sort at 1421 West End Avenue or with the phone number 555-2717.

I drummed fingers for a couple of seconds, then flipped back through the phone book pages to the R-E's. I marked Walter Remler's number with my finger as I dialed it.

The line was busy.

"Good," I said. "He's home."

"Who?"

"Remler."

"What were you calling *him* for?"

"More coincidences," I said. "Remler really should have less than no interest in a rigid notation box, but according to Jackson George he was positively fascinated by Harry's. I'm going to go ask him a few questions."

"Want me to come?"

I shook my head. "I'll do better alone with him. You can stop on your way home and check out this address; see if Wilma Ryan lives there."

"I'm on my way. Call me when you get back."

I carefully locked the door behind us, then followed Schwartz down the stairs.

Back in the 'twenties and 'thirties, Walter Remler's neighborhood was one of the most interesting in New York. The big apartment buildings on Riverside Drive were occupied by moneyed sophisticates who mixed and mated with Columbia University's intellectuals a couple of blocks inland. The sports and the profs would get together and take the A-Train a few stops north to the night spots of Harlem, to swing through the night with the Duke and the Count.

Though the area's gone scruffy, some of the grand old apartments are still very nice and a certain type of wealth clings to Riverside Drive. This type includes Walter Remler, theatrical impresario. That's impresario with a small i: Remler is no Hurok. Call him the King of Off-Off Broadway; everyone who knows him does, if not to his face. Why this King of Off-Off chooses to live where he does probably has to do with the fact that university students these days swing harder, higher, and farther than those pre-war jazz babies ever dreamed of doing.

That's no more than rumor, mind you, and for a good reason. Remler himself is not big bucks. *Mrs.* Remler is. Margaret Wilfong Remler's dowry came to the altar in a Brink's truck. That windfall was the foundation of both Walter Remler's theatrical enterprises and his spectacular collection of erotica. But there are limits to what you can explain away as art, even to an adoring spouse who happens to be as short on brainpower as she is long on money. Tedious evenings at little theaters will fly; so will accumulation of mechanical representations of sex acts. Orgies with college students definitely would not.

I got off the Broadway local at 125th Street and walked the few blocks to Remler's apartment building, where I charged up a short flight of brick steps onto a portico like the entry to the Lincoln Memorial. The heavy white columns were impressive not so much for their helical windings of tinsel and holly as for the astonishing fact that they were pristine white. Not a single line of graffiti to be seen. Undoubtedly the reason for this was the pair of gorillas in doorman uniforms who flanked the entrance. No one who didn't belong there was going to get past these characters to spray-paint naughty words on the columns.

I walked up to the simian on the left and smiled in what I hoped was an engaging manner. "I'm here to see Mr. Remler."

The guy looked me up and down with hostile, piggy eyes. He wrinkled his nose as if he might be checking my pheromones. "'Utsa name?" he gargled.

"Purdue," I said, and then as expediency triumphed over principle I added, "Dr. Purdue," giving appropriate subtle emphasis to the "doctor."

It worked; it always does. Which is why I hate to use it. Sarah likes to tell me that's another example of my perversity. I insist on making life harder for myself, another reason why she can't understand what goes on inside my head. As if that were my fault.

The gorilla seemed to relax, if slightly. He moved inside the doorway, picked up a phone, and dialed a four-digit number. "Mist' Remle'," he said. "Dokuh here to see you. Dokuh Puhdoo." He paused, then said, "Okay," and slammed the instrument back into its holder. Then he motioned me inside. "Mist' Remle' says go on up," he growled. "Pen'ouse. Twenny-fifth Floor."

"Thank you," I said, and moved past him toward the elevator, breathing a good deal more comfortably. Remler and I are no more than hello, how-are-you acquaintances. I'd have been SOL if he'd told the doorman to send me away.

My ears popped as I got off the elevator on Twenty-Five. I stood there long enough to look at the Hudson and the Palisades, shimmering through the huge plate of glass on the far wall. Who might have lived in this penthouse seventy years ago? On a warm summer night he might have had a party, windows open, lazy breeze blowing off the river, and Cole Porter entertaining the guests *ad lib* at the piano. Or on a Sunday afternoon in winter, Gershwin might have teased the ivories as the sun dropped lower and lower over the Palisades. It wasn't beyond imagination to picture the Duke and the Count, down from Harlem, coming halfway to meet George and Ira, up from Broadway.

But Walter Remler, The King of Pricey Sleaze, didn't even own a piano.

I took a deep breath and rang Remler's bell.

Walter opened the door. He blinked, whether at surprise to see me or because of the bright light in the hallway, I couldn't tell. Remler's pupils were unequal in size, the right bigger than the left. This condition is known as anisocoria and sometimes it's an indication of disease or injury to the brain. In Remler's case, though, it represented what we call an incidental congenital anomaly, a harmless deviation from normal in embryonic development.

A questioning smile oozed outward from the left corner of Remler's mouth. "Well, Thomas Purdue. What on earth brings you to my door?"

"I was in the neighborhood," I said. "Okay if I come in for a few minutes?"

Remler stepped aside and motioned for me to pass. As the door closed behind me, *I* blinked. The receiving hallway was darkened, black-light bulbs in twin sconces being the only source of light.

"Come in," Walter said. "You can meet my other guest."

He moved quickly past me. Remler was a creature of the night. I went carefully, trying to avoid knocking anything over and fighting the unsettling sensation of being led into the burrow of some lascivious gopher or prairie dog.

The living room was a temple to Remler's obsession. Thick oriental rugs muffled our footsteps. The windows at the far end of the room were draped in black silk edged with purple velvet; the furniture was heavy and dark, very late-Victorian. As my eyes began to adjust I could focus more clearly on the objects of my host's affection. Metal sculpture, wooden carvings, Oriental ivories, all fashioned in tribute to the physical act of coupling, mostly in uncommon postures. The good stuff, smaller automata, watches, and clocks were in the next room, mostly in locked glass cabinets.

As we came into the room a woman rose from an overstuffed armchair. "Dr. Purdue," Remler said. "This is Miss Morgan. She's been plying me with questions for the past half hour."

The last sentence came complete with open leer. Marisa extended her hand. "How are *you*, Dr. Purdue?" And then to Remler, "We've already met."

"You do get around, my dear, don't you?" Remler commented.

Couldn't have put it better myself, I thought. "Hello, Marisa. Is your head all right?"

"Oh, yes. Just fine." She laughed. "Accidents do happen, don't they?"

Especially when you're breaking and entering, I said to myself.

"Can I offer you something to drink, Thomas?" Remler asked.

I shook my head. "No, thanks. I'm fine."

Remler dropped into a chair and lounged insouciantly. "So what can I do for you?" He glanced at Marisa. "Is this a ... private matter?"

"No," I said. "Not at all. I was just wondering something. I understand you and Harry Hardwick had quite a little fight a couple of years back. Over a machine."

Remler smirked. "The Musical Maiden." He gestured toward the far corner of the room, then got up and walked in that direction. Marisa and I followed him.

As we came close, I could see a lovely young woman posed in the corner, her hands holding the edges of a filmy garment. In the dim light you'd swear she was a living person, but not so. She was a lifesized doll, fully five feet tall.

"My little musical maiden," said Remler. If his tone of voice alone weren't enough to disgust me, he ran his fingers through the doll's long, brown hair. "Phalibois, at his most inspired. Watch."

As if he were embracing the mannikin, Remler reached his right hand behind her to push the start lever. *Damn it,* I thought. Was *everyone* in New York right-handed except Broadway Schwartz and the killer?

The girl's hips began to undulate. Her fingers teased the

top of her nightie. Her head bobbed and her eyelids fluttered. Then her hands drew back the nightgown on either side until finally she held it fully open like a shimmering cape. As she stood exposed, her eyes opened wide and she blew a kiss in our direction. All this to the accompaniment of the beautiful "*D'Amor sull' ali rosee*," from *Trovatore*.

It was an uncanny performance; the doll couldn't have looked more alive. When she got no response her lips twisted into a pretty pout, she drew the nightgown back over her body, and lowered her head to sulk. After a moment she raised her head and regarded her audience with apparent fresh hope.

Remler reached to shut her off. "Impressed?" he asked.

It was impossible not to be. Henry Phalibois was justly famous for the lifelike, near-life-sized automata he created during the latter years of the nineteenth century. Whether the Musical Maiden came into being as a representation of Phalibois' wife or perhaps his mistress, or whether she stood as the personification of her creator's imaginative longings and desires, she was the undisputed masterwork of a distinguished career. No problem imagining Remler going to any necessary length to have her.

"I see why you and Harry had words," I said.

Remler snickered. "You're putting it politely. I'd been dickering price with the previous owner for some time when he called to say he'd been approached by one of Harry's scouts. He said if I wanted the Maiden I'd better say yes, right then. Of course I had no way of knowing whether or not the man was bluffing, but I was not about to take that kind of a chance. I said yes and wired my money. Next thing I knew, Harry was on the phone, accusing me of moving in on *his* deal. Well excuse *me*, I told him, but *I'd* been there first, and in case he hadn't gotten the message, the world didn't necessarily part like the Red Sea when Harry Hardwick raised his baton. Harry was not pleased, I can tell you that."

Story time. "I've heard it a little differently. Some people say it was *Harry* who was chasing the Maiden, and he asked you whether you'd seen her and if so whether she was real or a fake. And then you called the owner and bought her out from under Harry."

Remler just blinked mildly behind his shades. "People say all kinds of things. But consider this: even if it *was* true, Harry was a fool. He'd been around the block. If he decided—for whatever reason—to invite a competitor into the arena, well ... I think he'd have done better to direct his anger at himself."

Round to Remler. But the match was still on. "Whatever. Knowing the story I was surprised to see you at Harry's party the other night."

Remler didn't even pause. "The invitation surprised me at least as much as it did you. Harry called a week before. He said he thought it was time to mend fences. He apologized for the names he'd called me, and said he wanted me to be there." Remler made a fancy pass with his hand. "So I went. It's not in my nature to carry a grudge."

Walter Remler, Knight of the Generous Spirit. "Harry *was* a decent guy. So you went. Were you impressed by his rigid notation box?"

"Rigid notation box?" Remler was innocence itself. "Funny thing about that." He gestured with a flip of the hand toward Marisa. "Our young lady here was also asking me about a rigid notation box. But I'm afraid I can't be of much help to either of you. It's not the sort of thing I collect."

Marisa saw me staring at her. "I spoke to Mr. Jackson George yesterday," she said. "He told me Mr. Remler might be able to help me."

Remler gave a languid, helpless shrug. His blond hair fell forward into his eyes, making him look like a large, indolent spider. "You *do* know," he asked me, "don't you?"

I knew, all right, but I said, "Know what?"

"About Jackson George."

"*What* about Jackson George?"

"He was murdered today. Shot. I heard it on the radio this afternoon. They found him in his apartment. The police don't have any leads. No break-in; nothing apparently stolen." Remler leered at me. "Better save your pennies. First Harry, now Jackson. Some major items will be coming up for sale."

As I've said, a collector can't afford to be overly sensitive, but there are limits. This was definitely bad taste. Natural death is one thing: people die, collectors acquire. Either that or they don't collect much. But murder's something else. It makes the buyer's premium too high. You're inclined to not bid at all.

"I wonder why Jackson thought you'd be able to help Marisa find a rigid notation box," I said.

"I haven't the slightest idea," said Remler, shifting in his big chair. "I can't even remember the last time I talked to Jackson George."

I paused, the way you will when you're standing at the edge of a particularly icy swimming pool. Finally, I braced my feet and pushed. "I've been trying to get a rigid notation box for a long time. I talked to Sammy Shapiro about it; I thought he might be able to find me one. But he said I'd have to get around you first. He told me you were so fascinated by Harry's box at the party, you were bound and determined to get one yourself."

Remler's reaction was far milder than I'd imagined it would be. He just shook his head and tsked down toward his feet. "Shapiro wouldn't know the truth if it flew right up to him and perched on that big crooked nose of his. Believe what he tells you and you'll be chasing wild geese into Canada. Yes, certainly, I listened to that box at Harry's. I've never heard such nice music from a cylinder music box. But it held no collecting interest for me."

"All right, but I'd sure like to know where it is now. It was stolen when Harry was killed."

"I've heard." Remler was calmly non-committal. "You ought

to keep your fingers crossed. If it was stolen by another collector, you'll never see it again. But maybe it was ripped off by a junkie. If I were you I'd cruise every antique shop in the city for the next month. You might get lucky. But I'm afraid I can't help you–in spite of what my friend and yours, Shapiro, might have told you."

That was his story and now he was making it clear the tale was told. I couldn't blame him. I was surprised he'd let me distract him from Marisa even this long.

But I wasn't quite finished. "Maybe you're right. Maybe I *should* cruise shops. Would you believe Marisa, here, found a rigid notation box at a place called the Gotham Antiques Mart, just a couple of weeks ago? Then right after that, Marty Abramowitz, the dealer, got himself shot to death. You remember Abramowitz, don't you, Walter? Fat, bald, and greasy? He and Randy Nussbaum made a little noise a few years ago when they knocked together a Reginaphony and passed it off on a new collector."

Remler smirked. "I've never dealt with Abramowitz–but I do remember hearing about the scam. What of it?"

"I wonder where they got the phonograph parts for that machine."

An indifferent shrug. "Search me."

"The usual reliable source says the parts came from you, Walter."

"Well, what of it?" He was irritated, but the man had good control. "I don't remember that they did, but do *you* remember all the stuff you unload and to whom? Maybe I did sell some phonograph parts to Nussbaum, and maybe he and that dealer did cobble a Reginaphony out of them. But that's not my fault. Just what are you driving at?"

"Okay, Walter, thanks." I stood up. "If you can't help, you can't. Nice to see you, anyway."

Nice to see him. I'm don't think Remler believed my story anymore than I'd believed his. But he got to his feet and shook hands.

Marisa got up, too. I started for the door.

"Well, thank you, Mr. Remler," I heard Marisa say. "I won't trouble you any further, either." Then she was alongside me. "I'll take the elevator down with you, Thomas."

"It's a free country," I said.

As we stood waiting for the elevator Marisa hit me with the big smile. "I really would love to see your collection," she said.

"Maybe sometime."

She turned up her facial thermostat. "How about now? I'm free."

"No, you're not. You're very expensive. I don't know what the price actually is, but I'm sure I can't afford it."

She looked mortally wounded. "What's the matter? I was so surprised the other night to come out and find you ... gone. Did I insult you somehow?"

"Only my intelligence. Nothing serious."

"What–?"

The elevator door opened; she followed me inside. "Can it," I snapped. "First, you show up at Shackie's to ask about a rigid notation box he was supposedly fixing for you." I almost added it was also a box not catalogued in Shackie's log book, but caught myself just in time. "Then, you come sneaking into Shackie's–*breaking* in, actually. You have a talk with Jackson George about rigid notation boxes and next thing, Jackson's dead. Now you're at Remler's, still asking questions about rigid notation boxes. You'll have to excuse me, but I don't feel comfortable around a woman who's a half-step in front of both me and the Angel of Death everywhere I go."

"I've only been trying to find my music box. And I was ... so pleased when I ran into you. If I couldn't have my beautiful music box, I thought ... maybe I might find something even better."

She moved as if to put her arms around me but I pulled back a step. "Sorry. I'm nobody's consolation prize. You said

Jackson George sent you to talk to Remler. Who sent you to George?"

"A dealer in the antiques mall on Second Avenue. He had some music boxes, so I asked him where I might be able to find a rigid notation box. He said Mr. George collected rare early music machines and might be able to help me. But as it turned out he couldn't; he only collected miniatures. So I thanked him and left."

Winsome shrug for terminal punctuation, but it was cock and bull. For her next trick she'd offer to take me to the mall, so she could point at one of the three or four shops that have music boxes from time to time and describe a little man who wasn't there—but who *was* there the other day, really he was.

The elevator bumped to a stop. We got off and walked toward the front door. "I've had enough," I said. "You go hunt for your music box and I'll hunt for mine—by myself." And then, without thinking, I added, "And I'll get to Scotland before ye."

The silly line ran through my head all the way downtown on the subway, keeping time to the clack of the wheels on the rails.

It was getting on to eight o'clock. I felt hungry and discontented. A corned beef sandwich and a big slice of cheesecake at the Carnegie Deli helped the hunger. But the discontent remained as I walked crosstown, back to Gramercy North. All over the city, music box people were being picked off and I was getting nowhere fast. I can't say I was fond of Jackson George, but he was a character in his own right and I already missed him.

I found myself humming. When a tune works its way into my head it can play back at me for hours. *Oh, you take the high road, and I'll take the low road, and I'll be in Scotland afore ye ...*

Wait a minute, I said to myself. Not Scotland. England.

I stopped humming. The music had done its work.

Schwartz sounded surprised when I called and told him I was going to catch a quick flight to England. "It makes sense," I said. "That's where this rigid notation box came from, courtesy of Gordon and Maida Westfall. Then there's Marisa, who's English but doesn't want me to know it. For that matter, Muriel Hardwick's also a Brit. And those pictures–they were taken in England, weren't they? Britannia Rules, and the Union Jack? And there's one more thing: When I went to talk to Jackson George two days ago I found a matchbook from an English nightclub. But Jackson hates England, hadn't been there in years. Is that enough?"

"Hmmm." Schwartz was thinking half aloud. "Yeah, I'd say so. For sure, we ain't doing so good here."

"Like for instance you found out there's no Wilma Ryan at Fourteen Twenty-One West End Avenue."

"Like for instance there ain't *nobody* at Fourteen Twenty-One West End Avenue," said Schwartz. "'Cause there ain't no Fourteen Twenty-One West End Avenue, period. How'd you know?"

"Just a guess. All right, I'm on my way to the airport. If I get a red-eye I can be there working tomorrow afternoon. Otherwise I waste a whole day."

"You don't want to kill any time. Not now."

The golden rule of time management. Don't kill time. Then maybe time won't kill you.

With my one small suitcase hastily packed I stopped long enough to call Sarah. "*England*, Thomas?" she said. "Why on earth ..." Her voice petered out, then returned in full suspicious dress. "You *will* be back in time for Christmas, won't you?"

"Of course. Count on it."

There was a moment of silence. Then Sarah said, "I know I'm going to be sorry, but why? Why are you going to England the week before Christmas?"

"I've got to see a man. About a music box."

"Damn you! This is one of your stories, isn't it?"

I can't understand why she behaves that way toward me. How much more truthful could I have been?

"You're not really going to England at all, are you? You're going into hiding, that's what you're doing. Just so you won't have to help me serve dinner on Christmas Day. I *knew* you'd find some way to get out of your promise."

"'Bye, Babe," I said. "I've got to run." I made a few quick kissy sounds into the phone, then hung up. She can drag out one of these scenes for hours. And I didn't have hours for that. I had to see a man named Gordon Westfall about a music box.

TWENTY

A person can do many things on a seven-hour plane ride through the night, but only one makes any sense to me: sleep. As soon as the SEATBELTS ON sign went off, back went my seat, back went my head, and out went I. Out I stayed until the chime rang and they ordered SEATBELTS ON in preparation for landing at Heathrow.

The man in the next seat, a red-eyed, rumple-haired mess, glared at me as I stretched and snapped the seatbelt into place.

"Nice flight," I said. "Seemed to take no time at all."

"For you, maybe," he snarled. "Christ, how the hell can you sleep like that on a plane? All the way across you were snoring."

"Sorry. I've got something called narcolepsis aeronautica, this one-in-a-million condition of the nervous system. Vibrations from commercial jet airplanes seem to be in some kind of sympathetic sequence with my brainwaves, so as soon as the pilot revs up for takeoff my brain shuts down. I wasn't sleeping; I was actually unconscious. Sorry if I bothered you."

"Huh! I'll be damned! Well, I wouldn't complain if I were you," he said. "Sounds like a pretty good deal."

Speak with a straight face and complete sincerity, and people will buy any story you've got to sell. Fortunes are made by telling people halitosis can be cured by readjusting the lumbar vertebrae, and the right time for marriage can be determined by checking planetary alignment.

***

Off the plane, no luggage to retrieve. I cleared customs in a bound, stopped for a plate of scrambled eggs and a cuppa; then a quick layover in the men's room to give my little portable razor its morning exercise. While shaving I had a moment of uneasiness, that unpleasant sensation of someone behind me giving me the once-over. I looked around the room via the mirror, but it was no good. There were probably twenty men, either standing at urinals with their backs to me or washing their hands and faces at sinks to my right and left. None seemed to have the slightest interest in Thomas Purdue. I went back to my shave, then hustled on.

It's an hour's ride on the London Underground from Heathrow to Dr. Watson's, a small B&B a block and a half from the Baker Street Station. I checked in, left my suitcase on the bed, then went right back down and into the Underground. Ten minutes later I was at Gray's-in-the-Mews Antiques Centre.

The crowds at Gray's were a mob, but this *was* the week before Christmas. Lucky it wasn't a week later. England, native land of Tiny Tim and the rest of those soppy Cratchits, fairly shuts down on December twenty-fifth, not to reopen until after New Year's. Now, people were stocking up for the drought.

Gray's-in-the-Mews is composed of two buildings, one in front, one behind. The Westfall Music Box Shop is in the rear building, main floor. I knew the proprietors by name and sight, though I was never one of their regulars. I wondered how willing they'd be to give me the information I wanted.

I worked my way through the shoppers and peeked through the window. Gordon was waiting on a middle-aged couple. Maida was standing in the rear, hands clasped before her and friendly smile frozen on her face, ready to help a young woman who was looking at a disc music box at the far wall. There were three other potential customers in the small shop. No point going in now.

The sign on the door said hours were ten to five, Tuesday through Saturday. My watch said 4:03.

I let the crowd wash me back to the front building. Might as well look around in other shops for a while. Good old narcolepsis aeronautica, I felt fine.

I saw a few pretty things, but nothing to spend money on.

At twenty to five I worked my way back to the Westfalls' shop. Gordon was still with the same couple and Maida was strolling around, being generally helpful to three lookers. I started to feel uneasy. Tomorrow was Saturday, the last weekend shopping day before Christmas. The minute they opened the door the shop would be filled with people. I'd have to be more pushy than I'd originally intended.

I watched one customer leave, then two others. Finally the couple who'd been with Gordon walked out, the husband carrying a medium-sized cylinder box. My watch said eight minutes to five. If I'd counted right the shop should be empty now.

I pushed at the latch on the door.

It stuck.

I pushed again, then rattled the handle and pushed a third time before it occurred to me that the damn door was locked.

I shaded my eyes to look through the glass. Gordon was still sitting at the desk. Maida was standing with her back to me, leaning over and talking to him.

I knocked at the door.

Gordon sat up straight. Maida turned around and gave me a crooked smile. "We're closed, sorry," she mouthed, jabbing her finger at her watch. Then she turned back to Gordon.

I called up my reserve and knocked again, very firmly. Maida spun around, clearly irritated. I motioned her to the door. She narrowed her eyes, then started walking toward me. As she reached forward to turn the doorknob, no doubt primed to read me out good and proper, I saw recognition click. Her mouth shaped itself into a genuine smile.

The door swung open. "Why, Thomas Purdue. I'm so terribly sorry, really I am. I'd no idea you were over."

Gordon was on his way toward us. He's a big man in his early seventies, with a thatch of that silver-white hair that looks so distinguished over a three-piece tweed suit. "My word, quite an unexpected pleasure," he boomed. His handshake was near crippling. "Spending the holidays in England this year, are you?"

Sarah's face appeared in the air over his left shoulder. *Hah! I knew it all along!*

"Actually, no," I said, with far more reluctance than he could ever have understood. "This is a quick trip."

I could see Maida was about to tell me they'd had an awfully long day; could I p'aps come back in the morning? Better head her off. "I know it's a rough time of year for you," I said. "But I need your help. That's why I've come to England. Please, may I have a few minutes of your time–it shouldn't take longer than that."

They looked at each other, passing silent signals, trying to agree on the best way to handle this situation. I'd be smart to wrap things up quickly. "It's *terribly* important," I said, putting every possible ounce of verbal consequence into the second word.

That did it. Polite-but-determined New York will prevail every time over courteous London.

Gordon's eyes were grave. Maida locked her fingers behind her back and studied me. She was a small, round-faced squirrel of a woman with a heavy sprinkling of iron filings and diamond chips mixed into her sugar and spice. You hope women like that will be tough *for* you, not against you.

"Come sit down," she said and pointed at the desk. "I'll brew up a pot of tea." She turned the lock handle again, checked that the closed sign was facing outward, and marched off past a curtain into the rear of the shop.

Gordon led me to the desk, sat behind it. I settled into one of the two customer's chairs across from him. "Maida will be out directly," he said, his way of informing me we'd be engaging in a few minutes of pleasantries. "You've been well, I trust."

Sometimes, the best story is no more than a word. "Yes. And yourselves?"

"Oh, fine, just fine." Gordon opened the desk drawer, extracted a pipe, filled it with tobacco, and lit up. His ruddy face vanished momentarily behind a billow of white smoke. It's amazing that any Englishman lives past fifty. They smoke like pre-EPA chimneys, consume incredible quantities of eggs, butter, and red meat, put not just cream but clotted cream on their strawberries and into their coffee, and look with suspicion if not frank distrust upon anything remotely resembling aerobic exercise. Yet here was Gordon Westfall, easily in his seventies, thirty pounds overweight, but fine, thank you, just fine. God bless him and his fortunate genes.

Gordon looked around the shop. "People tell us, don't you know, that Maida and I should be thinking of closing shop. 'At our age,' and all that. Bah!" He leaned forward to fix a stare on me. "I think a man should die with a full shop. But then our children tell us, 'Whatever will we *do*–after all, *we* don't know about musical boxes.' Can you imagine such laziness? All that's required is to call Rob Matthews at Sotheby's. He'll clean this place out, hold the auction sale, and there's their bloody inheritance free and clear. I'll be damned if I'll close shop and spend the rest of my days sitting in a little room with my eyes glued to the telly."

Maida had come out with a silver tea tray while Gordon was going on. "Calm yourself, my dear; you'll have your blood pressure so high you'll give yourself a stroke, and fat lot of good that'll do you, eh?"

She set the tray down. Three china cups, saucers, and small plates, all matching the little tea pot, creamer, and sugar bowl, and a plate loaded with one-bite cakes. How they do it, and on no notice, I have no idea. At home I'd as soon drink warm dishwater as tea, but in England I make an exception. They brew their tea with regard; somehow that makes a difference.

"We'll muddle through," Maida said, smiling, as she poured

the tea into the cups. "Musical boxes are not nearly so easy to find as they once were–I don't have to tell *you* that, Thomas, now, do I? But then consider prices. A box that ten years ago was a thousand is now five. So we sell fewer musical boxes, but for more money the piece. And we get by ... don't we, my dear?"

The last sentence was addressed to Gordon. I caught the look between them. I hated to throw sand in their eyes, but it was either ask my questions or sit back and wait for a four-time killer to go after Victim Number Five. Who, by the way, just might be me.

I swallowed a raspberry mini-scone and washed it down with a mouthful of tea. "I'm sorry to bother you; I know it's inconvenient. But I'm in the middle of a very unpleasant situation back in New York–a very dangerous one, actually. I think you may be able to help me through it."

As if on cue they both put down their tea cups and stared at me. The English are great listeners; they give full measure in a conversation. I told them about Harry and Shackie and the rigid notation box.

They nodded. "Yes," Gordon said gravely. "We've heard. Terrible, what? Charles always seemed such a nice young man. I'd never have thought him a murderer."

"He wasn't," I said. "That's one reason I'm here–to *prove* he wasn't. The other is I don't think the real murderer's finished yet."

"Oh, dear." Maida's hand moved up to cover her mouth. "Murders over a musical box. Outrageous."

There's a finely tuned linguistic push-pull between England and the United States. The more we move toward hyperbole, the more the English dig in their heels and understate. It's unusual to hear a Brit say something is fantastic, awesome, or unique–because few things really *are* fantastic, awesome, or unique. Or outrageous. What the British say, they mean. Maida's indignation burned in her eyes.

"It *is* outrageous," I said. "Four murders, to be specific.

You probably haven't heard about the latest; it was only yesterday. Jackson George."

The world of dedicated music box collectors is a small one. "Jackson *Jawhdge?*" Gordon sputtered. "Not really?"

"I'm afraid so."

Maida, an eyeblink quicker than her husband, had already moved from shock to reason. "Odd, that," she said. "Jackson George, murdered over a rigid notation box. But he collected only miniatures."

"Yes," I said. "I think somehow he tumbled on to what was happening and said something foolish to the wrong person. It's a complicated story, difficult even to know where to start. But that's why I'm here. You see, the rigid notation box that seems to be at the center of all this is the one you sold to Sophie Soleski. She sold it to Harry."

I could never have predicted the reaction I got. I'd expected shock certainly, and probably horror. A smatter of defensiveness wouldn't have surprised me at all. But I got none of the above.

Gordon looked blankly at me, then at Maida, then back to me. "I say," he began. "The rigid notation box *we* sold to Sophie?"

"Yes. The one that reached her, oh, between two and three weeks ago. Harry got a line on it and as fast as it came in, it went out. To him."

"But my dear fellow. We didn't send a rigid notation box to Sophie. Not a month ago, not ever."

"But–"

"I don't think we've ever had a rigid notation box," said Maida. "Terribly scarce, don't you know. They go direct, one collector to the next."

"I realize that," I said. "But Sophie told me you'd shipped her four boxes–"

Gordon had been rummaging in the desk drawer. "Yes, that's in fact quite right."

He showed it to me: Four musical boxes, to Sophie Soleski, New York City, USA, shipped December 1. One Paillard sublime harmonie tremolo, #8768, c. 1885. One four-air overture box by the Lecoultre Freres, #29568, c. 1860. One Conchon 9-bell box, #17423, c. 1880. One four-air Nicole overture box, #35789, c. 1860.

I looked at the listing. "That's a four-air Nicole *Freres* box?" I said. "Not a four-air Francois Nicole?"

"Well, yes ..." Gordon said. "We'd not have been likely to mistake a Nicole Freres–good as it might have been–for a Francois Nicole rigid notation box. Would we, my dear?"

Maida shook her head. "No, not at all," she said, but in a very distracted way. I could practically hear gears turning in her brain.

"The serial numbers were also different," I went on. "The Francois Nicole was number four-thirty-two. We're definitely talking about two different music boxes here. You're *certain* it was the Nicole Freres you packed up and shipped to Sophie?"

Gordon began to bristle, if ever so slightly. "My dear fellow–after close to forty yaahs in this business I do believe I'd not mistake a Nicole Freres for a Francois Nicole."

I wasn't watching him, though. My eyes were on Maida. The shock and horror I'd expected had finally arrived; her eyes were full of both. She looked at Gordon and reached out to touch his hand. "Oh, my dear, *we* didn't pack those boxes, now, did we? And *we* didn't ship them, either."

The effect on Gordon was impressive. His mouth opened and closed three or four times and then he sat bolt upright. His face was the color of uncooked beef; his eyes bulged frighteningly. "That ... *blighter*!" he stammered. "That bloody blighter!" He jumped up from his chair and stormed around the room, waving his arms. "I knew we shouldn't have taken him on–why, I told you at the time, a man his age is out of new leaves to turn over." He slammed his right fist hard into his left palm. "I should have known bloody well better."

I tried not to think what Gordon's blood pressure might be. Maida trotted over to her husband and took him by the shoulder and arm. "Calm yourself, my dear," she said. "It's only a thought–at least so far. We don't *know* he did anything wrong, now. Do we?"

Gordon smiled wanly. He knew, all right, and so did she. Doubly cursed, both of them: totally honest *and* totally straightforward, they were completely at the mercy of the bitch goddess, Truth.

"Who packed the boxes and shipped them?" I asked.

They slumped into their seats. Gordon looked around the room, anywhere but at me. He seemed to be taking a mental inventory of his stock.

"Our repairman," Maida said. "Huey Fortune."

I'd heard of Huey Fortune. "*He's* your repairman?"

She nodded. Gordon looked back at me, wounded. "Bad choice, I'm afraid. We'd been using Michael Francis for years and years–but he died four years back, right about the time of the big snow. Left us badly up against it. We had unrestored boxes stacked like woodpiles against the shop walls. Our sales dropped alarmingly; we had nothing restored to sell. Then Huey, that drunken blighter, heard of our predicament and came by to beg me to take him on. He was off liquor for good, so he assured me. Not an easy situation. I knew he could do fine work ... when he was not under the influence. And I was desperate."

"We *were*, my dear," Maida put in. "We had no choice."

"'Twas Hobson's Choice, no better," Gordon said wryly. "I've spent as much time keeping Huey out of pubs and in the workshop as I have buying and selling my stock. He's put me at my wits' end more than once–but now this; I'll not tolerate further. Out he goes, first thing in the morning."

"Where does he work?" I asked.

Gordon pointed to the rear of the shop. "Back there, in the building across the court. He was living on the streets when he came to us. So, we had that space converted to living quarters and repair shop."

Maida raised a finger. "Another odd thing, now we've been talking about a rigid notation box–don't you remember, Gordon? The young lady, just last week? Came by the shop enquiring after a rigid notation box. Said she wanted to have one for her collection. We'd never seen her before."

"Don't tell me," I said. "Very attractive, wasn't she? About thirty, long black hair, big blue eyes. Lots of makeup, but well put on. And very brightly dressed."

"Why, yes, Thomas. I'd say that describes her to a tee. Know her, do you?"

"We've met. Just this past week in New York. She said her name was Marisa Morgan. And by the way, she's still looking for a rigid notation box."

Maida and Gordon shook their heads in tandem dismissal. "She never told us her name," Gordon said. "Which was one reason we thought it odd. People do tend to introduce themselves when they're genuinely interested in a major acquisition."

"I guess I need to talk to Huey," I said, and stood up. "Sorry to have had to upset you."

"Never mind," Gordon said. "Not your fault, certainly. But you'll not find Huey there. P'aps you'd best come back in the morning."

"I'm afraid the longer I wait, the greater chance someone else may be hurt. Do you have any idea where I can find Huey tonight?"

Again, they looked at each other. I wondered how two such guileless creatures had managed to survive so long and so nicely in this world. "Well ..." Maida began, but got no further. I thought she looked embarrassed.

"There's a ... a place he likes to go," Gordon said. "The George Sand Club. On Brewer Street."

Recognition dawned in stages. I pressed my fingers against my shirt pocket, felt the matchbook. "Huey's literary?"

Gordon coughed. Maida looked away. "It's ... well, it's not *that* kind of place," Gordon finally said.

I decided not to push the matter. I'd gotten better answers to my questions than I'd hoped for. Now, the thing was to find Huey and ask him some questions. I extended my hand. "Thank you. Believe me, you've been more than helpful."

They looked like shirts after a bad day at the laundry: unstarched and shoved willy-nilly through the wringer. My little story about being helpful didn't help *them*. No story could. They were hooked on truth, addicts of the most terrible sort. I felt sorrier for them than I did for Huey Fortune. As a taskmaster, old John Barleycorn's a breeze compared to Simon Pure.

They each shook my hand and wished me luck and safety. "Be sure to let us know how things turn out," Maida called after me.

I assured her I would. Knowing they'd get the word from someone other than me if things turned out badly was not comforting.

TWENTY-ONE

I didn't go directly from the Westfalls' to the George Sand Club. First I wanted to check out another lead, one that could not be researched late in the evening. I hopped the Central Underground Line to Lancaster Gate, then walked the few blocks to Craven Terrace.

I paused in front of a six-story whitewashed stone building with white curtains neatly framed into each window. Its address checked against the note I made after I'd knocked Marisa silly and gone through her purse. I walked up the wide stairs into the foyer, scanned the names next to each mail slot, then rang the superintendent's bell.

A tiny woman in a clean and ironed print dress advanced into the hallway like a slow-rolling wave. Old fracture of right hip or severe arthritis. She was eighty if a day. Even with her carefully-piled white coil of hair she couldn't have stood more than four-ten. "Yes, sir?" she sang up at me. "How may I be of assistance?"

Her blue eyes were piercingly clear but there was no animosity in her gaze. I asked whether she was the superintendent.

She nodded. "My husband and I, we are in charge."

No doubt firmly. I smiled as disarmingly as I could. "I wonder whether you can help me," I began, but she interrupted.

"I'm sorry, sir. We have no vacancies at the moment."

"No, no. That's not what I mean. I was looking for a friend, a young woman. Her name's Marisa Morgan. She said this was her address ..." I pointed at the rows of nameplates, doorbells, and mailslots. "But I don't see her name there."

"No." The old woman shook her head. "You won't. When did she give you this address, sir?"

"Last week. In fact, last Friday. A week ago today."

The woman's stare turned toward the critical. "You're an American, aren't you, sir?"

"Yes–from New York. That's where I met Miss Morgan, at a party for musical box collectors. She was over for a visit, she said. I told her I'd be in London on business this weekend, so she said I should call on her. She offered to show me her collection."

The old woman pursed her pale lips. Her eyes narrowed in thought, then she shook her head slowly. "I'm afraid you're out of luck, sir. Miss Morgan moved house at the end of last month. When she gave you this address I'm afraid she was either being a bit forgetful or, well ... shall we say more than a bit insincere?" I had to smile. The old woman's eyes softened. "Pretty little thing, isn't she, sir?"

"Very much so. I was looking forward to seeing her–*and* her collection. Have *you* ever seen her musical boxes?"

"We don't go into our tenants' rooms, sir."

"I'd very much like to find her." I considered slipping a piece of colored paper into the old woman's hand, but I was afraid that would only insult her. "Can you tell me her new address?"

The woman shook her head. "I have no idea, sir."

"No forwarding address? In case mail comes here?"

"We return it to the Postal Services, sir. *They* would have the forwarding address."

Sarah would love England, I thought. Neat. Tidy. Everything and everyone in its, his, or her place.

"Would you know where Miss Morgan worked? Maybe I could track her down that way."

Another headshake. "I believe she was some sort of consultant, sir. Worked on her own; came and went at unusual hours. I'm quite sorry. I don't think I can be of help to you."

I thanked her politely, went outside, and gave the red mailbox opposite the doorway a light kick. Nothing about this entire sitation seemed to make sense. But *everything* makes sense, everything in the world. If it seems not to, that's only because we're looking at it in the wrong way or from the wrong point of view.

Maybe a talk with Huey Fortune would put me on the right track. I checked my watch: nearly eight-fifteen. I started back toward the Underground station.

I came up into Piccadilly Circus and set off along Shaftesbury Avenue into the theater district. Crowds jostled on the narrow sidewalk under brightly-lit marquees. Once I turned onto Great Windmill Street it was easier going. A couple of blocks to Brewer Street and I stood in front of a pink sign with black lettering, identical to the cover on the matchbook in my pocket.

I walked into the George Sand Club and instantly understood the Westfalls' reaction. The walls were shocking pink, but more shocking were the pictures hung on them. Each featured women dressed in mens's clothing or vice versa, and most showed couples engaging in pretty inventive sex. The effect was disorienting. I became confused over which was man and which woman. It was like watching a snake swallowing its own tail over and over again.

Black-and-white formica tables filled the room, but only four were occupied. Beyond the tables was a bandstand behind a tiny hardwood dance area. The people at the tables sat quietly, drinking beer and talking.

A person came up to greet me at the door. He, she–I'm not sure–wore a purple woolen dress not quite long enough to hide a thicket of leg hair. A blond wig framed dusky stubble, pushing its way through a carload of powder and rouge. "Can I help you?" a male voice asked.

"Yes. I'm with Huey Fortune."

"Oh, yes?" The transvestite looked me up and down. "You appear alone to me."

"Funny," I said, and reached into my pocket. "One's eyes *can* fool one, can't they?" I pressed a ten-pound note into her hand. "Tell Huey Fortune I want to talk to him about a rigid notation music box. Got that? Ri-gid no-ta-tion. If he doesn't want to talk to me, that's fine. Tell him I'll go someplace else to peddle my stuff. Whatever, you can keep the money."

The hostess looked down into her hand, then gave me a cutting smile. "Wait here a moment."

She minced across the floor to a table where two men and a woman–or at least so I thought–were sitting around a pitcher of beer. As the hostess bent over and spoke into the ear of one of the men, the man's entire body stiffened. He swung his chair around to look at me.

Carpe diem. I waved at him and called out, "Hello, Huey. Got a minute?"

He pushed roughly to his feet and charged past the hostess to confront me. "Hey, mate, who the hell are you? And what the hell d'you want?"

Huey Fortune was scarecrow-thin, with a face like a quarter-moon. His jutting chin seemed to rise in greeting to a shock of greasy black hair. Chin and cheeks were covered with a two-day crop of whiskers. He wore a red flannel shirt, and his shapeless black trousers were held up at the waist by a length of string. He smelled like a urinal that had also seen hard use as an ash tray.

"I'm either your friend or your enemy, Huey. Which, depends on you. I want to talk to you–about a rigid notation music box."

He shook his head. "Sorry. I on'y do repairs. You want to buy, go see Gordon and Maida, the Westfalls. Over by Gray's." He turned away to return to his table.

"You also ship music boxes," I said.

For an instant I had that same feeling of being watched, like in the Heathrow bathroom. I looked around the club: not more than eight people there. Most of them had turned to look at us, but it would have been strange had they not.

My remark froze Huey.

"And you pack. Like for instance four music boxes to Sophie Soleski. Just a few weeks ago, remember?" I motioned with my eyes toward the door. "Let's go outside and talk for a minute."

"Sod off. Buggering Yank. I ain't going nowhere."

"You're forgetting what I told you, Huey. I can be your friend or your enemy. I'm good at both. You'd better make the right choice."

He swallowed hard and smacked his lips. "Come over there." He pointed at his table. "You want to talk, we can talk there."

I shook my head. "I need to talk to you in private. You don't want anyone to hear what I've got to say. Kapeesh ... friend?"

"What the hell *is* this? Blackmail?"

"That's ugly. Not a nice thing to say to a friend." I moved toward the door. "Come on now, I don't have all night. If you're not interested, I know people who will be."

Have you ever seen a coyote look at a chunk of bait in a trap? *I* haven't; I'm a city boy. But I know what one would look like. It would look exactly like Huey Fortune at that moment.

He swallowed again, rubbed the back of a hand against his lips, and nodded twice, a firm one-two. "I'll get me coat."

I watched as he walked over to the table, pulled a ratty navy pea jacket off the back of his chair, and put it on. He said something that looked like "Back in a couple of minutes," and then came over to me. I nodded at the hostess, opened the front door for Huey, and followed him outside.

The door was barely shut when he wheeled to face me.

"Okay, mate, what's on your mind, eh? You're keeping me from my beer."

Early evening during Christmas week is not quiet on any street in London. People passed on both sides of us, moving quickly but still clearly taking us in. I steered Huey toward a narrow alley on the far side of the Sand Club building.

"I'm not in a hurry, which means neither are you. Let's go over there."

"This 'ere's good enough for me. Hey, what the bleedin' 'ell, are you? A copper?"

"No, but screw with me some more and that's who you *will* be talking to. If you can still talk." I grabbed his elbow, twisted it, and shoved at the small of his back. "Let's go."

A couple of passersby glanced, but no one moved to interfere. I was surprised at how little resistance Huey put up. Maybe strong-arm was the way to go with this bloke. I spun him around, shouldered him against the wall, and moved my face up close to his. Which definitely hurt me more than it did him. Neurologic patients don't always bathe and brush their teeth as often as Miss Manners might suggest, but Huey could have given the worst of them a strong run for the Big Pew Prize.

"Where'd you get it?"

"Get what?"

I twisted his collar tighter. He coughed; I moved my head sideways to avoid the soggy fallout. "The rigid notation box. The one you shipped to Sophie Soleski three weeks ago. Your memory's not that short. Where'd you get it?"

"From Mrs. Westfall, you bloody fool. I packed what she gave me."

I twisted again and rammed my fist into his Adam's apple. Not so hard as to keep him from talking–just enough to give him the clue that every bad story was going to make him increasingly uncomfortable. Huey coughed again.

"No you didn't. Mrs. Westfall gave you four boxes, but you packed only three of them. The fourth was a Nicole Freres overture box; you took it out and packed a Francois Nicole rigid notation box in its place. So, where ... did ... you ... get ... that ... rigid ... notation ... box?"

"I'll yell, mate. I'm gonna yell for help if you don't get your hands off my shirt."

I ratcheted up the throat pressure, then jumped to the side as he choked, gagged, and threw up onto the concrete.

"Okay. Yell. Go right ahead. Then you can talk to the cops, and Mr. and Mrs. Westfall, too. *And* me, by the way."

Huey's inflamed eyeballs beamed hatred at me.

"Where did you get the rigid notation box? You steal it?"

"No, you bugger. I didn't steal it." Righteous indignation from the falsely accused. "I bought it straight-out."

"You bought it? Who from?"

"Well, I ain't gonna tell you that–"

Right there in that dirty London alley I lost it. Without thinking, in an unpremeditated fashion and in cold blood, I hauled off and slugged Huey Fortune.

It was a hard right, straight to the mouth. I felt pain in my knuckles, but obviously nothing compared to what Huey felt. He let out a howl as the back of his head banged off the brick wall; then he threw his hand over his mouth. When he cautiously removed it and took a peek, he let out a whimper. He moaned and spat. I thought I heard a tooth bing onto the pavement.

It was dark in the alley, but my eyes were adapted well enough that I could see Huey was scared silly. Probably afraid I was going to kill him.

The notion appealed to me. I grabbed his collar and twisted hard. "Who'd you buy that rigid notation box from?" I snarled in a voice I could hardly believe was my own. I shoved him sharply, slamming his head into the wall again. He let out a cry of pain. "Talk, you bastard."

"Freddie Fellowes."

I was so surprised I loosened my hold. "Freddie Fellowes? You got that box from Fat Freddie?"

"Honest, mate, now that's the truth. You can ask 'im, go ahead."

Freddie Fellowes is the Grand Old Man of British music box collecting. You can ask 'im, go ahead. Freddie's lived seventy-five years, and has been collecting, writing, repairing, and lecturing on music boxes for more than fifty. The idea of Huey Fortune buying a rigid notation box from Freddie Fellowes was incongruous but not inconceivable. Freddie isn't independently wealthy, and every now and again an unrefusable offer has been known to separate him from a treasure. But a rigid notation box?

"How much did you pay him?"

"Twenty-five thousand," Huey gasped past my hand.

"Twenty-five thousand?" Little Sir Echo playing avenging angel. "Twenty-five thousand *pounds*?"

"Yeah, twenty-five thousand quid, that's what I said. Now let go o' me, huh?"

Twenty-five thousand pounds for a rigid notation box would set a world's record with room to spare.

Huey writhed. I tightened my hold. He gagged again but managed to not throw up. "You don't look like you've got twenty-five thousand pounds sitting around in your pocket. Who staked you?"

"Sophie Soleski," he groaned. "Let go o' me, mate, wouldja? I told you everything I know. Sophie sent me the money, said I should buy the rigid notation box from Freddie Fellowes and ship it to her wid the boxes from Mr. and Mrs. Westfall. She said make it right on the invoice. So I took out the Nicole Freres–sold that one at the Bermondsey Market, I did–and put in the Francois Nicole instead. That's how it happened."

Bad story. Harry's reputed purchase price was about two-thirds Sophie's. Would Soph use a rigid notation box as a loss leader?

I punched Huey again, this time square on the nose. His legs crumpled; I held him upright by his shirt collar. With my free hand, I slapped him hard alongside the cheek. "Who staked you? And for how much?"

"Oh, you bleeding bahstid," Huey moaned. "It was an American collector, in New York. Rich chap called Charlie O'Shacker."

I was glad for both the darkness in the alley and Huey's fear. Maybe he'd mistake the expression on my face for anger. "Charlie O'Shacker? You know him?"

Huey shook his head. "Never met 'im. He just rang me up one day, told me to get the rigid notation box from Freddie Fellowes, and ship it off to Sophie Soleski. Sent me twenty-five thousand quid and a little extra for meself. You can kill me if you want but that's the truth."

"Why did he want you to ship it to Sophie? Why not to him?"

"How the sodding hell am I supposed to know *that*?"

Freddie to Huey to Shackie to Sophie? My killer back in New York could easily have represented himself as Shackie over the phone to Huey. Another dead end. Still, I *had* traced the rigid notation box back another step. Maybe next was to talk to Freddie Fellowes.

As I loosened my hold on Huey he slumped against the wall. His breath came rapidly and noisily through his gaping mouth. Unaccustomed as I am to pounding hell out of recalcitrant British slimebags, I looked down in amazement at my sore knuckles–and at that moment a bell rang.

Or better, a series of bells, a small carillon of recognition. Huey had gone to the table to get his coat. The face of one of the men who'd been sitting with him suddenly clanged loud and clear. It was Mr. Big Teeth, the guy about to be circumcised in Wonder Bread between Wilma Ryan's choppers. Then I remembered the face of the second man who'd been getting the old Union Jack off. No question. It was Huey Fortune.

I made a grab for Huey's collar again.

"You friggin' barmy sod," he whimpered. "Why don't you just kill me and be done?"

He tried to duck down and away from me but I pulled him up short and gave the back of his head a quick tattoo against the wall. "That wouldn't be any fun. I like to see a little squirming first ... know what I mean? Who were those guys sitting at the table with you inside?"

"Nobody special; just two er me mates."

"What're their names? Start with the guy who likes to stick his business in hot dog rolls and let pretty girls eat it. The same chappie who gave you a hand getting the Union Jack off. Remember? Or does your memory need a little help?" I pressed my knee into his groin.

"Naw, oh Jesus. Don't do that. They're just me mates like I said. Harold Marley, he's the one in the pitchers wid me. The other bloke's Glenn Graham. Okay?"

"Almost. Don't give me any shit about you and your mates just having a nice little stag party. Who's the boss? The guy who takes the pictures and sends them out for blackmail? Quick, now."

"I don't know bleeding nothing about no blackmail, but the guy took the pictures, he's Little Willie MacIntosh. Owns the place. Ain't nothing wrong with what I did. All consentin' adults. Not a bad way to turn the odd quid."

Now I had some names and ideas. There were probably rooms in the back of the George Sand Club, photographic studios turning out porn pictures for consenting adults, with a hidden camera here and there to catch well-heeled suckers like Harry Hardwick. *Not a bad way to turn the odd quid.* It occurred to me to go back inside and see about having a talk with Little Willie Macintosh, but I told myself no. Whoever and whatever Little Willie might be, he was probably a tougher nut than Huey Fortune and I might blow the whole show right there. Maybe smarter to check out Freddie Fellowes first.

I let go of Huey. He cringed against the wall. I aimed a finger at his heart. "Don't take any trips. And don't talk about this, not to anyone. Keep your mouth shut and you'll be okay."

As I walked down the alley toward the lights of the street I could feel Huey's eyes broadcasting malevolence at my back. Maybe he didn't like Americans. Bloody prejudiced bahstid.

I got back to the Underground as quickly as I could and rode back to Dr. Watson's. The desk clerk smiled as I came through the door. "You're back early, sir."

"Shave and a haircut, two bits," I said.

"Excuse me, sir?"

"An American expression." I waved at him and chugged up the stairs to my room. I got Freddie Fellowes' phone number from Directory Assistance but when I dialed it there was no answer.

Ordinarily I'd have just assumed Freddie was out, but these were not ordinary circumstances. Still, I couldn't go over there as I had to Jackson George's and either pick a lock or wheedle my way inside. So I got undressed and into the shower, then tried Freddie's number again. Still no answer. I'd have to wait until morning. I locked my door, pulled back the covers, and went to sleep.

TWENTY-TWO

A quarter past seven next morning I was wide awake. Hardly a decent hour to call Freddie Fellowes. Then I remembered: it was Saturday. Belly Day. My feet were on the ground before I'd completed the thought.

The giant Saturday Portobello Road Antiques Market—why not? No reason to just sit in my room stewing. I shaved and was on the Underground by a quarter to eight, balancing coffee and a pastry from one of the little shops as I rode down the escalator to the trains.

The instant I came out of the Underground at Notting Hill Gate I heard a faint hum—Belly shoppers a few blocks away. I hustled along narrow sidewalks, darting here and there into the street where crowds were thick in front of souvenir shops. The closer I came, the louder the buzz.

As I turned into the head of the market the sound all at once intensified. Through white clouds of exhaled air, I looked down rows of stalls and shopfronts on either side of Portobello as far as I could see. The white clouds thickened. Portobello Road: what treasure might be waiting for *me*? I took a deep breath and plunged joyfully into the mob.

Time abandoned its hold on me. I floated through the narrow spaces of the arcades, watching, searching. It could have been June as easily as December, or eight o'clock at night rather than in the morning. I tried to remind myself I needed to call Freddie Fellowes but that seemed to be a demand from another world.

Halfway down the first side of the street and an hour and a half along, I spotted something. Mechanical musical items must be wound and sometimes the winding mechanisms can be subtle. This was one of those times. I was looking at an old silver fob bearing an elegant scripted initial, a P no less. Among its companions it stood out because of a stem rising through its midsection to end at the top in a little knob. A *winding* stem and a *winding* knob. I asked to see it more closely.

"A good one, that," said the dealer as he took it from the glass case and carefully handed it to me. "A bit dear, I'm afraid. Musical."

Too bad, but not unexpected. I pushed a little button below the winding knob, held the fob against the wall at the side of the booth, and brought my ear close. The tune lasted for nearly fifteen seconds and was quite nice. When it clicked to a stop I said, "How dear?"

The dealer was a bald fellow in his sixties, with a thin wolfish face and three small wens bulging from the left side of his scalp. He'd been at his business long enough that he could smell sincere interest. "Eight hundred," he said. "That's the best."

I frowned and pretended to study the fob. Then I played the music again.

"You don't find many of these," said the dealer. "I shouldn't hope to happen upon another soon."

I shrugged. "It *is* a nice one," I said. "But I have a couple–"

"You collect these?"

I shook my head no and extended my hand. Since being in trade still bars a lot of respectable London doors, English dealers are a jolly fraternal lot. "Thomas Purdue," I said. "Purdue's Musical Antiques, New York. I like to carry good things, but you know how it is. Not the demand for something like this there ought to be."

The dealer smiled weakly, a forced acknowledgement. Kiss up, kick down. More contemptible than a tradesman is a customer with taste only in his mouth.

"Still, I like it," I said. "Which has to count for something. What's the very best trade?"

He picked up a small cloth-covered ledger. It might have actually been his inventory or it could have been his horseracing bets or even meaningless scrawls on a page. No matter. All part of the game.

"How about six-fifty, Mr. Purdue?" he finally said. "I've six hundred into it myself."

That was better. I smiled and nodded, then peeled off bills. He tipped his hand to his head, wrapped tissue around the fob, and handed it to me. I thanked him and put it into my shirt pocket.

Hearing the fob had reminded me of Freddie Fellowes and why I'd come to London. More than a little reluctantly, I went outside and looked up and down the street. Nearly directly across was a pub, the Earl of Lonsdale. I crossed and went in.

The smoke was blinding, the noise deafening. Fortunately the phone was up front, just inside the door. I dialed Freddie Fellowes' number. This time he answered.

"Freddie, this is Thomas Purdue. From New York."

There was a silent moment, then recognition exploded. "Oh ... Thomas. My word! How are you?"

"Fine, Freddie." At least so far, I thought.

"Where *are* you? I can barely hear you past the noise."

"I'm in a pub. On the Belly."

"Ah, the Belly, yes. You're here in London, then?"

Foolish questions, you should answer them in line. I'm traveling in Europe, I'm in Bingen on the Rhine. But I replied in my most civil manner, if a bit loud. "Yes. Freddie, listen. I came to London because I need to talk to you. May I please drop by for a few minutes? At your convenience."

In the United States, impromptu visits among collectors

are commonplace. But in England ... well, that sort of thing just isn't *done*. Which I knew, but what choice did I have? I couldn't very well ask Freddie to schedule me in some time after the holiday rush. So his answer wasn't altogether unexpected. "Well, my dear fellow. It would be just lovely to see you, don't you know. But this *is* rahther short notice–"

"I know it's short notice. I wouldn't ordinarily do things this way but I'm involved in a terribly urgent situation. Literally a matter of life and death."

"Well, my word! Quite a necessity, then, you'd say?"

"Right. I would say and I do. Please: how soon may I come over?"

"Life and death, my, my. Would one o'clock be satisfact'ry?"

Three hours from then. But Freddie was seventy-five years old and English. This was his limit of adaptability to a breach of etiquette. If I'd said I was hemorrhaging he'd have probably encouraged me to put on a tourniquet, keep a stiff upper lip, and come by at one PM. I thanked him and said I'd see him at one.

Back outside, the Belly was bustling. I was here; I had nothing else to do. Might as well stroll through the rest of the market.

An hour or so later hunger growled, sending me into a little sandwich shop. Nothing fancy, not on The Belly. White counter, little round white tables, people ebbing and flowing everywhere. I bought a cup of coffee and a Welsh pasty, which they whipped in and out of a microwave just long enough to get clots out of the grease. I sat down at a table and sipped at the coffee.

Absent-mindedly, I reached inside my pocket, pulled out the wad of tissue paper, and unwrapped the fob. I wound the stem a couple of times, set the fob down on the wooden table, and listened to its lovely arrangement of a 200-year-old French folk tune. Using one-third the teeth on a modern small Japanese or Swiss movement, some anonymous watchmaker of the early nineteenth century had created a piece of musical art. That watchmaker knew in his heart and guts what he did mattered. If he were alive and in his shop today, he'd be labeled a workaholic and advised to seek counseling.

As the music stopped I picked up the tissue paper to rewrap the fob but my hand was arrested by a question. "May I see that, please?"

A young woman had settled into the chair next to mine and she was staring at my fob with an enormous pair of green eyes. Her smile was luminous. I handed her the fob; she examined it carefully. "I've never seen one of these to be musical," she said. "Would you mind playing it again?"

I leaned in her direction and pushed the button on the fob. "Put it on the table," I said. "That amplifies the sound. Then put your ear down to it."

I watched her listen. With her head full of soft brown ringlets she looked like an enchanted child. As long as the music played she seemed to not be breathing. When it stopped she looked back at me. "Oh, that is just marvelous! *So* beautiful." She inspected the fob more closely. "And it's ... I should say circa eighteen hundred?"

"Right on. Very impressive."

She blushed, just enough. "We frequently have fine mechanical musical items in stock. Snuff boxes, watches, singing birds—but I've never come upon a musical fob. It's wonderful."

"You're a dealer?"

She nodded. "My da, mum, and I have a little place down Kensington Church Street, not a half-hour's walk from here. They watch the shop; you know how it is. They're older."

I looked at her. Mid-twenties, I guessed. "Sure. About my age, right?"

She colored up again, very pretty. "Oh good heavens, no. They had me late. Mum was forty when I was born and Da was forty-three. That must be about what you are now."

"Close enough," I said. We both smiled.

"Anyway, I go about, finding the stock. That's ever so much more fun than staying in the shop."

No argument there. "Buying *is* more fun than selling."

She extended her hand. "My name's Teresa," she said, pronouncing it Tuh-ray-zuh. "Teresa Carpenter." She snapped her purse open, fumbled inside for a moment, and came out with a business card. Carpenters Three Antiques, it said. Number Twenty-three-A Kensington Church Street, London. Vernon, Maisie, and Teresa Carpenter. High-quality small goods.

"Thomas Purdue," I said and shook her hand. "From New York."

"I could tell by your accent. Interested in these things, are you?"

At last the pitch. I couldn't help smiling as I nodded agreement.

"You're in the trade?"

I caught the ball and flipped it right back. "Purdue's Musical Antiques."

"Well, then. We have some really lovely things at the shop right now. Several snuffs, two or three early musical boxes. And a magnificent piano-shaped *necessaire* of tortoise shell and ivory decorated all round with marvelous gold metalwork. With a very fine miniature cylinder music-works and the complete original set of Palais Royal implements, gold and mother-of-pearl."

I raised my eyebrows. Teresa had just described a woman's fitted needlework box, roughly of the same age as my fob, an elegant creation of the artisans in posh shops near the old Palais Royal in Paris. Most *necessaires* were cased in wood; a gold-decorated tortoise shell case would have been exceptional. An early piece, highly desirable. Something to make my jaws ache.

"Sounds interesting, but I don't know whether I'd be able to buy it with enough room for resale."

Teresa smiled in a way that gave new meaning to the word fetching. "I shouldn't be too certain. Da and Mum prefer to deal with trade and they like to do lot-sales. Come by and see what they've got, why don't you?"

I checked my watch. "I need to be in North Kensington at one."

"Oh, heavens. No bother there. The shop's walking distance–come on, then." She took me by the elbow. "We can be there in not more than twenty minutes."

As we made our way toward the head of the market Teresa chattered away about how she'd been in the antiques game all her life, born to the trade, so to speak. By the time she was ten she was a fully qualified salesgirl, by twelve a master picker.

We turned out of the market area onto Chepstow Villas, walking more rapidly now that we were away from the crowds. Teresa was telling me about the time she'd socked it to a couple of slimy dealers who were so foolish as to think they could foist a load of faked ivories onto a cute little fourteen-year-old popsie. Teresa was gesturing with her hands and stepping high, pocketbook swinging frantically from her right shoulder, when all of a sudden she stopped and said, "Oh!"

I asked what was the matter.

"Nothing quite the matter. I just realized: Da and Mum will be off to lunch right now; they aren't expecting me 'til later this afternoon. Let me stop up to the flat"–she pointed toward the third floor of the building we were approaching–"I'll pick up my shop key. Take just a moment, I promise. Come along."

I followed her up five whitewashed stairs through an unlocked door into a small vestibule. A single bulb in an unshaded ceiling fixture gave off more shadow than light; every movement we made was transformed into grotesque undulations on the yellowed plaster walls. To the right were four mailboxes, presumably one for the inhabitants of each floor. At the far end of the vestibule was a second door, this one with clear glass for its upper panel. Teresa led me through it into a second, inner, vestibule. A few steps to our left, a metal stairway ran upward and out of sight. No elevator. Carpenters Three Antiques couldn't have been heavy in the carriage trade, I remember thinking.

Teresa unsnapped the lock on her purse. "Do you want me to wait here?" I asked.

Her smile dazzled me. "No, of course not. No need of that. Just let me get my key and up we go."

I'm still not sure exactly what happened then. The room seemed to implode. A sharp impact knocked me off balance, then there was a rain of glass as the door panel flew into pieces. I hunched against the wall, covering my head as well as I could with my arms and hands. I saw Teresa's purse sail into the air; she let out an odd grunt and flew back against the opposite wall.

Somewhere in the back of my mind I wondered whether London had been hit by a massive earthquake. As I lowered my hands and moved away from the wall, the shattered door slammed open and a very large man came lumbering through with surprising speed. He was at least six-four and had probably 250 pounds packed under a dark blue topcoat. Atop his head perched a classic black English bowler. He looked familiar but I couldn't sort out where I might have seen him, primarily because he was pointing a huge handgun at my chest.

"Don't move if you please, Dr. Purdue. Put your hands up on top of your head, there's a good fellow."

I did as I was told. I realized I wasn't breathing, and reminded myself there was no need to practice that; it would come quite naturally. But I was afraid to make any movement at all. Whether or not this English grizzly bear really needed any excuse to blow me away, I wasn't at all inclined to provide him one.

The big man moved quickly toward Teresa, who was now crumpled on the floor against the opposite wall. As idiotic as it sounds, it occurred to me then for the first time she might be hurt. The man bent from the waist and rummaged through her purse, all the while keeping his gun directed straight at me.

"Never mind, Dr. Purdue," he said. "You're quite ... ah! Here we are." He straightened up and turned full-face to me.

Could a situation ever get worse? Now the man was pointing two pistols at my chest. The second was a dwarf by comparison to the bazooka he'd dashed in with. Still, I had no doubt it could do a fine job of ventilating me if he twitched his trigger finger.

"Well, then," the man said. "As I was saying: you're now quite safe. She was going to kill you. See?" By way of emphasis he elevated the little gun ever so slightly.

Before I could mobilize my larynx into a reply the man gave me a quick pat-down, then lowered his weapons and shoved them away inside his coat. He motioned me toward the door.

"I think we'd best get away from here. My gun was silenced, of course. But someone may've heard the glass break."

My hands came slowly down off the top of my head; it was as if they'd frozen there. What the man said sank in by degrees: "My gun was silenced, of course." I looked down at Teresa. Her face was like white library paste and her eyes were wide open, staring at something I couldn't see. Perfectly placed in the middle of her forehead was a dark spot ringed by wormy streaks of drying blood. The wall was densely speckled red above and behind her at the level her head would've been when she was hit.

"Who *are* you?" I whispered.

The man smiled warmly. "Broadway Schwartz asked me to keep watch on you. He thought you might find yourself a bit of trouble."

It's nice to have friends. Especially friends with friends in places like this. "You're Al Resford? Big Al?"

He bowed almost imperceptibly, then opened the door and motioned me through. "I really must insist. It would be the worst of form to be here when someone comes in, don't you know."

For the first time, I noticed Big Al was wearing gray calfskin gloves. What the properly-dressed English gentleman will wear when he's out to kill a young woman and leave no fingerprints.

We hurried through the doorway into the first vestibule

and outside. A middle-aged couple walked past, the man's arms full of packages. The woman carried a green plastic shopping bag, loaded past the top.

"A good day at the Belly, I see," Al said genially.

The couple smiled at him.

I tried to mobilize enough saliva to stop my tongue and throat from sticking together. Talk about *savoir faire*. If Big Al was disturbed in the least by having just transformed a lovely young woman into Purina Buzzard Chow, he showed not the slightest evidence of it. He steered me in the direction we'd come. "Let's go back to The Earl of Lonsdale," he said. "P'aps you might like a drink."

The pub was packed. We worked our way up to the bar, took our pints and paid, then edged over to a narrow shelf inside a window.

"Crowds're the place to be if it's anonymity you're after. But you know that, of course. In New York no one has a clue what you're about, eh? But live in a small town and every time you have a few too many or try for a bit of fluff behind the wife's back–why, the entire populace knows practically before you've even done it, what?" He lifted his glass and clinked the edge against mine. "Chazz."

"Cheers," I said and took a long swallow, which seemed to set my brain back into motion. "I *have* seen you before–at Heathrow, in the bathroom. You were standing two washbasins away. And last night at the George Sand Club. You were at a table there, too."

"Oh, yes." Al's tone was casual. "And I watched while you uh, talked to Huey Fortune in the alley. But I wasn't required to come forth until today, was I?"

I felt embarrassed. "I got careless."

Al just smiled. He didn't have to say anything and was generous enough not to.

"But who *was* she? I mean ... the woman ..." I looked around. No one seemed to be listening.

"Teresa"–he too pronounced it Tuh-ray-zuh–"Carpenter. A bad one, all right."

"Did Huey Fortune put her onto me?"

"I'd say both yes and no. Huey probably hired her but not on his own screw. Huey's always servant, never master–you could see that for yourself last night, I'm sure. Teresa was taking you to Da and Mum's shop, wasn't she? To show you some magnificent antique–just as soon as she'd picked up her shop key."

I laughed. It wasn't funny but I laughed.

"Yes. Well. Da was a first-class blaggard from up Liverpool way. Mean, don't you know. He took care of difficult customers for years at Eddy the Weasel's card and dice room. Made only one mistake, that was getting a bit rough one night with a young MP, enough to break his neck and leave him paralyzed from the neck down. So Da's got lifetime lodgings at the state B and B up in Dartmoor. Mum was always, you'll pardon me, just a bit of the 'ore, but after they sent Da up she went badly to the bottle. She's in Brighton now, runs a rooming house ... well, that's what she calls it. Little Tuhrayzuh learned all she could from them both. And good, she was; I'll give her that."

Just then a cadaverous older man with a bristly cleft jaw shuffled past. He gave Big Al a friendly salute and said, "Howyer, Hedgey."

Al acknowledged him with a nod. "'Afternoon, Mick." Al looked at me and smiled. "Hedgey. People call me The Hedgehog."

Now that he mentioned it he did bear a resemblance, what with his round body tapering into a smallish head, virtual absence of neck, and slitty but attentive eyes. "What'll happen when they find Teresa ... er, Teresa's body?"

Big Al shrugged. "They'll investigate. But they'll find naught. It will go unsolved, just another underworld killing. Never mind."

I looked at my watch. It was twenty minutes to one. "How much of this business do you know?"

"Schwartz filled me in quite well, I should say," Al said. "And I believe I've not missed anything whilst you've been about your affairs over here. You need to be at Freddie Fellowes' at one, what? We'd best be on our way."

I didn't ask what he meant by we. I just drained my glass, got up, and followed him out to the street.

TWENTY-THREE

London's tough on the fixed-income crowd. Most older people there have two alternatives: move out to the country or go the genteel poverty route. Freddie Fellowes had taken Choice Number Two.

Freddie's place in North Kensington was in a mixed commercial neighborhood, shops on ground level and walk-up flats above. When he opened the door to our knock Freddie had on a white shirt and a carefully knotted plaid bow tie. But his blue sweater was frayed at the cuffs and unraveling over the left elbow.

"Well, Thomas." He greeted me with a firm handshake. "I'm glad to see you."

Freddie's face had the whitish cast of an old man who didn't often go out-of-doors. When I'd called a few hours before, he could have told me to just come right over, but then look at all the fun I'd have missed. He glanced past me to Big Al.

"Mr. Al Resford," I said. "My *very* good friend. Mr. Resford, Mr. Freddie Fellowes."

The two round men, one short, the other tall, shook hands and told each other they were delighted.

"Freddie, I don't want to impose on you more than is strictly necessary. Mr. Resford is ... uh, helping me with the problem I mentioned when I called you. Please feel comfortable with him here."

"Oh, yes, yes." Freddie rubbed his chin reflectively. His cheeks were smooth as a baby's. Prostate cancer, orchiectomy? I'd never know. The English cling to the quaint notion that all of a person's body parts ought to be considered private. More power to them.

Freddie jabbed a stubby finger. "You said this was urgent, Thomas? Matter of life and death, I believe were your words."

I shot a quick look at The Hedgehog. His little smile told me he'd not missed the joke.

"Yes," I said. "You see–"

"Hold on a moment." Freddie waved me silent. "Come in; sit down. We needn't stand talking in the hallway. Would you care for a drink?"

"Thanks, but we've just had a pint," I said. "Maybe later."

"Suit yourself, suit yourself."

We followed Freddie as he waddled into his living room. Instant transport through time, sixty years vanished. Dark mahogany chairs and a sofa heavily upholstered in green pile. In the far corner a large console radio–excuse me, wireless–with waterfall façade. Antimacassars applied more or less evenly to the arms of each chair and couch. These were the furnishings Freddie had put together when he'd left school and set up housekeeping; he'd never updated. But that had left him with more discretionary cash, and where *that* had gone was abundantly clear. The entire far wall was filled with shelves holding fifty or sixty fine cylinder music boxes. A few especially attractive ones were scattered on table tops throughout the room.

I sat next to a magnificent Nicole cylinder box; the engraved brass plate inside the lid told me it played a spectacular four-tune program of theme-and-variations pieces.

Freddie chuckled as he noticed me peering into the case. "That's all right; you may turn it on."

I pushed the start lever and *Last Rose of Summer* began to play. Big Al looked around the room, pointed at a drawing on the wall behind Freddie. "I say, is that a Rembrandt? The–"

Freddie silenced him with a glare that would have stopped a fully-wound clock. "Let us not have conversation whilst the musical box is playing, sir. This is *not* piped-in music."

Al nodded an apology. I smiled to myself. We sat silent and properly attentive for the remainder of the three-minute performance. The tune ended in a flourish, notes rushing madly up one part of the comb and down another.

As the stop-arm clicked into place, Freddie turned to Al, smiled amiably, and said, "No, Mr. Resford, I'm sorry to say it is not an original Rembrandt. Nice copy, though, isn't it?"

Al returned Freddie's smile. No hard feelings.

I coughed. "I appreciate your letting us come by, Freddie. I've got a real problem."

"Yes, so you said. Matter of life and death ... just how do you suppose I might be able to help?"

"You've heard about Harry Hardwick? And Charles O'Shacker?"

"Yes, quite. Shocking situation, what? Murder over a musical box? Unthinkable."

"It's getting worse. There's been another murder, day before yesterday. Jackson George."

Clearly, Freddie had *not* heard. His eyes bulged; his jaw dropped. "You don't say! Jackson Jawhdge, murdered as well? Over a musical box?"

"Not just any music box. To be specific, a rigid notation box. To be even more specific, Francois Nicole, Number Four-thirty-two."

Freddie never would have made a living hustling poker or pool. He appeared to be chewing on his thoughts. Then he looked straight into my gaze, eyes weighted with painful understanding. "Hmm, yes. I see why you've come here, now, don't I?"

"I'm afraid so. Not that I think you're involved in any way beyond the fact you owned and sold a music box which somebody wants in a terrible way. I'm hoping you can tell me something to help me find that somebody."

"I'll do what I can. But I simply can't imagine–"

"Let's start with Huey Fortune," I said. "He told me he gave you twenty-five thousand pounds for the box. Is that true?"

"Too true. Yes, he offered me twenty-five thousand; I was simply staggered. Mind you, it's an extraordinary musical box. But twenty-five thousand pounds? Huey said he'd a client who was keen to have it and money was not an object. Odd, that, I thought: one wouldn't think of Huey Fortune as quite the fellow to have such a client. But it *is* a funny game, collecting. So ... considering I owned two rigid notation boxes ..." He held out his hands helplessly.

"So you sold it. No one can blame you for that. Do you have any idea who that wealthy client of Huey's might have been?"

Freddie shook his head. "None whatever. Huey never mentioned his name and of course I never ..."

Again, his voice trailed out in a tone of annoyance and frustration. One doesn't intrude–but then one doesn't have important information when it's needed. The English Channel is full of rocks and hard places, two being unseemly probing and undue reticence.

"Of course, you didn't ask," I finished for him.

Freddie nodded sadly. "No. Huey had the money with him, five hundred fifty-pound notes in a plastic gymnasium satchel. We sat here and counted them out. Then he took away the rigid notation box, and I went straight-off to my safety deposit box ... Oh, I say." Panic was suddenly smeared all over his face. "You won't mention this to anyone, I trust." He looked at Big Al. "I mean ... Inland Revenue, that sort of thing."

"It's our secret, Freddie," I said. "But is that the whole story? Huey came in, paid you, took the rigid notation box, and left? Just like that?"

He said yes, then paused. "Hold on ... there *was* one thing, now you mention it. Immediately Huey was leaving he asked to use the toilet back there, behind my miniatures display room. He went, came back, and was gone in two shakes. All told he was not here longer than a quarter-hour."

Miniatures, I thought. Freddie Fellowes and his tiny treasures.

Jackson George and *his* tiny treasures.

Bingo.

Shackie's remark came back in a rush of comprehension. Pierre Legrande had told him what was wrong with the rigid notation box. Pierre Legrande, Francois Nicole's apprentice.

"Freddie," I said slowly. "There wasn't anything odd about the sound of that rigid notation box, was there? Was the music at all unbalanced–louder in some parts of the comb and softer in others?"

"Certainly not!" It was difficult to keep from smiling. I might as well have asked whether there was truth in the rumor his mother was a dowdy tart. "It played perfectly."

"Fine. Next thing: You haven't sold any miniatures recently, have you?"

"What? Oh, good heavens, no. I don't sell my miniatures at all. Never."

"Not to make you anxious, Freddie, but you didn't notice any missing after Huey left?"

"Good Christ! Oh, my word!" He was suddenly on his feet, running. "I hadn't considered that ... yes, he *did* go through there, didn't he? I certainly hope–"

Off he shuffled into the miniatures room, Al and I following. Freddie flipped the light switch as he entered, then stood in the doorway and looked around.

The display was beautifully laid-out on shelves built into all four walls. Ceiling track lights illuminated angles and corners. Every space on every shelf was filled with miniature music machines. There were snuff boxes, singing bird boxes, watches and small clocks, not to mention *necessaires* and miniature automata. I saw vinaigrettes, seals, and fobs. The idea of a thief loose there, or worse, a fire, made my chest tighten.

Freddie shaded his eyes and swiveled his head, looking for all the world like one of Vichy's comical automatons. He circled the room, peering into each shelf unit, left to right, top to bottom. His breathing was rapid and loud, almost a snore.

He finished examining the room, then released a huge sigh. "Nothing missing." He strolled to a small, round mahogany table at the middle of the room. "Four of my most outstanding pieces–and all here, I'm pleased to see."

I felt disappointed. It had seemed such a good idea.

Big Al scrutinized the four outstanding pieces, leaning forward from the waist and rocking slowly back and forth like a gigantic brain-damaged child. He hummed softly–"Greensleeves," I thought. Then he looked up at Freddie. "I say, these *are* elegant. Could you demonstrate them for me–would you mind terribly?" Mischief rose up in his eyes and spread out from the corners of his mouth. "I promise to be perfectly still while they're operating."

"Oh, pooh, pooh. Certainly. Of course."

Al's smile flickered just a bit brighter as Freddie picked up a small golden box and held it toward us. "A singing bird by Bruguier. Case gold, twenty-four-karat, with a beautiful chased design, as you can see. The bird's feathering is as good as any and it moves wings, tail, beak, *and* head. Listen carefully to the song. It begins as an intricate nightingale tune, then becomes an actual melody. Then nightingale song again. Watch closely."

Freddie pushed a small lever on the front of the case. From beneath an enameled elliptical lid a tiny bird popped up. With its complex movements, elaborate song, and iridescent green-and-blue feathers, the bird really did look and sound alive.

"Lovely," Al said as the bird dropped back into the case at the end of its performance.

"You like that?" Freddie smiled. "Look: here's a treasure for you. So to speak, of course."

He opened the box. Inside lay a treasure, all right: a tiny pistol made of gold and decorated tastefully with rubies, emeralds, and diamonds.

"Bird-pistol, Freddie?" I asked.

Miniatures don't come more elegant than the rare bird-pistols, manufactured during the late eighteenth and early nineteenth centuries by such master craftsmen as the Jaquet-Droz, father and son, and Jean Frederic Leschot. These tiny guns were molded and shaped in gold, in perfect proportion and complete in detail. Pull the trigger and a tiny bird flies out from the end of the barrel to sing its song. One of these baubles sold not that long ago at a European auction for well over a million dollars.

"Not exactly a *bird*-pistol, I'm afraid." Freddie, still in mischief mode. "'Tis actually a bit naughty. One pulls the trigger and out pop a man and woman. They then recline, you might say, and go through the motions of ... sexual congress. And all the while there's music from a very nice platform movement concealed within the handle. When the music stops, the lovers slide back inside the gun barrel. Charming piece."

"Wait a minute," I said. "Freddie ... you're not going to tell me this is the Farouk pistol?"

He flushed with pleasure. "Yes, quite. Astute of you to recognize it."

When King Farouk of Egypt was deposed in 1952, his incredible collection of mechanical music and automata was seized by the state and as the museum folks like to put it, de-acquisitioned. Somehow, Fat Freddie Fellowes was lucky or clever enough to pick up the erotic pistol.

"I've seen pictures of it in books," I said. "But I had no idea it was here."

"Well, my dear boy. It's not quite something one advertises, don't you know."

Understandable. Mechanical music values have skyrocketed during the past thirty years, and whatever Freddie paid for his treasure was peanuts compared to its present value. Three million dollars? Five? Certainly enough to keep an old man alive and in luxury for more years than he could possibly have left. But Freddie was a collector. To sell his Farouk pistol would be to sell his soul and toss in his heart as a premium. If the bobbies ever find Freddie Fellowes starved and frozen to death on the street, when they break down his rigor mortis they'll find a little gold pistol clutched firmly to the left side of his chest.

I extended one finger to touch the little pistol in its wooden case. Why? Why do people scramble through mobs to touch a politician or a pop singer? Why do they rub religious icons? A warm current seemed to flow into my hand, up my arm, and across my face. I stroked the pistol, first with one finger, then two. I felt as if my cheeks were flaming.

Freddie watched me, all sympathy. He understood.

Talk about a passion to kill for!

"Can you play it for us?" I asked him.

I saw pain in his eyes. "Awfully sorry, it's stopped working. Most upsetting. I must have it set right as soon as possible."

"Pity, that," said Al. "Might I examine it a bit more closely?"

"Certainly." Freddie took the pistol from its velvet-lined case and passed it to Al. The big man walked to the window, held the pistol up to light, and squinted at it. Then he laid it carefully on the mahogany side table below the window ledge and turned it this way and that. He peered up the barrel. Finally, he scrutinized the grip and made a final scan of the trigger region.

"Marvelous," he said, handing it carefully back to Freddie. "Simply amazing. Shame we can't see it in operation."

I couldn't have agreed more.

The third and fourth items on the table were a gorgeous musical automaton-watch and a wonderful *necessaire* in a case of gold-embellished tortoise shell, with a superb two-tune musical cylinder, circa 1815. Freddie tried to make up for the pistol by playing them for us but disappointment was inevitable. When the music stopped, I apologized for having burst in on him and thanked him for his help.

He waved me off. "No, no. Nothing of the sort. But I'm afraid I didn't add much to what you already knew when you got here, did I?"

"He really didn't," I said to Al.

We were sitting in a coffee shop on the way back to the Underground. "For a while there I thought I was onto something."

"Yes? Something like what?"

I felt silly but saw no way around it. "It had to do with Freddie's miniatures and what Shackie said about Francois Nicole's apprentice. The story is, in the old Swiss workshop system, apprentices were responsible for putting cement in music box cylinders to hold the pins in place and enrich the sound. Now, suppose when Huey went to the toilet he stuck a valuable miniature into his pocket, ran back to his shop, melted the cement out of the rigid notation box cylinder, and stuffed the miniature inside in its place. That would have unbalanced the sound of the music: It would've been louder where the miniature was stashed and softer where the cylinder was empty. *That* could explain why someone would've paid twenty-five thousand pounds for a music box and sold it for twenty-two thousand, five hundred dollars—after he'd taken out the miniature and put back the cement. But none of Freddie's miniatures were missing."

Al put down his cup. "Tell me, would that Farouk pistol have fit inside the cylinder of that particular musical box?"

I squinted into my mind's eye. "Yes, I think it would. The cylinder is twelve inches long and three inches in diameter. And the pistol wasn't more than four inches long and two, maybe two-and-a-half, inches wide, was it?"

"I shouldn't think so. P'aps your idea wasn't such a bad one after all."

"But the pistol—"

"—was a forgery."

All I could do was stare at him.

"Oh, yes." He chuckled. "The gold was plate, the stones glass. The barrel blind-ended about two inches up. I'd say our friend Huey *did* engineer an exchange there. Had he simply walked off with the genuine article, Mr. Fellowes would have noticed it right off and taken action. Clever, what?"

I felt pathetic. In not quite four hours Big Al Resford had made more progress than I'd made in a week, not to mention saving my life in the bargain.

"Al, please don't be insulted–but you *are* sure?"

Al smiled tolerantly and opened his huge hand to show me a straight pin with a tiny finger grip. "I always carry a few necessary tools in my pocket. This one's most useful. Bit of a scratch on the pistol grip uncovered cast base metal beneath gold leaf. Then up the barrel with the pin and as I said, the chamber ended blind. As to the jewels, well, I should say I *know* jewels. Right off I was quite certain they were not genuine. In the good light by the window it was obvious."

"Maybe Freddie bought a fake, years ago."

"A knowledgeable chap like him?" Al shook his head. "Not at all likely, I should say. He'd have looked it over too closely. I suspect Mr. Fellowes simply never made the connection between Huey's visit and the pistol's going out of order."

I don't know whether hedgehogs swallow canaries, but judging by Al's expression they might.

"There's another thing," he said. "It happens to be a fine forgery, really a lovely piece of work. Nine chances out of ten it was done by a fellow named Werner Ross. Had all his earmarks."

I practically upset my chair standing up. "There's where we can make the connection! Is Ross here in London?"

"Best slow down." Big Al smiled and pointed at my chair. "There, that's better. Now. For one thing I doubt Werner Ross could've added to our knowledge. Probably Huey was no more than messenger there as well. Brought Werner the money, took away the forgery."

"You said 'could've added'?"

"Yes, that's the second thing. Werner Ross died recently."

"How did he die?"

"Most unfortunate. Poor fellow had a heart condition. Seems to have had a dizzy spell, p'aps even a heart attack, and fell into his open forge. The workshop burned to the ground. Not much left of either it *or* Werner. Not a pretty picture, I'm afraid."

"Oh, great. When did that happen?"

"Just last evening. A little before midnight."

"In other words shortly after I talked to Huey Fortune."

Al nodded. "Odd coincidence, that. Accidents will happen, don't you know."

"Wait a minute." I'd hardly heard Al's last remark; his earlier comment was stuck in my ear, refusing to move aside for its successors. "'Not a pretty picture,' you said."

Al looked puzzled.

"About Werner and his workshop."

"Oh ... well, yes, I suppose I did. What of it?"

"You reminded me." I pulled photographs out of my pocket and handed them across the table to Big Al. "These were hidden in a box in Harry Hardwick's library."

Al's hooded eyes widened as he shuffled through the pictures. "Oh dear me," he said, and cocked his head to look at me in mock consternation. "Well, Little Willie. You've been naughty with your camera, now, haven't you?"

"Little Willie MacIntosh. Huey told me his name. The one who took the pictures."

"Took them, developed them, and sold them. Willie's a busy little man."

"I'd sure like to know who he sold them to."

Al lumbered to his feet. "Come along, then. You do have a few hundred-pound notes you could bear to part with, don't you?"

TWENTY-FOUR

Little Willie McIntosh's office was behind the bandstand at the George Sand Club. If Willie was there and listening the night before, he might have heard me pounding Huey Fortune's head against the wall outside. I doubt he'd have done anything about it, though: Little Willie didn't look like a peacemaker. His hair was brick-colored wire and he was missing his left central incisor. Tight charcoal trousers, shiny yellow silk shirt. I suspected Willie spent a great deal more of his school time in the principal's office than in the classroom.

If Willie's office was a fair indication he was also not a man to make pretenses. It was barren, walls mildly jaundiced with years of accumulated cigarette tar. Before Al had finished introductions Willie was already on his second smoke. He sat in a creaky swivel chair behind a cheap oak desk, its finish scratched and gouged scabrous. The only decoration was a picture-calendar on the wall to Willie's left, featuring a scantily-dressed young woman with a wrench in one hand and a dirty rag in the other, leaning over the hood of a little British car and saying, "Let us grease your valves and adjust your pistons." Willie must have liked the picture or the caption. It was a 1974 calendar.

Willie thumbed through the photographs I'd handed him, then pushed them carelessly back across his desk. They slid apart like a fan of cards. He studied me with eyes the color of a northern Minnesota pond in January, blew a mouthful of smelly smoke in my direction, then looked at Big Al.

"Never mind, Willie. You can tell him what he wants to know. Mat'r'fact I think 'twould be well if you do."

I wondered what it would take to cause Al to lose his aplomb and decided I didn't ever want to find out.

Willie leaned forward to rest his elbows on the desk top. "It'll be five hundred, mate."

"Five hundred pounds?"

"Aye." Willie regarded me with humorous contempt. "Coin of *our* realm, eh?"

I took ten fifty-pound notes out of my wallet and slid them across the desk. Willie's right hand came forward and picked them up like one of those metal-claw hands in an arcade game. Without taking his eyes off me he shoveled the bills into his shirt pocket.

"Worth the price," I said. "If the merchandise is sound."

Willie's face darkened toward scarlet but Al moved quickly. "*You* never mind, Thomas," he said. "You'll get proper value. Willie and I've known each other for a very long time. Ask him your questions."

Willie, sneering, leaned back in his seat. The chair gave a creaky protest.

"All right, Willie—these pictures. Huey Fortune said you took them."

"Huey talks more than's good for him. I'm sorry you didn't split his bloody beezer wide open last night. But, aye, 'twas me took the pictures, all of them. What of it?"

Al's avuncular smile didn't waver.

"I found them hidden in Harry Hardwick's library. You may or may not know, but someone killed Harry last week, along with a few other people. It might help me find the killer if I knew who bought the pictures from you."

Willie didn't blink. "Harry did."

"What?" The stupidity in my own voice embarrassed me.

"Harry bought 'em. The ones of him and Muriel, he bought 'em right after I took 'em, negatives and all. The other ones I sent him just last month. He didn't want the negatives for *them*, though. Just wanted every shot I had of *her*." He pointed at Wilma Ryan in the Union Jack-off picture.

"But why?" I asked. "What did he want them for?"

Willie spread his arms wide, palms up. "I don't ask customers questions, mate. People've got reasons. That's good enough for me."

"Who is she? You know her?"

Little Willie pursed his lips and clucked his tongue. "Name's Wilma Ryan," he said. "She ain't one of my regulars. Just something Huey Fortune drags in once or twice a year."

"Huey really gets around."

"Pfah." Willie's expression suggested Huey Fortune might be a plate of liver and broccoli. He dismissed the vision with a wave of his hand. "People come and go. I can't know 'em all."

"Okay. When was it you took the pictures of Wilma?"

"Last time she was here. September, I think. Yeah, that's right. Second week in September."

"How about the pictures of Harry and Muriel?"

"Mmm, lemme see." Willie stared at the blank ceiling. "Must've been ... oh, four, maybe five years ago. Close as I can come."

"Right about the time he married her," I said.

Willie leered at the world. "Aye. I told Muriel she was suckin' her way into a bloody lot of money that week." He shook his head and chuckled. "Right good girl that Muriel. Pretty and smart and a lot of fun, you know what I mean."

I nodded.

"She was a bleedin' lot better than Harry deserved, the phony bastard."

"Phony? I always figured Harry for a pretty straight guy."

Little Willie slapped his thigh and laughed. He rocked back and forth in his chair, then wiped around his eyes with a dirty handkerchief. "Oh, mate, that's a good one. Harry Hardwick straight? Maybe he was straight enough back in

New York, but when he went away he–what is it you Yanks say?–he let it all hang out. Four or five years ago he was getting ready to dump his second wife. Guess Muriel looked good to him."

"So you got him with a hidden camera. And the negatives went with the pictures for top dollar–sorry. Top pound."

"No, no." Straight-up in his chair, Willie waved off my conclusion. "No hidden cameras, mate, never. Harry *liked* doin' it for a camera and he liked havin' his little souvenir to look at afterwards. Far as the negatives go, he just wanted to make sure nobody else was ever going to have a peek. Can you blame the man?"

"No," I said, very quietly, but I *did* blame him. Probably Harry had intended to destroy the pictures before he died but death had overtaken him suddenly and unexpectedly. Too late, Don Giovanni; no time to make amends. I didn't care about Harry's sexual behavior but his thoughtlessness was unpardonable. Another person was in those photos. It's fine to kiss a girl in the dark, always has been. But it's never been good form to tell.

It would take time to fit this new image of Harry Hardwick into my mind. "Harry was one of your regulars?" I said to Willie.

"Aye. When he was over here. Came round with Huey, they were thick as pudding. Two of a kind, only difference was Harry had money and was better at pretending he was what he wasn't. Huey found 'im musical boxes and Harry paid through the nose. Why, not even a month ago Huey was here one night going on about how he was doing a big deal for Harry. Twenty-five thousand pounds for one little musical box, plus ten percent for himself."

Willie was too shrewd not to notice the glance that passed between Al and me. But he drew the wrong conclusion. "Oh, come on, mate. Twenty-five hundred quid one way or the other was naught to Harry Hardwick. Just his way o' makin' sure Huey kept showin' up at *his* door with the goods. Huey's a slob, but at least he's an honest slob. I'll take him before Harry any day."

Willie had honesty confused with bad storytelling. I remembered good times I'd enjoyed with Harry. I thought about how he'd helped Sophie Soleski after Peter died, and how generous he was with Shackie while my young friend was establishing himself in restoration work. Far more accurate and fair would have been to say Huey Fortune was a slob, if not pure then certainly simple, and Harry Hardwick had a slob side. But Harry also had enough sense and decency to try to keep that aspect of his behavior under wraps. Harry had a wart on his forehead but I rarely noticed it. His friendly smile always drew my attention.

But Willie MacIntosh didn't want to hear any of this and I didn't especially care to tell him. I reached across the table to take back the pictures. For the first time it occurred to me how good–*really* good–the photography was. I could count teeth in Wilma's brilliant smile, or hairs at the base of Old Doggie-Dick Harold Marley's giant pecker. Huey Fortune was clearly a fingernail-biter. I flipped through the stack. Every picture was the same. This was first-class photography.

Little Willie chuckled harshly and said, "You like me work, I see."

His tone was sarcastic, self-deprecatory. He probably expected me to shove the pictures into my pocket and sneer at him. I did put the pictures away but I said, "Yes, actually, I do. Not what's in them–porn's not my cuppa, I'm afraid. But the work itself is fantastic. Where'd you learn photography?"

Willie's face darkened. He ran a hand rapidly through his bricky hair.

"Really, I'm not putting you on. Whoever took these shots is one hell of a photographer. I'm curious, that's all. How you learned."

Willie slowly leaned back in his chair, all the while keeping me under close surveillance. "OJT," he said. "I like to watch. Well, a bloke can't just sit one night after the other holding his business in his hand while other people do the real thing. They get to sayin' what a queer sort you are, and problem is you start sayin' it about yourself. So I had me an idea. I went out and bought a camera and started takin' pictures. That made it okay—I wasn't just watchin'. But the pictures were a disgrace. I said to meself, Willie, what does it matter? Long as you're lookin' through a camera, you can watch all you want. But them photos just made me feel sick. So I picked me up some books and read them. I made friends wiv a couple of professional photogs. I bought lenses and tripods and lighting systems, and learned about film speeds and camera angles. And guess what? Me pictures kept gettin' better and better."

The change in Willie was astonishing. Suddenly gone were the hard lines around his lips; gone was his clipped cynical delivery. His words came rapidly, without effort. His face glowed.

"Funny thing. I thought maybe I could take pictures of other things, you know. Landscapes. The sea. Bowls of fruit or pots of flowers. Maybe I could even have me some shows. But they were terrible—no life to 'em. I tried people wiv their clothes on, but they looked like stiffs all ready for the hearse. So"—he leaned forward—"I'm tryin' different things. Here, take a look."

Willie opened his top right desk drawer, pulled out a handful of photographic prints, and handed them gently to me. They were of men and women, or men and men, or women and women, all in different stages of undress. Nothing outlandish here, no hot dog rolls or British flags. Just pairs of people undressing themselves and each other, touching each other, kissing, caressing, having intercourse in various positions. The photography was beyond flawless; it was inspired. In one picture a woman's leg was so masterfully shadowed as to appear velvet; I privately embarrassed myself by touching it gently with my finger.

I looked into Willie's wide blue eyes. "They're wonderful," I said, and meant it. "These expressions on their faces ... some of them make me want to cry."

"Aye," Willie said softly. "It's amazin', you come down to it. Ten minutes after we start, they don't know the camera's in the room and that's when *I* start takin' pictures. I'm doin' more of these all the time. Them things"–he aimed a finger at my coat-pocket stash–"they pay for film to do these."

An hour later, Big Al and I lounged at a table in Pashto, an Afghani restaurant a couple of blocks down the street from Dr. Watson's. My glass of Afghani red wine tasted quite good, drunk as it was toward the close of a day when I'd had my life nearly rubbed out, found evidence that my wonderful rigid notation box was a mere temporary hiding place for an erotic miniature automaton, and discovered that a longtime friend, now unavailable to answer charges, had fair streaks of kinkiness and thoughtlessness in his character.

"So Harry Hardwick bought those pictures himself, if I can believe Willie's story."

"I'd say you can," said Al. "Murder's not Willie's game, never has been. He'll give someone a good thrashing now and again, make no mistake. But that's as far as he goes. He should have no reason to tell you he sold those pictures to Harry Hardwick if in fact he did not."

"He also as much as told me it was Harry who gave Huey money to buy Freddie's rigid notation box. But why would Harry want Huey to ship the box to Sophie Soleski with the pistol hidden inside so he could buy it back from her for more than half again as much as he'd already paid for it, and then show it off at his party without bothering to take the miniature out of the cylinder?" I made a face. "It doesn't make sense."

Al nodded in amiable agreement.

"Harry and Huey. Huey and Harry. Maybe it's time to have another talk with Huey."

"I'm afraid that's not possible."

The waiter came up to the table.

"What? Are you going to tell me *he's* dead now, too?"

The waiter took an involuntary half-step backward.

"Lamb *biryani*, if you please." Al folded his menu and handed it to the waiter. Then he looked back to me. "No, just missing. But I think the waiter would like to take your order, Thomas."

"I'll have the same. What do you mean, 'missing'?"

Al watched as the waiter retired, a bit rapidly, I thought. "He's vanished. After your session with him last night and no doubt after his visit to Werner Ross, he appears to have gone underground. But ..." Al reached into his pocket and pulled out a long white envelope with blue lettering. "Here's something I found at Huey's flat."

I took the envelope. "You mean–"

"Oh, yes. I went there last night after I saw you safely back at your B and B. I hoped I might find Huey, but when I didn't I let myself in for a private visit. This was the only interesting item I found."

"A plane ticket. For New York. And *issued* in New York."

"Leaving January three, with next-day return. Evidently our friend Huey has–or had–business in the States after the first of the year. Something you might want to put into your pipe, now you're reassessing the situation."

"Harry had a business trip scheduled right after New Year's. But I don't know just when, or where he was going."

"I've taken down the dates and flight numbers of Huey's planes. And I've sent the American Express card number and date of issue of the ticket to your friend Broadway Schwartz. I expect he'll be checking with the agency directly. Here's a copy for you."

Al handed me a neatly-lettered notepad page. In return I handed him the ticket.

"Yes, that's right." He smiled. "I'll leave it back at Huey's. Just in case he returns and is still inclined to use it. We wouldn't want to–what is it one says now?–foreclose on any of our options? Yes, I believe that's the expression."

"It is, but I don't think I can afford to wait that long."

"I'm afraid that remains to be seen."

The waiter set our plates before us, then scooted away.

"It's time for me to go back to New York. Some trails there could stand re-exploration."

"I'll take you to the airport after dinner," Al said through a mouthful. He waved a fork at me. "Don't let your meal get cold. Airplane food is notoriously unsatisfying."

At the airport I ducked into a phone booth, called Directory Assistance, and got Clive Barnes' number. Clive is archivist of the International Musical Box Registry. When he answered I apologized for the intrusion, told him it was a bit pressing, and asked whether among the several thousand cylinder music boxes in his lists there was a machine by Lecoultre Freres, serial number 42,401, with four operatic airs.

"Pressing, eh?" Clive said. "Theft, is it?"

I said yes. The most useful short story there is.

I heard his computer beep and whir, then he said, "Sorry. Nothing Lecoultre between forty-two, three-sixty-two and forty-two, four-eighty-five. Anything else I can check for you?"

"How about Wilma Ryan? Any boxes registered under that name?"

"Wilma Ryan. Hmm. Let me look."

Another brief series of beeps and whirs, then another "Sorry."

I thanked Clive and hung up. Another dead end. Try another street, Purdue.

A few days before Christmas, the flights were packed. I

finally wangled a seat on a plane leaving at six AM. Then I found a quiet corner in the waiting area and stretched out on the carpet, my head on my suitcase. Five hours of sack time there, another six in the air. More than a good night's sleep. A quick shave in the airplane lavatory before landing and I was on my way.

Two steps into the terminal and I heard, "Jeez, Doc! You look as fresh as a daisy. Ain't you been up all night?"

"Schwartz. What the hell are you doing here?"

As if I didn't know.

"Oh, well." He shuffled his feet. "Al called and told me you were on the way. You find out anything?"

"Only what Al's undoubtedly already told you. Including, I'm sure, the way he saved me from getting shot to pieces. What, have you characters decided I need a permanent bodyguard?"

"Don't go getting bent outta shape." Schwartz took me by the elbow, edging me toward the exit. "Whoever these guys are, they're playing rough. Two heads're better'n one, right? Four eyes, four ears. Especially when somebody's maybe gonna sneak up on you."

As short as he was I had to work to keep step with him. Schwartz is pure energy.

"I appreciate it. But you've got things to do. Sunday morning, flea markets. An auction in Jersey today, right? You've got to eat."

He stopped and turned to face me. "If I ain't mistaken, doctors got to eat, too. So when you go back to seeing your patients I'll go back to full-time picking. Until then we're a team. Come on. Let's grab a subway back to town."

Trudy had cinnamon rolls in the oven to go with the cheese omelette she started as soon as we arrived. "It's Sunday," Schwartz explained. "She likes to make a big breakfast on Sundays. Today we held it 'til you got in."

"Guess I won't argue."

Trudy beamed happiness. Two guys to feed. All this and heaven, too.

I untied my shoelaces, slipped out of my shoes, and wiggled my toes. "Tell me something, Broadway–what does Big Al do? I mean, when he's not busy saving bunglers' lives."

Schwartz shot a quick glance toward Trudy at the stove, then looked back at me. "Antiques. High-end stuff: art, jewels, that kinda thing. Me and Al, we go back a long way together." He paused, then went on. "But I never ask Al a question if all I am is curious."

I nodded. "Forget I said anything."

"But, hey!" Schwartz, instantly re-energized. "Al says you found out something interesting about those pictures. Harry Hardwick bought 'em himself?" He shook his head. "I can't believe it."

"It's true. Sounds like Harry had a side we never got to see over here. What it means is we've got to forget about blackmail now. Also, knowing Harry and Huey were pals puts a new slant on the whole situation. I think Harry paid for the music box and Huey bought it for him. But Huey also stole something small and valuable, and hid it inside the music-box cylinder. And, Huey had an airplane ticket for New York on January third, with return on January fourth–"

The light coming on in Schwartz's eyes stopped me. "You just reminded me, Doc. That airplane ticket. Al called me yesterday, I checked it out. It was charged on Harry Hardwick's American Express card. And you know something else? *Hardwick* bought a ticket the same time, going to England January third–same flight as Huey, returning two days later. What do you think of that?"

"The obvious thing is they were working together. But on what I don't know. Or what went wrong. Until now I figured someone set Harry up, but try this for size: Harry paid Huey to steal a piece for his collection that just wasn't for sale, not even to him. And somehow it went wrong. Somebody tumbled–Jackson George? What I still can't fit in, though, are these two women, Marisa and Wilma." I tapped the tabletop as if that would help my neural connections to fall better into place.

"When I can't figure out what to do about something I sleep on it." Trudy smiled as she scraped a chunk of omelette from the pan onto my plate.

"Thanks," I said. "But it's a while 'til bedtime, and people are getting killed too fast. I've got to call Sophie Soleski. I hate to say it but I need to put the screws to her."

"Don't worry," Trudy said. "A person can't be Mr. Nice Guy all the time. Here. Have another cinnamon roll."

TWENTY-FIVE

I got a big hug from Sophie. "Thank you for getting back to me so fast. I've been worrying myself sick. If you can't help me ..."

Her voice trailed off as she watched my reaction. Sophie's eyesight isn't what it once was, but there's nothing wrong with her mind. She gave me that look, the one we get first from our mothers and our grade-school teachers, then from our wives.

"You *did* get my message, Thomas, didn't you–the one I left on your phone yesterday? Isn't that why you're here?"

The skin under Sophie's jaw hung slack. Her eyes were shot through with jagged red lines. Play it straight, I thought. "In a word, Soph, no. I've been out of town the last couple of days. Back just this morning and haven't even been home yet." I pointed to my suitcase by the door where I'd dropped it.

Sophie turned around and walked toward a large cylinder box in an elaborate carved-oak case, set on a matching table. She moved like a peasant woman with a yoke and two heavy pails of water across her shoulders. When she reached the music box she ran her fingers lightly across the lid, then raised it and pushed the start lever. Music filled the room, "*Suoni la tromba*" from *I Puritani.*

I watched Sophie watch me as the music played. This was one of her favorite boxes, an Ideal Soprano-piccolo by Mermod, with a cylinder twenty-four inches long and three inches in diameter. Each note and every chord seemed to flow directly into her bloodstream, a lyrical operatic transfusion. When the cylinder clicked off at the end of the tune she looked three inches taller and ten years younger.

"All right," she said. "Why are you here?"

I smiled. "Ladies first. What was your message about?"

A hand came to rest on the Ideal-piccolo lid. "It's about that big mandoline-basse box. The one at Shackie's."

"What's the matter? Has *it* been stolen now, too?"

She shook her head. "At least not as far as I know. No, listen, Tim Rutledge paid me eighty-five hundred dollars for that box and you know it's worth it. But the sale is contingent on its being put into top condition." She ran a hand distractedly through her hair, pushing stray gray strands back out of her eyes. "Part of the deal was that Shackie would have the work done by Christmas, and that's just a couple of days away now. If Tim asks for a refund I'm up the creek. It hasn't been easy since Peter died. No pension, not much insurance; I make do on Social Security and what I can earn selling music boxes. I don't even have Tim's eighty-five hundred dollars any more. I *can't* give it back to him."

"No problem. If that's the way Tim wants to be, let him go to hell. *I'll* buy the box from you. It's worth the price and I'd be glad to have it."

As I was talking she drew herself up even straighter. "That's kind of you. Sincerely, it is. But I've never taken charity in my life and I'm not about to start now. Anyway, that's only part of it. Tim's been one of my best customers for years. He can be a pain in the neck but he likes quality and he pays the going rate. If this deal falls through he'll probably never buy another music box from me."

"Sophie–"

"No, Thomas. Listen to me, please. Would you–can you–have that music box ready by Christmas, all cleaned and polished and dampered? You have no idea how I hate asking you something like that. But I have no choice."

It really is always something, isn't it? "Sophie, a rush job on a mandoline-basse box? Shackie was the best in the business, at least after Peter died. What the hell am I? A weekend hobbyist. An amateur."

"Bah!" Sophie waved her hand, an irritated dismissal. "Money has nothing to do with it. What is an amateur, if not somebody who does a thing for love? Whether or not he gets paid doesn't matter. What's important is whether he's a good lover–and you *are* good, Thomas. You worked with Shackie for how many years?"

"Almost twenty."

"Ah! How long did you have to study to be a doctor?"

The answer was eight years, four of medical school and four of residency. "It's not the same thing. Shackie had special gifts. If I worked with him 'til Judgement Day I'd never be as good as he was."

"Thomas, you're a very bright man but you don't understand. And when you want to be stubborn there's no moving you. Restoration work is not like a golf match or a game of tennis. Maybe Shackie *could* have done this job better than you, maybe faster, too. But God rest him, he can't do it at all now. And you can do it well enough–no, excuse me, I didn't mean it that way. You can do it well, period. Won't you please at least try?"

"Sophie, don't you think it'd be a better idea to give it to Lucas Sterne? I know what you think of him, but ..."

I heard my own voice and saw Sophie's face, and that was as far as I could get. Her expression told me: only an amateur, paid or not, was ever going to work on *her* music boxes. Even if it meant she'd go bankrupt. Better that than having to cook up a story for a celestial judge who wanted to know why she had put a marvelous mandoline-basse music box into the hands of a common whore. Check, checkmate.

"All right, Sophie," I said quietly. "I'll do my best. But no promises."

She walked over and kissed me. "Thank you, Thomas," she said. "I know you can do it, but even if I'm wrong you'll have my gratitude. You are a friend–in need, indeed."

Poor Sophie. About to get clouted alongside the ear by that Judas of the mind, Conventional Wisdom.

"Now, I've had my turn. What brings you here right off the ... what? The plane?"

"Yes, right off the plane. I've been to England the last couple of days. London."

Her eyes widened and her mouth opened. "Oh, my goodness," she said. "Two days. That's a–" There C. W. struck and silenced her. Some friend, indeed. With difficulty she finished her sentence, "short trip."

"Short but productive. I got help from a lot of people. Now I need help from you."

She tried the light-handed brush. "You're not still on this business about the murders, are you? Poor Harry and Shackie. The police closed the case; *they* seem perfectly satisfied. I can't understand why you're spending so much time and–"

"You're a very bright woman, Sophie, but you don't understand. And when you want to be stubborn, there's no moving you."

"I do not like to be talked to in that tone of voice."

Bad move on her part. *I* don't like being talked to in that tone of voice. "I'm spending this time because the police are wrong. Shackie didn't kill Harry or Abramowitz, the antiques dealer, or himself, for that matter. And he couldn't have killed Jackson George, could he? *Or* a forger in London named Werner Ross. And he didn't try to kill me."

I stopped and watched her reaction. Sophie was usually rock-steady but right then her hands were shaking like a Parkinsonian's.

"Yes, somebody tried to kill me," I said. "In London. Somebody's killed five people and tried for a sixth, all because of a certain rigid notation music box Huey Fortune packed into a shipment to you from the Westfalls. The rigid notation box you sold Harry Hardwick."

"I think I'm beginning to get angry, Thomas."

"You've got a long way to catch up to me," I said. "The Westfalls told me they had no idea you'd gotten anything other than the Nicole Freres overture box they'd listed on their invoice. They showed me that invoice, Soph; now I'll tell you what. Show me your copy. If it says 'Francois Nicole rigid notation box' I'll apologize and go straight out the door and you'll never hear another word about any of this business. What do you say?"

Now she was really shaking. She glanced at her Ideal Soprano-piccolo box but I think she knew she was beyond even that. Not that she was ready to back off.

"Thomas, I think you should leave now, and not come back until you've gotten this monkey business out of your system." She picked up my overcoat from the chair and handed it to me.

"Uh-uh, sorry." I shook my head and dropped the coat back onto the chair. "I'm not leaving until I see an invoice. If you won't help me I'll help myself. I'll tear this place apart—see what else you might be hiding, too."

She put a hand on the phone.

"Go ahead, call the police. Tell them a man is ransacking your apartment. When they'll come I'll tell them why."

Neither of us breathed, it seemed, for hours.

Finally, Sophie blinked.

"Listen," I said, much more gently now. "Somebody's been using you. Five people have been killed, and I think you're sitting on some important information. You know Shackie wasn't a killer. Could you face him if you just walk away from this?"

That hurt. I was encouraged enough to say, "Could you face Peter?"

She dropped into the armchair at her side. When she looked up her face was older than memory. I felt sorry for her, but not guilty. We live and die by the stories we tell, and when you tell a bad story you have to pay. But you pay most dearly when you won't tell a story at all. Leave open space and someone else will tell your story for you. Those are the hardest stories to untell.

"It happened too fast." Sophie's voice was a dull drone. "If only I'd had a little time to think about it ... Harry called me. He said there was a rigid notation box in Gordon and Maida's shipment, and he wanted it. He–"

"He called you before you even got the crate? How'd he know–did you ask him that?"

"Huh! Of course I asked him. I said, 'What, Harry, you're reading crystal balls?' He laughed, of course. Said 'I've got my sources'–those were his words. Well, sure he had his sources. I figured somebody in London must have got word, and quick gave Harry a call. The shipment came two days later and there it was, a Francois Nicole rigid notation box. And yes, the invoice did say Nicole Freres overture box. Satisfied? Ordinarily I would have picked up the phone and asked Gordon or Maida if there'd been some sort of mistake. But for one thing it was after five by the time I had everything unpacked, too late to call England. For another thing Harry called again. He said the shipment should have arrived and was his source right? I should have said yes, there *was* a rigid notation box but I thought there might've been a mistake and I'd have to call Gordon and Maida in the morning to check it out. But when a person wants to believe something, they will. Nicole–Nicole, so easy to mix up. A bookkeeping error, that's all it was. Why should I get the best customer I've ever had angry at me, and on top of that bother Gordon and Maida over nothing? So, yes, I said to Harry, it's here. He said he'd be right over and he was. He said how much; I said twenty-two thousand, five hundred. He wrote a check, picked up the box, gave me a kiss, and left."

She sighed. "So there I was, sitting with a check for twenty-two and a half thousand dollars and a headache a fistful of aspirin wouldn't do a thing for. But it was done. So I said to myself, forget it. If it really was a bookkeeping error, no one will ever say a word and what's the difference? And if they really did send me the wrong box, *they'll* call *me* and then I'll have to call up Harry. *And he'll know what to do*. God help me, that's what I said to myself. And I believed it. Now see what's happened."

I cracked my knuckles, something I don't often do. Sophie looked at me, surprised. "You said it; it's done. You never did hear from the Westfalls?"

She shook her head. "I didn't hear from anybody. Except you."

I took a couple of seconds to work up my nerve. "I hate to ask you this, but I want to look through your books. Checkbooks, savings accounts, business ledger. Everything from the past two years."

I thought she was about to object but she closed her mouth before words could get out. "Sure," she said, very quietly, then got up, walked to the back of the living room, and disappeared into her little office.

A few minutes later she was back, carrying a big ledger book, a bank passbook, and two small rectangular cardboard boxes, each filled with small slips of paper. She laid them down in front of me.

"That's everything?" I said.

"Everything!"

Soph left me alone while I looked through her papers. What I found—or maybe better, what I didn't find—reassured me. No large deposits, no big withdrawals. If anything the numbers showed even more starkly than Sophie's words how close to the line she'd been living. No way could she have bought a music box for roughly $40,000 and then sold it for twenty-two-five. Nor could she have put up anything like forty K to start with.

Our goodbye was considerably less warm than our greeting had been but I thought Sophie looked more relieved than angry. I promised to do my best to get her mandoline-basse box ready for Tim Rutledge by Christmas.

"No guarantees, though," I reminded her.

She smiled unpleasantly. "There's only one guarantee in this world, one we didn't ask for."

Schwartz was waiting downstairs. "Get anything?" he asked as I walked over to him.

"Yeah, another job to do. Come on, tell you about it on the way. I'm going to take Trudy's advice, at least for an hour."

Back in my apartment I checked the small pile of mail inside the door. A couple of bills, a notice saying I was in line to win the Big One from Publishers' Clearing House, and four or five medical journals. I tossed the handful of paper onto the dining room table, then played back the phone message tape. Supposedly there were seven messages but six were brief silences followed by clicks. The seventh was Sophie's.

I shrugged and looked at my watch. Just about half-past one. "I'll set my alarm for two-thirty," I said.

"Fine by me." Schwartz tossed his coat on a chair and grabbed the TV remote control. "I'll watch the Giants." He clicked the remote switch; the screen lit up with football.

I went into the bedroom, undressed to my underwear, and stretched out on the bed. A dull throb between my shoulder blades and in my legs told me I was going into a fade. I needed a jolt to my adrenal glands, something to set off a fresh burst of adrenaline and cortisol.

I pushed the lever on my special bedside music box and heard the first notes of the overture to *"La Forza Del Destino."* I was asleep before the music ended.

The alarm didn't wake me, though. The telephone did.

I blinked up at the clock-radio. Twenty after two; I felt surprisingly refreshed. "Thomas Purdue," I said into the mouthpiece.

"Well, Doctor. It's nice to finally catch you at home. You've been a bad fellow the last few days. Unavailable. Tsk, tsk."

It was a voice I'd heard once before, odd and definitely male, but with a strange electronic quality. Like a voice-mail operator.

"Can I help you?" I said. "Are you a patient?"

"Yes, you *can* help me," intoned the voice. "And I have been very patient until now. But I'm afraid my patience is gone."

I was wide awake, adrenaline rush in full progress. The power of positive sleeping. I looked around the room, wishing for a portable phone so I could go into the living room and signal Schwartz to pick up an extension. No luck. I was on my own.

"Why don't you tell me how I can help you? I'll see what I can do."

"Please don't be cute, Dr. Purdue," said the voice. "It ill becomes you. You're not going to keep me on the line for a trace. You have a music box I want–Francois Nicole Number Four Thirty-Two. I want it, and I want it right away. I'll give you a hundred thousand dollars cash; I'll also let you live to enjoy the money. What do you say to that?"

I couldn't say anything because I'd choked on an overwhelming tide of joy. *He didn't have it.* My rigid notation box was safe. Wherever Shackie put it, that's where it still was.

"You're assuming I have that box," I finally got out. "You tore my place and Shackie's to bits. Maybe all this time I've been thinking you've got it."

"*Do* you have it?" the voice asked.

"For me to know and you to find out," I said. "But if you don't have it and you do something foolish you'll never get it. Will you?"

"Dr. Purdue, I don't like to be unpleasant."

Have you ever heard a nasty voice-mail operator?

"But I may have to be. I do want that music box but at some point I may have to settle for just keeping you permanently quiet. You're not an easy man to threaten, Dr. Purdue, I'll give you that. But you'd be wise to consider the safety of others. Like that of your wife. Sarah, I believe her name is?"

Nasty turn in the game. "Listen, schmuck, do anything to my wife, even frighten her, and you'll never get anywhere near that music box."

"Get off the white horse, Doctor. It's a bore. If I can't get my music box I might as well have some satisfaction. It's up to you. I'm not going to wait very much longer. And, oh, Doctor. Please don't try to have your wife leave town. If she so much as sets foot in a bus terminal, a train station, or an airport, I'll kill her on the spot. That's all I have to say."

I was going to ask just how long he was going to wait but the phone clicked dead. I was staring into it when Schwartz burst into the room. "Mean son of a bitch. Hey, Doc, that's one scary guy."

I set the receiver into its cradle. "You heard?"

Schwartz looked puzzled. "Sure, what do you think? I was going to sit there watchin' the football game and not check out a phone call?"

"You must have picked up after I did. But I didn't hear a thing."

"'Course not, Doc. I'm good at what I do."

All of a sudden, time was not a luxury. I reached simultaneously for my shirt and the phone, punching numbers as I slipped my arms through the shirtsleeves. "Muriel," I shouted into the speaker. "Thomas Purdue. I need to speak to you—very important ... Good. I'll be over in an hour."

Then I dialed Sarah's number.

TWENTY-SIX

"Something tells me your wife ain't gonna be so happy about this," Schwartz said.

We were waiting for the elevator, to go down to the lobby and over to Sarah's. "Tell me something I don't know. Like who that phone call was from."

Schwartz looked disgusted. "Could be anyone in the world. Those voice-scrambling phones–if we'd gotten a good recording maybe some computer guy could unscramble it. But we didn't."

"We can at least rule out half the population of the world. It *was* a man."

"Not necessarily, Doc."

That earned Schwartz a healthy fisheye.

"No, really. Hey, with those scrambler-phones nowadays you can sound like anybody. Say you're a lady and you live by yourself and that worries you. So you push a button, and shazam–you sound like a man."

I hadn't thought of that. Over the phone you can't tell the players without a scorecard. The elevator door opened and a thought popped into my head. Telephones. Voice mail. Hardwick Electronix.

Sarah's apartment is neat-orderly and neat-uncluttered, not neat-interesting or neat-unusual. Living room furniture from Levitz, white-covered sofa and matching armchairs which get along famously with her teak coffee table and two end tables. Nothing out on those tables, either, save for a telephone and a couple of dishes of nuts and candy. Sarah doesn't collect anything, not even dust. Neat-boring.

"You sounded concerned. What's the matter now?"

Sarah was not pleased. I'd interrupted her Sunday afternoon. My wife has never been religious but on Sunday she rests. She spends all day with the massive *New York Times* or a book; she might flip on *Meet the Press*. Evenings, she wanders out to dinner, then maybe a movie or a concert. All the time we lived together this drove me crazy. How can you do nothing all day? She wasn't doing nothing, she insisted, and it wasn't her fault I was a compulsive doer.

"I'm sorry," I said. "But this business with the missing music box has really heated up. You need to know about it."

She rolled her eyes. Oh, stupid, impossible husband. "Honestly. You're like a dog with a bone between your teeth. Can't you let go for even a Sunday?"

While she was talking she kept Schwartz in corner-eye view. Bad enough I had to come by and pester her on The Day Off, catching her on the sofa in her yellow lounging pajamas. But did I have to add insult to injury by bringing that Schwartz character along?

"I can't, Babe," I said. "Five people are dead, and if it weren't for some good luck I would've been *numero seis*."

"Keep meddling and maybe you won't be so lucky next time." Then her eyes softened, her voice along with them. "I swear, you get worse the older you get. You're a doctor and a good one, but you're not the New York City Police Department or Interpol. I really wish you'd let go of this thing before you ... get hurt. You're impossible, but I'd miss you. Besides, you made a commitment for Christmas Day. Remember?"

"God forbid I should get shot so I can't ladle out turkey gravy to the homeless. Sarah, listen to me. Please. I just got a phone call from the killer. He thinks I've got that rigid notation music box."

"Do you?" Mother Sarah's classic gaze. Guilty, sonny, until proven innocent. Maybe even after that.

"No."

"I don't believe you."

Schwartz, on his best behavior to that point, jumped into the breach. "Believe him, Mrs. Purdue. He's telling you the truth. He ain't got that box."

Sarah's look suggested Schwartz might have been an unusually nervy cockroach who'd dared crawl out from under her sink and complain about the food. "Oh, really? Do you think he tells *you* the truth?" She turned to me. "What's he here for, anyway?"

"He's my bodyguard."

She thought that over briefly. "Why? Did you think you needed protection from me?"

I didn't have time for this pissiness. "Sarah, goddamn it, shut *up*. Listen to me: Whether you like it or not I'm in this too deep to do anything but keep going. I need to find that rigid notation box before the killer does–and I need to find the killer before he decides to take me as a consolation prize. I'm only sorry I've gotten you involved." Then I told her about the phone call.

I thought sure I'd get the full now-see-what-you've-done-with-your-thoughtlessness routine but Sarah dealt me a surprise. She looked at me mildly and said, "Is that all?"

"That's not enough?"

"It's plenty. But what do you want me to say?"

"That you won't go anywhere near Kennedy, La Guardia, Grand Central, Port Authority or the Saw Mill River Parkway. That you'll just go about your business while I get this thing figured out. That you'll let Schwartz stay here and keep an eye on you–"

That far and no further. "Oh no, absolutely not! Not on your life."

"Sarah, but–"

"No buts. Oh, honestly, I keep telling myself not to get involved in any more of your crazy schemes and games. But I do. If you'll remember, I was the one who stole those disgusting pictures. You didn't ask me to; I just did it. Because I knew they might be important to you–"

"They *are*. If I ever get this mess figured out it'll be more on account of those pictures than anything I've turned up on my own."

"Well, there it is then. You can't tell me I've been an innocent bystander. But I'm not foolish, you know that. I won't plan any trips and I won't take any. You just keep your bodyguard, though; he's not coming anywhere near *my* body. Go on now, get out of here, both of you. Go play detective. Let me enjoy what's left of my Sunday."

I looked at Schwartz. He shrugged. I got up, then bent to kiss Sarah on the forehead. She reached for my hand. "Thomas, you will call me, won't you, if you find that music box?"

"Sure. If you want me to."

"Good luck." She kissed my hand lightly, then picked up the *Times*.

Outside in the hallway Schwartz said, "You really gonna call her?"

"Of course not. For her own safety. Safer for her not to know I have it–if I do."

Schwartz closed one eye and narrowed the other. "You know, she's right–you *do* lie to her."

"Oh, well, excuse me. What would've happened if I'd said no, I won't call you? She'd have had a fit."

Schwartz shrugged. "So? You ain't ever seen a woman throw a fit?"

"Broadway, chill out. That's all I'd need ... all *we'd* need now. For her to get sore and do something stupid, maybe screw the whole thing up. That's the way I had to handle it. Okay?"

"Sure, sure. Suit yourself." Schwartz started toward the stairwell, then turned around. "I guess we all gotta handle things our own way, but I gotta tell you, I can't believe that wife of yours would ever do a stupid thing. An aggravating thing, yes. A pissy thing? Definitely. But stupid?" He shook his head. "Uh-uh. I think she's the most *un*-stupid person I ever met."

I might have been irritated but I thought of my rigid notation box curled up in a corner somewhere waiting for me, and all I could feel was a warm tingly glow. I also thought I had a fair idea where it might be, at least in a general way. But I wasn't going to mention that to Sarah. Or to Schwartz, yet, for that matter.

If Sarah had come along to see Muriel Hardwick this time she definitely would not have approved. The fair Muriel had clearly made a full recovery from the past week's distressing events. Her makeup was flawless and her long brown hair was piled in a beehive calculated to attract any drones in the neighborhood. She wore a one-piece black-and-white silk garment, a kind of upscale sheer leotard, and it was obvious if you opened the zipper in the back you'd find only skin underneath. Judging by the expression that grew on Schwartz's face as we followed Muriel into the living room, he'd drawn the same conclusion.

"You're looking good, Muriel," I said.

Her smile told me how well she understood I was not making an idle social remark. Sharp lady, Muriel. "Thank you. I feel good. Lawyers are making bundles on Harry's will but that's all right. They'll be done soon enough and there'll be plenty left for me." In case I was less perceptive than she'd just been she added an emphatic, "*Plenty*."

The room was much brighter than it had been on my last visit. Gone were the heavy maroon drapes on the far window bank. Late afternoon sun poured in unimpeded.

Muriel followed my gaze. "That's a beginning. Those bloody ugly drapes—I pulled them down myself. I've been thinking, actually: this place might not be half-bad once properly seen to. I've had a decorator in; she says she can make it ever so much nicer than a spanking-new condo. Take things right down to the support beams if necessary."

"Be a little pricey, I suspect." Soft grin. Teasing.

She was equal to me, no surprise. "I don't think I can spend money fast enough to keep it from growing. Harry had no children and no other close relatives, and his wives were never more than window dressing. I knew I could easily end up as ex-Number Three–so I made jolly well certain of a good prenuptial agreement. That way I'd at least get my pension when he decided to retire *me*. But I came up lucky, now, didn't I? The roulette ball stopped rolling right on my number."

"Very lucky. One might even say uncomfortably so. People could get the wrong idea."

"Like you for instance?" Left eyebrow arched skyward.

"Heavens, no. But some people might. Frankly, I'm surprised you're ... well, quite as open as you are."

Muriel laughed heartily, sending her well-packaged chest into an uninhibited shimmy-shake. "Sod those people. You needed to talk to me–urgently, I believe."

"Yes."

"What would you like to know? I'm nothing if not obliging."

I pulled out the two pictures of Wilma and passed them to Muriel. "For starters you can tell me whether you know that woman."

I'd thought Muriel was going to make an attempt at nonchalance but I was wrong. Her eyes flew open. "My, my, my," she said, taking quick stock of me. "You've been busy, Thomas."

"Not busy enough. I need to know a lot more about this woman."

"Why?" She set the pictures down on the end table and waited for my answer.

"I think she might've had something to do with the killings–Harry's, Shackie's, the others. She keeps turning up in odd places."

Muriel snickered. "Not surprising, that. But come now, you want information from me but you're holding back. Fair's fair. You're not the police; I don't have to talk with you. If you'll tell me what you know I'll do the same. Otherwise, no deal."

Schwartz looked doubtful but I decided to go ahead. "Okay, in chronological order: On the day Shackie was killed this woman left a music box with him for repair. Then a few days ago when I was returning boxes to Shackie's customers she showed up and managed to talk *me* into doing the repairs for her. But then I got hold of these pictures–"

"Wait just a moment. Just how did you manage that, pray tell?"

Time to dress up the story–but it had to be a careful fit. "A friend in England put me onto the George Sand Club–"

"Shit!"

Muriel's remark was no more than a whisper but it carried a wealth of power. Schwartz actually moved back in his chair. "You know how Harry and I got together then?"

I nodded. "But don't worry. That's not what I'm here about. It's our secret, I promise."

She glared at Schwartz, who quickly raised his right hand. "No sweat, Mrs. Hardwick. I learned a long time ago how to keep my mouth shut when it better not be open. You ain't got no worries."

Schwartz is one of the world's great disarmers. Muriel smiled.

"It's this Wilma Ryan I'm interested in," I said. "Willie MacIntosh said she wasn't one of his regulars; she just showed up every now and then. He was pretty sure she was American and he didn't much care for her. What else can you tell me?"

"I'm afraid not much. I only saw her the once–and I can't say I liked her, either. Very affected, a snide little bitch-transie, I remember thinking. She talked a great deal about other people but where she herself was concerned, she was definitely not forthcoming. I'm sorry."

"I shrugged. "All right, but if you don't mind I'd also like to talk about Harry. Willie said Harry was quite a kink, and frankly that surprised me."

Muriel cut loose a very undignified snort. Schwartz crossed his legs and coughed politely.

"Oh, my word," Muriel finally said. "Yes, of course–I *know* how Harry appeared to all of you. Good old Harry Hardwick, successful businessman and collector. Come to my house; play with my toys; have a drink of good liquor and some fine food. Get a big smile and a pat on the back from benevolent Uncle Harry. But he was an evil man."

"I know Harry had a big ego," I said. "He was entitled to it. He worked hard. That doesn't make him evil."

Muriel lit up a cigarette and blew out smoke as though it had somehow offended her. "Cross Harry–or even let him *think* you'd crossed him–and you were on his list forever. He destroyed people, but never directly, oh no. At heart he was a coward. Remember a to-do a couple of years ago, several young women accusing Senator Barford of improprieties?"

"Sure. Who could forget it?"

"That was the idea. Spicy stuff, eh? Indecent exposure, peeking though holes in walls of the Ladies', talk of some really different kinds of oral stimulation. Nothing ever proved but Barford lost the election, and his wife and family for good measure. That, everyone remembers. They *don't* remember Barford was sponsoring a bill that would have brought a large part of Hardwick Electronix under some unpleasant antitrust guidelines. In the commotion, that bill was dropped like a hot potato. Do you recall what Honest Harry had to say about that?"

"If I'm right it was something about sincerely regretting the turn of events," I said. "That he'd been looking forward to doing battle with Barford."

"And there was nothing in the whole world he loved more than a good fight. Remember that line, do you?"

"Yes."

"Harry loved a good fight, all right—but only so long as both his opponent's hands were tied behind his back. Sorry to disillusion you, Thomas."

I waved her off. "Let me ask something else about Harry and grudges: How upset was he, really, about losing that musical maiden to Walter Remler?"

Muriel stubbed out her cigarette and sat up straight. Her mouth opened wide and she chortled, a real ho-ho-ho. "Oh, my dear, need I tell you? He was simply beside himself. Wanted to tear Remler to bits. 'Never should have trusted the man' and all that. He swore he'd pay Remler back to the penny, with interest."

"But Remler was at the party the other night."

Muriel nodded agreement. "Yes. Odd that, I thought. In fact I said so to Harry. But he said it was time to make things up. For the good of the Association."

"I gather you didn't believe him."

She shook her head and chuckled. "Not a word of it. Harry make things up after a tiff? That's a joke."

"You and Little Willie tell the same story. He called Harry a phony—said he only let it hang out when he was away from home."

"Oh, that he did." Muriel lit another cigarette and took a deep drag. "He let it hang out so far I'm surprised he or that disgusting Huey Fortune didn't step on it. Thick as they were, we all wondered for a while whether Harry and Huey had a little something going between them. But Harry just liked having somebody at hand he could count on to run his sleazy errands and say 'Yes, sir' and 'Thank you very much, sir.' As for Huey there was nothing he'd not do for a few stray quid."

"If you don't mind my saying so, you seem to have seen Harry at his worst, but you still married him. Why?"

As I was speaking, the doorbell rang. Muriel glanced at her watch and said, “Oh–that’ll be Lucas Sterne.” She got to her feet. “Thomas, really,” she said, speaking quickly now. “I’m not daft. It was better pay than I could ever hope for at the Sand, and easier work as well. Only one customer and to be completely frank it was not all that often he came shopping.” She paused, hand in mid-air, then smiled. “And you can’t beat the retirement benefits, now, can you?”

As she left the room I flashed Schwartz a keep-it-shut look. We sat silent until Muriel came back with Lucas Sterne in tow. Lucas’ eyes looked unusually bright below his tangle of black curls.

“Lucas is here to talk with me about the removal and sale of Harry’s machines,” she said. “Thomas, I hope you don’t mind ... if you’d like to chat further I can see you tomorrow.”

I was about to say no, that was all right, I was finished. But what came out was, “I’ll be in touch.” Give them something to think about.

Muriel showed us out. As she was about to open the front door, I said, “Oh, one small thing. Did Harry’s company make telephones? Answering machines? That sort of thing?”

“Why, yes, of course.” She looked puzzled, amazed that I’d asked such a stupid question. “If it was electronic, Harry made it. There must have been ten pages of telephone equipment in the last catalogue.”

TWENTY-SEVEN

Shackie's place smelled musty. I turned up the thermostat, then stood in the doorway with Schwartz and swept the space with my eyes.

Schwartz frowned. "What was it again Shackie told you?"

"He said when he wasn't working on the rigid notation box he'd hide it so only Francois Nicole himself would be able to find it."

"The guy who made the box in the first place."

"Right. The master of the shop. It'd have to be somewhere an apprentice or employee wouldn't think of. Or go."

"Like maybe where the boss lived?"

"Sure. How about his bed? What would have been more off-limits to anyone but Francois Nicole?"

The slashed mattress and box spring were still on the floor upstairs. Schwartz watched as I knelt down and palpated the mattress, then percussed its upper surface, hoping to pick up a rectangular woody tumor deep within. No luck. I reached inside and pulled this way and that at the stuffing. Still no music box.

"Strike one," said Schwartz.

Strike two was the box spring. Same physical examination, same disappointing result. We spent the next hour looking for compartments under floor boards, behind clothes-closet walls, and in back of bureau drawers. We pulled every picture and mirror off its hook.

Finally Schwartz shook his head. "If he hid it up here he did too good of a job."

I couldn't argue the point.

We went downstairs to the workshop area, a space easily ten times that of the living area. "Okay," I said. "Somewhere in the workshop where only Francois Nicole himself would go."

We strained to shove the heavy drill press off its mooring but there was no compartment underneath. We moved the lathe. We wrestled the big band saw to the side.

Schwartz's hat was dark-stained above the band; he pushed it back and picked up a rag from a worktable to wipe at his forehead. "Whew!" He took in the room with a glance. "Glad that's all the big stuff."

"The desk," I said, pointing.

Schwartz groaned.

We shifted the desk and looked underneath. The flooring was solid. I checked each drawer for a false bottom. I didn't find one.

I moved my hands slowly across the work station at the east end of the room. None of the small power tools—mini-drill press, grinding wheels, mini-rip saw, jeweler's lathe—could have been used to hide something the size of that rigid notation box. The kiln, Shackie's efficient replacement for the nineteenth-century forge, was empty, save for the small sand dish and temperature-indicator cones. The ultrasonic cleaner was full of fluid. I emptied it and unscrewed the bowl from the power-unit base. Nothing inside but power unit.

Schwartz called from the north side of the room. "Hey, Doc. Come here—I got a thought."

He was standing in front of the woodstore, three shelves filled with blocks, chunks, and slices of wood of all shapes and sizes. Shackie saved everything. A piece of scrap wood or brass or steel often became precisely the item he needed for an essential repair.

"Could be under this stuff," Schwartz said.

"Whoever tore the place apart thought of the same thing. There was wood all over the floor when I got here. I had to toss it back in."

"Did you look behind it? Like for a panel in the side wall or the back?"

For answer I grabbed the piece of wood closest to me and tossed it back over my shoulder. Schwartz followed suit.

In ten minutes we had the shelves empty and Shackie's former home looking much as it had the day I stumbled in and got myself knocked stupid. But all the walls were solid. Silently, we piled the wood back on the shelves. Schwartz looked at me hopefully.

"Let's cover the rest of the shop," I said.

We covered it like a blanket, three hours of hard looking. Down on our knees to check the flooring. Up on chairs and stools to scrutinize high walls. Bending over to make certain every drawer in every work station was filled only with tools or supplies. No sign of a missing music box. The disturbing thought struck me that Shackie might have meant his remark literally: maybe *only* Francois Nicole could have found that music box. I was not Francois Nicole.

What I was, was tired and hungry. I nudged Schwartz. "Come on. Second Av Deli time."

Schwartz went through a giant corned beef sandwich like a bulldozer through soft earth. "There's something a lot more than business between Mrs. Hardwick and that Sterne jerk," he said between mouthfuls.

"Frank the Crank clued me in to that, but whether it matters to us is a different question. Muriel could have been working with Huey Fortune, sure. She certainly could've fronted the money. But if she and Lucas wanted to kill Harry and frame Shackie, why all this business about stealing the Farouk pistol and hiding it in the cylinder? What about the pictures from Harry's library? Where do Wilma Ryan and Marisa fit in?"

Schwartz wiped his mouth with the paper napkin.

"Let's go back to Shackie's," I said.

Schwartz's face dropped. "We're gonna tear the joint apart some more?"

"No–not right now, anyway. I'm going to put in some work on that mandoline-basse box for Sophie. She needs it before Christmas."

Schwartz looked at his watch. "It's almost seven. You get off a flight from London, then all day you run around New York. Now you're gonna fix a music box? Don't you ever go to sleep?"

"I slept on the plane. And for almost an hour back at my place, remember? I can put in a few hours at the workbench–in fact, it's probably a good idea. Relax, change pace. Anyway, it's too early to go to bed."

Schwartz looked across the room at the revolving refrigerated dessert cabinet. "We got time for a piece of cheesecake?"

I don't know where he puts it. "Sure. Cup of coffee, too."

On the way back to Shackie's Schwartz stopped at a stationery store and bought a couple of paperbacks. One was a thick John LeCarre spy story, the other *Mr. Sammler's Planet.*

I was surprised. "I didn't think Bellow was exactly your material."

He looked at the book. "Oh yeah, I like science fiction."

"Broadway ..." I began, trying to sound as tactful as I could. "You really don't have to go back to Shackie's. I know my way around New York. Why don't you go home and spend some time with Trudy? She must be–" The expression on his face stopped me. "Okay, come on."

At Shackie's, Schwartz threw his coat onto the hook near the door and started up the steps to the loft. "I'm gonna go stretch out on what you left of that mattress. Read my book there."

I went to the workbench, looked up at the big mandoline-basse box in its storage alcove, and for a moment wondered whether I was crazy. To try to restore a machine like this *and* track down a mass murderer in just three days did seem a bit of a push.

But the world doesn't stop. All you can do is keep juggling. Chin up, feet on the ground, balls in the air.

I pulled the mandoline-basse down off the shelf and set it on the workbench.

I thought of picking up with the damper replacement at the point Sammy Shapiro had interrupted me, but decided instead to go with general clean-up. It *had* been a long day, and dampering is meticulous work, demanding full concentration and good hand/eye coordination. So I disassembled the mechanism, put the pieces into plastic mesh baskets, lowered them into the ultrasonic bath, and turned the control dial. The machine started to buzz.

Now to check the tuning scale of the comb. I'd need a heavy vise to grip the comb base so the teeth pointed upward. I bent over the vise, comb in my right hand, while with my left I opened the vise jaws.

Right at that moment Schwartz sneezed.

You concentrate, you forget things. Like there being another person in the room with you. I jumped a foot, then spun around to look in the direction of the little explosion. As I did I felt the comb bang against the vise.

If you run a saw blade through your finger you're likely to wrap the wound in a handkerchief and squeeze it. Later, you'll congratulate yourself on your good sense in applying effective pressure to a hemorrhage—but that's applesauce. The reason you wrapped that finger so nice and tight was because then you couldn't see it. That's how I was with the music box comb. I couldn't bring myself to look down and assess damages.

From the loft Schwartz called down, "'Scuse *me*."

I couldn't bring myself to wish God's blessings upon him. I knew it wasn't his fault but I still wanted to kill him.

Without looking at it I set the comb on the table. Then I sat down. *Then*, I looked.

I wished I hadn't. The top eight teeth of the comb were stubs.

I thought I might return my dinner onto the workbench. My hands were covered with ice water; I felt dizzy; I tried to slow my breathing.

What the hell was I going to do now?

The answer came in Shackie's voice but from somewhere inside my own head: *Replace the teeth. What else?*

But eight teeth! If they're not done perfectly they won't look right *or* sound right. The box'll be ruined.

Of course you've got to do it right. But you know how. You've done it enough.

With you watching.

So? Do it the same way.

But eight teeth!

No. Don't do them one at a time. Make one block of eight teeth. Faster and *better.*

But *I* did the damage. My fault. That hurts.

Sure it does. But get off it. Remember when I was carrying the comb from Olive Martin's box and I tripped on the air compressor hose?

Now that you mention it, yes. And as I recall, you weren't in a party mood.

Of course not. But what did I do? I put in a block of six, a block of two, and three single teeth. When that box came in, it was a disaster, but when it left it was beautiful to see and hear. Come on. Get to work.

I stared at the mutilated comb. Then I walked over to the supply cabinet, took out a small square of steel and some grinding points for the flexible-shaft tool. Then I went to work.

Over the next couple of hours I ground and filed a slot into the comb base to receive the replacement tooth block. I measured the slot carefully, then cut a section of steel to size.

With a cutting wheel I slit the block into eight teeth, and ground and filed them to match their predecessors. I had to admit: they looked good.

But they also had to sound good. For these new teeth to ring clear, the steel would have to be hardened. First step was to heat the tooth-block. I took it across the room to the kiln, and opened the door.

Something wasn't right.

The sand dish should have been at the center of the kiln floor, ready to receive the tooth-block, with a temperature-inducator cone on each side to show whether the heat was both evenly distributed and at the correct temperature. But the dish was against the left wall of the kiln, four cones pushed into the sand, points upward.

I began to move the dish toward center but stopped part-way. Shackie always left the kiln ready for use. If the killer had moved the dish and cones when he ransacked the place, why would he leave them so nice and neat against the side of the kiln, cones all pointing straight upward?

Pointing straight upward at two loose bricks in the side wall.

I stopped breathing. My heart stopped beating. The earth stopped spinning.

My fingers shook as I reached out toward the loose bricks. Those *were* loose bricks, weren't they?

No, they weren't. As the thing came away in my hand I saw it was a piece of cardboard about eighteen inches long. Shackie had painted it on one side so it looked like two kiln bricks.

I slid my fingers into the cavity in the wall of the kiln. When I touched something firm and straight I went into overdrive. Fingers from both hands scrabbled against rough mortar, finally pulling out a tightly-sealed white plastic garbage bag. I couldn't undo the twist-tie so I tore into the plastic with my teeth and ripped it away.

There in my shaking hands was Francois Nicole's rigid notation box, serial number 432.

Put it down, I told myself. Before you drop it.

In the kiln, the goddamn *kiln*, he'd hidden it! Where Francois Nicole would have seen immediately something was not right. Where Thomas Purdue came within a few minutes of incinerating one of the greatest musical treasures in existence.

I opened my mouth and tried to call Schwartz's name, but no sound came out. My throat felt like that little dish of sand on the kiln floor. I tried again but could only push out a soft croak. I sank into the chair at the kiln workstation and lowered my head onto the table. A stream of melting ice ran off my brow and over my arm. I managed to pull the start lever on the rigid notation box; the room filled with music. *The Magic Flute.*

"Hey, Doc, what–?" I heard Schwartz call from far away.

Then I felt a touch on my shoulder. "You found it! Hey, you found it. Where was–"

I raised my head.

"Oh, hey, you okay?" He pulled a grotty handkerchief out of his pocket and wiped solicitously at my face. "Take it easy, Doc–it's okay. Take it easy."

Air began to flood back into my lungs. At the same time jubilation flowed into Schwartz's voice. "You did it. You found the sucker. Where was it–can you tell me?"

I pointed at the kiln. "In there. Shackie hid it behind a fake brick." I pointed at the cardboard panel in front of us on the table. "I damn near burned it up. I was going to start firing the kiln."

Schwartz gave another wipe to my forehead. "Well, but you stopped. What now?"

I felt a great tenderness for Schwartz. "I get a glass of water."

Talk about going on adrenaline. Less than an hour later Schwartz and I were sitting at the principal workstation. The rigid notation mechanism was out of its case on the table, its cylinder removed. Holding the cylinder carefully so as to not damage pin alignment, I showed it to Schwartz. "Look there—on the left end cap. A little scratch, bright brass. Someone's had this end cap off. Huey."

Schwartz could barely contain himself. "So open it up and let's see what's inside."

I was trying as hard as I could to not think about how Thomas Purdue, amateur restorer, was in the process of dismantling a rigid notation box. I had about as much right to unscrew and separate those components as I did to build a bridge over the Atlantic Ocean and tell people it was safe to drive across. I told Schwartz to rest his vocal cords and watch. Quietly.

I freed the pin at the end of the cylinder spindle, then pulled the spindle free and set it down. The cylinder felt light. I leaned back to hold one end up to the bulb in the gooseneck lamp, and peered through the near end as if it were a telescope. Where I should have seen a clean ring of light there was only a small irregular gleam.

"We're close to home," I mumbled, and motioned for him to take a look.

"Something's in there," he said.

"Guess what."

Now came a tricky part. Shackie had devised a tool that could be inserted through the central hole in a cylinder end cap; adjustment of a screw on the collar of the tool would set the apparatus firmly into place so it gripped the cap inside and out. By careful manipulation the cap could then be pulled free. But there was a catch. This procedure was usually done on cylinders as a preliminary to repinning, so you could handle the cylinder any old way you liked.

But my rigid notation cylinder needed protection. I rolled it in a thick blanket of plastic bubble-wrap. Then I handed the package to Schwartz. "Whatever you do, don't let go. Don't let me pull it out of your hands."

Schwartz tucked the cylinder under one arm and gripped the near end with both hands. I fed Shackie's puller-tool into the endcap hole, then started to twist and pull. Gently. Very gently.

Those fresh scratch marks on the brass told me which end of the cylinder Huey Fortune had worked from. He'd also have wanted easy removal. The ease with which the cap came free was the confirmation I'd hoped for. I ran my finger over the cap edge. Fresh grease.

"See?" I said, pointing inside the cylinder. "There's why it sounded funny to Shackie. Huey melted out the cement, and stuffed in his little treasure wrapped around with paper. So there was metal and paper inside some parts of the cylinder, other areas had just paper, and at the ends there was nothing at all. That made the sound range anywhere from tinny to full. Shackie was really going to put on a show for me."

But now I was the showman.

I extended a pair of long-handled forceps into the open end of the cylinder. Slowly, carefully, I teased out a small oblong package. But there was still something inside. I brought out a second package with the forceps, almost identical to the first.

I took the hollow bubble-wrapped cylinder from Schwartz and laid it carefully on the table top. Then I began to unroll brown padded paper from the first package. As I came to the end, Schwartz let out a whistle.

"That's it, Broadway. What everyone's been chasing."

The little gold pistol was a perfect image of the one I'd seen at Freddie Fellowes'. Four inches long and two inches wide, it gleamed in its padded paper cocoon. Rubies sparkled scarlet; diamonds twinkled. Hanging from the trigger cage by a thin wire was a tiny key.

"God, will you *look* at that," Schwartz breathed.

"You ain't seen nothin'. Watch this."

I sat down, fit the key into the tiny hole in the pistol stock and gave it a couple of twists. Then I pointed the barrel at Schwartz and with my fingernail pulled the trigger.

Music began to play. After the first couple of bars a tiny carved-ivory couple not an inch long emerged from the end of the barrel. The man embraced the woman and they moved together in perfect time to the music, an amorous horizontal dance. As the final notes sounded, the man rolled away and the couple slid gently back into the barrel.

Schwartz reached under his hat to scratch his head. "I thought they were even going to light up a cigarette when they were done. Who made a thing like this?"

"I'd guess Jaquet-Droz–a master eighteenth-century French automaton-maker. Probably a commissioned piece, something a wealthy nobleman gave to his mistress as a present. Lord knows how it came down to Farouk."

"Must be worth a fortune."

"At least. If Freddie wanted to sell it he could name his number. A seven-figure number."

Schwartz moved away as if the pistol might burn him.

I pulled the trigger a second time. Schwartz bent forward to get a better look. I sat and listened.

When the music stopped and the miniature fornicators had gone back to their intraballistic hideaway, Schwartz chuckled. Then he pointed to the second package on the table and asked, "What do you think's in that one?"

"One way to find out."

Roll by roll I unwrapped the paper and found myself staring in mental paralysis at another miniature pistol, a mate to the first.

"Jeez, how many of these things *are* there, anyway?"

Bingo. Connection established.

"At least three," I said, and reached over to take a spool of thin wire from its hook above the workbench. Slowly, I fed the wire into the barrel. It went only about an inch and a half. I fit the key to the winding arbor and tried to turn it, but no go. With my heart pounding I scratched the wire gently against the handgrip. A tiny flake of gold fell to the tabletop. Underneath was gray base metal.

"Another fake?" Schwartz looked up into my face.

"Looks like." I was running out of adrenaline. "But I think I've had it for a while. Time to quit."

"Okay with me. I wouldn't mind a time-out."

"Unanimous vote, then. The ayes have it." I stood up and stretched, raising my arms high above my head.

Then I went limp all over and plopped back into the chair. "Son of a *bitch*!" I muttered.

"Hey, what's the matter now?" Schwartz looked ready to give CPR.

I wrenched my photographs out of my pocket and quickly shuffled through them. "You don't know anyone who can do photo enlargements, do you? High quality ones, great on detail. In a hurry?"

Schwartz looked at his watch. "At this hour?"

"Emergency, Broadway. I'll pay double-overtime. Triple if I have to."

He held out his hand. "What is it you want to see?"

"The faces–I want to be able to make out every freckle, every little mole and beauty spot. I want to see the whites of their eyes, and the blues and the browns and the blacks, all sharp as a razor. You have someone who can do that?"

Schwartz nodded. "It'll cost you, but yeah."

I took five hundreds out of my wallet and put them on top of the pictures in Schwartz's hand. "That enough?"

He nodded again. "But you're comin' with me."

"No. It's late and we're both tired. You go get the pictures; I'll finish up here. I'll meet you back at my place a.s.a.p."

"But, Doc–"

"Broadway, things are happening too fast for both of us to row the same boat. Get me those pictures. When I'm done here I'll call a cab and I won't go down 'til I hear the horn blowing. Okay?"

His face said he didn't like it, but okay.

***

As Schwartz went out, I locked the door behind him. Then I went to work.

When I was finished I plucked the eight teeth on my newly-hardened comb section. They rang sweet and clear. Carefully, I put the section down on the workbench, then looked around. The kiln door was open and the sand dish and indicator-cones were back where they'd been, below the false bricks. It looked as if the kiln had not been touched since Shackie tucked away the rigid notation box a week before.

I called a cab. Then I walked back to the kiln and pulled the rubber tubing free from both gas inflow nipple and supply canister. "Accidents happen," I said to my own ears, and shoved the tubing into my pocket. "Whoever wants to heat up that kiln is going to have to bring his own tube."

Schwartz got back to Gramercy North about half an hour after I did. He bounced into the vestibule, a large brown envelope under his right arm. "Eleven by fourteens. And clear as a human being could make 'em."

"You got the negatives, too, I trust?"

"Doc, please. A little respect if you don't mind."

"Sorry."

I opened the envelope. There were my original photos, a bunch of negatives, and several 11x14 color glossies. I held the enlargements up to the light, one at a time, and stared at them.

Schwartz studied me anxiously. "They have what you need?"

"You bet. You just bet they do."

TWENTY-EIGHT

Next morning the phone once again beat the alarm to the punch. "I'm out of patience, Doctor," said that odd electronic voice.

I glanced at the headboard. Few minutes before eight. "You're not the only one," I snapped. "I've had it with you. You're dead; you just don't know it yet. Dead as Harry Hardwick. Dead as Charles O'Shacker. Dead as Marty Abramowitz. Dead as Jackson George. Dead and gone, null and void. So long, schmuck. Don't call anymore." I slammed down the phone.

Schwartz was in the room before the echoes stopped. He looked worried. "Jeez, what kind of a thing was that to do? That guy's gotta be mighty pissed now."

"I'm counting on it. Hold on."

I picked up the phone and hastily dialed Sarah's number. She answered on the second ring.

"Oh, good," I breathed. "Thank God you're still there."

"Thomas? That's quite a greeting."

"Sarah, listen."

"Don't tell me. You found the music box."

Don't tell me–that's what she said. I can follow orders. "Not quite yet. But things are coming to a head; the killer's about to make a move. I want you to stay in your apartment today. Don't go out, not for anything. If–"

"Are you crazy? I have to go to work; I'm leaving in ten minutes."

"No you're not. Stay home."

"I can't stay home from work. I–"

"Goddamn it, call in sick. How many sick days do you have?"

"It's not right to call in sick when you're not."

"It's not right to go out when some nut may take it into his head to hurt you or kidnap you or kill you. It's crazy, in fact. You've got to–"

"Call the police. Now."

"No. I can't."

"Why not? Why do I have to tell you this is police business, not yours? *You're* the one who's crazy–playing detective, risking your life, risking *my* life, and why? Because you think it's fun. Some great challenge you've never faced before–"

"Sarah, this isn't the time for amateur psychotherapy."

"If you don't call the police, I will."

"If you call the police, I'll never talk to you again."

There was a ridiculous standoff if ever there was one. Two grown people playing verbal chicken. In the lull I grabbed advantage. "Tell you what. Do what I tell you, just for today. If I don't have everything wrapped up by tonight I'll call in the troops. Fair enough?"

"Thomas–"

"Just one day, Babe. That's all. If I don't have it wrapped up by tomorrow–"

"If you don't have it wrapped up it could have you wrapped up. And me with you."

"At least we'd be cozy. Come on, just one day. It–" I almost said it wouldn't kill her to take a sick day but caught myself just in time. "One lousy day."

Deep sigh. Then very quietly, "Damn you."

"I love you, too. And I don't want anything to happen to you. Stay in your apartment. Doors locked *and* bolted. Don't answer the phone–and don't try to call me, either; I'm not going to answer the phone here anymore. If you need me, go through the hospital switchboard and have them ring my beeper. If I want to get hold of you, either I'll come over there or Schwartz will. We'll use your key to open the lock and we'll say ... let's see. What'd be a good password?"

"We don't *need* a silly password. I know you; I know Schwartz. If someone opens my lock and I'm not damn sure it's you or Schwartz I'll be on nine-one-one, screaming at the top of my lungs. Passwords, my God! I don't know why I keep getting mixed up in your insane life–*Thom*as ..."

That one word, that tone of voice. Trouble.

"I know why you don't want to call the police, don't I? It's because you *have* found that music box. And you're afraid they'll take it away from you. For evidence, or something like that."

"Sarah–"

"It's true, isn't it? You're risking your life and mine and Schwartz's and God knows who-all else's just so you don't have to hand over a music box to the police. *Aren't* you? Tell me the truth."

"It's more complicated than that."

"Stop and think for a minute, would you? To risk lives for a music box–I can't even *begin* to understand that."

Of course she couldn't. It had nothing to do with understanding. If you're a collector you just know it; if you're not, you don't. I knew it. Sarah didn't. She couldn't. There was nothing to argue about.

"One day," I repeated. "That's all I'm asking for. Okay?"

"Oh, I could–"

"What, kill me? Talk to you later." I hung up.

Almost immediately the phone rang again. Schwartz and I looked at each other. I switched off the answering machine. The phone rang ten times, stopped, then a moment later started ringing again. After four attempts, it stayed silent.

"This guy ain't going to be very happy at all with you."

"Good. I'm not very happy with him. Come on. We've got a lot to do."

***

Breakfast at a Second Avenue coffee shop, then downtown to Wind-Me-Up. We got there a little before ten, just as Frank the Crank was opening the door.

"Well, looky this," he said. "The good doctor again. I don't see you for a month, maybe two, but now three times inside of a week. To what do I owe the honor?"

I said a silent thanks that Frank was up. "To your singular skills. To your unique and strangely personal talents. In other words–"

"In other words you need my help again. What now?"

I looked around. "Can we come inside and talk?"

"Oh. Yeah, sure." He stepped aside to let Schwartz and me pass, then led us to the rear of the store.

"Oh, and Frank ..."

He turned around. He'd picked up on my tone. "What?"

"How about locking the door and leaving the closed sign up?"

"Jesus Christ. Two days before Christmas, my best time of the year, and you want me to lock out my customers?"

"Ten minutes, Frank. That's all, I promise. It's important."

He walked to the door, threw the bolt, pushed it shut, and flipped the sign around. As he walked back to us he said, "This *better* be important."

I didn't like the sound of that. This was not the time to lose Frank to his unpredictable bipolar derangement.

"It is," I said, in my best medical center baritone. "I need you to help me catch the guy who killed Shackie and four other people in the bargain."

That did it. Frank's black eyes glittered with curiosity. "What're you on to?"

"I know who it is, but I can't prove a damn thing. I've got to make him make a move. You're going to cast my bait."

Frank looked somewhere into the distance. "Anybody who'd do a decent guy like Shackie ..." He snapped back to us. "Who is it?"

"Not so fast," I said. "You hook him for me and I'll pull him in. Then we'll both know for sure."

"What do I do?"

"Activate the grapevine; make sure it's all over Music Box Town. Thomas Purdue found Harry Hardwick's rigid notation box and figured out why it sounded bad at Harry's party. He's throwing a big bash tomorrow night at his place to show off the box and tell the story. Oh, and one more thing, Frank. Important."

"I'm with you. All ears. Tomorrow night. Big Christmas-Eve Party."

"Tell them Purdue is over at Shackie's, working like a demon, today, tonight. Getting everything ready for the big performance."

Frank's face went from enthusiasm to moderate doubt. "I got it, but I also got one question. This character, whoever he is, he's killed four people already. You *are* gonna have cops there, aren't you? Watching?"

"No, I'm not. I told you: I don't have any proof. I can't count on the police being willing to go along with my hunch. Besides, what if they get pissed and decide to toss me a curve?"

Sly smile, scratch at ear. Frank's trademark expression of comprehension. "In other words, maybe they'd take away that rigid notation box and keep it for evidence."

"Tell it any way you'd like. But I'm the one who's going to catch this dirt ball. With more than a little help from my friends. Both of them."

Schwartz beamed and patted at the bulge over his left chest.

Frank nodded seriously. "Okay. You call the shots; I'll play along."

I clapped my hand against his arm. "Thanks," I said. "I knew we could count on you. Just watch out for the Black Angel, Frank. Don't let him screw this up."

Frank's face went through fear to anger and finally into

determination. His lips were thin and pale. "No way. If that bastard starts pullin' me under, I'll at least call you. And if you got to give me something, I'll take it. No way I'm gonna let you down. Or Shackie."

I thanked Frank again, then checked my watch. "We've been here twelve minutes; time for us all to go to work."

At Shackie's, I held up my new comb-tooth segment for Schwartz to see. He frowned. "Hey, not to offend you, but frankly it looks like hell. All that black stuff on it."

Funny. The first time I'd ever made a new block of teeth with Shackie I'd seen that same sooty scale and figured I'd botched the job. "It comes right off with a little sanding. Here's the important thing."

I rested the block on the wooden tabletop and plucked the upper tooth with my fingernail. A short sound went up, clear and bright.

"Hey," Schwartz cheered. "She rings."

"She sure do. That was the dicey part. Now it's just a matter of cleaning it, soldering it into the slot on the comb, and filing the teeth to proper pitch. Couple of hours, no more."

It actually took an hour and three-quarters. Schwartz held the repaired comb up to the light, turning it this way and that, squinting his eyes to assess the work. "You can hardly even see the line. Beautiful job. I didn't know you were that good."

"Neither did I."

Schwartz wanted to break for lunch but I shook my head. "You go get some food–maybe for lunch *and* dinner." I took a couple of bills out of my wallet and handed them to him.

That he didn't like. "Leave you alone here? When you're waiting for this guy to come in and I'm supposed to be hiding in the john ..." To finish the sentence, he patted his left chest again.

"It's too soon. I don't think we'll have company before tonight–certainly not before late afternoon. Go ahead. This's the time. I don't want you to faint from hunger when you may need to do your thing."

I locked the door behind Schwartz. I'd been in any number of life-threatening situations before, but in all of them someone else's life was under threat, not mine. Which makes a big difference, believe me.

With Schwartz out of the way, I went to the phone and called my lawyer friend, Melvin Madrid. Luck held; he was in. And after all the time and trouble I'd saved him, he was more than pleased to answer my short question.

I hung up the phone and walked to the ultrasound bath, where the components of the mandoline-basse box were still soaking. Once I had them cleaned and polished I could reassemble the mechanism.

The phone rang.

I reached for it but pulled back my hand. My throat was parched. I licked my lips. Finally, I picked up the receiver.

"Hello?" The anxiety in my voice annoyed me.

"Thomas?"

The voice was familiar but I couldn't place it. "Yes? Who's this?"

"Lucas Sterne."

Fancy that. Frank the Crank was nothing if not efficient. "Well, Lucas," I said, suddenly all brightness and cheer. "What can I do for you?"

"Just wanted to ask. There are little birdies flying around town, telling interesting stories."

"Oh really?"

"Yes. Stories about how you've found Harry's rigid notation box."

"I don't know, Lucas. You've got to watch those rumorbirds; they can cause a lot of trouble. But I'll tell you what: I'm having a little get-together here at Shackie's place, tomorrow night around seven. We can talk about it then."

"No advance info? No hints even?"

"No early birds. I'll see you at seven tomorrow. Right now I'm busy."

Schwartz got back and I told him about Lucas' call while I was rinsing the components and rubbing them with brass polish and a soft cloth.

"Didn't take him long, did it?"

"He's got to be worried. His whole career's riding on that Hardwick sale."

"Can't say I feel too sorry for him." Schwartz snickered. "The little twerp."

We broke for lunch after polishing and before reassembly. I made myself a roast beef sandwich and opened a can of Dr. Brown's Cel-Ray. Schwartz piled an inch of corned beef onto a slab of rye bread, then in an apparent afterthought added a few slices of turkey and Swiss cheese. He cut a slice of cheesecake, then sat down to the feast. I pulled up a chair opposite him. I'd just taken my first bite when the phone rang.

I stopped chewing. Schwartz froze, sandwich in mid-air.

I ran across the room, swallowing hard as I went, and grabbed the receiver.

This time it was Sophie. "Thomas, *what* are you up to?"

"My neck. In your mandoline-basse box. It's cleaned and polished and ready to go back together. Then I'll register the cylinder and do the dampers. I just might get it done for you ... but I did have a bit of a problem."

"What kind of a bit of a problem?"

"I'm sorry. I slipped and banged the comb against a vise and knocked out eight teeth." I heard a sudden intake of air at the other end. "I've already replaced them, made a block," I said, talking as fast as I could. "They look good to me and they sound good. And the line's almost invisible. It *should* be okay. But if Rutledge is unhappy I'll buy the box myself. My fault, my cost."

"I'm sure it will be fine. God bless you, don't worry about it. But that's not why I'm calling."

"I figured. You heard a story from the rumor-bird, didn't you? Something about a missing music box that's been found and a big show at a party tomorrow night?"

"Yes. I couldn't help wondering ... I feel like a fool. It's my own fault, but still. I can't help worrying–"

"Don't," I said. "You've got nothing to worry about. Just come by tomorrow about seven. I'm sure you'll be interested."

"I'm not worried about myself, but I've been at least partly responsible for four murders already. I don't want there to be a fifth. Especially if it's you. I'm sorry for getting angry at you yesterday. I had no right."

"Like I said, don't worry. I'll see you tomorrow. That's a promise."

"You usually make promises you ain't sure you can keep?" Schwartz asked.

"Never," I said.

Schwartz stopped chewing long enough to make sure I knew he'd diagnosed moral leprosy. "I think I might be starting to have some sympathy for that wife of yours," he said.

"There's a balance in the world, Broadway. Good and evil. Yin and yang. Positive-negative, black-white. Alpha and omega. Jobs have perks; jobs have hazards. No free lunches."

Schwartz looked at his sandwich and laughed. "And one and one don't always add up and make two."

Bingo again. I put down my sandwich.

Schwartz's face clouded over. "Now what? What the hell did I say?"

I reached across the table and shook him by his shirt front. "You just tied up the last missing link," I shouted. "One real Farouk pistol, two fakes."

After lunch I wrote out a guest list for the party. In addition to Lucas Sterne and Sophie Soleski there was Muriel Hardwick, Barton Moss, Walter Remler, and Sammy Shapiro. "Call 'em at home, call 'em at work if you have to," I told Schwartz. "Tell them seven o'clock, my place, Gramercy North."

"What if they can't come?"

"They can't, they can't. But I want to know whose ears Frank's put the word in. We already know Lucas and Sophie. Make sure to find out who else."

"Got it."

Schwartz went off to the phone. I went to the workbench.

Re-assembly's usually quick and easy. Within half an hour the mandoline-basse mechanism was back together, shiny and clean. The music was wonderful. Six airs from Italian opera, Verdi, Donizetti, Bellini. Booming chords from low bass notes supported a strummed-mandolin effect. Best of all, the notes from the replacement block of treble teeth were bright and clear, right on pitch.

Schwartz hung up the phone and turned to listen. "Sounds a hell of a lot better, you ask me. But you still got some of those noises–dampers, right?"

"Right, left, and in between. That's next. You call everyone?"

"Got 'em all and they're all coming. Every one'd heard from Frank. Shapiro even said he was gettin' pissed at you big-time 'cause you hadn't invited him."

"Great. We're on our way."

I'd taken the comb back off the mechanism and was ready to start dampering when once again the phone rang. Schwartz moved to answer it but I waved him off.

"Let's not tell anyone you're here."

I picked up the phone and said hello.

No answer.

I got that tingly feeling in the tips of my fingers. "Hello?" I said again.

"Doc ..." finally came through the phone. "Doc Purdue ..." It sounded like a seventy-eight RPM record played at forty-five.

"Frank?" I said.

"Who d'you think, dumb bastard? I said I'd call you, right? If the Angel got me? Well, he does, bad. But word's out; I talked to everyone just like you wanted. Job's done."

I pictured Frank the Crank at the other end of that phone line, slumped in his chair, bald head down on the desk. When the Black Angel dragged Frank down he dragged him all the way down, straight to the bottom of the sea. *You* try moving, let alone breathing, with fifty fathoms of salt water above and around you. I couldn't imagine how Frank had managed to take a telephone receiver off the hook and dial seven numbers.

"Great, Frank, thanks. I love you, man."

All I heard from the other end were snuffles. Frank was crying. After a minute or so, he said, "Doc? Maybe you *could* gimme something. So's I don't have to get like this all the goddamn time."

"Count on it, Frank," I said. "I'll come on by with some Angel poison, soon as I can. Hang in."

More crying. Then the line clicked dead.

Dampering a music box comb demands unwavering attention to detail. Pull holding pin, ream hole in damper anvil, insert wire of proper thickness, gently tap pin back home. Bend wire to proper shape. Start again.

It's hard on eyes and shoulders. When vision blurs and fingers stiffen, you need to stop and stretch. Otherwise you get clumsy. Then pliers slip or you miss with the hammer, and you're replacing more knocked-out teeth. So I worked, I stopped and stretched, I worked some more. I was taking a break about four-thirty when the phone rang. I snatched up the receiver and said hello.

"Dr. Purdue."

That voice again. I covered the mouthpiece and stage-whispered, "Schwartz! It's him." Then I growled, "What the hell do you want? I told you to piss off."

"You did. But I'm a generous person, Dr. Purdue. I'm at least going to let you know your time is up. I want that rigid notation music box and I want it now."

"I don't have it."

"I think you do. And I know if you don't turn it over to me you're going to be a very unhappy man. Now listen carefully: There's a phone booth outside the Union Square subway entrance, south side of Fourteenth Street. I want you to be at that phone exactly one half hour from now, with the rigid notation box in your hands. If there's someone in the booth, just wait. As soon as the line is clear the phone will ring and you'll get further instructions. Do you understand?"

I didn't say anything. I thought I could hear Schwartz breathing through the extension line.

"I wouldn't be cute, Doctor. If you don't follow my directions to the T you'll never see your wife again, except to identify her body. I assume it's you they'll call."

The sneer in the voice was infuriating. "Listen, you walking brain-death," I said. "My wife is a first-class pain in the ass. Why do you think I haven't lived with her for the last six years? You want to do me a favor and get rid of her for me, be my guest. Even if I had that rigid notation box I wouldn't give it to you. Now, get lost."

On the last word, I slammed down the receiver.

Schwartz ran toward me from across the room. "You're either the bravest guy I ever knew or the dumbest, and you want to hear the truth, I ain't sure which. That guy gives me the creeps."

"He should. He's not an example of perfect emotional health. Now get yourself over to Sarah's, quick. Don't leave her alone for a minute."

A frantic look around the room. "But, Doc—"

"Never mind. You can't be in two places at once." I pulled

Sarah's apartment key off my key ring and dropped it into Schwartz's hand. "I'll lock the door. If somebody starts kicking or shooting the lock I'll do a quick nine-one-one, and then I'm out that window there and down the fire escape. Go on now. If anything happens to Sarah I'm not going to forgive myself."

He smiled. "I didn't think you really meant–"

"*Go.*" I hustled him to the door and into the hall. Then I went back inside.

I walked to the rear of the shop and grabbed five large rags from Shackie's tatter-box. Three I used to cover small to medium-sized music boxes on the work-in-progress shelves. Then I went back to the main-station workbench and draped the fourth rag over Wilma Ryan's Lecoultre box on the shelf above. Finally, I wrapped the rigid notation box in the fifth rag, tucked the package under my arm, and charged up the stairs to the loft. Carefully, I slid my treasure through the slash I'd made into the box springs, cushioning it between two coils. Then I hustled back downstairs.

Nothing else to do now but wait. I sat down at the workbench and picked up the dampering where I'd left off. Pull pin, clean hole, place wire, tap pin, shape damper. Repeat. And again. *D. C. al fine.*

TWENTY-NINE

I was on a damper roll. My hands moved along the comb as if of their own accord, tooth by tooth, zip, zip. I worked myself into a countdown rhythm: like ninety-nine bottles of beer on the wall. Silly, but it worked. Ninety-nine dampers to put on the comb, ninety-nine dampers to shape. When one of those dampers is round like a dome, there's ninety-eight dampers to put on the comb. Ninety-eight dampers to put on the comb, ninety-eight dampers to shape ...

I was counting down from forty-two when a woman's voice behind me said, "Mr. Purdue." Not Doctor. I jumped off the chair onto both feet. "Oh dear, I'm sorry. Did I frighten you?"

Wilma Ryan leaned forward, clutching purse to chest, dog-eyeing me through rimless glasses.

"Well ... Mrs. Ryan," I said. "No, not really frightened, more like startled. I was concentrating."

She extended her neck to peer at the comb in my hands. "Is that from *my* music box?"

I shook my head. "Sorry, I'm not onto yours yet. This box has to be done for Christmas."

She smiled. "Oh, that's fine; I understand. And why don't you call me Wilma? Your name is Thomas, isn't it?"

"Yes," I said. "I actually did try to call you, Wilma. To tell you it would be a while before I could get to your music box. But the phone number Shackie put down was nonexistent. One of you must have made a mistake."

She put her hand over her mouth: silly me. "Oh, I'm sorry. I have to make a confession."

"Uh-oh. Slipped into moral turpitude somewhere, have we?"

"Oh, that's a bit strong, I think." She giggled. "No, it's just that ... well, I don't want my husband to know ... about how I'm going to have the music box restored. He didn't approve of my buying it in the first place and he wouldn't approve of spending more on it now. I didn't want Mr. O'Shacker or you, for that matter, to call and tip my husband off."

"Why didn't you tell me that? Or Mr. O'Shacker?"

Small pout. "I should have. But I felt foolish."

"Oh, well." I held out the comb. "Here's what needs to be done on your box–see the little wires under the teeth? They have to be put into place, then curved into shape."

She tiptoed forward, looked briefly at the comb, then shifted her gaze directly into my face. "Thomas, why are you looking at me like that?"

"Like what?" I put the comb carefully down on the table.

"Well ... like you're studying me."

"I have a curious nature. I wonder things. Such as how you got in here."

Without turning, she pointed behind herself. "Well ... the door was open. Unlocked, I mean. I knocked, but ... maybe not hard enough. No one answered. So I tried the door and it opened."

"And you thought you'd just come in and say hello. See how I was coming along with your music box."

Her face was like the sun slowly emerging from cloud cover. "Yes, that's it exactly. I hope you're not angry. You *will* still take care of my music box?"

"Yes, of course. But the sooner I can get this comb finished, the sooner I can get to yours." I pointed above the workbench. "There's your music box, right where we left it the other night. Not to be rude, but maybe you should let me get back to work. So I *can* get to your box."

She made no move to leave, just stood staring at the shelf. "Why do you have it covered, Thomas?"

She was holding her big leather purse at chest level and taking care, I thought, to stay out of my reach. When I'd shown her the comb she'd leaned forward from the waist, clearly more interested in my face than in wire dampers.

I ran my tongue across my lips. "It's a very fine music box. I cover special ones. Just a little extra care."

Wilma glanced around the room. "Those over there." She pointed to the storage shelves. "Are they also special?"

"Oh, yes."

"Show them to me."

There was something in her voice now, a quality I'd heard before but couldn't say where. An odd sound, like a structure slipping on its foundation.

"Well ..." I began, and scratched at the back of my head. "Those music boxes belong to other people. Besides, I really do have to get back to work. Otherwise I'll never get to your—"

"Show me those music boxes!"

Now I knew where I'd heard that vocal oddity. It was in my own voice when I was trying to get Schwartz out of Shackie's and over to Sarah's. Not that my marvelous insight was particularly helpful. Wilma was holding a pistol in her left hand.

"Get over there and pull off those rags," she barked. "Now!"

Lying in a tray or hanging on a wall, Wilma's pistol would have been unimpressive. But in the hand of a twitchy woman, her finger tight against the trigger, it looked big as one of Stonewall Jackson's cannons, capable of blowing a hole through me armies could march through. I didn't feel the least bit brave.

Wilma followed me to the storage shelves. She stood behind me as I slowly removed the covers, one by one. It was easy to see I had not shown her what she'd come for.

"All right," she said. "Where is it?"

Just then the phone rang.

Wilma waved the gun at me, fair warning. "Don't answer that."

We stood motionless during eight rings. Then, a brief pause, and ten more rings. Probably Schwartz, I thought.

Wilma tightened her lips and aimed the gun straight for my heart. "Time's running out," she said, gesturing with her eyes toward the phone. "Now listen, and listen carefully. Maybe we can still cut a deal. Or else you can tell me you don't know where that rigid notation box is, and the minute the words are out of your mouth I'll shoot you. Then I'll poke around here as long as I think I can. If I find it, good. If not ..." She shrugged, ever so slightly. "I'll keep thinking." Grim smile and a grimmer little laugh. No giggle this time.

I jerked my head toward the sleeping loft and said, "It's up there."

Doubt covered her face. "Is it?" She worked her tongue against her upper lip. "Then let's go get it." She gestured with a wave of the gun. "After you."

Hard as it is to stare into the barrel of a gun, it's harder yet to walk casually along with that gun aimed at your back, and not pull a Lot's-wife routine. I started up the steps.

"Faster," Wilma snapped. "You'd better not be kidding or you're going to die in bed. Just not the way most people do."

"You're not going to hang me in a closet?" I said.

She snickered. "Hardly. I don't think you'd forget all about me standing behind you while you looked over a music box. Your friend was easy: choke-hold for a couple of minutes, then drag him upstairs and hang him in the closet. But it's all right; I don't need you to look like a suicide. Just dead will be good enough."

I glanced back. Wilma was four steps behind me, gun up and ready. Too far for me to lunge and shove. I'd be Swiss-cheese before I had a finger on her.

"Turn around and stay turned," she snapped. "Keep moving." I stopped at the top of the steps. "Go on," Wilma said. "Make space."

I walked toward the bed. "After you killed Shackie you

took his keys," I said. "If we check the police report on the contents of Shackie's pockets we won't find a house key on the list, will we?"

"Forget the chit-chat." Wilma waggled the pistol. "Just get that music box. You've got one chance."

"It's there." I pointed at the bed. "In the box springs under the mattress."

Wilma moved back a step or two. The gun didn't so much as waver. "Fine," she said. "Get it."

I bent and tugged at the corner of the mattress.

"No sudden moves," Wilma said. "You don't want to make me jump."

The mattress was off. I reached between the springs, picked up the rigid notation box, and lifted it out.

"Nice and easy."

I turned to face her, holding the rigid notation box with both hands. Maybe a quick shove as I made as if to hand it over? She was standing with her back to the rail, only a step onto the flooring. I looked at her high-heeled shoes. Not sensible shoes for murder. If I hit her low enough she might go over and down.

Wilma smiled. "Well, what do you know? You did have it after all, naughty boy. Put it on the floor."

That'd be all she'd write. As soon as the box was out of my hands I'd be dispensable and dispensed with. It occurred to me I was holding a potential weapon, whether thrown, swung, or shoved. But the price tag on a soul is even higher than that on a life and I wasn't going to risk having that music box smashed beyond repair or blown by a bullet into permanent silence. I'd go with the ultimate defensive weapon, the old Thousand-and-One-Night Smoke Bomb.

"You'll have the music box," I said to Wilma. "But not what used to be in it."

"What?"

"I said you won't have what you really came for—what

used to be inside the cylinder where your friend Huey put it. It's not there now; I took it out. See?" I opened the lid, set the box on the floor, kept talking as fast as I could. "Sounds a lot better than at Harry's party now that it's got cement in the cylinder instead of two Farouk erotic pistols–the real one and a fake." I pushed the start lever.

The Magic Flute. Glorious music. The savage breast looked down into the music box, in the process slightly lowering its pistol.

"Wilma, you're screwed!" I suddenly shouted. "Wilma–Walter. Wilma–Walter! Wilma–*Walter*!"

The pistol wavered in Wilma's left hand. She started to transfer it to her right.

That's what I was waiting for.

I launched myself below gun-level, straight at her thighs. As I hit her, I heard a shot and groaned. *The Magic Flute* kept playing, though, didn't miss a note.

Wilma flew backward against the rail but didn't go over; the damned rail was too high. She let out a low-pitched scream and rebounded above me, hitting my right shoulder like a sack of potatoes. I straightened and heaved her forward but she was too heavy for me to get her up and over the four-foot railing. I held her pinned between my body and the rail, being sure to keep her gun pointing straight up. Fortunately it was my right hand against her left.

I lowered my head and butted her hard in the face. Again, she screamed. Her left arm tightened and the gun went off. Another hole in the ceiling; I could live with that.

But sooner or later one of us was going to make a mistake. I couldn't press her to the rail forever, and unfortunately she did still have possession of the gun. If she got her left arm free she'd win. I needed to do something to shift the counterbalance in my favor, maybe take a bit of a risk. Might call for some balls.

Of course.

I drew back my right leg and swung my knee sharply forward, scoring a direct hit on Wilma's crotch. This time the noise she let out was more groan than howl and I felt her go limp. I watched, fascinated, as the pistol seemed to float to the floor of the workshop below. Wilma dropped to her knees, white-faced behind her makeup. She writhed on the floor like a giant fetus in agony.

I dashed for the stairs. Whoever got to the gun first was winner and Wilma was clearly *non compos corporis*. In two huge jumps I was halfway down the stairs. I had it made.

Until the door to the apartment opened and I found myself staring into another gun barrel. Marisa Morgan was behind this one.

"Hold it there, Thomas," she said.

Wilma was still rocking and groaning upstairs. Without taking her eyes off me Marisa said, "You shot her, did you?"

"No. Just a knee in the balls."

She looked at me, full of suspicion. "You've an odd sense of humor."

"Flattery'll get you some things, but not what you came for."

"We'll see about that. Go on, now. Back upstairs."

In the loft Marisa pulled a pair of handcuffs from her hip-pack. "Here, pull her arms behind her and put these on her. And please don't do anything funny. I don't want to have to shoot you."

Wilma was breathing more easily now. She glared at me.

"Not my fault," I said. "You heard the lady. Only following orders."

Wilma raised her left hand.

"Hands together behind your arse–fast!" Marisa commanded Wilma. "You're as good dead as alive to me; it's your choice."

I bent down to put on the cuffs when suddenly Wilma grabbed my ankle. I twisted away, kicking at her face. A direct hit brought a scream; by reflex she twisted sharply away from my foot ... and off the edge of Shackie's sleeping platform. For the instant I could see, her expression was one I'd noticed before only on the face of Wile E. Coyote. For that instant her arms flailed, wing-like; but like Wile E. Coyote, Wilma was not aeronautically sound.

"I couldn't shoot," Marisa gasped. "I was afraid I'd hit *you*."

I didn't stop to say thanks, just charged down the step-ladder. There was still a gun loose on that lower floor. Marisa clattered behind me.

No need to have hurried. Wilma lay crumpled on the floor between the bandsaw and the lathe, a couple of feet past her gun. Her head was nearly one-hundred-eighty degrees off customary posture. Just for the record, I bent down, palpated her limp wrist. Her eyes were open and staring, both pupils dark and fully dilated. Death, the great equalizer.

Marisa looked at her pistol, dangling from her hand, as if trying to figure out how it had gotten there. Slowly, she slipped the weapon inside her jacket.

"Let me guess," I said. "Freddie Fellowes wasn't as thick as he let on. He *did* pick up on the fact his Farouk pistol had been switched for a fake, and hired you to find it. Guess Number Two is you're the Yard."

"Go with One." Marisa smiled. "I'm a private investigator. And I'm surprised at you, Thomas, a collector of your standing. Wouldn't *you* have noticed if your prize antique, the most important item in your collection, had been tampered with? Mr. Fellowes may be a crashing old bore but he's certainly not senile. He played that pistol every night, last thing before he went to bed. Early the morning after it was stolen, he was in my office. He didn't want to go to the police because he knew if word got out he'd tumbled, that'd definitely be the last he'd see of that pistol. It would vanish into some collector's basement in Amsterdam, Leipzig, or Singapore and that would be that. A low profile was necessary. Fortunately it worked."

"Almost."

She studied my face. "What do you mean?"

"Just that our fancy carrying case up there is empty now."

"Thomas ..." She looked upstairs, then back at me. "Don't mess with my mind, eh?"

"I'm not. You knew right from the beginning the pistol was inside the cylinder, didn't you?"

"I thought it was something like that," Marisa said. "Especially after I'd talked to the Westfalls. At that point it seemed easy. But after Harry Hardwick was shot and the music box stolen, things became considerably more complicated, didn't they?"

I laughed. "You might say. It took *me* a lot longer to catch on. Shackie knew there was something in the cylinder that didn't belong there, but Wilma put him away before he could show me. When I finally did dope it out I removed the pistol and hid it. Where no one will find it."

Except maybe Francois Nicole, I thought.

I took Marisa's elbow. "Come on back upstairs–I'll show you."

I set the rigid notation box on the night table, opened the lid, and wound the spring. The music picked up where it had wound down while I was wrestling with Wilma, partway through "*Idomeneo*."

"Sounds a lot better now the pistol and paper are out and the cylinder's evenly filled with cement. If you insist I'll open the cylinder for you."

"That won't be necessary. Unfortunately, I believe you." A crooked little smile grew across her face. "You tell a good story. But I *am* going to have to ask you to un-hide that pistol and give it over to me. Otherwise, you're going to be in the middle of some highly unpleasant legal complications. Mr. Fellowes will have his pistol back, whatever it requires. He's prepared to sell the remainder of his collection if necessary."

"Rather than the half it'll take to pay your fee?"

Marisa laughed. "I wish. No, my fees for this work won't be more than four or five thousand pounds, expenses included. About the price of one nice music box I'd say."

"There you are. We have room for an agreement."

"I'm sorry? I'm afraid you've lost me."

"Easy, I don't want the pistol; it's not my thing. Even if it were, I wouldn't want it under these conditions. It belongs to Freddie, it should go back to him. But ..."

"But there's something you do want."

"Two somethings: First, I want the rigid notation box. Freddie sold it, and for an outrageous price. Which is fine. Let him keep the money and I'll keep the music box."

"But it was sold to Harry Hardwick."

"Not your problem. Or Freddie's. I bought the box from a licensed antiques dealer; I've got a receipt. According to a sharp lawyer I know, that gives me a valid legal claim. If the matter went to court it could be tied up for years. But I think I can work things out with Muriel Hardwick. What I want is for you and Freddie to not say a word about the music box to the police. You'll have the pistol; just return it quietly to Freddie. Not one word to anyone about a rigid notation box."

She ran her tongue over the inside of her cheek and smiled, a very sexy maneuver. "I expect Mr. Fellowes would agree to that ... I'd have to call him, of course."

"Of course. But there's one other thing."

"Oh, right. Which is?"

"That you come to my party tomorrow night. I'm sure you got word about it."

She smiled but didn't say anything. She didn't have to.

"Come to the party and listen to everything I say. Especially what I say to my wife. Don't argue. Don't dispute anything; don't contradict me. Or else no deal."

She rolled her eyes. "Oh very well. If you need to play games I suppose I can play along."

"If we *are* playing games they're your games. Even the

rules are yours. Who was the old lady at the flats in Kensington where you're supposed to live?"

Marisa grinned. "My grandmum. She and Granddad own the building and rent out the flats. After you knocked me over the head I thought you might have gone through my purse. So I phoned Grandmum and had her put a false name in my mail slot. She told me you'd been by. Next time you're in London try me again."

"I don't think so." I closed the lid of the rigid notation box, stroked the smooth wood, and pushed the start lever. The tragic strains of "*Don Giovanni*" filled the room.

"Oh, you bloody crazy collectors!" Hands on hips, Marisa shook her head in disgust. "You're daft, all of you, absolutely insane. I'll be glad to finish this case."

"You'll be bored," I said, and glanced over the rail at Wilma's corpse. "Time to call the cops; you'd better get out of here. I'll tell them she ... he ... *she* came here posing as a client, then took me upstairs at gunpoint–wouldn't say why. I distracted her, grabbed her ... she went over. Let them draw their own conclusions once they undress her down at the morgue."

Marissa colored very prettily, I thought, then started for the door. "See you tomorrow night," I called after her. Don't forget–don't mention the music box. *Or* the pistol."

"For heavens' sake. Yes." She closed the door.

I reached for the phone, dialed Sarah's number. Schwartz answered on the first ring. "All over but the shouting."

I didn't bother to tell him whose.

THIRTY

It was the best party ever. Sarah was there, and Schwartz and Trudy. Lucas Sterne sauntered in, kow-towing to Muriel Hardwick but taking time between his acts of deference to check out every music box on my shelves. Sophie Soleski held court near my desk. For once, Sammy Shapiro didn't have a lot to say. Neither did Barton Moss, who hung in the background and kept close tabs on the kitchen table where I'd put the booze. Frank the Crank was swinging high, trying to make quick-time with Marisa. I asked Frank if he was ready to poison a Black Angel. He shook his head.

"But you said, yesterday–"

"I wasn't feelin' so good yesterday. Today, I'm fine."

"The Arkansas Traveler. His cabin never leaks when it doesn't rain."

Sophie Soleski chuckled. She looked twenty years younger than she had the day before.

Sarah looked puzzled. "I don't understand."

"Arkansas Traveler," I repeated. "The song."

She just shook her head. "I'll never understand the way your mind works."

I gathered everyone around my desk and played the rigid notation box through its full program.

"It does sound better now." Lucas said it grudgingly, but he said it.

"So does that mandoline-basse," said Sophie. "I'm impressed,

Thomas. The music is perfect and I can hardly see the join where you set in the teeth. If Tim Rutledge doesn't like it he can go straight to hell. I'll never sell him another music box."

"Good. If you need me for other restoration jobs every now and again I suspect I can handle them."

"We'll talk, my dear."

Lucas looked from the rigid notation box to Muriel. "Good thing he found it," Lucas said. "That'll help your net sales."

Muriel glanced my way, then shook her head. "No, I think not. Thomas bought that box from a dealer; he has proper legal claim. Besides, considering the trouble he's been to–"

"But Muriel–"

She cut him off with a laser-look. "Do be still, Lucas. I said Thomas will keep the rigid notation box and there's an end to it. He and I settled the matter this afternoon."

Lucas favored me with a bent smile.

"You snooze, you lose, Lucas," Schwartz shouted. "A person's gotta get up early to beat out the Doc. Hey, Doc–what was it that tipped you off to how Wilma Ryan and Remler were ... well, the same person."

"Same person, sort of," I said. "Basically he was Walter Remler, but over the years he must have developed the Wilma character to hide behind when dirty work needed doing. I should have had it figured a lot sooner. The pupil in Walter's right eye was bigger than the left. Any of you ever notice that?"

Only Frank the Crank raised his hand. "Yeah, now you mention it ..."

"That's right, Frank. Now I mention it. It wasn't ugly or disfiguring–nothing a person would pay particular attention to. Unfortunately, when Wilma came in last week, it was her Lecoultre I focused on, not her. But it must have registered at some level in my mind because when I looked at these pictures"–I pulled the two photographs of Wilma out of my pocket–"something clicked."

"That's why you wanted me to get the blowups," said Schwartz. "To see her eyes better."

I opened the worktable drawer and took out the 11x14s. Sophie covered her open mouth. I heard her mumble, "Oh, dear."

"Sorry, Soph," I said. "But look at her eyes. Two people, same initials, both with anisocoria. Pretty big coincidence."

"Where did you get these pictures?" Good old Lucas on the uptake.

"Just stumbled across them," I said lightly. "They were hidden in a book in Harry's library."

Lucas glared at Sarah. She looked away very quickly, but I swore she smiled.

"Were these the only ones you found?" Lucas added.

"Yep," I said, not missing Muriel's smirk and half-wink. "But they were enough. Along with a matchbook I found in Jackson George's apartment a few days ago, they got me to the George Sand Club, a cross-dress bar in London. Huey Fortune hung out there and whenever Harry was in London he went with Huey. When Remler was in London Wilma went too, of course. Harry and Remler were both over for that big miniatures auction at Sotheby's last September, and Harry saw Wilma at the Sand. How Harry made the connection I can only guess. He was a sharp man; maybe he noticed the unequal pupils. Or maybe Huey tipped him. In any case, Harry got wise and bought the pictures from the club owner, the man who'd taken them. At first I thought Harry might have been trying to blackmail Remler. Imagine what Remler's wife would have done if she'd found out he was a cross-dresser who posed for pictures like these."

Sophie clucked. "Oh, the poor woman."

"Remler's big time collecting, not to mention his theatrical career, would have been down the drain in a hurry. What I couldn't figure, though, was *why* Harry would be blackmailing Remler. Harry certainly didn't need money. Then it occurred to me. What you said, Frank. About–"

"You mean how Remler aced Harry out of–"

"The Musical Maiden," Muriel finished. "*That's* why you were so interested. Oh, my God, yes. I have never in my life seen a man as furious as Harry; I don't think he slept for a week. But all of a sudden it was over. Let bygones be bygones, he said. Which did puzzle me a bit. But I'm not a collector, now, am I? So I just let it go by."

"But you were right," I said. "Harry never would have forgiven being screwed over like that–especially on such a major item. He sent Huey Fortune a big chunk of change–enough to get two top-quality replicas made of the Farouk pistol and to buy the rigid notation box from Freddie Fellowes. A rigid notation box was impressive enough to serve as a smokescreen, an excuse to get Huey into Freddie's flat. While he was there he stopped on his way to the bathroom to swap one of the fake pistols for the real one. Then a fast run back to his workshop. Dismantle rigid notation box, put real pistol and second fake inside cylinder, switch Nicole rigid notation box for Nicole overture box in Sophie's shipment. No customs inspector in the world would pick up on that. Then ship the crate to Sophie. Let Harry know it's on the way. Harry buys the box from Sophie and takes it home."

"I don't think I ever saw Harry so pleased with a purchase," Muriel said.

"I'll bet. I'll also bet when Harry invited Remler to his party he told him he had a purchase in process for the ultimate piece of musical erotica, the Farouk pistol, and he'd show it to Remler as soon as he had it, right after the holidays. Then Huey would come over on the third of January, open the rigid-notation cylinder, take out the two pistols–the real one and the second fake–and call Remler to say something like, 'Harry's away for the day and wouldn't you like to make a quiet buy–quick enough for me to get back to London before Harry gets back home.' Huey would've met Remler on a street corner or in a hotel lobby, given him the fake pistol, taken the money and run. Literally."

"But it wouldn't have taken Remler long to figure out he'd been had," Sophie said. "Then what?"

"Part of Harry's plan. It's illegal to carry more than ten grand in currency on international flights; I don't think Harry would have wanted to take a chance on Huey getting nailed with three to five million dollars in a satchel. Huey probably would have dropped the take in a locker or a big safe deposit box, then made straight for the airport. Remler would've spent the day stewing, tried to call Harry in the evening, but by then Harry would have been on his way to London with Huey—and the real Farouk pistol. They'd have gone to visit Freddie Fellowes, all very friendly, and switched back the real pistol. Presumably Freddie would never have been the wiser. Then back to New York for Harry to laugh himself silly at Remler's expense. He'd have pulled out these photographs—"

"Oho!" Frank the Crank raised a finger. "I think I'm gettin' the picture, Doc."

"Like Remler would have. Harry would have given him a great big 'Gotcha!' and said there were more of these pictures where the first two came from. And if Remler wanted to make noise, Harry would make a louder noise."

"Which Remler's missus wouldn't exactly take very kindly." Frank the Crank snickered. "End of the line on the gravy train."

"That's how I see it," I said. "At that point, Remler wouldn't have been buying condom tins, let alone Farouk pistols."

Sarah looked puzzled. "But that's not what happened."

"No, I think that was the original script. But Huey must have gotten greedy. Maybe he wanted to make a killing ... so to speak. Or maybe he was just tired of being Harry's lickspittle. Either way he decided to play both ends against the middle. He tipped Remler off, told him how Harry was planning to pull a fast one. By the night of Harry's party Remler must've put two and two together, and figured out the pistol was inside the rigid notation box. Now, Frank—when I saw those old men in your shop ..."

"Listenin' to the Edison, you mean?"

"That's right. I'd have sworn I'd seen them before. Problem was, I was working off *déjà vu* once removed. Jackson George told me how Remler was practically drooling into the rigid notation box and Sammy here was making fun of him. That just didn't make sense."

"I couldn't figure out why Remler was so interested in a cylinder music box," said Shapiro. "Any cylinder music box."

"He either got impatient or he just wanted to turn the tables once and for all on Harry," I said. "After the party he shot Harry and grabbed the rigid notation box. If he'd been able to get the pistol out of the cylinder right then, before he went any further, he'd probably have gotten away with the whole business. But fortunately he wasn't a restorer: if he'd tried to take that mechanism apart and open the cylinder he'd have destroyed the rigid notation box. That would've ruined the rest of his plan–which was to cover himself by framing Shackie. Early next morning he sold the box to Abramowitz. He told Abramowitz his name was Charles O'Shacker so if the police ever followed a lead to Abramowitz it would've looked like Shackie killed Harry, stole the box, and fenced it. Next, Remler dressed as Wilma and started off back to Abramowitz's. He was going to buy the box, take it home, bash it open, and if the pistol *was* there, just dump the music box into the East River. Then he'd know he didn't need Huey any more. Could've kissed him off, paid him off, or knocked him off. But he didn't figure on Schwartz tipping me, especially so early in the day. As I was running out of Abramowitz's shop I nearly knocked over a woman going in. It took me a while to remember that, but once I did I also remembered her face. Wilma."

"But how was Jackson George involved?" Sophie asked.

"I'm not sure," I said and looked at Marisa.

"I'm afraid that was my fault," she said. "Thomas–Dr. Purdue–has put things together quite nicely. Mr. Fellowes found out about the theft of the pistol just a few hours after it was done. He didn't want to involve the police so he came to me for help. Fellowes knew Huey had stolen the pistol but never imagined it was hidden inside the rigid notation box. He had no reason to think Hardwick was involved; he told me the two likeliest contacts for Huey would have been George and Remler, as collectors of miniatures and erotica. So I came to New York and tried to find out what I could, as quietly as possible. After Hardwick was killed, I decided to get more active. I went to see Mr. George–"

"And left the Sand Club matchbook in his study," I said. "Careless."

"Very. But my questioning was even more careless. I didn't tell Mr. George the entire story, of course, but he was far from unperceptive. If the pistol was stolen and not offered to him, he knew to whom it must have been offered. I expect he called Remler, said something ill-advised, and Remler killed him."

"Poor old Remler." Frank the Crank chuckled. "Just one damn thing after another."

"You can say that again," I told him. "Once the rigid notation box was sold, Remler had to shut Abramowitz up or risk having the police trace the box to me. Remler knew I had it–remember, I bumped into him dressed as Wilma, on my way out of Abramowitz's shop with a package under my arm? When Wilma went inside to ask about a music box for sale, Abramowitz probably thought it was a riot, telling her yeah, he did have one, but just a minute ago he sold it to me. So Remler called Abramowitz that night, pretended to be Shackie, made up some excuse about having to see Abramowitz right away. Then he–maybe as Wilma, I don't know–went to the shop and shot Abramowitz.

"Now Shackie was nicely framed for both murders, and at that point Remler was back in business. He tore my place to pieces, didn't find what he was looking for, and then probably remembered the fuss Shackie made at Harry's about the way the box sounded. He also knew what good friends Shackie and I were. So there went Wilma again, off to search Shackie's, carrying along a Lecoultre music box as an excuse in case Shackie was home. Unfortunately, he was. She killed him and set it up as an apparent suicide. Then I showed up. Wilma would've killed me, too, but at that point I was the only remaining link to the rigid notation box. She had to be satisfied just to brain me, get out of there, and hope to be able to get the box away from me later."

"So where'd you finally find it?" Frank the Crank was nearly hopping with excitement.

"In a safe place."

"Aw, Doc!"

"Nope, sorry, Frank. Can't tell. That part of the story's not over yet. The Farouk pistol's hiding where Shackie stashed the music box. It's the safest place I can think of until we can get it back to Freddie Fellowes."

"We? Who's 'we'?" Sarah was all suspicion.

"Marisa and I. That is, at least Marisa and I. We're taking the late night flight to London to return Freddie his pistol. You can imagine how grateful he is. He's throwing us a real bash of a celebration."

"The cops're lettin' you go outta the country?" Schwartz misses nothing, thinks of everything.

"Released on my own recognizance. I'll be guest star at the inquest but Melvin Madrid, the lawyer, says there won't be any problems. And 'til then, no restrictions."

Sarah's eyes locked with mine. "Why do you have to go?" asked my wife. "She's a detective. Why can't she take it herself?"

"Couple of reasons. Added security. But mostly just to get it quietly back into England, the way I think Harry was going to do it. Getting it out of New York should be no trouble–if they spot it on X-ray, I'll demonstrate it and that'll be that. Security guards won't know a priceless antique from a dirty little trinket. Going into England might be trickier. Marisa'll be a returning British citizen; customs could decide to take a good look through her stuff. But on Christmas Eve a Yank with one small piece of hand luggage can say he has nothing to declare and he'll be in like Flynn."

Sarah was working up to a doozie. "Oh, I just knew–"

I interrupted her. "Freddie's invited us all." I pulled a handful of airline tickets out of my pocket and waved them in the air. "Five days in London, all expenses paid, for any of us who want to go. Freddie wants to say thank you. He said considering all the money he got from selling the rigid notation box it's the least he could do."

There was a general uproar, cheering, and that sudden burst of animated conversation which always follows an unexpected development.

Except for Sarah.

She marched over to me like a Salvation Army Colonel, fixed me with a withering glare, and said, "You bastard." Just like that. "I *knew* you'd find a way out of helping me serve dinners on Christmas."

"What?" I shouted, all righteous spluttering. "What do you think? I rigged these murders? Just so I wouldn't have to–"

That's as far as I got. Sarah swung her big black purse. What she actually was aiming for I'll never know but the purse was huge and full and on a long strap, and as she brought it forward it caught me right below the ribcage, a solar plexus bulls-eye. I let out a grunt and went down in a heap on the floor. Airline tickets fluttered down around me like confetti.

"Oh, Thomas!" The scent of Sarah's face powder came through the red haze of pain. I was making horrible crowing sounds, trying desperately to draw air into my lungs. I felt as if I were being sucked into a huge black hole.

Sarah pulled at my arm. "Thomas. I didn't mean to ... oh, damn you, anyway–Thomas! Are you faking?"

I'd have laughed if I could have. Later when I remembered it, I did, for a long time. But right then all I could do was gasp for breath. From above Sarah's shoulder Marisa caught my eye. No question, she was enjoying herself immensely.

THIRTY-ONE

The gathering at Freddie's was boisterous and enlightening.

Big Al Resford told us how he'd tracked down Huey Fortune. "Hiding in his mum's cellar up at Lincolnshire," Al said. "Two days of cold and damp, living on naught but potatoes and gravy–and nothing to drink but water–he was ready to talk. More than ready, I should say."

Huey's story confirmed my guesswork nicely. The original plan *had* been a big-time bait-and-switch on Remler, but Huey saw his chance to make a bundle. He called Remler and told him he'd hidden the pistol "somewhere safe" for Harry, and after the first of the year he'd be coming to the States, at which time he'd be able to sell the pistol–the real pistol–to Remler. Then, instead of leaving the real pistol at Freddie's according to Harry's plan, Huey would have left the second fake. Harry'd never know. At some point Freddie would find out, but so what? He'd have no way to pin the fake on Huey.

So, I figure when Remler heard Shackie fussing about how the sound of this brand-new-just-arrived rigid notation box was unbalanced, that told him exactly where the pistol was hiding. Next thing Huey knew, Remler was on the phone telling him Shackie had apparently killed Harry and made off with the rigid notation box. Then Huey had to confess: yes, the bird-pistol was in that damned cylinder. Remler pretended to be mightily upset; he swore he'd find the rigid notation box, bring Huey over, and go on with the deal. I'll bet he would have brought Huey over—but only to put him out of the way. Another dead drunk on the Bowery; who'd have noticed? But when Huey called and told Remler I'd showed up in England and punched him around, Remler thought I might be onto something, so he told Huey to get rid of me. Enter Teresa Carpenter. Then after I came home alive and Huey dropped out of sight, Remler must have decided to make one last try at getting the pistol, but in any case to be sure to finish me.

I looked at Big Al. "Where's Huey now? Did you turn him over to The Yard?"

Al blinked mildly. "My understanding is Mr. Fellowes wishes no publicity. I don't imagine Huey will be a bother to anyone any longer."

I caught Schwartz's eye. No further questions.

Freddie, of course, was thrilled, the pompous old poop. He said he was delighted I was the new owner of "his" rigid notation box. "Harry Hardwick wasn't a *real* collector," he said. "He had a lot of money—but not the slightest genuine taste or proper appreciation, you understand."

I understood fine. A person with enough brains and drive to make a ton of money is by definition too crass to appreciate life's finer things. But who was I to take offense? Some of my own stories don't make much sense to other people.

Like Sarah.

I thought about her all the time I was in London. First thing back I called and asked her to have supper with me the next night.

She hesitated, then said, "I can't, Thomas. It's New Year's Eve."

"Oh. Mr. Harold."

"Well, yes. He's picking me up at nine."

"All right. Tell you what: I'll come by at five-thirty. We'll have a light supper at the Brasserie. You'll be back in plenty of time."

"But why, Thomas—"

"I just want to see you," I said, and hung up the phone.

From our table in the back corner, we had the Brasserie nearly to ourselves. Sarah looked lovely. Just angry enough to have high color in her cheeks and sparklers in her eyes. The small loudspeaker above us swung into bouncy music: "A Cup of Coffee, A Sandwich, and You."

Sarah slammed down her fork. "Damn it, Thomas–if you're going to take me out for supper at least stop humming. Get your head out of the music long enough to spend a *little* time with me."

"Oh. Sorry." I reached across and patted her hand. "That's Roger Wolfe Kahn. One of the best hotel orchestras."

Surprises without end. Sarah's face lit. "Well, for heaven's sake."

"What?"

"That's where Harold is taking me tonight."

"Where?"

"To hear *him*." Sarah pointed at the speaker. "Roger Wolfe Kahn. He *is* supposed to be wonderful, isn't he?"

I nodded. "He sure is. Where's he playing?"

Sarah waved her hand, trying to clear the air. "One of the hotels; I'm not sure which. I don't know whether Harold actually said."

"Hmm, Roger Wolfe Kahn. Maybe I'll go myself. I'll look it up in the paper."

"Oh no," Sarah said, very quickly. "You can't ... you couldn't. It's sold out–has been for weeks, Harold said."

I laughed. "Just teasing. I wouldn't spoil your date."

Something came forward in her eyes, then receded. "Thomas, why was it so important for you to take me to dinner tonight?"

"I want to go to bed with you. Seems like the least you could do after the way you slugged me last week."

"Damn it!" She put her cup of coffee down hard. "You're always doing that to me."

"Doing what?" I swallowed a last mouthful of wine.

"That. Just what you're doing now. Putting me off. I can't believe a word you ever tell me."

"Then believe everything I tell you. Make it easy on yourself."

And on me, I thought.

She reached across the table and took my free hand between her two. "I ..." she began, but got no further. "Forget it. I'm glad you had a nice time in England."

"Would have been nicer with you there."

"I don't back down on *my* commitments," said Ms. Prim. "You should have seen the expressions on those poor people's faces."

"I saw some nice expressions myself. Can you imagine: everyone there got exactly what they wanted. Freddie had his little golden pistol back. Muriel had her inheritance unencumbered, along with a pile of ashes from a bunch of ugly pictures. And–"

"And you had your rigid notation box free and clear. Now I understand. More than a coincidence. More like a nice convenient *quid pro quo*."

"That's what it was. But not the way you think. I gave Muriel those pictures with no strings; we burned them together. Afterwards, I told her how I'd gotten the rigid notation box, and offered her what Harry paid Sophie for it. She said forget the money–twenty-two thousand bucks plus or minus didn't mean much to someone sitting on hundreds of millions. She said she thought I'd earned it. I thanked her. That's the story."

Sarah looked at best doubtful.

"Believe me. Lucas Sterne was definitely happy; he's going to get ten percent of the selling price of Harry's collection, which should keep him comfortably in business forever. Sophie was ... well, put it this way: She's been around long enough to know sometimes you just have to forgive yourself and everyone around you, and move along. Frank the Crank said it was the first real Christmas he's had since he was a kid. He wasn't down once, not in five whole days. As for Schwartz, Trudy and Al, that was a real old home week. Just being able to watch them was worth every penny. A good time was had–"

"Wait a minute. What do you mean, 'worth every penny'?"

"Just what I said. Why?"

"Because when someone says that, they're usually talking about money *they* spent."

"I was," I said, and started to smile.

"But you said Freddie paid–"

"Sure I did. But that tight old bastard wouldn't dream of dropping thirteen grand on a five-day party. I *had* to say that. If everyone thought I was paying they'd have felt uncomfortable."

"But, my God! Thirteen thousand dollars! Where did you get that kind of money to throw around?"

"I'm getting sixty thousand a year from Shackie's trust. So why can't I spend thirteen to brighten my corner? You turn on your lights by serving a thousand plates full of turkey and mashed potatoes in a mission. We don't live on the same corner, Babe."

"I know." Her voice was very small and sad. She looked down at her plate. A tear ran down her left cheek.

I squeezed her hand. "Nothing to cry about," I said. "I don't dig your neighborhood, but I like you. I'll come visit you; you visit me. Fair enough?"

She looked up, trying to smile. "If I'd gone to London ... would you be telling me this now?"

"Of course not. You'd have a fit."

I couldn't tell whether she was crying or laughing. I'm not sure she could, either. She pulled a small handkerchief out of her pocket and wiped at her eyes. Then she looked at her watch.

I swallowed the rest of my coffee. "Okay. It's eight-thirty; let's go. Don't want to keep Mr. Harold waiting."

***

After Sarah went inside, I took off on the run for Gramercy North. I was up to my apartment, down with a Gristede's bag under my arm, and back in front of Sarah's building again within ten minutes.

I stood at her doorway and looked around. The grocery store on the corner was still open. Two buildings down was a bar, doing a land-office business. I thought of going inside and having a drink but told myself no.

I walked up the block to 25th Street, then back down to 24th. Then I retraced my path. A young couple walked past, arm-in-arm. They looked at me. I smiled. I thought the girl winked at me, but in the dark I couldn't be certain.

The cold was more bracing than chilling, whether because of lack of wind or the workings of my mind, I couldn't tell. No threat of snow tonight: a crescent moon hung low over the East River, just visible above the apartment roofs on the opposite side of Second Avenue. The sky was filled with stars, signaling Morse-like as they do across the black void of creation. Directly opposite where I stood, a Christmas tree in a top-floor apartment blinked out a similar message on its white bulbs. I stood and watched, head back, until my mind began to spin and my vision softened, and I could no longer tell which sparkling lights were stars and which tree-bulbs. Somewhere in my head a glowing baritone sang. *Must it be ... forever inside of me? Why can't I let it go? Why can't I let you know? Why can't I let you know the song my heart would sing?*

I walked my beat undisturbed until I saw by the clock inside the bar it was 11:30.

Time.

I gripped the icy steel in the pocket of my topcoat, took out my keychain, and with Sarah's apartment key let myself through the outside door and into the vestibule.

Up the two flights of stairs I went, on my toes, slowly and quietly. When I got to the third-floor landing I worked the key into Sarah's door lock. Carefully, very gently, I turned the key. The door opened noiselessly.

I slipped inside, closed the door, and flipped the deadbolt.

I heard the sound of the TV from around the corner in the living room. "New Year's Eve, from the world-famous Waldorf Astoria Hotel. With Gordon Gentry and his silk-smooth Society Serenaders."

I tiptoed the few steps around the corner and stood silently in the archway.

Sarah in pink lounging pajamas sat on the couch opposite the TV. Her eyes were red; she sniffled. I told myself I could still change my mind: turn around, tiptoe out, sneak back to Gramercy North. Instead, I took a deep breath and swallowed hard.

"All right," I yelled. "Where is he–the son of a bitch?"

Sarah shrieked–what did I expect? Her hand went to her throat. "Good God, Thomas! What are you doing here? You scared the life out of me."

"Where *is* he?" I repeated.

"Harold ..." A murmur, not really a question.

Every blood vessel in her face emptied. She was white, terrified.

"Don't try telling me he stood you up. I know better than that." I charged into the bedroom.

Sarah was a half-step behind me. "Have you finally gone completely crazy? What–"

I stood in the middle of the room and looked around. "Come out, you bastard, you son of a bitch. I know you're here."

Sarah stood frozen, staring at me. As I pulled the gun out of my pocket her eyes went like dinner plates.

"Ah! I heard that." I ran over to the closet and flung the door open. "You dog!"

Then I aimed the gun and fired.

There was a monster explosion. I heard Sarah scream.

I turned to face her, holding out the gun so she could see the little white sign extending from the end of the barrel. BANG, BANG. YOU'RE DEAD.

"Teach *him* to mess around with my wife. That's the end of Mr. Harold."

Sarah leaned against my shoulder, breathing heavily. If I didn't know her as I did I'd have been sure she was going to faint. But Sarah would never do a thing like that.

I dropped the gun, opened the Gristede's bag, and took out a CD which I held up for Sarah to see. "Bring Back Those Dancing Twenties" was the title and beneath that was a photograph of a large dance band. The men wore sleek mustaches and tuxedoes with wide lapels. The sign on the bandstand was easily legible: Roger Wolfe Kahn and his Hotel Biltmore Orchestra. From Original Recordings Made at New York's Biltmore Hotel, 1925 to 1929.

"If there's anything I can't stand it's a liar. Telling his girl he was taking her to hear Kahn and not meaning a word of it–he deserved to be shot. *I* can do better than that."

I took my portable CD player out of the paper bag, put the CD into the player, pushed the switch, and set the machine down on the tabletop next to the bed. That bouncy music of "A Cup of Coffee, a Sandwich and You" began to play.

"Dance, my dear?" I extended my arms.

Sarah looked straight into my eyes. She rested a hand gently on my arm. Then she said, "Aren't you going to take off your coat? Give it to the check-girl?"

I tossed my topcoat into the corner. Sarah laid her head against my chest and we began to glide around the floor of the bedroom. Sarah lifted her mouth to my ear. "You know ... Harold really was awfully dull. You *are* more fun, damn you. What you said in that hotel bar after I'd stolen the pictures was right. I was having fun. I hadn't had such a good time in years."

I remembered what Schwartz had said. *An aggravatin' thing, yes. But stupid? Uh-uh. I think maybe she's the most unstupid person I ever met.* So Sarah's remark about going to hear Roger Wolfe Kahn–was that really a blunder? Or was it a setup all the way, something she'd said knowing full well I'd pick up on it?

Who the hell cared?

The music stopped between selections. We applauded politely. Then, as the orchestra swung into a dreamy rendition of "Imagination," I said, "Tell you what. You can help me get rid of the body. We'll dump him in the East River and watch the piranhas eat him."

She started to giggle, then noticed the gun on the floor near our feet. "Where on earth did you get that?

Uh-oh. "Schwartz."

Her eyes flared but then the penny dropped and her whole expression changed. From pissed to stunned in nothing flat. "You're not going to tell me, are you, that *that* was the gun Schwartz was carrying last week? When you sent him over to my apartment?"

"The very one. I didn't know it until afterwards. I should've, but I didn't. Schwartz couldn't carry a real gun if ... well, all right. If his life depended on it." I picked up the toy pistol and waved it in Sarah's direction. "But you can be sure if he'd had to use this silly thing to save your life he'd have done it somehow. You were safer with Schwartz and his popgun than you would've been with Bugsy Siegel, Baby Face Nelson, and a pair of tommy guns."

Sarah sighed but she was smiling. Not a sad smile, either. The color was fully back in her face. Her cheeks glowed.

"Dance?" I held out my arms.

She looked at me with glistening eyes. "I don't know. If you want the truth I'd just as soon go to bed with you." She looked toward the closet. "Why not? Harold's dead now–rest his boring, tedious soul."

With that she unbuttoned her blouse, tossed it aside, then stepped out of her pants.

The music is sweet. The words are true.

The song is you.

Sarah pulled back the corner of the bedcovers and looked back over her shoulder at me. "You're not going to just stand there holding that silly gun and gawking, are you?"

"No. Absolutely not."

I flipped Schwartz's weapon into the closet with Harold's body, and closed the door.

"You know," I said, as I started to unlace my shoes. "I've been thinking. Shackie's loft. I won't need all that open shop space for repair work. We could redesign the place so we'd each have our own living area. *Mi casa, su casa*, but one address. Be a lot cheaper than living this way, wouldn't it? Nicer, too."

She laughed, a lovely light sound that reverberated into my ears from somewhere far down the long corridor of time. "Shut up and get into bed with me."

I didn't say another word.

But silence doesn't mean a story's over, only that some parts of stories are best told by silence. People die, sure. Good stories go on forever.